ALSO BY KATIE RUGGLE

Fish Out of Water

ROCKY MOUNTAIN SEARCH & RESCUE
On His Watch (free novella)
Hold Your Breath
Fan the Flames
Gone Too Deep
In Safe Hands
After the End (free novella)

ROCKY MOUNTAIN K9 UNIT
Run to Ground
On the Chase
Survive the Night
Through the Fire

ROCKY MOUNTAIN COWBOYS
Rocky Mountain Cowboy Christmas

ROCKY MOUNTAIN BOUNTY HUNTERS
Turn the Tide (free novella)
In Her Sights
Risk It All

BENEATH THE WILD SKY
The Scenic Route

Crossing Paths

KATIE RUGGLE

sourcebooks
casablanca

Published by Sourcebooks Casablanca, an imprint of Sourcebooks
P.O. Box 4410, Naperville, Illinois 60567-4410
(630) 961-3900
sourcebooks.com

Cataloging-in-Publication Data is on file with the Library of Congress.

Printed and bound in the United States of America.
KP 10 9 8 7 6 5 4 3 2 1

To all my anxiety-ridden readers—here's a book-shaped hug.

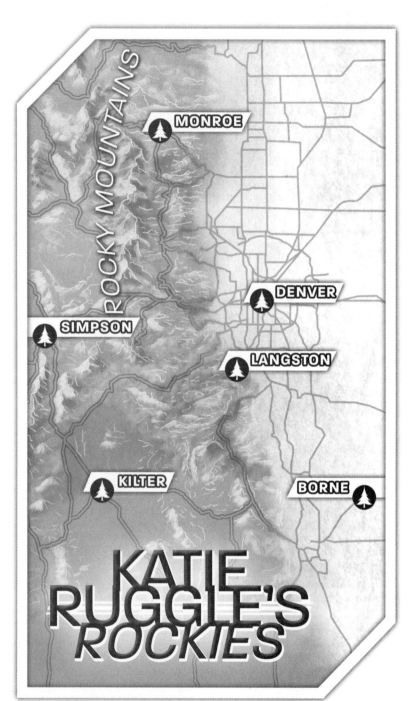

MEET THE CHARACTERS

Crossing Paths is the second book in Katie Ruggle's latest series, Beneath the Wild Sky...but along the way, we get the chance to see some familiar faces. If this is your first time dipping into Ruggle's extended quirky-yet-uniquely-action-packed universe, here's a handy run-through of everyone you'll meet:

LOU & CALLUM FROM *HOLD YOUR BREATH*

Lou, a chatty East Coast transplant determined to make her own way in the Rockies at any cost.

Callum, a taciturn (and charmingly uptight) dive rescue instructor who doesn't know whether he wants to strangle her or kiss her. (Spoiler: He wants to kiss her.)

These opposites attract when Lou stumbles across a headless dead body and begins a mystery that will lead to hijinks, danger, drama, and the formation of a certain Murder Club.

RORY & IAN FROM *FAN THE FLAMES*

Rory, a highly competent, no-nonsense gun shop owner. Raised by mountain doomsday preppers, Rory knows how to do just about anything but deal with people.

Ian, an almost impossibly hot firefighter struggling to reconcile his criminal background with where he wants to be in life. He's been head over heels in love with Rory since they were children.

These childhood sweethearts have their hands full when the local MC comes calling and strange arsons begin spreading out of control.

ELLIE & GEORGE FROM *GONE TOO DEEP*

Ellie, a sweet city girl with zero survival skills but enough grit to have her going toe-to-toe with the most grizzled survivalist.

George, a towering mountain of a man with a reputation for being something of a gruff hermit…until he falls in love at first sight.

This virgin lumberjack of a hero will do anything to help his heroine survive a trek through the Rockies in search for her father: even if he has to wrestle a bear to protect her.

DAISY & CHRIS FROM *IN SAFE HANDS*

Daisy, a kindhearted woman struggling with agoraphobia who witnesses a crime nobody will believe.

Chris, the devoted best friend who will stand by her side no matter who turns against them as a result.

When Daisy witnesses a leader of the community committing a shocking crime, only her best friend is willing to believe her. But the secret that has kept their mutual spark from truly igniting for years may be enough to end their story before it can ever begin.

MOLLY & JOHN FROM *IN HER SIGHTS*

Molly, the oldest of five sisters, is a bounty hunter by both necessity and choice, keeping her family afloat despite the way people whisper about them.

John, a rival bounty hunter and the biggest pain in her rear. He's always underfoot and getting beneath her skin with that obnoxiously handsome grin and cheeky wink.

When her criminal mother puts up the family home as collateral for her latest legal trouble—and then immediately skips bail *with* the stolen jewels in tow—Molly and her sisters vow to track her down and save the lives they worked so hard for. Too bad Molly's archnemesis is determined to stick by her side every step of the way.

CARA & HENRY FROM *RISK IT ALL*

Cara, one of five bounty hunter sisters, always dreamed of becoming a kindergarten teacher. But if she can bring in a target with a high payout, maybe she can retire from the family business guilt-free.

Henry, the man Cara is determined to bring to justice, is innocent. If only he could convince the beautiful bounty hunter on his trail of that…

When Cara goes after a high-level criminal, she never antici-pated him to be so gentle…or so protective of her when the true villains came back for revenge.

FELICITY & BENNETT FROM *THE SCENIC ROUTE*

Felicity, the most driven of her sisters, determined to save her family by finding their criminal mother at all costs.

Bennett, a PI hired to find Felicity's mother, pulled against his will into the sisters' orbit…and under the thrall of the beau-tiful bounty hunter he's been tailing.

When Felicity Pax realizes a PI is on her tail, she says goodbye to her sisters and leads him on a merry chase up into the Rocky Mountains in a desperate bid to keep him from digging up any dangerous dirt. But when things take a turn for the deadly, Felicity and Bennett find themselves on the same side…and closer than either is willing to admit.

CHARLIE FROM *TAKE A HIKE* (COMING SOON)

Wild-child sister **Charlie** loves nothing more than working for her family's bounty hunting business…until she's pulled into a mystery that'll have her losing her heart and her head.

ONE

"Pax Bond Recovery," Norah answered her cell phone.

"Which of you Pax girls is this?"

At Barney Thompson's distinctive voice, she made a face. She would've rather talked to pretty much anyone other than the slimy bail bondsman who held the deed to their family home. *Thanks for that, Mom.*

"This is Norah," she answered. "What can we do for you, Mr. Thompson?"

"Norah…Norah… Oh, you're the mousy blond! POS's kid. How's he doing?"

"Fine," she lied, not wanting to go into the gory details of the mess her dad, Dwayne "POS" Possin, was currently making of his life—especially not with Barney Thompson of all people. The only reason they were giving Barney the time of day was because they still hadn't found their currently-on-the-run mom, and he could make their lives miserable if she missed her first court hearing. "What do you need?"

"All business, aren't you?" he asked with a stiff laugh.

She scrunched her nose at the two out of four of her sisters who were watching with a mixture of sympathy and apprehension. Norah could barely deal with talking to people outside her family. Making nice with a scumball like Barney was not part of her skill set.

"I have another job for you," Barney continued.

Her relieved exhale was silent. Even though he sounded a bit peeved, at least he was willing to get down to business. "Who's the skip?" she asked.

"Devon Leifsen."

The name didn't ring any bells, so she repeated it for Molly and Cara to hear. Both of them gave her a blank head shake. "What did he do?"

"You mean what is he *accused* of doing?" Barney corrected archly.

"Sure." There was a snap in her voice that she couldn't help. Barney was quickly wearing through her thin veneer of patience.

"What with your mother's…situation, I would think you'd be more of a stickler about the whole innocent-until-proven-guilty thing." He paused as if waiting for her to comment, but she held her silence until he finally answered sullenly. "He's *accused* of being a hacker. He was arrested for deactivating home security systems so his buddies could burglarize the places."

Norah felt cold rush through her as her gaze flew to Cara. Her sister had been kidnapped a few weeks ago after their security system had been disabled. Maybe it was just a coincidence, since there were lots of hackers in the world, but Langston,

Colorado, wasn't a huge place. Cara gave her a questioning look as Norah asked, "Is he local?"

"If you call Denver local, then yeah." Barney sounded bored now that she hadn't risen to his earlier bait. "Look, it's all in the file I sent over. Find him fast, or you're not going to like the consequences."

Norah was already opening her email app and pulling up the business's account. If there was a chance that this guy helped kidnap Cara, then she was going to relish her part in bringing him in.

"Hello?" Barney's voice echoed faintly from her phone, and Norah twitched her shoulders in irritation. He'd said that everything was in the file. Why hadn't he ended the call already? "Hello? Did you hang up on me, you little—"

Returning to the phone display, she pressed the end button. A snort from Molly brought her gaze from her phone screen to her sister's amused expression. "What?" Norah asked.

Cara sighed, but the corners of her mouth twitched in a way that meant she wasn't really that exasperated. "Don't hang up on clients, Norah."

"It was Barney." She turned back to her phone, wanting to read the file.

"True," Molly agreed, the laughter in her voice slipping away. "But as long as he may have the ability to evict us in the near future, it might be a good idea to say 'bye' at the end of conversations."

Distracted by the contents of Devon Leifsen's file, Norah just grunted an acknowledgment. "The skip is a hacker who's been disarming residential security systems so his friends can burglarize homes." She heard Cara's sharply indrawn breath as Norah continued to scroll through the information. Even though she'd barely glanced at the file, she knew in her gut that Leifsen had to have been at least partially responsible for her sister's kidnapping. Cara had almost *died*.

For that, Devon Leifsen was going to pay. Norah would track him down so her sisters could make sure of that. She looked up as she promised, "I'll find him, Cara."

"Of course you will," Molly said, giving Cara's shoulder a comforting squeeze. "And then I'll bring him in. He's as good as locked up."

"I know," Cara said, although her voice shook slightly.

That tremor made Norah even more determined to locate Leifsen. Even though she wouldn't be the one physically chasing down the skip and dragging him back to jail, she could at least do her part by discovering his whereabouts. He'd try to hide, but Leifsen would soon discover what hundreds of other skips had learned—the Pax sisters were very good at their job.

———

After dinner, with her belly full and her brain already occupied with Devon Leifsen's file, Norah settled back on her bed with her laptop warming her thighs. Probably hoping for leftovers, their dog, Warrant, had chosen to stay downstairs with Cara as she did meal cleanup. Although Norah appreciated having the space to stretch out her legs, she missed the furry beast's warmth.

She read through the bare bones of Leifsen's entire file,

letting the information settle into her brain. He had a few possible connections in Langston, although his home base and main associates were in the Denver area. He was young—only twenty-three—but he'd managed to rack up a solid list of suspected offenses in the five years since he'd been a legal adult. Norah was pretty sure his sealed juvie file would be interesting reading as well.

Like Barney had said, he'd been arrested most recently for his part in three Denver burglaries. One of his accomplices had given him up as part of a plea deal. Before that, he'd been accused of numerous crimes, from bank fraud to planting cameras in the dressing area of a local beauty pageant. Norah's nose wrinkled at that last one.

Not only is he a thief, he's a sexual predator too. Gross.

Most of the charges against him had been dropped immediately, and he hadn't been convicted of anything. He'd never been married, and there were no known girlfriends or boyfriends—past or present—listed. His mailing address matched his parents' house in Golden, and they'd been the ones to bond him out before he skipped bail.

After scanning through the last page of his file, she started searching online for information, starting with his parents, Karen and Bryon Leifsen. They owned several auto body shops along the Front Range, and the couple's names popped up quite a bit in the Denver social scene. Karen had a few speeding tickets, but otherwise the pair seemed to be generally law-abiding—or at least were good at not getting caught.

A light knock on her bedroom door made Norah jump, her

laptop bouncing with the sudden movement. "Come in," she called, and Cara stuck her head in.

"I'm heading to bed," Cara said. "Find anything?"

"Not really." Norah had taken in a lot of information, but she wasn't ready to start processing it yet, so there were just a bunch of facts about Devon Leifsen floating around her brain.

"Don't stay up too late." Cara always told her this, even though she knew Norah almost never took the advice.

"I won't," she responded as usual, although she'd probably still be digging deeper into the rabbit hole far into the wee hours. Once she found a trail, it was almost impossible for her to stop chasing it, even for critical needs like eating and sleeping. She worried that if she took a break, she'd never be able to pick up where she'd left off, and that lead would be gone forever.

Once Cara withdrew and softly closed her bedroom door, Norah moved on to searching for information on Leifsen's few friends mentioned in the file. One of them, a Chloe Ballister, was in a modern rock band that played at a bar in Langston on a semiregular basis.

"Of course it's Dutch's," Norah muttered as she made a note of it. The local bar had been a hot spot for trouble over the past few years. "Everything shady seems to come back to that place."

Chloe was also a regular at open-mic nights at Chico's Coffee, one of Norah's favorite places. She wondered if she'd ever been at the coffee shop at the same time as Chloe—or even Leifsen—without knowing it. The thought gave her a shiver. Norah was happy to track skips remotely—she was really good at it, in fact—but the idea of confronting them in person like her sisters did made her want to go hide in a closet.

A faint beep drew her eyes back to her laptop. A black text box with a flashing cursor opened in the corner of the screen, and she blinked at it as confusion slowly morphed into understanding. As letters appeared on the screen—letters that were not typed by her hand—she could only stare in horror.

Hi Norah!

Someone had gained access to her computer.

Her brain couldn't wrap around this fact. Despite layers and layers of top-notch security, someone had managed to hack into her heavily protected system. Her hand hovered over the touch pad, unsure if she should engage or do her best to kick out the interloper. They didn't seem to be attempting to access her data, however, and the cheery greeting—including an exclamation mark—threw her off guard.

Who is this? she typed, even as certainty settled inside her. It had to be Devon Leifsen, the hacker she was researching at this exact moment. Anyone else would be too much of a coincidence.

Devon. Nice to meet you.

Her heart was thundering now. She balled her hands into fists, taking reassurance in the bite of her short nails into her palms. Despite the confirmation, doubt took hold. Could it be a prank? Someone pretending to be Leifsen? The only people who knew she was investigating him were Molly and Cara, and neither of them would do something so cruel and pointless. Barney knew, but Norah was willing to bet her left kidney that he didn't have the know-how to hack her computer. In fact, she was reasonably sure he had to have help sending an email.

What are you doing? Her shaking fingers made it hard to type accurately.

Chatting with you! ☺ She'd never seen such a sinister smiley face.

Why did you hack my laptop? The voice in her head was now screaming at her to shut him down, but she had to know.

Because I wanted to introduce myself to the beautiful woman who's investigating me now. *waves* Hi pretty bounty hunter!

Norah's gaze flew to the dark window for a terrified second before she looked back at the small, circular lens at the top of her laptop screen. *He's not watching you*, her brain tried to reassure her. *He's just trying to scare you.*

It was working. She was full-on terrified. Her safe world, hidden behind her laptop screen and passwords and firewalls, had been broken into, and she'd never felt more vulnerable and exposed. With just a few lines of text, Leifsen had destroyed the anonymous security that'd allowed her to help her sisters. How could she do her research work now that the very skip she was looking into had virtually walked into her bedroom to confront her?

With trembling fingers, she closed the text box and then

shut down her laptop. As soon as the screen went black, she closed the computer and kept her hands pressed against the top as if to keep Leifsen from remotely opening it, as impossible as that would be. She mentally vowed to cover the laptop camera before booting it up next time. Her gaze darted around her shadowed room, dark without the light from her laptop screen, and landed on the black window again.

Forcing herself to put the computer aside and slide off the bed, she moved to the window, her heart hitting her ribs so hard it felt as if it was going to break out of her chest. The darkness of the room spooked her, but she couldn't turn on a light, not if he was watching her.

He's not out there, she tried to convince herself as she drew closer to the glass pane. *He's holed up somewhere miles away, messing with your head from the safety of a friend's couch.*

Despite the logic of that and the high likelihood that he was nowhere near her house, the shadows took on a menacing quality. Someone could easily be lurking in the darkness, staring up at her, taking delight in her fear.

Her breaths came quickly, fogging the glass, and she couldn't drag her gaze away from the thousand and one possible hiding places right outside her home. Wait—was that a flash of light? She blinked rapidly, but that just made it harder to tell if she'd imagined the glow or not. Her stomach twisted as his typed words ran on repeat in her mind. He could be just a few steps away from her house. If he picked the lock, disabled the alarm, and crept up the stairs, he could be outside her tiny bedroom in mere minutes.

At the thought, her gaze flew to her closed door. *Is that creak just the house settling, or did someone take a stealthy step?* She went completely still, listening. It felt like the house held its breath along with her. All she could hear was the rapid thud of her heartbeat in her ears, telling her to run.

But she was trapped in her closet of a bedroom. There was no escape.

Her first instinct was to text her sisters. She knew they'd come running to protect her, and they'd deal with the problem so Norah could return to her safe comfort zone, but something in her rebelled at the thought. Leifsen had broken through *her* security on *her* laptop. Unintentionally, she'd left a back door unlocked, and he'd used it to slither into their home. Leifsen was her mess, and she needed to protect her sisters from him rather than expose them to danger.

You can handle this. Fear still filled her, vivid images of terrible possibilities flashing rapid-fire through her brain, but she forced herself to shove those unhelpful thoughts away. Grabbing hold of the tiny kernel of anger inside her, she focused on making it grow. Leifsen had destroyed her safe, happy place, ruined the only thing she could do to help her sisters, and she wasn't going to let him get away with it. He'd dragged her out from behind her screen…so he'd have to deal with the consequences.

Because now Norah was mad.

TWO

NORAH STARED FIXEDLY AT THE fist swinging toward her face, even when the knuckles got so close she went cross-eyed. She wanted to close her eyes, but they refused to cooperate.

The fist stopped abruptly, close enough that Norah's eyelashes brushed against the battered knuckles. The gym was completely silent until her belated indrawn breath broke the quiet. For the thousandth time, she mentally gave thanks that no one else was ever there during her sessions. It limited the potential embarrassment at least. Physical pain, Norah could handle. Mockery, not so much.

"If you're not going to block, you should at least move your face." The voice had a compelling raspy edge, and it took her a moment to actually register what he was saying, just long enough for her eyelashes to flick against his knuckles three more times.

When the meaning of his words finally registered, she pulled her head back and moved her focus from that huge, scarred fist. She hadn't expected the almost hit to come so fast. It hadn't given her time to think through each step of blocking his punch, so she hadn't done anything—not even duck. That had always been her issue when her sister Felicity tried to teach her self-defense. If she wasn't able to run through her mental what-to-do checklist, her brain froze until it was too late. That was probably part of the reason she'd watched her sisters come very close to dying multiple times recently.

Now she was on her eighth training session with Dash, and she was still freezing whenever a fist headed in her direction. The strength and agility training he put her through was tough but doable, but the part where she actually had to learn to fight… That wasn't going so well.

Dash dropped his arm to his side and regarded her with his head cocked slightly to the right. Although he was frowning, that had been his default expression since she'd walked into his gym seventeen days ago, so she didn't take it personally. "It's better to move *before* the punch lands."

When he paused, she figured he was waiting for her to say something. There really was no necessary response, however, since everything he'd just said made sense. Still, in the interest of moving on to the next step, she gave a nod and said, "Okay."

His scowl deepened. "Don't just agree. *Do* it next time."

She studied him as she mentally debated how to respond. It was an interesting face to look at, with his almost-black irises and prominent cheekbones and the scars mottling the left side of his neck and jawline, but she couldn't really enjoy it because the majority of her focus was on what to say next. *Okay* hadn't gone over well, so that was out, but that was usually her go-to when she wanted someone to stop staring at her and continue.

"I will," she tried.

To her satisfaction, that seemed to do the trick. Although his expression was still snarly, he took a step back and settled into the defensive position he'd just shown her—base solid and hands ready to protect his face. Despite his burly form, he looked light on his feet, and she knew from their training sessions that he could move surprisingly fast. One of his slashing black brows lifted in a soundless command. Twitching her tank top into place, she moved to mimic his stance.

She'd been working with Dash less than three weeks, but the position already felt natural. It just made physiological sense, and there was nothing Norah appreciated more than when things were logical. If only punches didn't come so quickly, she was pretty sure she'd actually be able to remember how to counter them.

"Let's try this in slow motion," he said as if he'd read her mind. He started extending his arm, the muscles stretching out from their bunched positions. Even when he wasn't flexing though, his arms were huge. As his fist gradually drew closer to her face, she ran through the steps in her head.

Shoulders up, tuck my chin, thrust palm, connect with the side of his wrist, shove his arm away, move my face in case I miss, and return hand to guard position.

"Good." The compliment was a mere grunt, but it still warmed her insides. "Again."

Over and over, slightly faster each time, he threw punches at her face. Gradually, her movements became automatic, and she didn't have to think about each step. Her body just started doing what needed to be done.

"Okay," he said, shifting his balance back.

Norah felt a line of sweat tickle her spine, and she wished she could take off another layer. If she took anything else off, however, she'd be down to her underwear. Just the thought of being that close to naked in front of the intimidatingly self-possessed Dash made her flush.

"Let's work on breaking some holds." His voice was even as he continued, either ignoring the fact that she'd turned bright red or not noticing that she suddenly resembled a stop sign. As warm as the gym was, he probably just thought she was overheating because of the physical effort rather than embarrassment.

He was waiting again, so she gave him a slight lift of her chin in response. That seemed to be what he'd been waiting for, because he shifted closer and waited for her to imitate his ready stance.

"If I grab you, what's your first impulse?" He closed his fingers around her forearm, the rough rasp of his skin in direct opposition to the gentle, careful way he held her.

She blinked down at his hand, surprised that she wasn't more upset. Normally, she wasn't a big fan of strangers touching her. Her gaze moved to Dash, and she wondered why it was different with him.

"Your first impulse is to stand there?"

She felt her cheeks warm again, but he sounded surprised rather than mocking.

Norah tried to think how to explain that he didn't trigger

the usual alarm in her brain, but she couldn't even understand it herself. If anyone except her sisters—well, apparently her sisters or Dash—touched her, she would've yanked away. "No," she answered belatedly. "I'd pull back. If someone else grabbed my arm I mean."

The revealing heat was returning to her cheeks, annoying her. *Why am I being extra awkward today?*

Luckily, he didn't seem to notice anything off about her as he increased the pull on her arm. His fingers stayed gentle, even as he hauled her close. She wondered if she was supposed to fight back, but her brain was still preoccupied by her strange reaction to him, so she couldn't organize her mind enough to figure out the best way to get free from his hold. As careful as his grip was, it was still firm and unyielding. Her forearm looked tiny and frail in contrast to his thick, rough-looking fingers.

He pulled her closer until their chests were almost touching. She kept her gaze on his face, checking for clues about what he wanted her to be doing in response. All she knew from looking at him was that his eyelashes were black and thick enough to be in a mascara ad, and he appeared to be...baffled.

"Why aren't you pulling back?" he finally asked, yanking her attention away from her study of his eyelashes.

"Am I supposed to?" she asked.

"No."

She blinked.

"Most people do, and we have to drill a different reaction into them. You're the first person I've trained with such a... passive response."

Norah frowned. "Passive?" She didn't like to think of herself as passive. Even with her less physical role in her family's bounty hunting business, her contribution felt active, like she was accomplishing something. Her method of chasing skips might be computer-based, but it was its own type of hunt. Though she had to admit that she hadn't done very well in the field. Maybe if she hadn't been so *passive*, she wouldn't have ended up on the wrong end of a gun so often.

Her chin set as determination coursed through her. This was why she was here after all. She wanted to get better at the physical stuff so she could do her part to protect her sisters. She was tired of always being the one tied to the railroad tracks. She wanted to be the hero riding to the rescue for once. "What should I do instead?"

The corner of his mouth twitched in something so close to a smile that she blinked, startled. "Just what you did," he said.

Shaking off her distraction, she looked up at him, confused. "I thought I was too passive."

"Not in this case." He stepped back without releasing her arm. "Like I said, most people pull back when someone grabs them. That's what the assailant expects you to do. If you step in closer instead, it throws them off guard."

Norah could understand why the attacker would be thrown, but there were still holes in his logic. "I haven't gotten away though."

"That's the next step." He pulled her in again, and she allowed herself to be tugged toward him, even as the word *passive* rang sourly in her brain. This close, she had to tilt her head back to meet his gaze. "Now you're in a position to get some hits in. You could knee me in the groin or stomp on my foot or do a palm heel strike to my nose. All my tender bits are at your mercy."

The words *tender bits* coming from cranky Dash made her smile, but his meaning sharpened her grin. "Nothing passive about smashing your...tender bits."

This time, he really did smile, and it looked just as fierce as hers felt. "Nope. As tiny and fragile as you seem, they won't see it until it's too late."

Her surge of confidence faltered. "See what?"

He gave a light tap on her sternum. "Your ferocious inner badger."

Her smile returned at full force, and she started asking him to show her how exactly to crush his bits when a thunderous knocking made her jump. His scowl snapped back into place before he released her arm and headed for the entrance.

She watched him flip the dead bolt and yank open the door as butterflies danced around her insides. When she'd walked into the gym for the first time a few weeks before, the most she'd been hoping for was to possibly learn to throw a punch. All she wanted was to never again be a liability in a fight, but Dash made it seem like even *more* was possible. With time and training, she might become a true badass. It was a powerful feeling.

"What?" Dash snarled, but even his cranky tone couldn't erase her smile, especially since his ire wasn't directed at her.

"Why's the door locked?" another voice, almost as deep as

Dash's but not half as gravelly, asked. "This place is never closed. I thought you were dead or something."

"Private session. Come back in an hour." Dash swung the door shut, ignoring the other man's protests, and clicked the dead bolt back into place.

As he joined her where she waited in the center of the gym, she felt a twist of anxiety, thinking that all the usual gym clients were locked out, waiting in the alley, getting more and more annoyed because she was having yet another private session with Dash. They met three times a week, since a sense of urgency pressed on Norah. Devon Leifsen wouldn't sit around waiting for her to figure out how to fight. There was no time to waste. Not for the first time, she told him, "You don't have to close the gym down just for me."

He gave her a level look. "You don't need a bunch of gym bros staring while you try to learn this stuff. He's right—except for our sessions, this place is almost always open. He can come back later."

The thought of having an audience as she struggled through the motions made her nauseated, and she gave him a grateful nod. "Thank you."

With a grumbly noise, he waved his hand as if dismissing her thanks. "Let's not waste this time then. Palm heel strikes, when you do them right, can be even more effective than a punch…"

As Dash continued, Norah focused on him, filing every word into the proper place in her brain. At the back of her mind, she was almost giddy with the knowledge that he'd closed down the entire gym for her because he knew she'd be uncomfortable with people watching. The happy, hopeful butterflies in her belly took flight again, but she batted them down, determined to concentrate.

After all, empty-gym time was precious and not to be wasted.

THREE

NORAH PEEKED AROUND THE DOOR before stepping into the entry of her house, feeling the usual guilt that she was learning self-defense from someone other than Felicity. There usually wasn't anyone around after her sessions, so she was able to grab a shower and get a few hours of research done before any of her sisters returned. Today, rather than the mostly empty house she'd expected, it sounded like all her sisters were home—and all were speaking at once. Giving up on her plan of slipping in unnoticed, Norah stepped inside, curious as to what was happening.

"Norah!" her oldest sister, Molly, called from where she was pacing the kitchen, a cell phone pressed to her ear. "You're home. Good. Cara and I need some help in here."

Charlie spun around from where she, Felicity, and Bennett—Felicity's brand-new husband—were deep in discussion by the bottom of the stairs, their heads so close they were almost touching. "Wait your turn, Moo. *We* need Norah. We're so close to finding

Mom. If she slips away one more time, leaving us wandering around Nebraska again, I'll... Well, I don't know what I'll do, but it'll be bad." Charlie crossed the living room and grabbed Norah's shirt as if to lock her in place.

Eyebrows shooting up, Norah met Charlie's amped-up gaze. "What's happening? You really have a lead on Mom?" Her stomach twisted with a mix of emotions. Although it hadn't been exactly a surprise when Jane had disappeared after using her daughters' home as collateral on her bail bond, Norah still felt sick every time she thought about it. She also hated the thought of her mom going to prison, and she was annoyed at herself that she even cared. After all, Jane didn't seem to mind that her actions were about to make her daughters homeless.

"Yes." Felicity was the one who answered as she bounced across the room to join them, Bennett close behind. He gave Norah a chin lift in greeting.

Although her other sisters had thought Bennett was strange at first, Norah had liked him right away. He didn't seem weird to her—just quiet like she was.

Judging by the excited gleam in Felicity's eyes, she wasn't feeling the same messy mix of feelings about their mom that Norah was. "It's a good lead too. Do you remember Evan Sage?"

The name rang a bell, but Norah had to think hard before saying, "He was a deputy who moved away sometime last year."

"That's the one." Charlie grinned as she cast a sideways glance at Felicity. "He got a job with the police department in a small town in North Dakota—"

"South," Felicity interjected.

"Right." Giving a little shrug, Charlie accepted the correction with good grace. "I always get those two confused. I wish they'd just merge into one big state called Dakota. Anyway, apparently he's *still* obsessed with our Fifi here."

Bennett made an unhappy grumbly sound, but Charlie ignored him.

"He texted her when he spotted Jane on some security footage, taking a five-finger discount at their local Walmart just an hour ago. Store security didn't manage to catch her, so they passed the case to the local PD."

"He's not *obsessed* with me," Felicity said mildly, giving her husband a reassuring pat on the arm.

Without pausing, Charlie continued, "Obsessed Deputy Evan sent over the video files from inside and outside the store. Could you go through them and make sure it's Mom and if you can spot what she's driving?"

"Of course," Norah said, shoving her conflicted feelings aside as a spark of excitement grew inside her. As much as she knew she needed to learn the self-defense skills Dash had started teaching her, her first love was doing research, safe behind her computer screen. Although Leifsen had been popping up on her screen regularly with terrifyingly upbeat messages and menacing happy faces, she'd beefed up her laptop's security even more, and she was pretty sure this time he wouldn't be able to hack in. "Are the files saved in our shared drive?"

"You know it." Releasing Norah, Charlie grabbed hold of Felicity's and Bennett's arms and towed them toward the door where their travel bags were waiting. "Text us if you find anything. We're going to get on the road and head toward Dakota."

"That's not a thing," Felicity complained as she freed herself from her sister's hold in order to reach for one of the bags. Bennett got there first, hoisting up all three, making it look as if they barely weighed anything. Giving him a smile of thanks, Felicity turned back to Charlie. "You can't just change two states' names to make up for holes in your geographical knowledge."

"But it makes so much sense. Thanks, B." Charlie headed out the door, and her voice grew fainter as she crossed the front porch. "Think of how much embarrassment it would save people. I can't be the only one who gets those two confused."

"Bye, Norah," Felicity said, rolling her eyes.

Norah smiled, liking that she'd been included in the joke.

"Bye, Molly and Cara!" Felicity called.

The two in the kitchen chorused their goodbyes, and Molly added, "Keep in contact, and don't do anything stupid."

Holding the door for Bennett, Felicity called back, "I never do anything stupid."

Molly stuck her head into the living room. "Try to keep Charlie from doing anything stupid then."

"I heard that!" Charlie yelled from outside.

"Good! Then you'll know not to do anything stupid!" Molly shouted back, although she was smiling.

With a final quick wave from Felicity and another brisk chin lift from Bennett, they left, the screen door closing with its usual *bang* behind them. The sound, as familiar as it was, made

Norah jump. It seemed to emphasize the finality of their exit. This might be the last time they had to chase after Jane.

Norah pulled her gaze off the closed door and headed into the kitchen. It seemed a lot quieter without Charlie, Felicity, and Bennett there, even though Molly was still talking to someone on her cell.

"Ready to research?" Cara asked with a smile that turned puzzled as she studied Norah. "What have you been up to? You look like you just ran a marathon or fell into a pond. Possibly both."

Norah hesitated, nervously fingering the medical alert bracelet she'd gotten back when her asthma wasn't yet under control. Although she hadn't had to go to the ER for a bad flare in years, she still wore the bracelet. It had turned into a security blanket for her. She was reluctant to answer Cara's question, but she wasn't sure whether that was because she felt guilty for going to a trainer other than Felicity or because she wanted to keep Dash and her newly sprouted ambition to become a badass to herself for a while. Her giddiness over the second option made her uncomfortable, so she quit her mental debate and just blurted out, "I was at the gym."

Cara's eyes widened. Even Molly, who was supposed to be paying attention to the person on the other end of the line, looked intrigued. "What gym?" Cara asked, the corners of her mouth lifting as her eyes sparked with interest.

Before Norah could answer, Molly was saying into the phone, "Gotta go. Potentially fascinating things happening here." There was a short pause before she snorted a laugh.

"Yes, more fascinating than you. It is possible, you know. Love you. Bye." Ending the call, she shoved her cell into her pocket without looking away from Norah. "You went to a gym? Why? Doesn't Fifi torture you enough?"

"Who was that on the phone?" Norah knew her stalling tactic wouldn't work—at least not for long—but she needed a few moments to get her thoughts together. Molly and Cara would feel the guiltiest if Norah explained her true reasons for wanting to learn how to fight. After all, she'd been their backup when her inability to defend herself had become glaringly evident. Also, she didn't want to be taken off her current case. She had to keep Leifsen away from her sisters, plus it was personal now. She was going to bring him down.

"John Carmondy, of course." Cara was the one who answered. "Who else does Molly love except for us, and we're all here—well, we *were* all here before Fifi, Bennett, and Charlie left."

"It could've been Lono," Norah argued. "She loves her dad."

"Quit stalling." Molly narrowed her eyes into the stern glare that was guaranteed to make Norah fold. She should've known that her sister would see right through her. "What's going on?"

"I…um…I wanted to take some MMA lessons?" Her voice turned up at the end, and Norah knew she'd failed. Her sisters wouldn't believe her weak excuse for a second, and then she'd have to tell them the truth about her stalker and that she didn't want to be the weak link anymore. She couldn't live with the idea that she might be the reason they were killed or injured, all because they trusted her to act as backup and she'd failed miserably. Both Cara and Molly were eyeing her suspiciously, and she braced for the coming inquisition.

"Why would you suddenly decide that you're interested in fighting of any sort?" Molly asked. "You don't even duck our punches when we spar."

"Uh… It's actually an interesting sport? An art form even. He's—I mean, *it's* beautiful." Norah resisted the urge to close her eyes and sigh at her utter hopelessness.

The silence from her two sisters was charged as they looked at each other and then back at Norah. The sheer glee in their expressions made her pretty sure they hadn't reached the correct conclusion, and she let the air out of her lungs in a quiet breath of relief.

"Is all this"—Molly sketched a circle in the air, encompassing Norah's entire sweaty and bedraggled form—"because of a *guy*?"

"A really fit MMA guy?" Cara, who was usually her steadiest and most practical sister, sounded positively giddy. "One who insists that the only way to learn is if he puts his strong, sinewy hands on you to guide you through each movement?"

Even Molly's eyebrows flew up at that, and she turned to stare at Cara. "Where'd that come from?"

"That movie Henry and I watched the other night. The one with the hot Samoan boxing coach?"

"Oh, right," Molly said.

Both of her sisters refocused on Norah, their obviously eager anticipation of what she was going to say next making her panic a little. She didn't even know how she felt about Dash. How could she explain him to her sisters?

"It's not... I mean, there *is* a guy, but that's not... He's not..." She trailed off, caught by her inability to explain Dash's allure. *Hot* was the wrong word, conjuring up an inaccurate Hollywood-pretty-boy image. Dash was compelling and solid, and he laid out ideas in a way she could understand. He was capable of building her up and giving her hope, something she'd never expected from gym sessions filled with drills. *This* was why she hadn't wanted to share him yet, while the idea of him was so unformed yet potentially life-changing.

As her tongue-tied silence lengthened, her sisters' expressions grew even more pleased and excited, making her face burn. She knew her normally light skin was currently bright red, digging her deeper into the hole she needed to climb out of.

Just go with it, her inner voice urged. It was an easy way out of having to explain her true reasons, which would only make her sisters feel bad or worried enough to sideline her yet *again*. Saying she found Dash enormously hot felt dismissive, as if she were reducing him to nothing but a flat image. It would be a small price to pay to protect her sisters from hurt though.

With a sigh, she held her hands up in a shrug. "Fine. He's... *hot*." It tasted like a lie on her tongue, but it did the trick.

A sound that could only be described as a squeal emanated from her sisters in stereo, and Norah winced from both the decibel and the attention.

"It *is* a guy! You voluntarily went to a gym because you're interested in a guy!" Cara was positively giddy. "What about the sinewy hands thing though? Was I right about that part?"

"Our little Norah is all grown-up," Molly cooed, making

Norah cringe. Molly's delighted laugh was contagious though, and she found herself giving her sisters a reluctant smile.

"Well? Spill!" Cara prodded.

Norah stared at her blankly. She'd already spilled about the whole gym thing. What more did her sisters want?

Cara rolled her eyes affectionately as she clarified, "What's his name? Description? How'd you meet him? Are you dating or just *working out* together?" Cara's eyebrows bobbed up and down suggestively, making Norah choke on a laugh.

The truth was she'd found out about Dash's gym online, and it was rated the best in the area for mixed martial arts training. She hadn't set eyes on Dash until she'd forced herself to walk into his gym, but that didn't fit with this version of events she was letting her sisters believe.

With perfect timing, Molly's phone beeped, distracting her and saving Norah. After Molly read the text, she looked up at her sisters. "New plan. John's picking up a skip and asked me to act as backup, so you two are it for research until I get back. Norah, you'll tackle the security footage of Mom while Cara takes over investigating the hacker."

"No!" The protest was out before Norah organized her thoughts, sheer panic filling her at the thought of Leifsen turning his attention to sweet Cara, who'd already been through so much. When both her sisters turned surprised faces toward Norah, she scrambled to think of a way to justify her protest. "Um…she's already working on that embezzler case. Besides, I'm at a…ah…sensitive spot in my research. The security footage of Mom won't take me long." *I hope.*

Her sisters looked baffled by her muddled explanation. Molly sent a look toward Cara, who shrugged, so Molly turned back to Norah. "That's fine, I guess?"

Relieved, Norah stood, wanting to get away before they questioned her. "Okay. I'm going to look at the store footage."

She headed upstairs, motivated to get through the store footage as quickly as possible. Not only was Leifsen a creepy stalker, but he'd likely had a hand in stealing Cara away. Helping to bring him in would be doubly sweet.

———

Hours later, Norah decided that one circle of hell had to be watching store security footage nonstop. She wasn't sure what terrible thing a person would have to do to get sentenced to an eternity of that though. Her eyes were having trouble focusing, so she blinked rapidly and looked away, taking in the dimly lit details of her tiny room. It was officially a largish closet, but sharing a room made her anxious and unable to sleep, so she'd converted the tiny space into an improvised bedroom as a teenager.

The closet window showed the fading light of evening. Norah stared outside, still blinking to get her distance vision back after spending half the day staring at her computer screen. Just enough sunlight remained to emphasize the dark shadows. Usually she appreciated living on the edge of a national forest, but at this time of day, when the trees stood stark and spooky against the indigo sky and her imagination inserted monsters into every creeping shadow, a part of her wished for the constant ambient light of a big, never-sleeping city.

Her stomach growled, making her jump and then laugh at her momentary startle. It was pretty sad to be scared by her own body's noises, and it definitely meant she needed a break. Standing, she stretched out the kinks and then headed downstairs to the kitchen.

Sitting at the small table that worked as a desk, Cara looked up from her laptop and blinked. Norah had to smile at her sister's cloudy expression, sure that it matched hers from just a few minutes ago. The transition from research mode to reality wasn't an easy one.

Cara smiled back before transitioning to a yawn as she glanced at the clock on the microwave. "Whoa, where'd the day go?"

That wasn't really a question that Norah could answer, so she just shrugged and stuck her head into the fridge. Felicity's insistence on all of them eating healthily made it harder to find a quick meal, but there were eggs and cheese and veggies, and Norah could make something with that.

"Molly isn't home yet?" she asked, her brain instantly filled with terrible scenarios of what might've befallen Molly and John.

"She's spending the night at John's. The skip pickup went off as planned, but I'm assuming they have a lot of adrenaline to work off now." Cara smirked.

"Oh." Norah wasn't sure how to respond to that, not wanting to picture her sister having sex, so she stayed quiet and opened the egg carton.

"What'd you find?" Cara asked, her tone carefully diffident. When Norah glanced over, her sister was studying a sticky note with more intensity than it deserved.

"Mom stealing things," Norah said baldly, feeling guilty when she saw Cara wince before her sister quickly smoothed it away. "Want an omelet?"

"Sure. It really was her then?"

"Yeah." Picking up an egg, Norah held the cool, smooth oval in her hand as she studied Cara. Even though Jane had proved to her daughters over and over that she wasn't a reliable person, it still came as a shock every time she did something like this. Norah wasn't sure if they'd ever get used to their mother's disregard for the law—or for her own children. "She took a bunch of travel toiletries and a few smaller electronics and then drove away in a red Honda Accord with a Colorado plate. I think the last letter was an L, but I'm not one hundred percent sure about that. She left the parking lot and headed west on the frontage road next to the store, but she could've gone anywhere from there."

By the time she'd finished summarizing what she'd found, Cara's expression had returned to her usual calm. "You let Fifi, Bennett, and Charlie know?"

"Yes." Norah cracked the egg she held into a bowl and then added three more. "I wish I could've gotten the entire license plate number."

"You gave them a lot to work with," Cara assured her. "With that and a place to start, they're going to track her down in no time."

I hope so. We don't have much time to spare. Jane's first court appearance was coming up in thirteen days. Norah didn't say that out loud though. Cara knew as well as she did that they were down to the wire. Instead, Norah changed the subject. "How's your research going?"

"Eh." Cara wiggled her hand from side to side in a so-so gesture. "Okay. The guy's slippery, but he thinks he's smarter than he really is."

"They always do."

"Right?" After a short pause, she asked, "How are those omelets coming?"

The gentle reminder made Norah realize she'd stopped beating the eggs as they'd talked, so she refocused on the meal prep. "Sorry."

"No problem. Your brain's busy." Cara's sigh was almost soundless. "Lots going on right now."

Norah focused on the eggs so her sister couldn't see her expression. *Even more than you know.*

———

Norah tried to research Leifsen, but she kept expecting messages from him to pop up on her screen. Although none had—yet— that evening, the possibility ruined her concentration.

After a few hours of fruitless attempts at working, she couldn't face any more time in her closet bedroom. The walls were pressing in on her, trapping her, while the tiny window made her feel exposed. It bothered her that Devon Leifsen could make her feel that way about her beloved space, but she couldn't focus on research while jumping at every tiny noise.

With a huff, she packed up her things and hurried down the stairs. Cara was curled on the couch with her cell phone pressed to her ear, ignoring the laptop open in front of her. From the soft look on her face, Cara had to be talking to Henry. Not wanting to have to explain why she'd been chased out of her room, Norah just mouthed "Chico's" to her sister and headed toward the front door.

Cara gave her an acknowledging wave and pushed off the couch, moving toward the alarm panel. Without pausing in her phone conversation, she disabled it to let Norah out. Once she was on the porch, Norah waited until she heard the faint beep of the security system being turned back on before she headed down the porch steps. Even though the alarm had been circumvented several times—including once by their mom—they still used it religiously. It'd protect them from break-ins by non-tech-savvy fortune hunters at least.

It was a chilly night without a visible moon, and the streetlights seemed too far apart to cut through the surrounding shadows. Clutching her laptop bag strap with both hands, Norah hurried toward the intersection. As she passed Mr. Petra's house, she glanced over to see his entry light was on, and her neighbor's slight form was silhouetted in the window next to his door.

Rather than feeling reassured by his presence, she shivered and hurried her steps. Mr. P's featureless glare felt menacing, and she let out a breath of relief once she'd moved out of his line of sight. She didn't slow her quick pace for several blocks until Chico's came into view.

As she stepped inside the coffee shop, her heart finally returned to its usual rhythm. Although Chico's was a bit shabby, it was cheerful and wonderfully familiar. When Norah was young and Jane had her sketchy friends over to the house, Molly would bring her sisters to Chico's. The baristas never seemed to mind having a group of kids hanging out for hours and even snuck them hot chocolate with extra whip, pretending they'd messed up an order and would otherwise have to throw the drink out, even when no other customers were in the shop at the time.

The coffee shop was about half-full, with people scattered around the mismatched couches and armchairs as well as at the more traditional wooden tables and upright chairs. The sound of milk being steamed and the muted chatter of the customers drove out any lingering worries, and Norah's shoulders lowered as she relaxed.

Although she hated that anxiety about Leifsen had driven her out of her house, visiting Chico's had been a good idea. Not only would she get the security of being in a crowd, but she could also justify the visit. After all, one of Leifsen's connections, Chloe Ballister, was known to frequent the place. Norah could pretend to herself that she was doing a little field research rather than just running away from Leifsen's looming shadow in her too-quiet, too-solitary bedroom.

She ordered her usual drink—hot chocolate with extra whip—and waited until it was ready. Large ceramic mug in hand, she wove her way through the mishmash of furniture to the overstuffed armchair in the back. When she saw that a twentysomething guy reading a battered paperback had already claimed her favorite seat, she settled in the corner on her second choice, a love seat, and took a sip of her drink before putting it on the convenient end table.

The hot chocolate was sweet enough to make her teeth hurt, but the happy memories it brought back made it worth it. Pulling out her laptop, she settled it on her knees and booted it up.

The love seat bounced as someone settled on the other side. Internally, she cringed, bracing herself to rebuff an interested guy. When she turned her head, she had to blink a few times in surprise. The person sitting next to her was none other than Chloe Ballister, friend—or at least former friend—of Norah's skip and stalker, Devon Leifsen.

"Oh, sorry," the tall woman sharing her seat said. "I should've sat somewhere else, shouldn't I?"

Still startled that a person of interest—Norah's very excuse for running to Chico's—had just dropped down next to her, Norah didn't reply.

Chloe made a face as she glanced at the empty chairs surrounding them, making her long blond braids fly out as she turned her head. "Yeah, I just made things awkward. Good thing I don't have the equipment to use a urinal. I'd be guaranteed to pick the one next to the only other person in the bathroom."

Norah gave a choked laugh, recovering enough from her surprise to start to feel hunted. *Did Leifsen send her in here after me?* Pushing down her panic, she forced herself to speak. She tried for nonchalance, but her words came out squeaky. "It's okay."

"No, it's weird."

Despite her racing heartbeat, Norah was starting to feel a little excited. This was the perfect opportunity to find out more about Leifsen's whereabouts. She'd wanted to do field research; here was her chance dropped right in her lap—or at least right next to her lap. Taking a steadying breath, she tried to channel one of her more outgoing sisters. "Well, a little, but I'd rather you sat here than some person who was trying to hit on me." Norah frowned. "You're not going to hit on me, are you?"

Chloe laughed, the sound full and irresistible.

To her surprise, Norah found herself smiling back.

"Well, *now* I'm not." Chloe laughed again. "I'm Chloe, by the way."

"Norah." She wasn't sure whether to offer a hand to shake, so she just sat there and gave a sort of awkward nod. Part of her felt the usual discomfort of not knowing what to say to a stranger, while the other felt a panicky urgency to see what Chloe knew about Devon Leifsen. "Are you…um…meeting someone here?"

"Nope, so don't worry." Chloe settled back on her side of the love seat. "No one will want to kick you off your half."

Her complete acceptance of sitting so close to a stranger while not trapped in an airplane somehow made the experience humorous rather than uncomfortable. Instead of wanting to flee, Norah found herself relaxing back against the cushions, even as she reminded herself to keep her guard up. This had to be a setup engineered by Leifsen.

"How about you?" Chloe asked.

"Oh no." Norah's mind raced, trying to think of an excuse to be there, before she remembered that she honestly *wasn't* there under false pretenses…well, not completely. "I just needed to get out of the house."

"Same." The way Chloe smiled at her made Norah feel like a member of an exclusive club. "Also, coffee tastes better when someone else makes it."

Norah considered that for a moment. "True."

"Don't let me stop you from working."

Chloe waved a hand toward her laptop, sparking a flare of panic in Norah. She pictured opening up Devon Leifsen's file, the information she'd gathered on Chloe in full view, and her stomach twisted with hypothetical embarrassment.

"That's okay." As she closed her laptop with a firm click, her brain hunted for some reason to keep it shut. "I'm trying to avoid work, actually. I have a stalker who keeps sending me messages." She held her breath, waiting to see how the other woman responded.

Chloe's happy expression disappeared, replaced by a concerned frown. Either she was a good actor, or she didn't know about Leifsen's messages. Despite herself, Norah hoped it was the latter. Chloe was just so easy to like.

"A stalker? Have you reported him to the police?"

Norah couldn't imagine giving the Denver detective investigating her mom's case any more ammunition against her family. "No, but it's fine." Even as she said the words, she could feel how thin and untrue they were. It really *wasn't* fine. "Just some guy online, and he never really says anything threatening. Just overuses smiley face emojis."

"Hmm..." Chloe didn't look convinced. "Well, keep a record of everything he sends you. And if you need me to kick his ass, I love a good brawl." Her contagious grin returned.

Even the thought of Devon Leifsen couldn't kill Norah's answering smile. She promised herself she was staying skeptical about Chloe's motives, even as she allowed herself to answer honestly. There was no harm in becoming friendly with a possible lead to Leifsen after all. It would only help her research. "I'm actually learning to fight," Norah said, enjoying the chance to talk about that without having to worry about giving away her true motivation to her sisters.

"Of course you are," Chloe's tone made it clear she considered Norah a budding badass. "If you ever need backup though, I'm your woman."

"Nice."

The unexpected male voice made Norah flinch, afraid that Devon Leifsen was standing right in front of them. When she looked up, her shoulders dropped in relief. The man there was a white guy, but he was taller than Leifsen and had darker hair and a thick beard.

"There room for me in the middle?" the stranger asked with a leer. "I'd love to be the middle of a hot blond sandwich."

Norah instantly tensed again. He might not've been the specific creep she'd expected, but he was definitely a creep. Her throat closed as she scrambled for the best way to offend him just enough to make him go away but not so much that he made a scene or waited for them outside or anything. As she hesitated, his smile grew, as if he was enjoying her mute panic.

"Zero room." Chloe, on the other hand, didn't hesitate. Her flat, disinterested tone was the perfect dismissal, and Norah tried to tuck the memory of it into her brain so she could use a replica next time someone hit on her. Chloe moved closer so her leg was just an inch from Norah's, bending her head in a way that completely shut the looming man out of their conversation. "You were telling me about your self-defense training. Have you gotten to the knee-to-the-balls move yet?"

Norah was shocked she was holding back a laugh. Normally, she would be stressed and anxious for hours after some guy tried to hit on her, but Chloe made her feel like the guy's approach was nothing—less than nothing. She felt a surge of liking for Chloe, although she quickly tempered it with the reminder that she didn't know the other woman's motives yet. Chloe was—or at least had been—friends with Leifsen after all.

Chloe gave her a subtle nudge, reminding Norah to answer the question. "Oh yes. We spent several sessions on our knee-to-the-balls technique, as well as elbow, fist, and foot. We even worked on headbutts to the balls, though the logistics of that move aren't usually as useful as the other four." She peeked sideways, relieved to see the guy was gone.

Chloe erupted into giggles, leaning into Norah's side in a way that should've felt intrusive. Instead, it seemed like they were a connected team, working together to get rid of the creepy guy, rather than feeling like Chloe had shooed the guy off while Norah'd sat passively.

"That was perfect," Chloe told her, still grinning in that wonderfully conspiratorial way. "I knew *immediately* that you were amazing, and I'm always right about these things. My people radar is on point. We're going to be best friends. I can feel it."

Norah wasn't sure how to respond. Even despite knowing Chloe likely wasn't what she appeared to be, Norah desperately wanted it to be true.

"You don't believe me yet," Chloe said, not sounding offended as she reached out a hand. "But you'll see. When we're eighty and starting brawls at the nursing home, I'll be able to tell you I told you so."

The mental picture of exactly that was so vivid Norah couldn't hold back her smile.

"Give me your phone."

Tentatively, Norah handed it over and watched as Chloe entered her number.

"There," Chloe said with satisfaction, handing it back. "Now you can text me when things are about to go down, and I'll come running to be your backup. Less dramatic than the bat signal but more efficient." Chloe's phone rang, and she bounced up from the couch as she answered it. "Mom! I just randomly met the nicest person at Chico's. Hang on. I'm heading outside. It's rude to talk in here."

With a wave, she headed for the door, leaving Norah feeling stunned and ebullient and fighting to stay objectively suspicious. After all, it was just as likely Chloe was talking with Leifsen. Norah just really wished that it was in fact Chloe's mom. Even if she *was* talking with Leifsen, however, Norah was proud she'd made a connection with Chloe as a possible lead. She'd actually done fieldwork successfully, and that was something to celebrate, no matter Chloe's motives.

It took several minutes before Norah remembered the work

she needed to do and opened her laptop again. Resisting the urge to pull up Chloe's picture just in case she returned after finishing her phone call, she opened the file with Leifsen's financial records instead. It was less than a minute before the dreaded text box popped up on her screen.

You met Chloe! Isn't she hot? ☺

Norah's fingers lifted from her laptop, hovering above the keys as she stared at his latest message. Her heartbeat picked up as her breath caught in her chest. Her gaze flicked up to the tiny, neat square of electrical tape she'd used to cover the laptop camera, and she ran her thumb over it to make sure it was securely in place. It was, which somehow made Leifsen's knowledge even more disturbing, and her fingers shook slightly as she returned them to the keyboard.

How do you know that?

The thought that Chloe had told Devon Leifsen about her made Norah's stomach churn with an odd betrayal. It seemed that the whole meetup had been engineered by Leifsen after all.

How do I know everything about you? I'm always watching you, silly.

Where are you? she asked without much hope he'd actually tell her.

Wouldn't you like to know?

She rolled her eyes. Sometimes he was so cliché she felt like she was in some cheesy horror movie.

I'm enjoying our date, he wrote, making her shudder. **I'm pretty old-fashioned, so I insist on paying.**

Too late, she wrote, feeling a little satisfaction that she could have the upper hand, even on something as small as this. **I already paid for my drink.**

Check your account. Large hot chocolate with extra whip, right?

Her fingers trembled as she shut down her laptop and grabbed her phone to check her balance. There, in a pending transaction, was a transfer of $5.61, exactly the cost of her drink.

Shoving all her things back in her bag, she headed for the door, setting her half-full mug in the dirty dish container while trying very hard not to look up at the security camera, just in case he'd hacked into the feed. Her mind whirled, taking in all the ramifications of what had just happened. Devon Leifsen had access to her bank account. He'd known what she'd been drinking. He'd known she'd met Chloe or had even arranged their encounter. She'd always prided herself on being smart, but it seemed as if Leifsen was one step ahead of her in every interaction. She was in over her head.

As she pushed through the door and left the ruined comfort of Chico's behind her, Norah finally admitted she needed help. She was going to have to tell her sisters.

FOUR

"What's wrong with you?"

Norah stared at Dash, not sure exactly what he was referring to. Without more information, she wasn't able to answer his question, especially in her current overtired condition. With Devon Leifsen invading her computer, her privacy, her favorite coffee shop, and now her bank account, she'd lain awake all night, jumping at every creak of the old house. Even after she'd given up and scurried to Cara's room to take Charlie's empty bed, she'd still been unable to sleep. Now her brain was too muzzy to work right, so she just flat out asked, "Can you be more specific?"

He started wrapping her hands and wrists again, and she tried to concentrate on his technique so she could imitate it at their next session. Her sleep-deprived state made this difficult, especially since his efficient yet gentle touch lulled her into a comfortable haze. Normally, she didn't mind—even preferred—a regular lack of human contact, but she was starting to understand a little more clearly why some people were touchers. The brushes of skin against skin awoke a raw ache inside her that seemed to both worsen and improve with more contact. *Odd.*

His grumbly voice brought her out of her musings. "Why are you so out of it? Can't sleep?" When she shook her head, he asked, "Insomnia?"

"No. I usually don't have trouble sleeping." A yawn interrupted her answer. "Just last night."

His hands paused. "What happened last night?"

There was a deep stillness to him that caught her attention, even as sleepy and distracted as she was. Studying him, she was quiet for several beats before she realized he was waiting for her explanation. There was a solidness to him, a security, that made her think she could tell him anything. She didn't even hesitate before the truth spilled out of her mouth. "A skip keeps hacking into my computer."

His expression barely moved, just a slight narrowing of his eyes and hardening of his mouth, but Norah suddenly spotted *his* inner badger. "Skip?" was all he said, but his voice was so silky in the deadliest way that she felt her eyes widen, and contrarily, she started to smile. Sometime during their eight and one-tenth training sessions, she'd decided she liked Dashiell Porter, and his protectiveness warmed her insides.

"I do research for my family's bail-recovery business," she explained.

He gave a bare nod that was just the slightest lift of his chin. His lack of confusion or surprise made her wonder if he already knew. She hadn't told him what their family business was before—except for a brief mention of the possibility of her sisters getting shot or blown up—so she deduced that he'd researched her. She didn't mind. In fact, she approved. After all, she'd done the same to him before she'd even walked into his gym.

"You do research. That means you don't have any contact with bail jumpers," he said, that silky edge still in his voice.

"I don't—usually." She had to qualify it in order to be honest. After all, the occasional meetings with skips were why she was here, learning to protect herself and her sisters. "This wasn't actual face-to-face contact though."

"This one hacked your computer?" Holding eye contact with her, he finished wrapping her hands without looking, something she found disproportionately impressive.

"Yes," she said, pushing her hand into the boxing glove he held open for her.

"Why?" He helped her put on the second glove.

"I don't know." She'd thought about it a lot, especially while she couldn't sleep last night, but she hadn't reached any conclusions. "I did a complete system check, and he didn't access any of my files. All he does is…chat."

"Chat?" The way he spat out the innocuous word made it sound almost brutal.

"Yes. He introduced himself. With smiley faces. And waves. Then last night, he deposited $5.61 into my account."

He was grimly silent for several moments as she waited patiently for his response. "I don't like this," he finally said.

"Me neither." Her home and her computer were her

sanctuaries. Leifsen had violated her sense of safety in both of them.

"What's his name?"

She considered him as she absently bumped her padded gloves together. The muffled contact was an interesting sensation. "What are you planning to do with this information?"

"Find him. Have a chat."

There was a slight edge to the word "chat" that made her fairly certain Dash meant "punch" instead. As appealing as that sounded, she reluctantly shook her head. "My sisters and I need to find him first. What you want to do would be very satisfying, but it would almost certainly cause him to leave town quickly. My sisters have had to take too many trips lately."

"I could find him, have a chat, and then dump him on your doorstep so your sisters could bring him in."

She considered that. "You won't make it obvious that you're searching for him? Skips are harder to find if they're spooked."

Dash looked offended. "I can be subtle."

Looking at his huge form and the brutal, slashing lines of his face, she had a hard time imagining that. If she heard even a whisper of a rumor that Dash was out for her blood, she'd leave town—and the state—so fast there'd be a cartoon-style dust cloud in her wake.

When her silence went on for too long, his scowl deepened. "I *can*. He won't even know I'm searching for him until I pounce."

She paused. "How hard are you planning on pouncing?"

He studied her face as if checking what he'd be able to get away with. "A moderate pouncing?"

Norah was tempted—her sister had almost died after all, and Leifsen had very likely been partially responsible—but her conscience niggled at her.

He must've read her face, since he gave a disappointed huff. On anyone else, his expression would've been a pout. "Fine. A *light* pouncing."

"Okay," she agreed. He seemed so solid and reliable that every word out of his mouth had a sincere ring to it. "But if you spook him and he runs, you're the one going to New Jersey or Tasmania or Mars to pick him up."

His scowl disappeared as a rare smile touched his mouth so quickly that she wondered if she'd just imagined it. "Deal. Name?"

"Devon Leifsen."

"Got it." The badger look was back, and Norah felt a bit worried for Leifsen but more gleeful that the hacker was going to get at least some of what was coming to him. After all, Dash had promised to take it easy on him. "Ready to hit something?"

Perfect. She could pretend the punching bag had Leifsen's face on it and get some revenge for her terror and sleepless night. "Very."

———

By the time she got home, Norah was a little concerned about her decision to give Leifsen's name to Dash. All she had was Dash's word that he wouldn't scare off Leifsen. She and her sisters had to keep Barney happy, at least until Charlie, Felicity, and Bennett dragged Jane back in time for her first court appearance.

Besides, her *sisters* didn't even know about Leifsen stalking her. Norah had always shared everything with them, and keeping this a secret—even though her motives were good—seemed extra wrong now that she'd told Dash.

She stewed about it all afternoon as she closed her checking account and reopened a new one. It continued bothering her as she reviewed Leifsen's file yet again, staying disconnected from the internet. Even sitting at family dinner that evening, she was still tightly wound, vacillating between aggravation and a growing sense of guilt.

"Sooo…" She dragged out the word.

Molly and John, along with Cara and her boyfriend, Henry, immediately gave her their full attention.

Since she'd only said the one word, Norah figured her tone must've tipped everyone off that she was about to say something momentous…or at least moderately interesting. Being the sudden focus of four people nearly startled her into forgetting what she was going to say, but she managed to get the words out with only a slight stammer. "I–I might have done something… um…well, unadvisable."

John's eyes lit up. "*You* did something unadvisable?"

Her only response was a grimace.

"Well?" John asked. "What was it, little sister? Don't keep us in suspense."

Norah was already regretting mentioning it, but it was too late to back out. Even though John was the only one pressing her for an explanation, the others looked just as eager to hear what she'd done. In fact, as she allowed the pause to lengthen, she could see the interest in their expressions intensify. She groaned, stabbing at her chicken breast. "Dash—the trainer I'm working with?"

"His name's *Dash*?" Molly grinned. "That's such a great name."

"Does *Dash* have sinewy hands?" Cara asked, making Norah's face inexplicably warm. The only good thing was that both guys turned their heads to stare at Cara, taking some of the heat off Norah.

"Why are you asking that?" Henry lifted his hands, flipping them over to examine both sides. "What does that even mean?"

"That boxing movie we watched?" Cara reminded him. "The one with the hot boxing trainer and all the touching? He had the best hands." Glancing at his face, she cleared her throat. "*Second* best hands, I meant."

Ignoring their interaction as well as Molly's and John's muffled snickers, Norah forged ahead with her story. Now that she'd started, she knew she had to finish. If she didn't get it all out immediately, the conversation could take hours, and she had some more research to do that night. The day without internet had put her behind. "I told Dash the skip's name," she blurted out.

Everyone quit talking about sinewy hands and paid attention. That was one good thing about usually staying quiet, Norah figured. When she did talk, everyone shut up and listened.

"Why?" Molly asked.

"And why's that a problem?" Cara asked before Norah could answer Molly. "Unless he moonlights as a bounty hunter?"

Realizing that it was time to tell her sisters about Leifsen's stalking, Norah organized the story in her mind before speaking. "The skip has been hacking into my computer, and last night, he accessed my bank account."

That was all she managed to get out before everyone was talking at once.

"What?"

"Your computer? Don't you have a virtual jungle of impenetrable security on that thing?"

"Why?"

"Your bank account? Did he clear it out?"

"Which guy is this?"

"Barney's skip?"

"What did he do after he got in?"

Holding up her hands, Norah waited until the questions trailed off into silence before she answered the last one asked. "He introduced himself, and he just chats. Last night, he put enough money in my account to cover my hot chocolate at Chico's."

There was a pause before John said, "That's…ah…polite, I guess? Who is this guy?"

Molly gave a short shake of her head. "More creepy than polite. He's a hacker, one of Barney's bail jumpers. Devon Leifsen. Norah's been looking into him. Have you contacted the bank about your account?"

"Of course," Norah answered, a little offended that her sister had to ask.

"My stalker alarm is blaring," Cara said, sharing a concerned look with Molly. "And not the cute kind of stalker that Bennett started out being. What did Leifsen say exactly?"

Even though she'd tried to erase the event from her mind, Norah remembered every word. She recounted the gist of the conversations as the other four listened with growing frowns.

"He's challenging you." Henry was the first one to speak after she finished. "Reminds me of the way some serial killers make contact with law enforcement, trying to turn it into a game."

Norah widened her eyes as she stared at Henry. "It's reassuring that he's following the serial killer handbook."

Giving her a rare smile, Henry said, "I doubt he's killed anyone...directly at least. I'm guessing he sees you as his worthiest adversary and wants the same sort of cat-and-mouse interaction with you. He thinks he's smarter than everyone, so he imagines himself running circles around you as you try to catch him."

"*I* don't want to catch him," Norah protested. "Not in a confronting-and-cuffing way. I'll leave that to you two." She waved, indicating Molly and John. As much as she wanted to protect her sisters by dealing with Leifsen herself, she realized how far outside her skill set bringing him in on her own would be. She could find him, but physically chasing him down and tackling him? She knew she would just get in the way if she tried. Pushing away the thought that she was a failure, she reminded herself that there was a reason all her sisters worked for their business. They each had different strengths, and together they were unbeatable.

"Until we bring Leifsen in, I think we should use the buddy system." Molly had a line between her brows, a clear indicator of how upset she was. She was leaning forward in her chair, the food in front of her forgotten, and John rubbed circles on her back. "No leaving the house alone." She was looking at Norah but then added, "That goes for everyone."

Clearing her throat, Cara said, "As someone who was snatched out of this very house…"

"Gah. You're right." Molly grimaced and then got a familiar determined expression.

Norah knew that look. Molly was in full-on protective older sister mode.

"No leaving alone *or* staying at the house alone. Buddy system's mandatory wherever you—we—are."

Norah swallowed a groan. She should've known that sharing the Leifsen situation would lead to full lockdowns.

Still rubbing Molly's back, John gave a slow grin. "I like this plan. Figure I'll take advantage of that time-share I have."

"What?" Norah was confused. "You're going on vacation?"

A hint of red touched Molly's tan cheeks. "No. He's talking about my bedroom. He's not nearly as funny as he thinks he is."

John's grin widened. "Actually, I'm funnier."

"Let's go back to this very bad buddy system idea," Cara said, and Norah gave a nod of agreement.

The thought of having one of her sisters—or worse, Henry or John—along when she went to one of her training sessions with Dash made Norah cringe with preemptive embarrassment. Everything seemed to be snowballing, making her wish she'd kept her mouth shut. Leifsen hadn't done anything *dangerous* yet, and she had Dash to help her. Instantly, she felt guilty for wishing she'd kept the secret from her sisters. It was just that everything was getting so *complicated.*

"It's not practical to drag someone else to all my classes," Cara said. "I'm not forcing anyone else to sit through a two-hour lecture on the psychology of education. That'd just be cruel. Besides, we should focus more on protecting Norah, since she's Leifsen's target."

"I know it's not ideal," Molly said.

From the firm set of her chin, Norah knew her sister was going to dig in. When it came to the safety of her family members, Molly could be unyieldingly stubborn.

"But—"

"I—*we*—can all carry pepper spray," Norah blurted, not caring if she sounded desperate. She *was* desperate. She *liked* her training sessions with Dash, how strong they made her feel, and she didn't want to cancel them until they rounded up the troublesome Devon Leifsen, which could take *weeks.* Bringing a sister along to the gym wasn't going to happen, however. She would be teased for infinity, and even an audience of one would rob her of any sort of concentration. "Tasers too. And we can stay in public areas when we're out."

"We should make sure to keep our phones within easy reach," Cara added, taking some of the focus off Norah, to her relief. "I learned my lesson the hard way about having a cell handy." When she shivered, Henry covered her hand with his and squeezed. Cara offered him a grateful smile.

Norah felt a slight twist in her gut. It wasn't jealousy, really. She didn't want Henry for herself, but she had to admit she wanted what he and Cara had, their easy closeness. She wondered what it would be like to have a person who looked at her like she was their whole world.

"How about regular text check-ins?" Norah racked her brain for other options, but Molly hadn't lost her look of determination yet, and she was starting to despair.

"I like the buddy system," John said, wrapping a huge arm around Molly and hugging her against his side. With a surprised grunt, Molly grabbed his shirt to catch her balance as the motion nearly slid her off her chair. "Just think, Pax. You and me together constantly, twenty-four seven, not a moment apart for days, *weeks* even. It'll be like a honeymoon but with more togetherness. *Constant* togetherness."

"Urgh." The sound Molly made was disgruntled, but Norah noticed she tugged her chair closer to John's rather than trying to escape his enveloping hug. "Fine. No buddy system. Phones, Tasers, pepper spray, *and* check-ins."

Relief filled Norah, and it was hard holding back a delighted laugh when she caught the subtle wink John threw in her direction. Her sister's boyfriend acted like an easygoing goof most of the time, but he noticed things, and he had Molly pretty well figured out. It wasn't really a surprise, since he spent most of his time focused on her. A tiny twang of envy pinged through Norah again, but she ignored it.

Molly leaned forward, her gaze intense on Norah. "I know we all tease Bennett by calling him a stalker, but you can see how this is different, right? Bennett respected Felicity's boundaries, even at the beginning, when he was just a PI tailing her in hopes of finding Mom. Leifsen blasted through your legal and personal boundaries so hard, he left a Kool-Aid-man-shaped hole in them."

"I know they're not the same."

"Good." Molly sat back into the curve of John's arm. "And you'll follow the safety precautions, no exceptions or whining?"

Norah was about to agree to Molly's terms when the doorbell interrupted her.

They all went still. Norah tried to avoid answering the door as a general life rule, but Cara had a good reason for going pale and stiff at the chiming sound. After all, the doorbell had sounded the start of her kidnapping.

Molly extracted herself from John's hold and stood. "I'll get that."

As she moved out of the kitchen, John followed closely. Norah, Cara, and Henry stayed silent, listening as the two crossed the living room to the front door. Norah felt a bit silly, since Cara—and even Henry, by association—had a good reason to be tense about visitors, but Norah didn't have that excuse. She just had her ingrained hermit-like tendencies to blame. From her spot at the table, she couldn't see the front door, so she strained her ears to hear what the new arrival was saying.

"Can we help you?" Molly asked, sounding cautious but not overly concerned.

"Hi!" The bubbly voice was oddly familiar, and Norah frowned as she ran through her mental databases, trying to remember where she'd heard it before. "Is Norah home?"

Cara and Henry looked at her, their eyebrows raised in exactly the same way. Norah wanted to laugh at how quickly they'd become *that* couple, but she was too preoccupied with trying to place the woman.

"Depends." That was John, his happy-go-lucky tone not hiding the implacable thread of steel in that one word. "Who are you?"

"Laken Albee." Despite the familiarity of her voice, the name still came as a shock. "Norah and I are friends from way back."

"Isn't that the girl who picked on you in high school?" Cara whispered, her eyes sparking with mama-bear fierceness.

"No. She mostly just ignored me in high school." The need to be completely honest made Norah amend her answer. "She picked on me in *junior* high." From Cara's expression, the distinction didn't help.

"Maybe she wants to make amends," Henry suggested, giving a small shrug when they both looked at him doubtfully. "Most of us were nasty little beasts in junior high."

Cara's scowl deepened. "Did you used to be a bully?"

"No," he said, although he frowned. "I was always a sucker for the underdog, but I did other things I'm not proud of. Plus, I didn't discover deodorant until I was fourteen. That's a crime against my classmates right there."

"Hey, Norah." Molly's voice in the kitchen doorway pulled her attention away from Henry and Cara. "Laken Albee is here to see you. Want me to tell her to go away?" From her protective expression, she'd remembered Laken's name just like Cara had.

It was tempting to have her sister run Laken off for her, but

Norah decided to act like a grown-up. After all, Henry might be right. Maybe Laken had a change of heart and wanted to make amends for what an unpleasant little brat she'd been a decade ago. They were both adults now. They should be able to have a civil conversation. It was just that Norah didn't really enjoy having conversations with near strangers, civil or not.

When Molly gave a nod and turned back toward the door, wearing her fiercest expression, Norah knew she'd hesitated too long. Holding back a groan, she shook her head. "I'll talk to her." Standing, she moved to the entrance to the living room and frowned when she saw the closed door. "Did you shut her out on the porch?"

"Of course," Molly said. "Cops, vampires, and junior-high bullies. Never invite them inside. Life rule number seventeen."

"That's a good rule." John's face was completely serious as he gave an approving tip of his chin.

His solemnness almost made Norah laugh, but the unpleasant task of talking to Laken killed her amusement. Straightening her shoulders, she tried to channel some of the toughness she felt when she was blocking Dash's punches or pummeling the heavy bag. Despite this, her stomach still churned as she walked to the door. Taking a deep breath, she pulled it open, revealing the grown-up version of her junior-high nemesis.

"Norah!" Laken crowed, her expression changing from irritation at being left on the porch to bright enthusiasm. "Look at you! You haven't changed a bit."

"Hi, Laken." Norah eyed the woman through the screen door before forcing herself to step out onto the porch to join her. "You've chang—*oof*." Her comment was cut off as Laken grabbed her in a tight hug. Norah's hands hovered over Laken's shoulders as she debated whether to just let them be or give the woman a few back pats. Laken's perfume wasn't bad, but it was strong, and Norah felt her lungs tighten in warning. She hurried to step back before the scent could trigger her asthma. Laken clung to her for another awkward, endless moment before finally releasing her.

Digging her albuterol inhaler out of her pocket, Norah took a puff as she put several feet of space between them. She hadn't started wheezing yet, but better to be safe than sorry.

"Oh, there's the Norah I remember," Laken cooed, as if chronic asthma could be sentimental.

"What are you doing here?" It probably wasn't the most tactful thing Norah could have asked, but she was feeling off-balance, and her social skills weren't the best even on her most comfortable days. It was a bit surreal to have her junior-high nemesis on her front porch, and it was throwing Norah off her game even more than usual.

"Just visiting some friends." Laken gave a casual wave as she leaned against the porch railing. "We were talking about you, so I thought I'd look you up."

"Who's 'we'?" Norah asked, her shoulders stiff with tension. She didn't even try to lean against the railing, since she knew her awkward pose would expose just how uncomfortable she was. Besides, after her sleepless night, she was feeling rather exposed and vulnerable, and hearing that some random strangers were discussing her was not reassuring in the least.

Giving another wave—a backhanded one this time—Laken gave a chiming laugh that tensed Norah up even more. She'd heard that laugh too many times, and it had often been directed at her. "Just some friends from school. It was like a mini reunion at Dutch's the other night. I was having drinks with Kenslee, and then Carson and Pike showed up... Anyway, someone mentioned that your family still lived here, so I thought I'd swing by to catch up."

"How did my name come up?" Norah was even more suspicious after Laken's rambling nonexplanation. "I highly doubt that I'm a frequent subject of conversation between you and Kenslee."

Laken's face scrunched in a grimace of discomfort just for a moment before her expression smoothed back into unbothered perfection. "Langston isn't that big. We're able to get around to everyone on a pretty regular basis. Besides..." Her gaze dropped in a way that seemed abashed on the surface, but Laken's underlying note of slyness made Norah brace for the verbal hit. "Honey, you have to know everyone's talking about...well, your mom."

Norah had no response to that. Of course everyone knew about Jane's latest—and greatest—crime, and of course all the kids who'd picked on her in school had grown into adults who gossiped gleefully about them. She had no doubt that Laken and her friends knew every painful detail—that Jane had stolen a valuable necklace, that she'd used their family home as collateral for her bail, that she'd bolted the moment she was out of jail, that Norah and her sisters were frantically trying to track her down and drag her home before they were evicted.

Her spine felt as brittle and cold as an icicle. She searched for words, knowing that every second her silence stretched, it was more and more obvious Norah actually cared what Laken and Kenslee and their whole group said about her. All she could muster was a low grunt, a *huh* that she hoped sounded more unconcerned than panicked.

"So." Laken clapped her hands together, making Norah jump. "You have to come to Dutch's with me tonight. Everyone's meeting us there. It'll be like we're sixteen again—except our IDs will be legal this time."

Laken gave another one of her musical laughs, and Norah shuddered again. Her reaction to the sound was so Pavlovian that she might have smiled in any other circumstances, but right then, she was so aghast at Laken's invitation she couldn't find the tiniest bit of humor in anything.

"Have some drinks, set the record straight about your mother, dance a little…" Laken grabbed Norah's arm and gave it an enthusiastic shake. "We're going to have so much fun!"

No no no no no no no no… Norah's brain repeated the short refrain until she realized a few of those noes had escaped her lips, and Laken was staring at her, that perfectly full and made-up mouth open in a slightly startled O. "Uh…sorry." Norah knew she had to explain what she meant. There were regular Norah levels of rudeness, and then there were just plain unacceptable levels of rudeness. "I just…um…have to work today. Tonight. Today and tonight. Big case. No time to dance and…well, talk. To everyone." Deliberately, she pressed her lips together, attempting to keep more nonsensical words from escaping her mouth. What was it about Laken Albee that turned Norah into that awkward junior-high student again?

"Oh." Laken's mouth drooped at the corners in a way that would've convinced Norah Laken was truly sad, except that years of daily interactions with a teenage Laken had taught her better. "But we'll miss you. Isn't there any way you could get out of work?"

"No." Norah gave a shrug and attempted to look disappointed to soften her bald refusal. "You caught us at a busy time."

That gleam from earlier returned to Laken's gaze, making Norah immediately regret mentioning how busy they were. After all, it was only because half their workforce was chasing down their mom, plus the jobs Barney insisted they do, plus the fact that they'd need as much cash as possible over the next few weeks and months if Barney ended up yanking their house out from underneath them, and she wasn't about to share any of these facts with Laken Albee of all people.

"Well, I'm going to have to insist on getting together before I leave." Laken pushed her lips out in a pout.

Norah felt the prickle of nervous sweat on the back of her neck. If Laken wasn't giving up, that meant the odds were high that Norah would end up partying with her former classmates very soon. She was terrible at turning people down. She racked her brain for excuses to allow her escape from the social scene, but panic made her mind blank.

"How about coffee?"

Laken's suggestion was so unexpectedly simple and almost

not horrible compared to partying with a crowd of her high-school nemeses at Dutch's of all places that Norah found herself not hating the idea. Besides, she'd stepped out of her comfort zone with Chloe, and she'd managed to possibly get a new friend—or at least a lead to Leifsen—out of it. Maybe she should give Laken a chance. "Okay."

"Great!" Laken gave her a wide-eyed, excited look as if she was just as surprised by her acceptance as Norah was. "Ten a.m. tomorrow?"

"I can't at ten." The thought of Dash and her next training session made her smile, if only for a split second. The sensations she felt when Dash popped into her mind were novel. She'd never experienced warm, fluttery feelings like this before, and she wondered if this was what a crush felt like.

"Oh? Why not? What was that smile for?" Laken's coy questions were like a spray of Raid, immediately killing off every butterfly dancing in Norah's stomach, and she felt her smile slip away as the other woman continued throwing out questions. "Are you doing something fun? Can I come?"

Laken's casual nosiness made Norah's eyebrows shoot up—along with her anxiety level. The thought of bringing Laken along to her training session was even more horrifying than the idea of one of Norah's sisters accompanying her. "Gynecological exam." The words were out before the heat in her cheeks caught up.

Despite the embarrassment, Laken's taken-aback expression made Norah give an amused snort. She'd obviously chosen the right fake excuse if it had knocked Laken back a few steps.

"Before that then." To Norah's dismay, Laken wasn't slapped down for long. "I'll see you at the Java Bean around nine."

No good excuse came to mind, so Norah let all the air out of her lungs in defeat. "Sounds…" She couldn't say *good*, because it wasn't good. Not at all. "Sounds like a plan."

As Laken beamed, Norah tried to hide her dismay. She was already dreading the next morning.

———

Sitting on her bed that evening, Norah stared at the black screen of her laptop, her stomach churning. For the past half hour, she'd been unable to boot the thing up. She felt like her computer had betrayed her, which was stupid, since it was an inanimate object. It was her fault for not making her system secure enough, for allowing Devon Leifsen to keep wiggling in through holes she'd unknowingly left open. If she couldn't turn it on, then she couldn't figure out how he'd gotten in, much less patch those holes.

Even knowing that, she couldn't bring herself to boot up the laptop. With an impatient huff, she moved it off her thighs and onto the bed. Feeling like an abject failure at life, she got up and went downstairs to see Cara heading for the garage door.

Her sister paused, looking surprised. "Everything okay? Usually you don't emerge out of your research cave this quickly."

"Fine. Just having technical difficulties." *More mental difficulties than technical, but the technology doesn't work if I can't bring myself to turn it on.*

"Feel free to use my laptop," Cara said, opening the door.

"I'm going out with Henry tonight." She actually blushed a little, and Norah had to smile.

As strange as all the recent changes had been, she had to admit that Cara and Henry were objectively adorable together. Henry seemed like a really good guy now that they knew he was an FBI agent rather than a sociopathic murderer.

"Okay, thanks." Norah realized that using Cara's computer might be perfect. There was no way for Leifsen to tell that it was now Norah using the device, not her sister. As her brain whirred with her rapid thoughts, she realized that Cara was still hovering half in and half out of the doorway. Norah cocked her head in question. Figuring Cara might be waiting for her to say goodbye, she added, "Have fun tonight."

Cara smiled, creating deep dimples in her cheeks. "Thanks. Molly and John just ran to pick up a few things. Will you be okay here alone until they get back?"

"Sure." The reassurance came easily even as a cool prickle ran up her spine. The sun would be setting in just over an hour, and the thought of being in the house by herself, not wanting to turn on any lights just in case Leifsen was outside watching, was nerve-racking. Even though she knew there was a very minimal chance he was actively stalking her rather than just creeping into her laptop, she was still spooked by the whole thing. As much to reassure herself as her sister, she pulled her cell phone out of one of her hoodie pockets and a small Taser out of the other.

Giving the phone and weapon an approving nod, Cara said, "It's good you're smarter than me. I'll see you tomorrow."

"I'm not smarter," Norah protested. "I just learned from your experiences."

Cara blew a raspberry as she moved into the garage. "You are *so* smarter. Bye!"

"Bye." The door swung closed on the word, and Norah moved to lock it behind her sister. As she heard the automatic garage door opener kick on, she moved to the alarm keypad. Another thing her sister's experience had done was make her lose trust in the security system, especially since disarming systems was Leifsen's thing, but she still set it on *occupied—armed*. Even flawed protection was better than none.

Warrant padded after her as she checked to make sure the front door was securely locked and then returned to the kitchen for Cara's laptop. She spent more time than actually required to create a perfect square out of electrical tape and affix it over the camera. Once the lens was covered, she knew she had to take the next step. Without allowing herself to think about it, she jabbed the power button, turning it on before she could wallow in her doubts and anxiety. As it booted up, she busied herself with other tasks—getting a drink of water, scratching Warrant behind the ears, settling into a kitchen chair, lining the edge of the laptop to run perfectly parallel to the edge of the battered kitchen table, and arranging herself to allow for premium comfort. Even though she knew keeping her eyes off the screen wouldn't help if Leifsen decided to hack Cara's computer too, she still wouldn't watch. The tiny illogical part of her brain was insistent that she should keep her head buried firmly in the sand if she wanted to stay safe.

When enough time passed that she was sure the computer was fully booted and she was starting to feel silly, she forced herself to focus on the screen. Logging in, she took her first full breath in what felt like an hour when she didn't see the text box she'd been dreading. Wiping her palms against her jeans, she lifted them to the keyboard.

As soon as she dove into her usual research sites, her stomach untwisted, and she relaxed into the comforting familiarity of her job. Since Cara's laptop wasn't hers, she felt like it was a mask she could wear, a way of disguising her identity—albeit thinly. She saw that Chloe Ballister's band would be playing at Dutch's that weekend, and she added a note to the report she was preparing for Molly. It would be worth having someone there to talk to Chloe and check to see if Leifsen had tagged along.

Using the username and password she'd *borrowed* from one of the sheriff deputies, Norah logged into the DMV database and checked to see what vehicles were registered under Devon Leifsen's name. When that search turned up empty, she tried his parents. They had five—two newer luxury SUVs, a vintage sports car, a utility trailer, and an older Toyota Corolla. Norah noted all the colors, models, license plates, and VINs, but she circled the information on the green Toyota. Unless it was the car they let their housekeeper drive, it had to be the one they got for their failed-to-launch adult son.

When the dreaded text box popped up in the corner of the screen, Norah jerked back as if Leifsen had reached through the monitor and slapped her.

Hey Norah!

Are you trying to avoid me? LOL

Instinctively, she moved to sever the internet connection and then shut down Cara's computer, but she hesitated and just logged out of the DMV site instead. With late-evening sunlight still filtering through the window above the sink, she felt braver than last time, when darkness had surrounded the house. Now that she wasn't visible through a window, safe behind locked doors and an armed security system, the urge to ask questions permeated the heavy layer of anxiety she felt.

Her hands hovered over the keys, her gaze locked on the blinking cursor. *Just ask.* Channeling the self-confidence she felt during her sessions with Dash, she hammered out a quick question.

Where are you?

There was a tiny pause before he responded. **I can't just TELL you. That would be too easy. What's the fun in that?**

Biting the inside corner of her lips, her brain raced as she tried to come up with the best line of questioning. Usually, she had plenty of time to develop a plan and finesse it until all the details were perfect. Thinking on her feet wasn't her strongest skill. She finally typed one word, hoping it created the reaction she needed. **Scared?**

The pause before his answer was longer this time. **No. LOL. I'm not the one who should be scared. You don't even know where I am.**

Norah cocked her head as her gaze ran over his words. She wasn't the best when it came to reading people, and this format made it even harder to judge his emotional state. Had she made him defensive? She wondered at the sudden lack of exclamation points and happy faces. As she considered his answer again, more words appeared in the text box.

I know exactly where you are. Are YOU scared?

Swallowing down the sudden lurch of panic his question caused, Norah hurried to type, not wanting her hesitation to read as fear. **Not really. Why would I be scared of some dude who hides behind a computer?**

Her heart hammered from the confrontational words she'd just typed, and she forced down a semihysterical laugh. Leave it to her to be more afraid of arguing with Leifsen online than the possibility of him breaking in and killing her.

The longer the pause continued, the faster her breathing got until her brain was buzzing with too much oxygen. When his response finally appeared on the screen, she had to blink a few times before she was able to read it through the black spots dotting her vision.

What are you saying, pretty Norah? That you WANT to meet me? Want a more intimate repeat of our date last night?

Her heart skipped before taking off again, even faster than

before. Her eyes shot to the small kitchen window, but all she could see was a square of the dusky blue sky. It reassured her that there was no way for him to see her, and she pressed the tape a little harder against the covered camera lens underneath.

Realizing she'd never responded, she typed, **Sorry. Got interrupted.** She paused for a second, trying to think of how to answer his earlier question in a way that was least likely to get her killed but at the same time would annoy him enough to make him careless and maybe let some helpful information slip. Nothing immediately came to mind, and she frowned, wishing one of her sisters were there to help. Giving up, she ignored his previous question and asked another of her own. **Why are you so interested in me anyway?**

Because you're just like me.

She frowned at the line. Why would he think she was a creepy stalking hacker? **Why would you say that?**

It's true. We're both too brilliant to bother with the rest of the peons.

They're not peons. Norah knew it was futile to argue, but she couldn't stop her fingers from flying over the keys. **Why would you think we're better than everyone else?** She couldn't imagine having that kind of misplaced confidence.

Because we are. It's obvious. You're trying to fit in, but

you don't see how we're miles above all those cockroaches.

Annoyance flared as she read his words, and she quickly wrote, **You better not be calling my sisters cockroaches. How are you any better than them...specifically?**

We're on a higher cerebral plane. Have you read Plato? The allegory of the cave?

Norah hoped he couldn't see or hear her, because she rolled her eyes and muttered, "A higher cerebral plane? Please." Feeling like she finally might be able to get some useful information out of him, she played along. **Sure.**

Everyone else is a prisoner, staring at shadows, but the two of us...we've managed to break our chains and turn around. We see the truth.

With a snort, Norah paused to think of a leading response rather than telling him that she could barely muddle through life as one of those shadow-watching peons he was so disdainful of. She was pretty sure if she suddenly knew the secrets of the universe, she would hide under her bed with Warrant and a bag of peanut M&Ms and never come out.

Don't you have any family or friends who are enlightened like us? she finally typed, not thrilled with her response but knowing she couldn't delay any longer without seeming like she was working too hard. She didn't want to have a philosophical discussion with him about what was "the truth." She wanted to figure out where he was so she could send Molly after his stalking ass.

You're not paying attention, Norah. I already told you you're the only one.

What about Chloe? she asked, holding her breath, hoping he wouldn't say anything incriminating about her potential friend.

She's hot...but still a cockroach like the rest of them. We're the only ones, Norah. That's why we belong together.

Norah's stomach churned as her fingers hesitated over the keyboard. Before she could type a response, he beat her to it.

I know you can't see it yet, but I'm patient. I'll help you realize the truth.

She knew she wouldn't be able to get any location details out of him, but maybe if she made him mad, he'd slip. If he came after her, as terrifying as that would be, it would bring him out into the open and give her sisters the opportunity to catch him. It was obvious he wanted her to be with him, and as scared as she was, she was willing to act as bait if that would get him back into jail where he belonged.

With shaking fingers, she typed, **The truth is you're a stalker and a peon, just like the rest of us. Quit hacking my computer. Bye.**

After disconnecting the internet, she closed Cara's laptop with a decisive click. Just as she usually did after ending a conversation with Devon Leifsen, she stared at the top of the computer. This time though, she was able to mute her panic enough to be able to think things through. She had no idea if what she'd just done would be helpful in bringing Leifsen in or if she'd just made things a hundred times harder for her and her sisters. Blowing out a puff of breath, she sat back in her chair and moved her gaze to the window. Her thoughts still churned as she stared blindly at the darkening sky.

Warrant, who'd made himself comfortable under the table, groaned and rolled over onto his back. Absently using one foot to rub the dog's belly, Norah made herself take a long breath and release it slowly. Although her stomach was still twisted into a knot and her heart continued to pound too quickly, she felt a little calmer.

Glancing down at Warrant, who was wallowing in the bliss of her tummy rub, Norah gave an amused snort that sounded too loud in the quiet house. "It'd be nice to be able to hide under that table with you. All day tomorrow too." At least then she could avoid her coffee date. Warrant thumped his tail at her words, making her smile again.

Maybe not all *day tomorrow*, a sly thought interjected, and she felt her face heat at the truth of it. There was no way she was going to miss her time with Dash.

She was looking forward to their training session a little *too* much.

FIVE

When Norah walked into the coffee shop, the familiar smell of roasted beans and sweet things made her smile. The Java Bean wasn't as cozy and familiar as Chico's, but she needed a break from the latter place after Devon Leifsen ruined her last visit.

"Norah! Over here!" Laken waved from her spot at a tall table, and Norah's smile threatened to turn into a grimace.

How did she beat me here? Norah took a surreptitious glance at her phone to see that she was, as planned, fifteen minutes early—*seventeen* minutes early, even. She preferred being the first to arrive so that she could pick a spot with her back to the wall and avoid the awkward few minutes as she ordered while the person she was meeting stared at her back.

By the time she made it to the table with her cup in hand, her stomach snakes had already woken up and were writhing around. Laken had taken the seat against the wall, so Norah slid into the chair opposite, already feeling squirmy from not being able to see the room without turning around. Even though her logical mind knew it was highly improbable that everyone was staring at her, the insecure part of her could feel dozens of pairs of judging eyeballs boring into her back. Resisting the urge to keep her backpack on her lap as a sort of squishy protective shield, she hung it on the back of her chair.

At least Laken hadn't jumped up to hug her like she had the day before. Norah had been braced for that very thing and had even taken two precautionary puffs from her inhaler in case Laken's perfume attacked her lungs again. Instead, the woman just beamed at her from her coveted spot against the wall as Norah settled in as best she could with every nerve on high alert.

"Sooooo good to see you, Nor!" Laken's smile ramped up another few notches.

Although she eyed the woman across from her with some suspicion, Norah couldn't help but wonder if she'd misjudged Laken. Maybe she *had* changed from her horrid teenage self. It wouldn't be fair, Norah figured, to judge the woman on what she'd been like as a child. Keeping that firmly in mind, she gave Laken a cautious nod. "Thanks."

"What have you been up to the past five years?" Laken gave her an expectant look over the edge of her coffee cup.

See, Norah told herself. *She's changed. The old Laken would've just talked about herself.* Unfortunately, the question was one guaranteed to make her mind blank. It was just so *broad*. A lot had happened in those five years since high school, and most of it wasn't anything she wanted to share with Laken. She took a sip of her coffee, trying to use the delay to come up with a response, but all she managed wasn't really an answer to that question. "I've been good."

There was a pause that felt extraordinarily awkward, but Norah didn't have any other words to use to fill it, so she just kept her eyes on her coffee cup and ignored Laken's expectant gaze.

"Working with your sisters, that must be fun," Laken finally prompted.

"Yes." Norah knew it wasn't enough, so she dug deep for more words. "It is."

"And you're a bounty hunter. How exciting!" This time, Laken picked up the conversational ball right away, and Norah felt a surge of appreciation.

"Yes," she said, even though Laken hadn't really asked a question. Honesty made her add, "I don't really do any of the actual fieldwork though."

"Still, you do research for your sisters, right?"

Norah studied the other woman's animated and interested expression. Although her research duties weren't a secret, there was no reason for a former classmate who lived in a different town to know her role in the family business. Even allowing for maturation and personal growth that could've happened between their teenage years and now, Laken's behavior was odd. It was like her personality had changed completely, and Norah felt distrust push aside her appreciation for Laken's new, personable ways. "Where'd you hear that?"

Laken's eyes rounded. "Oh! Is it not true?" Her laugh rang a little too loudly, drawing the attention of a couple sitting a few tables over. "I should know better than to believe any Langston gossip I hear."

Tipping her head, Norah frowned. "Who was talking about what I do for my family's business? That's really boring gossip."

Although Norah didn't mean it as a joke, Laken threw back her head and laughed.

Still puzzled, Norah waited impatiently for the woman to give her an answer.

"You know this town," Laken said with one of her dismissive hand waves. "There's not much happening, so all gossip is fair game. But enough about boring hometown rumors. Tell me what it's like to bring in wanted criminals. Your work must be so exciting!"

It took a long moment before Norah could respond. The conversation was taking odd turns she wasn't prepared for, and Laken's attempts to redirect felt more like evasion than Norah liked, but she reminded herself to give the other woman a chance. "It's satisfying but usually not very exciting."

As she said the words, Leifsen's creepy messages flashed through her mind, but she pushed them away. Everything in her brain needed to focus on getting through this encounter without suffering humiliation. This wasn't the time for her to get paranoid.

"Oh, I can't believe that," Laken said coyly. "I think you're just being modest."

Frowning yet again, Norah shook her head. "It really isn't exciting. Maybe a little more for my sisters, but for me it's just a lot of hours in front of a computer."

Laken hid a tiny frown behind her coffee cup as she took a sip. Catching that brief downturn of the other woman's mouth, Norah studied Laken, curious about her unexpected reaction. Norah had always loved solving puzzles, and she felt some of her tension fade as she set her mind to figuring out what was going on with her former classmate.

"Tell me about your sisters' jobs then." Laken said, affixing her smile back in place as she lowered her cup. "Have they ever chased after anyone famous?"

"Not really." Norah shifted, uncomfortable with talking about the business. Even giving that evasive nonanswer felt wrong, like she was breaking confidentiality rules.

"Well…" Another of Laken's micro expressions flickered across her face—frustration this time—and the puzzle solver in Norah added it to the other clues. "Who are they after now? Anyone I've heard about?"

Norah didn't want to talk about Leifsen for several reasons, so she just raised one shoulder in an awkward half shrug. "Just a…white-collar criminal. No one interesting."

This time, Laken's mask dropped for a solid two seconds as she glared at Norah. "What about your mom?" she asked. "Have your sisters had any luck tracking her?"

Oh. That's her plan. The pieces clicked into place, and Norah couldn't hide her grimace. It seemed that Laken wanted the good gossip straight from the source. "I really don't want to talk about Mom," she said flatly, and Laken's head jerked back slightly, as if she wasn't expecting to be so bluntly refused.

"I didn't mean to touch a nerve." Laken plastered on a look

of sympathy, and Norah wondered how she'd ever thought the woman was being sincere. Laken hadn't changed since high school. She'd simply gotten better at disguising her true motives. "I just wanted to make sure you were doing okay with everything that's happened. I mean, being forced to hunt down your own mother... That must be so painful."

"You didn't touch a nerve," Norah said, unable to hold in a sigh. For a short while, she'd thought this coffee date wouldn't be excruciatingly uncomfortable, but now she knew the truth. It was going to involve Laken trying her best to dig her manicured nails into Norah's family business so she could rip everything open, exposing them for the entertainment of their former classmates.

She knew she couldn't sit there much longer without saying something that was truly rude. Glancing at her bare wrist as if she were wearing a watch, she abruptly stood and shouldered her backpack.

"I need to get to my appointment." As Laken stared at her, eyes wide and mouth slightly open, Norah grabbed her coffee cup and turned to leave. "Bye," she tossed over her shoulder, not able to conjure up a "good to see you" or an "it's been fun." Both would've been lies.

"Wait..." Laken said faintly, but Norah didn't stop, barely slowing to toss her paper cup into the recycling bin.

As she charged through the door into the autumn sunshine, she felt as if a fifty-pound weight had been lifted off her shoulders. Except for her abrupt departure, Norah thought she'd handled the time with Laken pretty well, and now it was over. She just had her session with Dash to look forward to.

Feeling the corners of her mouth tip up, she resisted the urge to bounce with every step. It was hard though. Excitement bubbled through her, lifting her buoyantly until she felt as if she could just float to the gym. A tiny, serious voice in her head warned her that the higher she flew, the farther she had to fall, but she ignored it and simply wallowed in the joy of leaving Laken behind for the prospect of punching Dash.

———

She arrived early. Uncomfortably early. Instead of looking at her nonexistent watch, she should've checked her phone and then hid out in an alley for forty minutes, because when she stepped inside the gym, it was packed. She froze, feeling claustrophobic. After previously training with just Dash, the movement of a dozen people—all big men—along with the clamor of clanging weights and grunts and the heavy pulse of rock music was overwhelming.

Norah wasn't sure how anyone could function with all the distractions, much less learn something. She took a step back, bumping her heel against the door. Her close proximity to the exit reassured her. No one had noticed her yet. All she had to do was slip back outside, linger in the alley for a while, and then return after Dash had kicked everyone out.

Her gaze swept over the place a final time as her hand reached for the door handle. Before she could put her escape plan into motion, however, she spotted Dash…and his eyes were locked on her.

Mentally cursing, she debated whether she should continue

her plan to bail and pretend that she'd forgotten a vital item in the car or something. The only problem was that it wouldn't take forty minutes to retrieve a lost item, so she would just have to deal with walking into the crowded gym again if she did that. Grumbling under her breath, she resigned herself to staying. Now she just had to run the gauntlet of sweaty, curious strangers to get to the other side of the gym where Dash was waiting.

Straightening her shoulders, she locked her gaze on Dash. *Just think of it as a video game*, she told herself. Dash was the prize she needed to capture, the treasure chest waiting for her at the end of her quest. All she had to do was weave her way through the mats and benches and weight racks while ignoring the grunting beings between her and her pot of gold.

Not allowing herself to hesitate a second longer, Norah strode forward, not taking her eyes off her prize, even as his expression turned quizzical. She only made it halfway when a muscular form stepped in front of her, blocking her path.

"Hey, pretty lady. You must be new."

Without engaging or even looking up at his face, she slipped around the obstacle and fixed her eyes on Dash again. His expression was now slightly amused, the right side of his lips twitching upward in a tiny, lopsided smile.

"Wait!" the obstacle behind her protested. "We can work out together. I'll help you with your form."

She ignored his words, just as she ignored all the other sounds filling the gym as she maneuvered through the second half of her treasure trek. No one else tried to stop her, and she found herself almost disappointed as she neared Dash's stock-still form. As quests went, that one had been fairly uneventful. Still, her heart was trying to pound its way out of her chest, and a triumphant grin stretched her lips as she stopped right in front of Dash.

Norah felt as if she should do something to show she'd claimed her treasure chest, like boop his nose or write her name on his forehead with a Sharpie or make him wear a *Property of Norah* T-shirt or something.

Unable to think of any claiming gesture that wouldn't be brutally embarrassing, she just stayed still and quiet.

He watched her with that intently focused stare, his amusement fading as his expression settled back into unreadable lines. "I didn't have time to kick everyone out."

"I know. I'm early. I was forced to make a dramatic exit from a coffee shop." That didn't seem complete, so she tacked on a simple, "Sorry."

His left shoulder lifted, wordlessly brushing off her apology. She expected him to question her about why a dramatic exit had been called for, but he simply asked, "You okay training with other people in here?"

She was still buzzing with the adrenaline it took to cross the gym, creating an illusion of invincibility, so she gave a firm nod. "I'll just keep focusing on you."

His gaze sharpened even as the corner of his mouth twitched up again. For a moment, he looked like a deeply satisfied lion who'd just eaten his fill of antelope. "Do that." His eyes flicked down to take in what she was wearing. She almost caved in her shoulders when she remembered she'd bought a new workout top and was wearing it for the first time, but she caught herself just in time and straightened her posture. To her relief, he didn't comment on the way her new shirt hugged her slight curves. Instead, he just met her gaze and asked, "Ready?"

"Yes."

"Then let's go."

———

After a workout so intense she'd actually forgotten about her larger-than-normal audience, Norah tried to decide whether she loved or hated assisted stretching. As Dash pressed on either side of her lower back, encouraging her to stretch just that little bit further, her hamstrings locked up in panicked protest before finally grudgingly releasing. His hands burned her skin through the fabric of her top, and she mentally grumbled at Cara for putting the term "sinewy" into her brain. Before that excruciating conversation, Norah had never put much thought into men's hands, and now she couldn't stop obsessing about Dash's.

Thanks to her twisting thoughts, she didn't notice when Dash released her, and she stayed bent over in the stretch until a clearing throat made her straighten. One of the gym members hovered over her, offering a smile and a hand up. Norah hid a grimace. She wasn't a fan of touching people, especially complete strangers—and sweaty strangers at that. Pretending she didn't see the oversize mitt, Norah got to her feet under her own power. Once upright, she concentrated a little too hard on dusting off her leggings just so she wouldn't have to make eye contact.

"Are you done hogging the new member?" the stranger asked, and she recognized his voice as belonging to the man obstacle she'd dodged when she'd first arrived at the gym. "And are you going to introduce me?"

"No," Dash said flatly, and Norah ducked her head to hide her pleased smile.

"Why not?" From the laughter clear in his voice, the burly stranger wasn't offended by Dash's curtness. "It's the least you can do when your gym is basically a sausage fest."

Ignoring the last part, Dash gave an annoyed grunt. Unlike the other man, he didn't sound at all amused. "She doesn't want you hitting on her. This is a gym, not Tinder. Stop bothering us, and go practice your side kicks. They still need work."

Norah couldn't hide her smile that time. She was the worst at turning away unwanted attention, but apparently Dash was the best—even better than Chloe Ballister. If he wasn't Gigantor-size, she'd carry him around in her pocket so she could pull him out to act as a buffer for any awkward social interaction. It would be so wonderful not to have to deal with pushy guys when all she wanted was a cup of coffee or groceries or to work out in peace. If only he'd been there during her encounter with Laken last night, he could've sent the woman scurrying away, and their unpleasant coffee date might never have had to happen.

With a good-natured grumble, the other guy finally took the hint and wandered off. Norah watched him go, but the sight of the other gym patrons eagerly taking in the encounter made her stomach tighten. She snapped her gaze back to Dash. It was much easier to pretend they were alone in the gym if she didn't look at everyone else.

"Good job today," he said gruffly, and Norah blinked. "What?"

"Good job." He spoke the words a little louder this time, and she allowed the praise to soak in and warm her from the inside out. "Especially with an audience." He swung an arm to indicate the people around them.

Although everyone had returned to whatever they'd been doing once Dash sent the pushy guy away, Norah still felt the burn of many eyes on her. It had taken a boatload of concentration to push her self-consciousness away and focus on what Dash was trying to teach her.

"Thank you," she said, tucking his praise into a safe place in her mind where she could take it out and bask in it later when she was alone. "See you on Friday?"

"Yeah, but not here," he said. "I'll text you the address."

Norah blinked, startled by this change in their routine. She knew he had to have a good reason to switch training locations though, so she just nodded.

His mouth tightened a little. "Heard anything else from the hacker?"

"Yeah." Norah grimaced. While floating in a happy sea of endorphins and Dash's attention, she'd forgotten about Leifsen for an hour. Real life returned with a crash. "Last night."

At her words, Dash seemed to grow another couple of sizes as he drew himself up. "What'd he do?" he growled. Before she could answer, he glanced over her shoulder and asked, "Hungry?"

"Uh…yeah?" The quick change in conversation made her answer tentative, and she glanced behind her to see what he was looking at. A couple of guys were stretching on nearby mats, but they appeared to be minding their own business.

"Let's go." Putting a hand against her back, he ushered her toward the door. "Davies!" he called across the gym.

"Yeah?" a guy responded, using his glove to stop the speed bag he'd been pummeling.

"Going to lunch. Watch the place." Dash waited for the other man's nod before grabbing his jacket and Norah's bag from one of the storage cubbies and using his back to push open the door.

"We're...going to lunch?" Norah felt a little like she'd been swept up in a muscle-bound tornado.

"You're hungry, I'm hungry, and I don't want an audience to hear our conversation." Without dropping his hand from her lower back, he steered her left. "Especially those gossip-loving drama queens."

She snorted a laugh at the description, startling herself. Everything was happening really fast, and her mind was buzzing. The heat from his hand on her back soaked into her muscles, giving her a lot to process. Add in the fact that she was pretty sure this could be considered a date, and her frantic thoughts refused to fall into any sort of logical order.

Worried about what might pop out of her mouth if she opened it, she kept her lips closed and concentrated on walking. It was another gorgeous fall day, and the sidewalk was busy. She expected to have to dodge other pedestrians, but everyone was quick to get out of Dash's way. When she noticed the odd way people glanced at him and then carefully averted their eyes as they gave him a wide berth, she turned her head and studied him. Was it his size? His obvious strength? Or was it the severe downward twist of his mouth that made people wary?

"What?" he asked.

Blinking as she was pulled out of her thoughts, she met his gaze. "What?"

"Why are you looking at me like you want to dissect me in a lab?"

Another jolt of laughter escaped, and she marveled at how easily this grumpy man could get her to laugh. "I was just trying to figure out why people seem scared of you."

Giving a grunt, he turned his head to face forward again. "Because I'm scary."

She laughed again. Despite his sour expression, the man was funny. "No, you're not."

"I am." He sounded almost offended that she didn't find him terrifying.

"You're objectively not scary."

"Objectively?" The corner of his mouth tipped up, making him even less intimidating. "If you're the only one who believes that, then you can't say objectively. That's pretty much the definition of *subjectively*."

When she couldn't think of a good counterargument, her shoulders twitched in a shrug. It had been an uncharacteristically inaccurate word choice for her to make, but she was feeling weirdly protective of the man by her side. "They're idiots then. I don't know how they survive if they're that bad a judge of who's scary."

"Who do you think is scary?" He guided her across the street through a break in the traffic, giving her a good idea of where they were headed for lunch. Sure enough, he opened the door to her favorite Thai place, and her mouth immediately started watering as she walked inside. The hostess showed them to a red booth in the corner, and Dash waited for her to sit before sliding into the seat across from her. After the hostess handed them menus and left, he looked at her, raising an inquiring eyebrow.

"Who do I think is scary?" she repeated. She was distracted enough by the menu that she answered without filtering her thoughts first. "Leifsen, although I pretend he isn't because he wants me to be scared, so showing fear would be letting him win. Sonny Zarver, a skip my sister brought in who liked to set booby traps and wrapped me in explosives once. Stuart Powers, one of the treasure-hunters trying to find the necklace Mom stole, because he's an amoral worm who'll do anything—no matter how awful—for money, but he always seems to manage to wiggle out of punishment. I could keep going, since most people scare me, but you don't. You say what you think, and you've never actually punched me in the face, despite all the opportunities you've had. You're the opposite of scary." Settling on an entrée, she glanced up from her menu and saw that Dash's expression had gone ice cold.

"Wrapped. You. In. Explosives." Each word was carefully enunciated with a pause in between, clipped rather than his usual grumbly rumble. "Where is Sonny Zarver?"

"Why?" she asked, a little surprised that she felt pleased by his ferocity on her behalf rather than nervous. It was a novel feeling to have someone want to fight her battles for her. "So you can find him and kill him for me?"

"No." The coldness in his expression lightened, although she could tell he was trying to hold on to his frozen rage. "So I can find him and kill him for *me*."

A laugh escaped her, and curiosity and amusement erased the last of the fury in his eyes, although his scowl stayed in place. "You're too late. My sister caught him and dumped him back in jail."

He grumbled a little but subsided when a server approached. As soon as their orders were taken and their menus swept away, Dash continued their conversation as if there hadn't been an interruption. "Let me know when he gets out."

Leaning back, she studied him. "I doubt he's going to get out anytime soon. Probably not for fifty or sixty years."

He mirrored her action, resting against the bench seat. His knees brushed hers under the table, and she jumped at the contact before shifting her legs out of the way. After working with him for ten sessions, she'd gotten used to how big he was, but seeing him take up an entire bench seat startled her anew. She wondered what it was like to constantly take up so much space. She'd always felt overly conscious of staying out of people's way, and she was small.

"Things don't always go the way they should," he said. "Let me know."

It seemed silly to argue about an improbable hypothetical, so she just gave a half shrug and nod of agreement.

"Good."

The word was basically a grunt, which made Norah want

to smile again. Even though John, Henry, and now Bennett had been around the house a lot recently, she wasn't used to spending much time with men, especially such an oversize and utterly masculine example as Dash was proving to be. It was a little like studying an alien species, discovering the similarities and differences. She was intrigued but still a little uncertain as to how to act, especially now that they weren't punching each other.

"Tell me about the hacker."

Norah frowned slightly, confused. "I already did."

"You said he was harassing you again last night. What exactly did he say?"

She paused, mentally debating whether she should share. Since he already knew about Leifsen, she decided it wouldn't hurt to give him more details. "I was working on Cara's laptop last night, and the same type of text box popped up. He asked if I was trying to avoid him. So I asked where he was, and he said it wouldn't be fun if he just told me. Then he asked if I was scared—"

A low sound from Dash interrupted her. When she paused and raised her eyebrows, he just gestured for her to continue.

"I asked why he thought I'd be scared of a guy hiding behind his computer—"

This time, Dash's interruption was a short laugh.

"He asked if that meant I wanted to meet him and said a bunch of nonsense about us being super geniuses while everyone else is a cockroach, and then I told him to stop hacking my computer and shut it down."

Dash's sharply cold gaze had returned, and he was frowning so severely that his mouth had turned white at the corners. "Don't like that."

Unbidden, her smile came again. It seemed like an odd time to be amused, but there was something about the way Dash so calmly understated things, even while his true emotions were evident, that both reassured and entertained her. "Me either. Especially because I think he helped the people who kidnapped my sister."

Nothing changed in his face except for a small tic beneath his left eye, but Norah could somehow *feel* the fury pouring off him. "Explain." It sounded as if his teeth were locked together.

"We don't have any proof," she felt compelled to say in order to be completely honest, "but Leifsen's been charged with deactivating alarm systems in a number of burglaries. When Cara was taken…" She had to pause for a moment to swallow against a suddenly tight throat. It had been too recent and too terrible, and the memories threatened to overwhelm her. Dash's hand settling over hers brought her back to the moment, away from those torturous hours when they didn't know if Cara was alive or dead. He squeezed her fingers gently before withdrawing, and she had to stop herself before she caught his hand again.

The server arrived with their soup, and she was grateful for the time to get herself together. She took a few spoonfuls before looking up at Dash again. "The alarm was disabled at our house right before Cara was taken. It's only supposition, but there's a chance that Leifsen was involved."

His fingers tightened around the handle of his spoon, and she found his white knuckles strangely appealing. His shared outrage that Leifsen was running around town, harassing her and committing who knows what other crimes, made Norah feel as if she wasn't alone. She and her sisters had pretty much raised themselves, and it had been the Pax sisters against the world for her entire life. There was something so tempting and wonderful about them having actual help.

Despite his obvious outrage, he deliberately ate a mouthful of soup before speaking. "Got any ideas where this…guy might be holing up?" The way he paused before saying "guy" made her think he had swallowed a much harsher term.

"Actually, I do." The thought of actively looking for Leifsen rather than waiting passively to see if he'd come after her was surprisingly satisfying. She smiled as she reached for her bag. She dug out her notebook and placed it on the table. "I haven't written up a formal report yet, but all my notes are in here."

Cocking a brow at her, he allowed one side of his mouth to curl up in a way that had her beaming back at him. "Want to go hunting?"

If anyone else had asked, her response would've been an enthusiastic *no*, but the thought of joining forces with Dash and dragging creepy Devon Leifsen out of whatever hole he was hiding in wasn't as terrible as it could be. Leifsen thought he'd left her cowering in her bedroom. She might be scared, but she wasn't helpless, not anymore. Besides, being with Dash made her feel both protected and powerful. He'd keep her safe until she felt ready to step away from his solid bulk to throw a couple of unexpected punches…and maybe a knee to the groin. This was *her* stalker after all, the guy who helped kidnap her sister. She knew she couldn't go after Leifsen alone, and she'd accepted that, but here was Dash, offering his services as coach, moral support, and bodyguard. How could she pass up the opportunity?

"I guess?" she said, making Dash bark out a laugh. "One of his associates is in a band that'll be playing at Dutch's on Saturday night. I was going to tell Molly so she could check if he shows up, but we could go instead?" Her nerve broke, turning her last statement into a question.

"Saturday night then. We'll track him down."

His eyes gleamed, and she felt her stomach jump in response—either in nervousness or excitement for the upcoming chase. Her first instinct was to analyze the new sensations she was experiencing, but then she mentally cut herself off. She was going to roll with it, allow herself to do something without examining everything that could go wrong.

After all, if she got into trouble this time, she'd be with Dash, and she'd bet he could keep them both safe. She felt her smile grow, stretching across her face until she knew she was beaming as she flipped open her notebook.

"Here's what I've learned about Leifsen so far."

———

As Norah cautiously got out of Cara's car, she wondered for the fiftieth time whether she'd entered the address Dash had sent her into the GPS wrong. The directions had taken her out of Langston and into the foothills, telling her she'd arrived at the

Devil's Thumb trailhead. Even when Dash rounded his parked SUV and walked toward her, she still felt off-kilter, like she was in the wrong place.

"Why are we here?" she asked, eyeing the trees bordering the small parking lot suspiciously. Mountain peaks poked up over the tops of the evergreens, looking beautiful and majestic but also making the location feel extra...wild. She wasn't very comfortable with *wild*. She did much better with places that'd been domesticated and tamed, like Dash's gym or her bedroom.

"Training." Before she could ask why they couldn't have stayed in civilization to train, he was already walking toward the start of the hiking trail. She hurried to catch up, looking around suspiciously for bears or moose or, even worse, ticks. There was a reason she didn't hike unless Felicity was in drill-sergeant mode. Even though Norah lived right next to a national forest, she still felt ill at ease in trees or open fields or mountains or... well, anywhere *nature-y* basically.

"What's wrong with training in the gym?" she asked, watching her feet as she scrambled up a rocky incline.

"Too controlled." He didn't sound winded in the slightest as he strode along the uneven, uphill trail as if he were walking on a paved sidewalk. "You need to be able to defend yourself in real-life situations."

Although she couldn't argue with that, she still wasn't excited about more wilderness time. Felicity dragged her and her other sisters through the woods on a regular basis. Couldn't that be considered sufficient outside training? "What if I promise to stay in heavily populated areas?"

He turned his head enough to give her some serious side-eye. "When your sister was kidnapped, where'd they take her?"

"Into the mountains," Norah answered, confused by the non sequitur.

"So you stayed home and let your other sisters go after her?"

"Of course not." Norah frowned at the idea that she wouldn't at least attempt to rescue Cara, then sighed as she got his point. "Fine. Let's do this then."

She could see the corner of his mouth quirk up the tiniest bit. Despite her discomfort with all things outdoorsy, she still felt a dart of pleasure that she'd almost gotten him to smile.

They hiked on in silence, broken only by the occasional clink of a disturbed piece of shale or the whistle of a bird. As always when she was with Dash, that quiet felt comfortable. Norah peered up at the endlessly tall evergreens, the patches of sky between the branches an almost dizzying deep blue. When the trees thinned, she could catch glimpses of the mountain peaks towering over them. Despite her continued unease, she had to admit to herself that it was breathtakingly gorgeous.

Her toe caught an uneven rock, making her trip. Dash glanced back as if checking on her. Once he saw she'd regained her balance, he turned to face front again. She kept her eyes on the trail in front of her after that.

"This way," Dash said, turning off the path into a small clearing.

Happy to not be hiking uphill anymore, Norah followed, looking around. The grass was sparse on the rocky ground, and she hoped they wouldn't be working on grappling during this outside training session. Rolling around on shale would be painful.

"You're almost always going to be smaller than your attacker," he said, facing her.

Since this was a statement of fact and not a question, she stayed quiet and waited for him to continue.

"What move gives you the best chance of survival if you're attacked?"

The answer seemed too obvious, so she paused for a second to review what he'd asked in case she'd missed a trick. The question seemed honestly straightforward, so she said, "Running away."

Although his expression didn't shift, she could still tell he was pleased by her answer. "Exactly. I've been neglecting your running training."

"I don't feel neglected," she hurried to say, holding back a grimace. Norah didn't understand the appeal of running. During all the miles Felicity made them do, she always waited for the promised endorphins to kick in, but they never had.

He barked a laugh at that but quickly regained his usual stern expression. "Here's what we're going to do. I'll put you in a hold. You'll break it and run. Then I'll chase you."

A shiver ran through her, not from her usual anxiety but from something like...anticipation? "You'll chase me?" she echoed. Saying the words gave her another not-fear shiver.

His chin tipped up in one of his short nods. "See how long you can evade me before I catch you."

Catch me? She couldn't say the words out loud, worried

that they'd hold some of the eager excitement that seemed to be taking over her body at the moment. She could only stare at him silently as he stepped toward her and grabbed her wrist. *Easy one*, she thought, her muscle memory moving her body before she even consciously planned it. Stepping closer, she lifted her knee for a groin strike, careful not to actually make contact. At the same time, she twisted her wrist so her thumb was toward her face, pulling free of his grip.

Once she was out of his hold, she hesitated for a fraction of a second, not used to the new next step of the exercise, until Dash growled, "Run."

His command unfroze her legs, and she darted out of the clearing, weaving between the trees, her heart pounding more from adrenaline than exertion. As she turned right sharply, her shoe slid on the grit covering the hard ground, and she almost went down to one knee. She caught herself, launching off the other foot back into a run, but it was too late. Strong hands gripped her waist, lifting her off the ground.

She shrieked with surprise, but no part of her was afraid. After all those sessions in the gym, she knew Dash's grip, and she felt completely safe in his hold—despite the fact that she was dangling off the ground. He lowered her to her feet, and she gave an exhilarated laugh as she turned to face him. "Again. I can do better."

"I hope so." Although he was frowning, she was pretty sure he was amused. "I caught you in just a few seconds. And run toward the main trail next time. More likely to find other people there."

This time, he put her in a choke hold, his right arm snug

around her neck but not so tightly that she couldn't breathe. She paused for a moment, surprised by how strangely comforting it was having him wrapped around her like he was her weighted blanket. The thought seemed so out of place and deeply weird that her hesitation lengthened until he asked, "What's wrong?"

Except for unexpected emotions, there wasn't anything *wrong* really, so she answered, "Nothing."

"Why aren't you freeing yourself then?" he asked without loosening his hold. "I know you've got this one down."

She did have it down. They'd drilled escaping choke holds over and over until she was pretty sure she could do this in her sleep. "Just…stuck in my head."

"Well, get unstu—" He broke off with a grunt as she tucked her chin and pressed her hands against his elbow, turning to the right and taking his arm with her. She snuck in a hammer punch, pulling it so her fist just tapped his back over his kidney. Free from his hold, she bolted immediately, determined to evade him for at least a few more seconds this time.

As she ran, that same excitement built inside her. She knew this was training and completely safe, but it felt more like a game with the slightest edge of danger. The knowledge that someone was likely right behind her, ready to grab her, should've terrified her. It *would've* terrified her in any other situation or, more accurately, with any other person.

Dash was different. He was safe.

Taking his advice about heading back to the main trail, she turned and ran parallel to it, not wanting to give a hiker a heart attack by crashing through the underbrush right in front of them. Her lungs tightened a little in warning, adding a slight wheeze to her exhales, and she knew she needed to find a hiding spot before her asthma kicked up a fuss about the extended sprint. She managed to keep her feet under her this time as she ran, even though she was scoping out the trees in front of her.

Not that one. Or that. Nope, not that one either. There! She saw just what she needed and would've smiled if she wasn't sucking air. *Perfect.*

Making a beeline to the cottonwood tree with conveniently low branches, she started to scramble up. She only made it five feet off the ground before a large hand wrapped around her ankle and gave a tug. It wasn't a hard pull, but it was just enough to send her off-balance, and she toppled right into Dash's arms, giggling as she fell, trusting him completely. There was no way Dash would let her hit the ground.

He laughed—short and rough—as he shifted her in his arms so they were face-to-face and her feet were still dangling above the ground. His amused expression faded, replaced by one that looked...hungry, maybe? Norah stared at him, a part of her mind registering how close their faces were, but most of her was focused on the way his pupils were dilating until the dark brown of his irises had almost disappeared. Her mouth felt dry, and she swallowed, her tongue darting out to lick her bottom lip. His intense gaze dropped to her mouth, which made her stop breathing for a second.

He set her on her feet abruptly, startling her. "Better," he said, his voice gruffer than usual. "Got to be careful about hiding instead of running though. You don't want to be trapped."

Off-balance, Norah just continued to stare at him, uncertain of what had just happened but not wanting to overthink it, especially since she was pretty sure he'd experienced a moment of attraction.

Attraction to *her*.

In fact, there'd been a moment, right before he'd broken the spell, when she'd wondered if he was going to kiss her. Her face went hot at the idea.

"Ready?" he asked.

Her first thought was that he was asking if she was ready to be kissed, and she felt her skin flame hotter.

"You did great on escaping the choke hold, so let's do a double wrist grab this time."

"Right!" The word came out too loud, startling a nearby bird into silence. "Training. I'm ready to…train."

As his fingers wrapped around her wrists, somehow managing to warm her entire body in the process, she forced herself to concentrate on the drill. Even if he *had* considered kissing her for a brief moment, that had passed, and she needed to focus on the reason they were here in the wilderness.

Training. He was her trainer, not her boyfriend. Even as she broke from his hold and ran through the trees again, she couldn't help but wonder what it'd be like to have Dash for a boyfriend.

She couldn't hold back a beaming smile at the thought.

Amazing. It'd be amazing.

SIX

"WHERE ARE YOU GOING?"

At Molly's question, Norah's shoulders dropped in a sigh. She'd almost made it through the door. She'd been planning to text her sisters to let them know her plans once she'd gotten safely out of the house—well, an abbreviated version of her plans at least. That way, she could put off the third degree for a few hours until she returned home. Reluctantly, she turned to face her sister.

"Out?" As soon as the one-word question left her mouth, she knew it was the dumbest way to start this conversation. She could actually see Molly's expression shift as idle curiosity changed to intense interest.

"Out?" Molly raised her voice and called up the stairs. "Cara, you're going to want to get down here for this! Norah's being weird in an interesting way again!"

Another sigh escaped Norah, this one feeling like it came all the way from her toes. She might as well spill everything, since she knew her sisters wouldn't let her leave until their avid curiosity was satisfied. "I'm—"

"Hang on." Molly made a shushing motion. "Wait until Cara gets down here. She won't want to miss this."

Feet thundered down the stairs, and a grinning Cara passed Molly and plopped down on the couch, looking as if she was fully ready to be entertained. All she was missing was a bowl of popcorn.

All afternoon, Norah had debated whether to tell her sisters the full story of why she was going out tonight. She'd promised to ask for backup if needed, but with Dash, she already had a very burly person to help her out if things got hairy. On the other hand, she wanted them to know where she was going to be, since even the biggest guys could get in trouble, and she'd only started getting a handle on this hand-to-hand combat thing. She was pretty sure her small successes in the gym wouldn't translate to winning a street brawl. If she told her sisters the truth, however, they'd just worry...and probably either lock her in her room or insist on going with her. Besides, if she and Dash got into trouble they couldn't handle, she could always text her sisters. Better to ask for forgiveness than permission after all.

Her sisters' expressions were getting more gleeful the longer she hesitated, and Norah realized she'd been doing that a lot lately—figuring out which truth would keep her sisters safe while minimizing her own embarrassment. She missed the days just a month ago when she'd been an open—albeit boring—book. Now she had secrets coming out of her ears.

"I'm going out."

"You're stalling," Cara said.

Norah couldn't wait for her sister to have her own class of kindergartners on which she could focus her stern expressions rather than using them to keep her family in line.

"Yes." Norah figured she might as well admit it. Her sisters already knew her tactics.

"Why?" Molly tagged in, dropping down to sit next to Cara to present a united nosy front. "What don't you want to tell us?"

"It's not that I don't want to tell you," Norah said slowly, picking through her thoughts as she spoke. "It's that I'm not sure what it is."

There was a pause before Molly asked, "What *what* is?"

"I'm meeting Dash—"

"Mmm...sinewy hands guy," Cara interrupted.

Norah flushed for some reason. "I don't know if they're *sinewy*, exactly." It was unsettling how easy it was for her to picture his hands. "They're really big though."

When her sisters exchanged smirks, Norah felt her face grow even warmer.

"So you're meeting Dash." It was a relief when Molly got the discussion back on track. "For...a date?"

"Of course it's a date," Cara said before Norah could respond. "Why else would she be meeting a guy on a Saturday night right around the time she usually goes to bed?"

Norah made a face, a little offended by that. "I stay up later than nine."

"Sure, but you're *researching*. That's like staying up late watching Netflix," Cara explained with more condescension than necessary for someone who'd researched and studied for class on Saturday nights up until not even a month ago when she'd met Henry. "It doesn't count as a social life."

Filing away the argument for a later date, Norah knew she had to redirect the conversation back to the original point. If she let it, this discussion with her sisters could stretch late into the night, and she had to be outside in seven minutes so she could meet Dash when he pulled his car up to the curb. If she waited too long, he'd park and come to the door, and then the sisters would want to meet him, and there'd be inside jokes about his hands, and Norah would burn up from embarrassment until she was just an awkward, charred husk on the floor.

"We're working, so it's probably not a date," she said.

"Working? Do you mean working out?" Cara looked puzzled.

Here came the part her sisters wouldn't like. "No, I'll be working. He'll just be helping. Backup, if you will."

"Norah Valentine Pax!" Molly had her sternest big-sister face on. "Are you chasing skips? Didn't you learn anything from Cara's mistakes? I thought we talked about this."

Grimacing a little at the triple naming, Norah shook her head. "We're just going to follow a possible lead on Leifsen."

"Your stalker?" It wasn't reassuring that Molly switched from loud and angry to quiet and calm. Norah knew that was when she was the most irate. "You're going to go after your stalker on your own?"

"Not on my own." Norah seized on that part, knowing the seconds were ticking away before Dash's arrival. Opening the front door, she backed out of it, talking quickly. "Dash is going to be my muscle. If we spot Leifsen, I'll text you. I promise. Better go so I'm not late. Bye! Love you! Don't wait up!"

Before she closed the door, she heard Cara snort a laugh as Molly repeated, "He's her...*muscle?*"

As Norah trotted down the porch steps, she blew out a long breath. For a moment there, she wasn't sure she was going to escape the house without Molly following. Date or not, having her older sister tag along would've been weird and awkward. Her phone chimed as she saw headlights turn onto her street.

Glancing at her phone, she saw Molly wasn't letting her get the last word. Text us the second you see Leifsen, or else I'll draw on your face with Sharpies while you sleep.

Giving a huff of amusement, Norah sent a quick I will! response before pocketing her phone. As she headed toward the SUV pulling up to the curb, she had a sudden worry that it wouldn't be Dash. The vehicle rolled to a stop as she took a hesitant step back, watching with building dread as the passenger window slid down.

It wasn't until Dash leaned over from the driver's side to pop open the passenger door that she exhaled and stepped forward again.

He cocked his head, studying her carefully. "Okay?"

"Yeah." She slid into the seat, feeling both relieved and a little silly for her moment of doubt. "I just wasn't sure if it was you at first."

He glanced around at their sparsely inhabited cul-de-sac. "You get many strange guys rolling by here?"

"Surprisingly, yes." Her tone was dark with memories of

shady detectives and mysterious unknown vehicles cruising by at all hours of the night, their occupants hidden by darkness. "Or not really surprisingly, I guess." When Dash lifted his eyebrows in a silent question, she explained, "The rumor around town is that the necklace my mom stole is hidden in our house. We get a lot of traffic."

Even in the dim illumination from the streetlight, Norah could see Dash's eyes flare with a fierce emotion. "Does this... *traffic* ever stop?"

"Sometimes." She lifted her shoulders in a shrug that wasn't as nonchalant as she tried to make it look. "The number of break-ins has decreased since John's friend installed the security system though."

"Glad the *break-ins* have *decreased*." He shifted into drive almost violently, but the SUV rolled forward gently, so at least he wasn't taking his rage out on the gas pedal. Still, Norah eyed him warily as he continued, "Is this the same security system Leifsen disarmed in order to *kidnap* your sister?"

Something in his chilly words made her feel defensive, but she reminded herself he was angry because he didn't want her in danger. She wasn't sure why he cared about someone who was just a client, but she knew she'd hate it if someone hurt or threatened Dash. As the glass house, she wasn't about to start chucking stones. Besides, it felt good to be valued.

"Yes." She didn't try to soften her bald honesty, even though his knuckles were white and she could see the muscles move in his cheek as he clenched and unclenched his jaw. "However, very few petty criminals have the same skills as Leifsen. I'm not sure how my mom managed to disarm it, but she's always been wily about things like that."

The sound he made, a sort of muttered *hmph*, was decades too old for him, as if he'd been momentarily possessed by his grandpa. Norah curled her lips in to hold back her smile, since she didn't think he'd approve of her levity while they were having a Very Serious Conversation. At least it was on his end. Despite her best efforts to keep a straight face, she was pretty sure he knew she was amused, judging by the sideways glare he was giving her.

She cleared her throat. "We also established safety protocols after Cara was…taken." It was still hard to say without her throat closing up, so she concentrated on the dashboard as she spoke, working hard to keep her voice steady. "We're rarely home alone now."

By his grunt, he wasn't appeased by this.

"We also carry Tasers, pepper spray, and our phones at all times."

Turning his head briefly, he eyed her as if looking for weapons. "You have all that on you now?"

"Yes." Patting her pockets to reassure herself that they were still there, she felt a rectangular shape that reminded her of what else she carried. "Also a pocketknife in case we get restrained with zip ties. According to Cara, more people carry zip ties around than we think."

The steering wheel squeaked in protest under Dash's grip.

"Don't break your nice car."

"It's fine." From his tone, he didn't think *anything* was fine, but Norah let that go. "I want a list."

She blinked. "A list of what?"

"Every single…person who's even thought about breaking into your home."

"I'm not giving you a kill list. You already get to lightly beat up—I mean *chat with*—Leifsen if you find him first." She eyed his profile. It was odd, but she actually preferred looking at him from the left. From the right, he appeared to be intimidatingly perfect, someone she would never have had the courage to speak to that first day at the gym. His scars made him more human, less godlike. "You can swear around me, you know."

It was his turn to pause. "What?"

"I can tell you're self-bleeping. My ears won't fall off if you curse." The SUV turned into the lot at Dutch's, distracting her. She'd been so focused on watching Dash that she hadn't paid attention to their surroundings as he drove.

"Maybe they won't fall off, but you don't need to hear that… stuff."

Unimpressed, she made a scoffing sound. "Women swear. We don't need to be protected from hearing bad words."

"I try not to swear in front of anyone." He parked and turned off the SUV before shifting to look at her fully. "My gran was a stickler for manners."

"Your gran?" This was the first personal thing he'd shared with her, and it felt like he'd given her something fragile and precious.

"Yeah, my little sister and I moved in with her when I was twelve and my dad went to prison."

Norah blinked as she processed that short, matter-of-fact

statement just loaded with information. "My dad's been to prison too. Several times."

He dipped his head in a nod, and she suspected he'd already known that.

"Your mom?" she asked.

"Took off soon after my sister was born. I was two."

It was Norah's turn to nod. She was careful to keep any trace of sympathy or pity from showing, since she hated that reaction when other people found out about her parents. "Do you ever feel like it's genetically inevitable that you'll commit a crime and be locked up?"

He paused, his usual scowl easing into bemusement. "No?"

Just me then.

"That's why I try to act how my gran taught me. I know that's my way out of that life."

Her chest warmed at the idea. "I'm glad you had her. If I didn't have my sisters, I'd probably be right there in the getaway car with my mom."

"Nah." His voice was certain. "You're stronger than that."

Even though she doubted the truth of that, she liked that he'd said it anyway.

"Ready?" He jerked his head toward the bar.

She resisted the urge to tell him to drive them home. Dutch's wasn't her favorite place. "I guess."

"Don't worry." He must've picked up on her reluctance. "I'll keep you safe."

Norah frowned. The whole reason she'd started training with him was that she was tired of being the weak link who couldn't keep *herself* safe. "Please don't treat me like I'm fragile. If you hadn't noticed, I have several sisters who already do that."

He eyed her for a long second before finally raising one shoulder in a partial shrug. "Nope. Can't help it. I'm going to keep protecting you." Leaving her momentarily speechless, he opened his door and got out.

"You can't just..." She trailed off when she realized he'd already closed his door and was three-quarters of the way around the front of the SUV. Realizing what he was about to do, she fumbled for the door handle, but it was too late. Her door swung open, and Dash waited for her to get out, looking rather too pleased with himself.

"Smug is not a good look on you." Even as she said it, she knew her words rang false. Everything was a good look for Dash. His mouth twitched up at the corner as if he knew what she was thinking. With a sigh that was embarrassingly close to a huff, she slid out of the SUV and allowed him to close the door.

As she crossed the parking lot, she tried to come up with a plan to convince Dash to quit treating her like she was breakable. She couldn't figure out how a guy who she paid to beat her up—albeit gently—on the regular had turned into a white knight who opened her car door and wouldn't even swear around her, not to mention his insisting on beating and/or killing all her harassers.

"Need to see your ID."

Norah jerked her head up to see the huge bouncer right in front of her. She'd been so distracted by thoughts of Dash that she hadn't even noticed him or her trek across the creepiest, shadowiest parking lot in town. Normally, just the idea of going to Dutch's made her want to hide under her bed, but this time, she'd marched right up to the terrifyingly huge and scowling bouncer without even a shiver of apprehension. She darted a quick glance at Dash next to her. Despite his annoyingly excessive protective side, she had to admit he was an excellent distraction.

She pulled out her license and handed it to the bouncer, whose frown deepened as he read it. "No."

"What?" Genuinely startled, Norah stared at him. "Why? I'm over twenty-one."

"You Pax women are trouble."

She grimaced. Jane's bad reputation had stained the whole family. Norah was used to everyone thinking she and her sisters were trash just because Jane played a little fast and loose with the law. "I'm not like my mom, I promise. I've never stolen anything in my life."

He rolled his eyes as he returned her license. "Your mom never caused any trouble here. Your sisters though…"

"Oh!" Norah was startled into smiling. For once, her sisters were the cause of the trouble, not her sticky-fingered mother. "Don't worry. I'm the quiet one."

"That's what the one who blew up the bar said."

"Technically, Sonny Zarver was the one—"

"And that's what the one who caused a brawl, a shoot-out behind the bar, *and* a visit from the feds said." Peering at her face more closely, his eyebrows drew together until they touched. "Hey, you were here that night!"

"Yes, but only because I was *dragged* here against my better judgment."

Dash coughed, but it sounded like he was disguising a laugh. He held out some folded bills. "We won't cause trouble."

For a long moment, the bouncer eyed the money as if debating whether it'd be worth whatever drama Norah and Dash would cause, but then he heaved a silent sigh and accepted the bills. "If either of you even breathes funny, you're out, and I won't be gentle about it."

Norah opened her mouth to protest the unfairness, since her sisters hadn't caused any of the previous chaos at Dutch's. Well, they hadn't caused *most* of it, and what they had started was for a good and fairly lawful reason. Before any words could escape, Dash wrapped an arm around her back and swept her through the door.

"One more strike, and you and your hundred and one sisters will be out for good!" the bouncer called after them.

The door swung shut behind them, cutting off her chance to respond, and she gave Dash a reproving look.

"I know," he said. "But arguing was just going to piss him off." His mouth quirked up as he looked down at her with amusement mixed with approval. "Didn't think you were the type to fight with the bouncer."

She shrugged. "No one can say anything bad about my sisters except for me."

Letting out a quick bark of laughter, he steered her deeper into the bar. It was busier than usual, probably because of the band setting up on the small stage, and Norah could feel the usual stares. Tonight they felt more hostile, and she wondered if that was because the Pax sisters' reputation was growing. Dash must've noticed the negative attention she was receiving, because he shifted closer until his body brushed against hers with every step. Sometimes, she had to admit, having some protection was a good thing.

He directed her wordlessly to a back booth. There was a young guy sitting there who looked familiar. As they drew closer, Norah sucked in a breath. "Stuart!"

The worm must've recognized her at the same time, because he shot out of his seat and lost himself in the crowd before she could do anything more than glare at him. Although Dash gave her a questioning look, he didn't ask until after they'd reached the booth Stuart had been occupying.

When Norah moved to sit in the seat across from Dash, he clasped her wrist, drawing her back to his side of the table. She gave him a confused look but slid across the cushioned bench, her pants catching on tears in the cheap vinyl. Once he sat down next to her, she raised her eyebrows in question, and he bent so his mouth was close to her ear.

"This way, we can talk without being overheard," he said, his lips brushing against her ear.

A flush of heat, quickly followed by a shiver, rippled down her spine at the contact, and it took her a few seconds to comprehend his words. Once they sank in, she gave a slight nod. It made sense, although she was pretty sure his lips didn't have to actually touch her ear in order for her to hear him. She eyed him suspiciously, but his face was in his usual set frown as he scanned the crowd.

Had he been flirting with her?

Norah cursed her lack of dating experience. She hated being clueless about anything, and she felt completely thrown by Dash. Although he'd been totally professional in the gym, the way he'd acted at lunch the other day and tonight made her wonder. Plus there was the almost-a-kiss moment at Devil's Thumb—unless she'd just made that up in her head. She wished she could ask one of her sisters without the inevitable teasing, but the idea made her mentally cringe with anticipated embarrassment.

Shaking off her thoughts, she focused on the band members. There'd be plenty of time to obsess about every move Dash made when she was lying sleepless and anxious in her narrow bed later that night. The thought made her grimace. Leifsen had been stealing too many hours of rest from her lately.

"Who'd you chase from the booth?" Dash asked, way too close to her ear again.

Rather proud of herself when she didn't outwardly react to the contact, she said, "Stuart Powers."

"Right. You've mentioned him."

Surprised, she turned to look at Dash and instantly regretted it. His face was *right there*, closer than she'd ever been to him, even in training. His lashes were thick and lush, and she couldn't help but think of birds. The females had no defense against the lure of the males, with their flashy, striking colors and dramatic patterns. It just wasn't fair. How was she supposed to keep her mind away from flirting and…other things when he was so close and so very fascinating?

"Does terrible things for money and always gets away with it."

"Right." It was an effort to pull her mind back to the awful person they were discussing. "That's Stuart in a nutshell."

"Add him to my list," he said in a voice so dark and deep she could've drowned in the sheer decadence of it.

"He's already on there."

His lips pressed together as his gaze ran over the crowd again. "He broke into your house."

"Yes. He was the first…well, besides Zach Fridley. But Zach was there to steal Molly's car, not looking for the necklace—the first time at least. The second time, he was Mom's backup when he hit Fifi over the head and knocked her out." Anger filled her at the reminder. "I really don't like Zach Fridley."

Ever so slowly, Dash turned his head until his flat black gaze met Norah's again. "Fridley goes on the list too."

Even though she'd had no intention of giving Dash her enemies list, she still found herself nodding, hypnotized by the way he stared at her. He was so deadly yet so matter-of-fact at the same time. It was both frightening and reassuring, and Norah had to look away, unnerved by the tumult he caused in her usually well-ordered emotions.

"That's Leifsen's friend?"

At his question, Norah met his eyes again. Although he was still much too close for comfort, being able to focus on details helped settle her pulse to a more normal rhythm. He tipped his head toward where Chloe, who was wearing a glittery tank top that showed off her two full-sleeve tattoos, was tuning her guitar. Her colorful skin paired oddly with her long, milkmaid-like blond braids. Even though she wasn't playing or singing yet, she exuded self-assurance, drawing the crowd's full attention before she'd even started performing.

"Yes." Norah studied the musician, wondering how the confident woman on the stage and the hacker so chicken he had to stalk Norah from behind a computer screen managed to become friends. "I'm not sure why. Unless she's faking it, Chloe seems awesome, and Leifsen is definitely *not*. It was three years ago, so maybe she was going through a rough patch."

Dash's raspy chuckle made her turn and look at him. He was still watching Chloe, so Norah had his profile again. Realizing she was staring, smiling like an idiot just because she'd managed to make him laugh, Norah quickly directed her thoughts back to their mission. This wasn't a date—*probably* wasn't a date. If it were a date, she hoped he would've brought her somewhere other than Dutch's.

"Do you see Leifsen?" she asked, determined to stay on task.

"Not yet." His usual grim expression returned as he looked around the bar. "You need to get me that list. I'm sure some of those…people are here tonight."

Even as she looked around for any unpleasantly familiar faces, she let out an amused huff. "That was an almost swear, wasn't it?"

He shrugged affirmatively.

Chloe spoke into the mic before Norah could respond. It was a ridiculous discussion anyway, but their silly back-and-forth made her heart thump harder. To her surprise, Norah was actually having fun. If someone had told her a few weeks earlier she'd be staking out a skip at Dutch's and enjoying herself, she never would've believed them.

"How's everyone doing tonight?" The crowd gave a more enthusiastic roar than Norah had expected, and Chloe grinned. "We're the Lost Marbles." The band immediately jumped into an upbeat song.

Norah cocked her head, surprised. She hadn't expected to actually *like* Chloe's band's music, but the bouncing beat was irresistible, as was her husky—almost raspy—voice. Norah glanced at Dash to see his fingers tapping the beat onto the tabletop. His obvious enjoyment freed her to move her shoulders and bounce a little as she danced in place, weirdly happy despite being in Dutch's, normally her least-favorite place to be.

"C'mon." Dash slid out of the booth and then offered her a hand.

A little confused by what he was planning, she still accepted his hand and allowed him to help her out of the seat. Once she was standing, he didn't let her go. Instead, he used that firm yet careful grip to tow her through the crowd closer to the stage. Still puzzled, she eyed his back. Was he thinking they'd have a better chance of spotting Leifsen in the crowd? At the thought, she snorted. Maybe Mr. Ginormous had a view over the crowd, but all *her* short self managed to see were upshots into the nostrils of the people right next to her.

Dash stopped once he reached a spot close to the band. As he turned toward her, she opened her mouth to ask what the plan was but closed it before she bothered. The music was much too loud for him to hear anything, even if she shouted, and yelling about their plans at the top of her lungs didn't seem very strategic. Instead, she raised her eyebrows in a silent question.

Bending so his lips were next to her ear, he said loudly, "We're dancing."

Although his words were clear, she was pretty sure she'd misunderstood. "Dancing?"

He must've read her lips, because he tipped his head in a nod as the corner of his mouth twitched up.

"*Nooooo.*" Norah drew out the word as the horror of his proposal hit her. *Dance? Her? In public?* Uh…nope. No way. Not happening.

His small smile just grew in response, which was not boding well for her escaping. He gripped her hips as he started moving to the beat. *Yes,* he mouthed, still grinning at her.

"I can't dance," she said. She wished she could. Dancing with Dash would be incredible.

Dash must've managed to read her lips—and her wistful thoughts—because he gave her an encouraging smile before he bent to speak directly into her ear. "Yeah, you can. If you can fight, you can dance."

"But I don't really know how to fight yet," she protested, but he'd already straightened again. From his teasing expression, he wasn't about to let her wiggle out of it. The song ended, and she hoped for a moment she'd get a reprieve, but then the band immediately dove into the next one, which was sultrier with a slower bass beat. Somehow, the thought of dancing to this song was more intimidating than the previous one.

Without releasing her hips, Dash stepped closer. His clean, spicy scent surrounded her, muting the usual stink of beer and body odor that filled the bar. She met his gaze and then couldn't look away, the gleam of heat and humor so different from his normal expression...yet much too intriguing. She couldn't remember any other man ever looking at her with such interest, and she couldn't wrap her mind around the idea that beautiful, fascinating, talented Dash was the one to finally do so.

"See...easy." His loud words somehow managed to sound intimate. She realized that without thinking about it, she'd automatically started moving with his hands' suggestions, swaying her hips back and forth in rhythm with the heavy beat. As soon as she noticed, her muscles locked up, and she went stiff. Dash just gave her that tiny, private smile and kept moving.

Overwhelmed by his intensity, she dropped her gaze from his face, but looking at his body didn't settle her nerves at all. He moved with an unselfconscious grace despite his heavy muscles, shoulders and hips rolling even as his hands urged her to follow his movement. Letting out a shaky breath, she forced herself to unlock her frozen body. Her side-to-side swaying started out stiffer and less fluid now that she was thinking about what she was doing and how she looked. She closed her eyes, pretending the crowd was gone and she was at home with her sisters, having a dance party to the music on someone's phone. Her movements smoothed out, became easier, more natural, but something still wasn't quite right.

Although she could block out the sight of all the strangers surrounding her, the heat and flex of hands on her hips made it impossible to mentally erase Dash. In her mind, her innocent family dance party shifted to something a little more wicked—just the two of them alone in the darkness, music filling the room as they swayed closer and closer together…

The music ended abruptly with a final thump of the bass, and Norah's eyes flew open as she realized she'd lost track of time. She immediately looked at him, her face heating. Her imaginings had been so vivid, she felt as though he should've been able to see what she'd been thinking. The urge to put some space between them—possibly miles—rose up inside her, and she started to take a step back. She needed to think about what had just happened, to repeat the events of this night in her mind until they made sense.

Before she could pull away, Chloe introduced the next song, and the band jumped into one even bouncier than the first. Norah, a little disoriented by the dramatic mood change, looked at Dash. He raised a shoulder in a half shrug and then grabbed her hands and started dancing again. The sight of him bouncing to the perky beat made her stare at him for a long moment before a laugh burst out.

His willingness to look absolutely ridiculous broke down a barrier inside her, and she joined in, bouncing along with him. It was so freeing not to think about how she appeared as she moved, whether she looked sexy or just awkward. Either way, there was no chance she could look sillier than Dash as he bopped to the beat. Raising their clasped hands, she danced right along with him, smiling the entire time.

Even when the next song slowed and Dash gathered her

against him, her nerves didn't return. She just melted into him and swayed, closing her eyes—not to imagine being somewhere else but just to enjoy the feel of him.

They danced until Norah's throat was dry from exertion and laughter, and she shifted away from Dash. He immediately reeled her back in, frowning.

"Water," she shouted, gesturing toward the bar. Instead of releasing her, he headed that way, keeping hold of her hand so she followed behind in his wake. It woke her up, reminding her that they were at Dutch's, not a friendly, safe bar where she could wander through the crowd on her own. No matter how much fun she was having, they were there to find Leifsen.

Not a date, not a date, not a date, she repeated in her mind, pressing down all the feelings that dancing with Dash had awoken in her. *This is work, this is work, this is work.*

Dash wedged his shoulder between two people at the crowded bar, and the redheaded bartender immediately made her way over to him. Watching, Norah was glad she hadn't tried to get water on her own. It would've taken her ages just to get noticed, and she didn't have Dash's bulk to be able to push her way through oblivious people like that. The couple to Dash's right left, and Norah claimed one of the stools while keeping hold of Dash's hand. Enjoying her slightly elevated position, she looked around the bar. It was even busier than when they'd first arrived, but she still didn't see any sign of Leifsen. The bouncer was standing inside the entrance now, and he saw her glancing over. He pointed at his eyes and then her in the *I'm watching you* gesture. Norah ducked her head to hide her smile.

"What?" Dash asked in her ear, leaning in as he handed her a bottle of water. Instead of taking the other open stool, he stood next to her, close enough to brush against her every time he shifted positions.

"The bouncer." She'd never seen anyone in real life actually use that gesture in a non-joking way. Instead of having to yell the whole explanation, she just waved it off. "I'll tell you later."

He gave a nod as she opened her water and took a drink. It tasted amazing, so cold it almost hurt her throat, but she still sucked it down as fast as she could. She'd been having so much fun she hadn't realized how thirsty she'd gotten. She offered the half-full bottle to Dash, but he shook his head, holding up his own.

Sipping more slowly, she turned back to her appraisal of the crowd. The dim lighting made it difficult to make out people's features, and she wondered if she'd looked right at Leifsen without realizing it. Coming to the bar while Chloe's band was playing had seemed like a good idea, but maybe it would be more effective to stake out her apartment building to see if he showed up.

Norah finished her water as she mentally ran over some options. This field trip to Dutch's was actually good in another way, besides just getting to dance with Dash. It would help her determine the best ways for her sisters to run down skips. There were some things she couldn't learn by researching rather than going out into the field. She felt a rush of gratitude for Dash. It was only because he was with her that she felt comfortable enough to go to Dutch's. Last time she'd been here was with

Cara, and her sister had almost been killed because Norah had frozen.

Dash took her empty water bottle, distracting her from the painful memory, and placed it with his on the bar. "Dance?" he asked, his small smirk a challenge that something inside her immediately rose up to meet.

At her nod, he towed her back to their spot close to the small stage. He rested his hands on her hips, but she didn't need his urging this time to start moving to the music. Still, she didn't object to his hold. She was surprised by how much she liked the pressure and heat of his broad palms and the firm grip of his fingers. It felt like he was a protective wall, keeping her safe from the crowd surrounding them.

Even as the image crossed her mind, someone bumped against her back, fully groping her butt before shoving her against Dash's chest. His arms closed around her as he twisted, turning her so that his back was to the threat, protecting her. She peered around him, catching a glimpse of a slim man in a bulky jacket and baseball cap disappearing into the crowd. At the last moment before he ducked around a leather-clad biker, he turned his head, showing his profile.

Devon Leifsen.

Norah sucked in a breath as she recognized him. She moved to dive into the crowd after him, but Dash caught her back.

"Let me go after him!" she yelled. "He's going to get away."

"Let me go first," he ordered, tucking her behind him before plunging into the crowd. Norah grabbed the back of his belt, grateful once again for the way people—even drunk ones—stepped out of Dash's way. All she could see was his back as they wove through the throng, and Norah resisted the urge to push him to go faster. Leifsen had been right within grabbing reach, and startled by the grope and shove, she'd let him get away.

When Dash stopped abruptly, Norah almost crashed into his back. "I can't see him," he said loudly enough for her to hear. Her stomach sank as Dash craned his neck to see deeper into the crowd, but then she had an idea.

Moving around in front of him, she turned so her back was against his front. "Lift me up," she shouted. He immediately complied, grasping her waist and hoisting her up. Her small squeak as he lifted her higher than she expected was thankfully drowned out by the music and noise of the bar. She scanned the crowd, but Leifsen's baseball hat was nowhere to be seen.

Realizing that he could easily have removed the hat, she looked around again, trying to hurry before Dash's arms gave out. As steady as they seemed, he couldn't hold her above him forever. Scanning the crowd, trying to examine each person as quickly as possible, she finally saw a bare blond head of someone determinedly working their way toward the exit. The person glanced back, meeting Norah's gaze for only a brief moment, but it was enough for her to identify him as Leifsen.

Tapping Dash's forearm, she pointed. "Blond, no hat, ten feet from the door!"

His head snapped in the direction she indicated. "I see him." He carefully lowered her and tucked her behind him again before charging toward Leifsen. Grabbing his belt again,

Norah kept pace with him, her heart thrumming from the chase. If she could always have Dash with her, she wouldn't mind doing fieldwork. A big part of her was completely terrified, but there was also that small bit that was…having fun? She was starting to understand the thrill her sisters got from chasing skips.

The crowd thinned as they got closer to the exit, and the remaining people jumped out of Dash's way. Peering around him, Norah saw Leifsen at the door. The skip looked over his shoulder and blanched, staring at Dash barreling down on him for a beat before shoving open the door.

An excited buzz ran through her. They were so close. She was starting to believe they'd actually catch Leifsen. Dash shot toward the door but stopped abruptly. This time, Norah couldn't halt in time and bashed her face against his back.

Reaching back, Dash wrapped his hand around her arm as if reassuring himself that she was okay. "Move," he growled.

Rubbing her throbbing nose that had taken the brunt of the crash, Norah looked around Dash's wide chest to see the bouncer blocking the exit, his arms crossed over his chest.

"I said no causing trouble."

"No trouble." Dash's voice was emotionless, but Norah could feel how tightly he held himself, most likely resisting the urge to physically move the bouncer in a violent way. She understood that desire, since she would've tackled the man if he hadn't been three times her weight. "Just leaving."

The bouncer stared at Dash for what felt like an eternity before shifting to the side.

Dash didn't waste time charging outside with her in tow, but it was too late. Leifsen was gone.

"We were so close," she said, her voice sounding too loud in the sudden silence.

Wrapping an arm around her shoulders, Dash pulled her against him in a side hug. "Don't worry. That...*weasel* thinks he's smarter than us, but he's wrong. We'll get him."

With a sigh, she relaxed into his side, disappointed yet reassured that Dash wasn't abandoning the hunt. "More almost swearing?" Her tone surprised her. She hadn't realized she could sound quite so...flirty.

"Yep."

Despite the abruptness of his answer, she still smiled, safe under the comforting weight of his arm as he steered her toward his SUV. They might've failed to bring in Leifsen, but somehow the night had still managed to be amazing.

———

Even as Norah was standing in her bedroom a half hour later, emptying her pockets of pepper spray, Tasers, and knives, she couldn't stop smiling. She kept replaying how it felt to dance with Dash and how incredible he had looked as he'd moved, even when he was bouncing around like an idiot.

Sliding her hands into her back pockets in an automatic check, even though they were too tight to hold much, her fingertips hit a folded piece of paper.

What is that? She knew she hadn't put it there. Her besotted grin faded in confusion as she pinched the paper between two fingers and fished it out of her pocket. It was indeed a folded sheet of paper, one torn from a notebook, judging by the rough edge. For some reason, her fingers shook as she unfolded it. Paper couldn't hurt her, but having it slid into her pocket without her knowing felt like a violation.

There were just a few short sentences scrawled in a scribbly hand.

Naughty, naughty, Norah. Who's the meathead? Lose him, or you'll be sorry. ☺

The menacing happy face confirmed what she already knew: Devon Leifsen was responsible for the note. Her mind flashed back to the moment right before he'd shoved her, when he'd groped her butt. That was when he must've shoved the note into her pocket.

Placing the note on her bed, she took a picture with her phone and texted it to Dash. It was only after her message was sent that she wondered why her immediate reaction hadn't been to wake up one of her sisters to show them the note.

The buzz of an incoming text from Dash brought her out of her thoughts.

Where'd you find that?

She hesitated for a brief moment before typing Pants pocket.

The dots indicating that Dash was replying flashed on her screen for several seconds before his next text appeared.

Free tomorrow for some stalker hunting?

Yes. It was Sunday, but she'd just planned on doing more research on Leifsen. If Dash was with her, she could take that research into the field. She was surprised he could get away from the gym though. It seemed he spent most of his time working. Don't you have to be at the gym?

Davies works Sundays. Any leads on where to start looking for Leifsen?

She smiled. Meet you at Green Valley Apartments at 9am? That's where Chloe lives.

I'll pick you up.

Okay. She hesitated, figuring she should leave it like that, keeping things professional. Then her fingers took over, typing before the cautious part of her brain could stop them. Good night, Dash.

During the pause that followed, Norah's heart pounded as hard as if she'd just downed three espressos. She'd overstepped, gotten too personal. Dash was just her trainer, with a casual interest in helping her bring in Leifsen. Everything else—the dancing and intense eye contact and the careful touches to her lower back—hadn't really meant anything. Her love-hungry brain had taken his friendliness and made it something more, and he was probably trying to think of the best way to let her down gently. She squeezed her eyes closed with embarrassment, jumping when her phone buzzed. She tried not to look, but she was unable to bear the suspense. Cracking one eye open, she peeked at the screen.

Sweet dreams, Norah.

She opened both eyes and read it again. Even as inexperienced as she was, she was pretty sure that wasn't something he'd say to let her down gently. Those were the words of someone who was interested in her.

Realizing she was grinning at her phone like a fool, she forced herself to put it down on the bed. The note rustled, and the reminder of Leifsen erased her smile. She wondered if he was outside right now, looking up at her tiny bedroom window. She had to resist the urge to peer outside. Even if he *was* out there, watching her, she wouldn't be able to see him in the shadows. She shuddered, her eyes glued to the piece of notebook paper. It should've been innocuous, but it was menacing instead. Just like when he hacked into whatever laptop she was using, he was shoving his words in front of her without her permission. Both the note and his text boxes on the screen were invasions, violating her space.

Picking up the note with two fingers as if it were covered in slime, she tucked it into Leifsen's file that she'd placed on the small strip of floor next to her bed. She wished she could burn it or at least shred it, but it was evidence. The memory of Dash promising they'd bring Leifsen in eased the tight ball of tension in her stomach. She wasn't alone in this. Whether Dash was her trainer or a friend or even something more, he was there, cutting a clear path for her and lifting her high above the crowd.

Despite her dread that Leifsen lurked somewhere outside her dark window, Norah's smile returned. She might have a stalker, but she also had Dash.

SEVEN

THEY'D ONLY BEEN SITTING OUTSIDE the Green Valley Apartments for three and a half minutes before Chloe exited and headed for the tenants' parking lot, her distinctive blond braids bouncing against her back with each long stride.

Norah straightened in her seat, her heartbeat speeding up as she spotted her.

"I see her," Dash said, and Norah realized she'd grabbed his arm in her excitement.

Clearing her throat, she released him and pulled her hand back into her lap. "Sorry."

"For what?"

As Chloe opened the driver's side door of an older white cargo van, the hinges squealed a protest loud enough for Norah to hear all the way across the lot to the service road where they'd parked for their stakeout.

"Um…grabbing you." Now she was feeling even more awkward than if she'd just let go and not said anything.

"You can grab me anytime." The corner of his mouth that she could see quirked up.

Norah stared at his too-perfect profile, marveling at his self-assurance. It was like he didn't ever get anxious or feel awkward. She wondered what that would be like, to live without the two things that seemed to rule her existence.

"Ah…okay." She had no idea how to respond to his invitation, so she just waved—awkwardly, of course—at Chloe's van as it rolled out of the parking lot onto the main road. "Should we…follow?"

"Planning on it." He waited until Chloe turned right at a cross street before heading toward the road she'd just left. He followed the van, leaving so much distance between them that Chloe's vehicle was barely in sight…and sometimes not visible at all.

Every time the van disappeared, Norah resisted the urge to yell at Dash to go faster. Although she thought she was containing her feelings well, only squirming a little when they fell too far behind, Dash gave her a raised-eyebrow glance and the tiniest smirk.

"What?" she asked, the word coming out stiff despite her effort at nonchalance.

"We won't lose her." He slowed down as a box truck merged in front of them, cutting off any sight of Chloe's van, and Norah clenched her teeth to hold back a frustrated exclamation. Dash made a sound low in his throat that sounded suspiciously like a chuckle. "If we do, we'll just wait for her to return. It's not like she's planning to murder someone." He paused. "Probably."

"But what if she's going to meet up with Leifsen?" To Norah's relief, the box truck merged into the turn lane, and the distant back doors of Chloe's van were visible again.

"Doubt it."

"Yeah." As much as Norah hoped things would be that simple, she had to agree with Dash. "She didn't look around at all or act nervous while she was walking to her van."

He tipped his head in a slight nod.

"There!" Norah felt her heart accelerate again as the white van pulled into the parking lot next to a brown brick building. She recognized the place, since they'd adopted Warrant there. "Why is she at the animal shelter?" The chance of Chloe meeting up with Leifsen seemed even slimmer now, unless he'd gotten very creative in where he'd holed up.

Dash kindly didn't state the obvious—that Chloe was probably there to adopt a pet—as he cruised past the shelter's entrance and took the next turn into a strip mall parking lot. He parked around the side of an automotive supply store, angling them to face the shelter across the short span of green space.

They didn't have to wait long before Chloe reemerged, holding the leashes of two large dogs. She turned away from the road toward a stand of trees.

"She's walking shelter dogs." Although it was obvious, Norah said it out loud, a little thrown by the additional evidence that Chloe Ballister, alleged friend of a creepy, felonious hacker/stalker/groper, seemed like such a *nice* person.

Dash gave one of his affirmative-sounding grunts.

"How is she friends with someone like *Devon Leifsen?*"

Norah asked with true curiosity, watching through the car windshield as Chloe's canine companions towed her farther away from them. "She's so much better than him."

In her periphery, she saw Dash lift one shoulder in a shrug. "Maybe it was bad info?"

Pushing back her immediate offense that she'd pass along *bad info*, Norah attempted to consider his words objectively. "I suppose it's possible." The perfectionist in her hated to admit that. "Several people linked them together though, and he showed up at her gig."

"Maybe he was just a bad decision on her part," he suggested before turning on the car. "Gave him too much benefit of the doubt. Doesn't seem like they're good friends now, so she probably figured him out."

Norah frowned. As nerve-racking as fieldwork could be, she was disappointed that her time with Dash was over already. She wouldn't see him again until Tuesday, which suddenly—and ridiculously—felt like a long time away. "Are we done for the day?"

He shook his head, making her stomach give a little swoop of anticipation. "You have a dog, right?"

"Yes." Norah cocked her head at him, wondering how he knew that. She didn't think she'd mentioned Warrant to him during their training sessions.

In answer to her unspoken question, Dash reached over and plucked a single coarse white hair from her shirtsleeve, holding it up so she could see.

"Oh. That's very Sherlock-y of you."

His mouth twitched up as he put the SUV in reverse and pulled out of their parking place. "We'll go pick him up and come back here."

"Why?" she asked.

"Give you a reason to be out walking." When she stared at him, her stomach dropping to her toes, he continued. "Plus he'll give you a topic of conversation."

"Wait." She held up a hand, clutching her stomach with her other one as if she could hold it in place. "Wait. You want me to...*talk* to her?"

He glanced at her quickly before returning his attention to traffic. "Yes?" It was the first time she'd ever heard him sound even a tiny bit uncertain.

"Yeah, no. I can't do that."

"Why not?" He sounded more curious than annoyed. "You've already met her."

Norah realized she was shaking her head and forced herself to stop. All she had to do was explain *reasonably* why what he was asking her to do was impossible, and he'd drop it. "Just the once, so she's still pretty much a stranger...so no. I don't...I mean...especially Chloe. She's so... She's confident and in a *band*, with tattoos, and she walks shelter dogs in her free time, with that great hair... I. Can't. No. Just can't. Impossible."

His lips tightened in an obvious attempt to hold back a smile at her horrified ramblings, but Norah didn't care. As long as he didn't make her strike up a conversation with someone who seemed infinitely too badass and awesome and girl-crush-worthy as Chloe Ballister, he could laugh all he wanted.

"Why don't *you* approach her?" Norah asked, even as her stomach twisted at the thought of dangling Dash in front of Chloe like delicious, delicious bait. "You can borrow my dog."

She didn't realize it was possible to scoff with a grunt, but somehow Dash managed. "She wouldn't talk to *me*."

It was Norah's turn to give him a disbelieving look. "Of course she would. A hot guy with a cute dog? She'd be much more likely to talk to you than me."

He paused, and she had a hard time reading his expression as he flexed his fingers on the steering wheel. "You think I'm hot?"

For some reason, her face was heating up, and she knew she was blushing. Unwilling to meet his gaze if he glanced at her, she stared through the windshield, her back poker straight. "Of course I do. I mean, you're objectively attractive. I'm not giving you an emotion-based compliment. It's just a fact." As hard as she tried to keep her voice steady and her words clinically cool, she felt herself growing more and more flustered until she finally shut her mouth.

Dash seemed to take pity on her and resumed the less-embarrassing portion of their conversation. "If I approach Chloe, she's going to be either annoyed or scared."

"What?" The absurdity of that made her forget her earlier awkwardness and turn her head to face him again. "First of all, Chloe doesn't get scared."

He actually laughed—if you could call the rusty coughing sound he made a laugh. "How do you know? Of course she gets scared. Everyone does. And I'm a scary guy."

"Not Chloe." Norah set her chin in a stubborn tilt. "She sat next to a stranger at Chico's. She sang in front of a huge crowd at *Dutch's*. There's no way she'd be scared, especially of you." She wasn't sure why he'd called himself scary. Even the first time she'd met him, she hadn't been afraid of him, and she was the biggest scaredy-cat she knew. The only thing she'd felt when she'd first seen Dash was reassurance and safety.

"Fine." She was pretty sure he would've rolled his eyes if he did that sort of thing. "Let's say she wouldn't be scared. She'd definitely be *annoyed*."

"Why?" Norah couldn't fathom being annoyed if Dash approached her, especially if he had Warrant, the most adorable dog in the universe, in tow.

"Weren't you annoyed when Tucker approached you at the gym?"

"Tucker?" She drew a blank. The only person besides Dash she knew from the gym was Davies, and she only knew his name because Dash had shouted it.

"The 'objectively attractive' man who hit on you after your session last week until I sent him to work on his side kicks." His description held more than a hint of sarcasm.

"Oh!" That last part rang a bell. "The obstacle."

"What?"

"Never mind." She definitely didn't want to explain that the only way she was able to walk through the crowded gym was to pretend all the other people were obstacles on her hunt for her Dash-shaped prize.

"My point is that you thought he was annoying, right?"

"Well, yes," she had to admit. "But he wasn't *you*."

His huff of laughter sounded like he couldn't decide whether to be exasperated or amused. "Very few people share your reaction to me."

She twitched her shoulders in a shrug. "You're just trying to get out of talking to Chloe."

"So are you."

"Well, yes." When he laughed again, she gave a reluctant smile. "Why don't we see if one of my sisters will talk to Chloe? They're both good at chatting with strangers."

"Fine." He pulled his SUV up to the curb in front of her house. "But I think you're wrong about her not wanting to talk to you. I bet you could be friends."

Just like the first time he'd suggested it, the thought of initiating a conversation with the extremely awesome-seeming— despite her potentially terrible taste in past friends—Chloe made Norah's brain freeze with panic. All she could manage to stumble out was, "No, I...she...no."

The mortifying thought of approaching Chloe kept her locked in her thoughts until her door opened and Dash's smug expression unfroze her.

"If you want to be protective," she said, getting out of the SUV, "you'd protect me from terrifying hypothetical encounters with almost strangers I'm supposed to somehow befriend."

He coughed another rusty laugh before escorting her toward her front door with his hand on her back. "She'd love you. I don't know how you don't see it."

"She'd love *you*," Norah countered, raising an eyebrow at his doubtful expression.

He opened his mouth to respond but then frowned, staring at the front door. Following his gaze, Norah saw that the inner door was ajar. The sight made her stomach tighten. She told herself it was probably nothing, that it was a beautiful Sunday morning and one of her sisters had likely just left the door open a bit to air out the house, but that logic didn't track. Her sisters were just as paranoid as Norah, and she couldn't see any of them being relaxed enough to leave the door not only unlocked but open. Not anymore.

Molly and Cara. Her stomach twisted with fear as she started to rush up the porch steps, only to be caught and pulled back by Dash. He tucked her behind him and moved to the front door, surprisingly silent for such a big guy, his feet not making any noise on the normally creaky wooden porch. She found herself grasping the back of his belt like she had in the club, trying to move as quietly as Dash. She was fine with him going first. His fists were much bigger than hers, and he had a lot more experience using them.

The screen door squealed as Dash opened it, and Norah could see his back muscles stiffen at the loud sound. She grimaced. They'd been trying to fix the squeaky hinges ever since Norah could remember, but they refused to be silenced—even under the intimidating glare of the sneaky ninja man in front of her.

With Norah close behind, still clinging to his belt, Dash stepped inside. As he paused, taking in the empty living room, her gaze flew to the alarm system. The steady innocuous green light next to the display showed that the alarm had been deactivated. Her sisters wouldn't leave it unarmed—not after everything they'd been through.

Dash prowled forward, yanking her attention off the alarm display. She peered around the room, looking for anything out of place, but the comfortably worn furniture looked as it always did. Squares of sunlight lit up the rug, the bright cheerfulness of the house working overtime as if to make her worries about her sisters and a possible intruder seem silly.

A *thump* from upstairs set her heart racing. She was tempted to call out, to see if one of her sisters had made that sound, but common sense and Dash's tense posture kept her silent. He moved quickly yet stealthily across the living room to the stairs, shooting up them at a pace that left Norah panting with adrenaline and physical effort, a slight wheeze underlying each breath. Still, she kept up with him, trying to quiet her breathing, not wanting to be left downstairs while Dash checked out what had made the sound on the second level.

She realized that Warrant hadn't shown his fuzzy face. He wasn't the most energetic dog by any means, but he normally stirred himself to greet his people and any visitors. His absence added to the churning in her gut, and her fingers tightened around Dash's belt. It was one thing to mess with their house or even one of her adult sisters, but if someone had hurt their innocent dog… A flash of rage jolted through her, burning up her fear and filling her with determination to find the intruder and make them regret breaking into *her* house.

As Dash turned left at the top of the stairs, Norah released her grip on his belt and turned right, still fueled by fury for anyone who might harm her sisters or her dog. Whipping his head around to glare at her, Dash gestured for her to return to her spot behind him, but she shook her head and darted into the twins' room, knowing he wouldn't call out for her and give their position away.

Although she moved quickly into the room, intent on not letting Dash stop her from helping to search for the possible intruder, she came to an abrupt halt just inside the doorway. Like the living room, Cara and Charlie's bedroom was filled with cheery sunlight, making it seem impossible that the bright room could hide someone with nefarious intentions. Still, she moved carefully around the space, checking under the beds and holding her breath as she reached for the closet door. Her fear had crept back in, shoving over her righteous rage to make space, and her fingers shook as she slid the wooden panel to the side.

The door slid silently on its track, exposing some of Cara's pastel tops. A relieved exhale escaped as Norah pushed it open farther—only to reveal the hulking form of a man.

EIGHT

SHE FROZE, STARING AT THE pockmarked, bulldog-like face of her mom's friend Zach Fridley. It only took a second for his presence to register, and she dragged in a stuttering, wheezing breath, preparing to scream. Before the piercing sound could escape, he lunged for her. She jerked back, but she was too slow, and he was too close. Wrapping a thick hand that smelled like grease and nicotine over her mouth, he turned her around and yanked her back against him.

For the second time in just a few seconds, her muscles locked up, refusing to move. He chuckled in her ear, just a breath of sound.

"Good thing the mousy one found me," he muttered, his lips pressed tight to her ear. It seemed like a mockery of when Dash did the same thing but with completely different motives.

Something about the too-familiar gesture unglued her frozen muscles, and she jabbed her elbow into his gut.

"*Oof*." The air was forced out of his lungs, blowing hot and disgusting across her cheek.

Twisting in his hold, she managed to kick him in the shin and thrust her palm upward toward his nose, although he turned his head in time to avoid the worst of the impact. Instead of breaking his nose, the heel of her hand glanced off his cheekbone.

Grabbing a handful of his hair, she yanked his head down as she lifted her knee, once again aiming for his nose. Instead, her kneecap connected with the tip of his chin. His head snapped back, and he howled, making her realize that she hadn't even had the time—or the breath—to scream for help. Shoving Zach back into the closet with both hands, she twisted around to run and almost crashed into Dash.

He grasped her upper arms before they could collide, actually lifting her off her feet and setting her to the side. As she caught the breath that had been stolen by her tussle with Zach and Dash's unexpected move, he grabbed a fistful of Zach's jacket and yanked him closer…right into his balled fist.

After just one hit, Zach went limp. Norah eyed him warily, not sure if he was actually unconscious or just playing possum so he didn't get hit again. If he was faking, he was a good actor, because the man was *limp*. "Is he out?" she asked.

Dash gave the man in his grip a shake, and Zach flopped like a rag doll. "Yeah." He turned his attention to her, giving her an intense head-to-toe visual inspection. "You okay?"

"Yes." She must've still been floating on the adrenaline high, because she grinned at him. "Did you see me beat him up?"

His mouth twitched up in one of his familiar smiles. "Just the end of it, but what I saw was impressive."

Her chest warmed. There was something about being useful in a dangerous situation that was more satisfying than being good at anything else. Her clumsy, semi-effective take-down gave her a huge thrill…but then she remembered her family.

"Did you find Cara or Molly? Any sign of our dog?"

He shook his head, and Norah's stomach clenched again. Did Zach have help? Did his accomplices have her sisters? Before she could start thinking up every worst-case scenario, a voice from the bedroom doorway made her whirl around.

"We take the dog on a quick walk around the block, and all hell breaks loose. I'm guessing this is Dash," Molly said, and Cara craned to see over her shoulder from her position behind Molly. "We'll need to see his hands."

"Oh, he's on our side," Norah hurried to say, taking a step sideways to put herself between her sisters and Dash. Warrant wiggled his way past her two sisters to lean his heavy body against Norah's legs. She'd never been more grateful to see the big furry beast. "Zach Fridley was hiding in the closet, and Dash knocked him out."

"You beat him up first," Dash said, and Norah gave him an appreciative smile over her shoulder. It was nice of him to share the credit.

"Oh, we don't need to check if he's holding a weapon." Molly sounded amused, which made Norah worry what was coming next.

Sure enough, Cara leaned to the side to get a better view of Dash. "We want to see if his hands are sinewy."

Norah groaned as her sisters laughed. She refused to look at Dash, since she didn't want to explain what they meant. She didn't even know if she *could* explain her sisters' goofiness. Instead, she focused on Zach's still limp form. "Should we call the cops? An ambulance?" she suggested doubtfully. Her lungs still felt tight, so she absently pulled her inhaler from her pocket and took a puff.

"You know that Denver detective will show up as soon as the dispatcher gives our address," Cara said, her mischievous smile disappearing as she wrinkled her nose.

"Cara's right." Molly's grin dropped away as well. "Detective Mill will use this as an excuse to search our house again, and he'll just let Zach walk anyway. That'll just make him more confident about breaking in again." She eyed the unconscious man as if she seriously wanted to get a couple of kicks in.

"Can you call Sergeant Blake?" Cara suggested. "She'll be on our side at least."

Looking gloomy, Molly shook her head. "She's on thin ice after mouthing off to Mill after the chief ordered everyone to be on their best behavior. Besides, Lieutenant Botha told her she can't respond to our family's calls anymore, at least until the stolen necklace case is closed. The local cops want to give the appearance of objectivity now that everyone's eyes are on them because of Mom's theft."

"Your neighbor home?" Dash asked, drawing everyone's gaze. Even Warrant abandoned Norah to sniff the newcomer.

Dash used his hand that wasn't still balled in Zach's shirt to scratch the dog behind his ears, making his heavy tail thump happily against the hardwood floor.

"Which one?" Molly asked. "Mr. Petra?"

"He the sour guy always peeking through his window blinds?"

Norah had to snort at the accurate description. Using her inhaler a second time, she dropped it back into her pocket.

"That's Mr. P. Yes, he's gone. He always golfs on Sunday mornings," Cara answered.

With a short nod, Dash shifted his grip to the back of Zach's shirt and started dragging him toward the hallway. Norah quickly moved out of his way, trusting that he had a plan, but Molly held her ground, blocking his path.

"What's the plan?"

"Having a plan is important to Molly," Norah explained as Cara made a noise in her throat that sounded like a laugh turned into a cough.

Dash lifted his shoulder in a shrug. "Dump him on the sour neighbor's porch and pick the lock. Call the cops and tell them I was jogging by and saw him breaking in. He came at me, so I put him down."

Molly studied him as he stood calmly, waiting for her response. Finally, she stepped aside. "I like how your Dash thinks," she said to Norah approvingly.

Norah felt her face warm as she debated whether to argue that he wasn't technically *her* Dash. She wasn't sure what would give her the right to full possession, but his lips had touched her ear multiple times, they'd danced together, and he approved of her somewhat bumbling fighting technique. It was starting to feel like she had at least a minor stake in him.

As she mentally debated the point, Dash dragged Zach out of the room and down the hall. Shaking herself out of her introspection, she trailed after him. "Want help?"

"Do you care if he has a few bruises tomorrow?" he asked in response.

She met Molly's and then Cara's gazes, and she knew their opinion on the matter matched hers. "Not at all."

"Then I'm good." He started down the stairs, dragging Zach behind him. Every bump of Zach's body against the hardwood steps made Norah wince yet, at the same time, also made her unreasonably satisfied.

"Seriously, Norah," Molly said under her breath as they followed the two men down the stairs. "This one's a keeper."

Norah swallowed a smile before moving to catch up with the man in question.

When he reached the front door, Dash hauled Zach onto his shoulders in a fireman's carry. Norah and her sisters clustered behind him, ready to follow him over to Mr. P's, but he shook his head. "Better not take the chance that any of you are seen."

"How're you getting him next door without the Villaneaus spotting you?" Norah asked.

"Oh, they're gone too," Cara interjected before Dash could say anything. "Sunday brunch at the Hotel Royale, remember?"

"Right." Norah had known that. She blamed her unusual absentmindedness on the stressful morning she'd just had.

Moving to the picture window, she looked out onto the street that was empty except for Dash's SUV. "You're clear." Glancing over, she felt a tug in her belly. "Be careful. Thank you for doing this."

"Yes, this is really nice of you," Cara added as Molly nodded in agreement.

He shrugged off their thanks as well as he could with an unconscious person draped across his shoulders. Molly opened the door for him, and he stepped outside, the screen door screeching as usual. Norah was pretty sure she'd never be able to hear it without remembering the fear from that morning. As soon as Molly closed the door behind him, Norah hurried to set the alarm.

"Did you set the alarm before you took Warrant for a walk?" she asked, trying to take comfort in the *alarm armed* message and red light that indicated the security system was on.

"Of course," Cara said with a bit of an offended huff. "It's not like I'd forget after being *kidnapped* and all."

Molly patted her sister on the shoulder, getting that fiercely protective look she always wore whenever Cara's abduction was mentioned. "It was definitely set. I triple-checked it."

Norah frowned. She would've felt more secure if they'd forgotten to set it. "It was off when Dash and I arrived, and the front door was open."

Leaving her sisters to process that disturbing news, Norah moved to a small side window so she could watch as Dash carefully navigated the lawn that separated their house from Mr. P's. "I should've offered to pick the lock for him."

"Something tells me that man can pick a lock," Molly said, squeezing next to her so she could watch out the window as well. "I'm telling you. He's a find. Knocks out a bad guy with one punch and then cleans up the mess? Winner, winner, chicken dinner."

Maneuvering between them, Cara joined them. "He has really nice hands too. Not quite as nice as Henry's but still an honorable mention."

Norah gave her sister a poke with her elbow. "You and your hand obsession." It was hard to see well from their vantage point, but she could tell that Dash had dumped Zach unceremoniously onto Mr. P's porch and looked to be making a call. It was short—the police, she guessed. Once he returned his phone to his pocket, he started working on the front door lock. "I still think I should've offered to pick the lock for him. It would've only been polite when he's doing all the work just to save us some hassle."

"If any of us should be picking the lock, it's me," Cara said. "I got the best time last practice."

"When did you two become so interested in fieldwork?" Molly asked. "And can you please stop? Worrying about the pair of you is giving me an ulcer."

Leaning forward so far that her nose almost touched the windowpane, Norah sucked in a breath. "Looks like Zach's waking up." His hands moved to clutch his head, and Norah couldn't hold back her smirk. "Good. I hope his head hurts."

With a snort, Molly said, "Look at you, Miss Ruthless."

"He broke into our house…for the *third* time. Also, he stole your car and sold it to a weed dispensary that painted marijuana leaves all over it. *And* he hit Fifi over the head." As she listed just some of Zach's recent crimes against them, Norah found herself growing angry all over again. "Plus he *stinks*. Just wait until you smell how bad Cara and Charlie's closet reeks now."

Cara groaned. After a slight pause, she asked, "Think Dash needs us to knock the bastard out again?"

Norah seriously considered going to help, but Molly just said dryly, "He has it under control. Look."

Sure enough, Dash had Mr. P's door unlocked and was currently hauling a groggy Zach to his feet and twisting one arm behind his back. He pushed him up against the house next to the slightly open door and held him with one hand while using the other to wipe the lock picks he'd just used on his sleeve. Tugging his sleeve over his hand, he used the improvised glove to tuck the tools into Zach's pocket. As the man wriggled in his grip, Dash pulled his phone from his pocket.

"Dash is an ice-cold badass," Cara said as if making an announcement of vital importance. "And I say that as someone who is dating another one."

"Agreed." Molly was watching Dash handle the burglar with professional approval. "Look how he's keeping him pinned with only one hand. Sometimes I wish I were that big. It would make my job so much easier."

"Maybe." Cara didn't sound convinced. "You'd lose the element of surprise though. If you were six four and covered in muscle, all the skips would see you coming and either run or grab their guns. Dash was able to get the jump on Zach because he was just expecting to deal with us *poor, defenseless ladies.*" She cooed the last three words, her mile-long eyelashes batting innocently.

"Plus, I'd just beaten up Zach, so he was off-balance because of that." As admirable as Dash was, Norah felt a little miffed he was receiving *all* the credit.

"Right," Cara agreed. "And it was easier for Norah to pummel him because he wasn't expecting it. Our small adorableness is part of our disguise, hiding the ferocious warrior women within."

Molly appeared to be considering that when Norah's phone buzzed with a call. Her tightly strung nerves made her jump, but she quickly recovered and pulled out her phone. As she'd expected, Dash was calling her.

She accepted the call and immediately asked, "Why are you on your phone? Don't you need that hand for other things right now?"

He gave one of his rusty, short laughs. "I've got him. Just figured you and your sisters would want to listen in."

In the background, she could hear Zach's groggy questions growing increasingly louder and more heated. The sound of a faint siren joined his complaints.

"We would. Thank you." Turning the phone on speaker, she placed it on the windowsill in front of them.

"It's like a drive-in movie," Cara whispered, making Molly laugh.

"Quiet. You're on speaker," Dash warned.

The command in his tone made Norah press her lips together

as if preventing words from accidentally leaking out. A sideways glance showed her sisters both covering their mouths with their hands, and Norah had to smother a nervous giggle. They were like two copies of the "speak no evil" monkey. It wouldn't be the worst idea to mute their side of the conversation, but she didn't want to lose the option of being heard. What if they had to shout a warning?

A marked police car pulled up at the curb in front of Mr. Petra's house, and Dash casually dropped the hand holding his phone to his side. Before the first cop had even managed to get his door open, an all-too-familiar unmarked sedan parked behind him. Norah winced at the sight, holding back the groan that wanted to escape. Just as they'd thought, Detective Mill had heard the dispatched call and come running, even though the address wasn't theirs. She was so grateful to Dash for taking the heat. Even the thought of Mill and the other cops tramping through their house again, tearing things apart in a poorly concealed effort to find any hint of the necklace, made her stomach hurt.

The uniformed cop, a balding man in his fifties, was one Norah vaguely remembered from her infrequent research-related visits to the police station to get copies of incident reports. He eyed Mill with obvious resentment but also a heaping helping of resignation before moving toward where Dash had Zach restrained on Mr. Petra's porch.

Mill followed a step behind, his gaze darting from the pair of men to the Pax house. Norah resisted the urge to pull back from the window, knowing that the motion would just catch the detective's eye. Also, there was nothing illegal about gaping through the window at the neighbors' police drama. If it had been, Mr. P would've been a repeat offender.

Cara's elbow poked her in the ribs, making Norah glance at her sister. *He's the woooorst,* Cara mouthed, and Norah nodded vehemently in agreement. Even though he'd been cleared of the crimes his former partner had been charged with, Mill still seemed shady, and he tried his best to make the Pax sisters' lives as miserable as possible.

"Sir, release him and step over there." The officer stopped at the base of the porch steps, ignoring Mill now that all his attention was focused on the two men.

"He'll run," Dash warned, and the rather portly cop seemed to reconsider. Norah couldn't blame him. Of all the tortures Felicity put them through during their early morning training sessions, the sprints were the worst. Sprinting with Dash chasing her in the mountains hadn't seemed so bad though. In fact, that'd been…exhilarating. Her face immediately burned hot, even though her sisters couldn't hear her randy thoughts.

The officer seemed to decide he didn't want a foot chase and climbed the porch steps, skirting the ceramic pots filled with fall flowers. Once he got a hand on Zach's free arm, he nodded to Dash, who released his hold and stepped away from the two men. Just as Dash predicted, Zach twisted around, trying to tear free of the cop's grip. The officer gave a shout as he struggled to pin Zach back against the wall, and Mill rushed up the steps to help.

Molly reached behind Cara and poked Norah. Once she had both of her sisters' attention, Molly mimed eating popcorn.

Norah muffled a laugh behind her hand, hoping that any sound that escaped was covered by the wrestling match happening next door. When she looked through the window again, she saw that the cops had gotten Zach down on the porch floor. The uniformed officer had a knee pressed into his back, and he and Mill managed to yank Zach's arms behind him.

The cop grabbed his handcuffs off his belt and moved to put them on Zach's left wrist, but Zach wiggled around like a fish, torquing his body so his feet swung around toward the steps. Grunts and breathless shouts echoed from the phone speaker, followed by a loud crash as the flowerpot on the top step went flying, a victim of Zach's flailing feet.

Norah met her sisters' equally wide eyes. Mr. Petra was going to be pissed when he saw that. She felt a small pang of guilt for dumping their problem on his doorstep—literally—but quickly dismissed it. Mr. P had caused their family enough hassle over the years. He could deal with a scuff on his pristine porch and a lost flowerpot or two.

The cops finally got Zach cuffed, and the uniformed officer pulled him to his feet, puffing hard enough for Norah to hear his breathing through her phone.

"He attacked me for no reason!" Zach was the first one to suck in enough air to speak. "I don't even know him, and he hit me hard enough to knock me out. I think I have a concussion thanks to him."

The cop ignored his ranting, donning gloves before patting Zach down. When he pulled out the lock picks, holding them up so Mill could see them, Norah squirmed with excitement.

Things had been going so badly for them the past several weeks. It was such a relief to have something finally go right.

Finishing his search, the cop shoved him toward Mill. "Stick him in my car, would you? We'll talk to this guy first." He gestured at Dash, who was leaning against the porch railing far enough away that he was out of reach if Zach tried to kick out but close enough to allow Norah and her sisters to hear everything.

Although Mill looked sour, likely from being treated like the uniform cop's lackey, he did as he was asked, hauling Zach down the steps toward the cars parked at the curb. As they reached the sidewalk, Zach swore, kicking out at the decorative glass globe next to him. It exploded with a crash that made Norah jerk back with a wince, that sliver of guilt for messing with Mr. P's property poking at her again.

The cop copied Dash's name and other information off his license before handing it back. "So what happened here?"

"I was on a run and saw that guy breaking in." He gestured toward the door that still sat ajar. "I stopped him. He tried to hit me. I punched him in the face. Knocked him out for a bit. Called 911. He came to, so I pinned him against the house until you arrived."

Norah had to smile at his Hemingwayesque way of telling a story. She appreciated that about Dash. Everything was laid out clearly and succinctly with no room to agonize over hidden meanings.

The cop eyed the phone still in his hand. "Were you video-ing us earlier?"

"No. Called my girlfriend. She was worried."

Norah felt her face warm at the "girlfriend" mention, and she very carefully didn't look at her sisters. Even though he was just making up a story, the word still made her stomach flutter in a new way she wasn't sure she fully approved of.

"Knocked him out in one hit?" At Dash's affirmative tip of his chin, the cop continued. "You in law enforcement?"

This time, Dash shook his head.

"Military?"

Dash gave a short nod. "Now I own a gym."

"Ah." The cop seemed to relax a little now that he had an explanation for Dash's skills. "You were on a run? You're a long ways from home."

"Five and a quarter miles." Norah saw Dash's shoulder lift in one of his familiar shrugs. "Today was a distance run."

"Huh." The cop sounded skeptical, but Norah was pretty sure he didn't doubt Dash's story. He was more confused by why anyone would purposefully run without being forced. She could relate. "You know the homeowner?"

"No."

"How'd you know that guy was breaking in then? Maybe he just locked himself out."

"He was picking the lock." Dash didn't hesitate in answering. "When I approached him, he tried to hit me."

"Do you know anyone who lives at that house?" Mill's question made Norah jump. She'd been so focused on Dash's interview she hadn't noticed him returning to the porch after locking Zach in the back of the squad car.

Dash turned and focused his flattest, most intimidating stare on Mill. "Who are they?"

"The last name's Pax. A mother and five grown daughters."

"There's a Pax who trains at my gym."

Norah had to admire Dash's ability to so coolly misdirect without actually lying. If she were being questioned by the cops, she knew she'd turn red and stammer horribly, even if every word out of her mouth was true.

Although it was hard to tell from a distance, Norah got the impression Mill had perked up at Dash's admission. "What's her first name?"

He did his usual one-shoulder shrug. "I'd have to look it up. Why?"

"Why isn't important. Let me know her full name once you have it." Mill handed Dash a business card. "And whatever else you know about her—when she usually comes to the gym, who she hangs out with, any details you can think of, even if you don't think they're important."

Although Dash accepted the card, he didn't promise the detective anything.

The uniformed officer, obviously unhappy with Mill butting into his interview, cleared his throat. "What do you—"

His question was cut off as Mr. P's new Infiniti flew past the cops' cars and up the driveway in a streak of shiny black. He screeched to a stop just short of the closed garage door.

"What's going on?" Mr. Petra shrieked as he tried to get out of his vehicle, only to become tangled in the retracting seat belt. Once he'd fought his way free, he ran toward the porch. When he saw the destroyed globe, he came to an abrupt stop. "What *happened?*"

Mill and the other officer exchanged a look. "Why don't you talk to the homeowner while I finish this interview?" the cop said.

"Why don't I take over the interview?" Mill suggested, condescension heavy in his voice.

If Norah hadn't already seriously disliked Mill before eavesdropping on this latest encounter, just this would've made her loathe him.

When the uniformed cop's jaw set mulishly and he started to protest, Mill raised a hand to silence him. "I'm the detective here." He waved toward Mr. Petra as if telling the other cop to go clean up a mess before turning to Dash.

With a shake of his head, Dash maneuvered around Mill and started down the steps. "I have to go. Call if you have any other questions."

"Wait—" Mill's protest was quickly drowned out by Mr. Petra, who'd given up on trying to piece his precious yard ornament back together.

"Who are you?" Mr. P demanded, loud enough that Norah could hear him in stereo from the phone speaker and through the window. "What are you doing on my porch? Are you responsible for this...*destruction?*" He moved in front of Dash, blocking his way, and Norah held back a laugh. Mr. P's slight form looked very small compared to Dash, giving the impression of a Chihuahua trying to stop a mastiff.

"The one responsible is handcuffed in the back of my car,"

the cop said. "This is the Good Samaritan who appears to have stopped the burglary."

Mr. Petra didn't seem to be appeased by this. If anything, his voice got louder as he turned to glare at the squad car. Sunlight reflecting off the windows made it hard to see inside. "Who is it? It's one of *those women* isn't it?"

He flung a hand toward Norah's house, and she found herself flinching back from the sheer venom in his voice. It made her regret feeling any sort of guilt about Mr. P's involvement. He was an awful, unpleasant man who didn't deserve a single intact lawn ornament.

Mill and the other cop both turned to look at the Pax house, and Norah drew back farther, positive that they were glaring right at her. A glance to her right made her see that her sisters were doing the same.

"Why would you think that?" Mill asked, sounding almost eager.

The uniformed officer cleared his throat, but Mr. Petra, probably sensing an ally in Pax hate, quickly spat, "They're the source of all the trouble in this neighborhood and most of it in this town. Not a day goes by that the police or some disreputable trash person isn't hanging around. And the state of their place brings all our property values down. I pray every day that they decide to sell."

Norah literally bit her tongue to hold back a torrent of defensive words that wanted to escape. Normally, she wouldn't dream of arguing with anyone, even over the phone, but he had crossed a line. No one could say bad things about her family...

well, except for her. She turned her head and saw that both of her sisters were struggling to hold in laughter, and some of her wrath dissolved. She was still annoyed when she turned back to the show on her neighbor's porch though.

"Let's get Mr. Fridley's statement before making any more accusations against your neighbors." The uniformed cop interrupted Mr. Petra mid-rant. Norah was starting to think the officer wasn't half-bad, at least compared to Mill. He turned to Dash. "You're free to go. I'll call with any follow-up questions."

With a short nod, Dash circled around Mr. P with what Norah considered great restraint. If she'd been the one out there, she didn't think she could've resisted a solid shoulder check after the way Mr. P talked about them.

As Dash walked away from the others, the cop's voice faded. The last thing they heard before he got too far away was the cop speaking to Mr. P. "Why don't you stay here with the detective, and I'll go talk to the suspect."

Both Mill and Mr. P looked sour about that plan, but they stayed in place as the cop headed for the squad car. Dash reached the street first and started jogging away from Norah's house. She watched his muscular form move out of sight before speaking.

"Sorry you have to run."

His amused huff didn't sound out of breath at all. "Just walking now. I'll find a coffee shop or something to wait out the cops."

"Hopefully Mill or the other cop won't run the plates on your SUV parked out front," Molly said, and Norah felt her eyes grow wide. She hadn't thought about that, but it was something

Mill was likely to do. There was no doubt he had a record of all their vehicles and probably what John, Bennett, and Henry drove too.

Dash just grunted in response. Without seeing his face, Norah wasn't sure if the sound was skeptical or agreeing. Either way, Mill still stood next to Mr. P on his porch, who was crouched by the broken flowerpot, but the detective was staring directly at their window.

"The detective is looking at us." Norah picked up the phone and moved back. She wasn't sure whether Mill could see them or not, but she wasn't about to take any chances. "As soon as it's clear, I'll call you back." After another grunt—this one she was pretty sure was in agreement—she ended the call and saw that both her sisters were smirking at her. "What?"

"He's such a caveman," Molly said.

"I thought you liked him." For some reason Norah didn't want to examine too closely, it was very important that her sisters like Dash.

"Oh, we do," Cara assured her, although she was grinning in a way Norah didn't quite trust. "Being a caveman is not a disqualifying trait."

"Definitely not." Molly said over her shoulder as she headed for the stairs. "Take it from someone whose boyfriend never shuts up. I love him, but the man is an extrovert."

"Where are you going?" Cara asked.

"My room. We can watch through the blinds without a nosy detective spotting us." Molly took the stairs three at a time.

Even though she groaned, Cara followed her up the steps.

"When did we become *that* neighbor? Shouldn't this behavior wait until we're in our nineties?"

Smiling despite the rock sitting in her stomach, Norah climbed the stairs after her sisters.

NINE

WATCHING THE SHOW NEXT DOOR was boring without any audio or wrestling matches. The only excitement occurred when the uniformed cop pulled Zach out of the back of the squad car, presumably so that Mr. P could get a look at him to see if he knew him. Mr. Petra let out a bellow of rage loud enough for Norah to hear before barreling toward a handcuffed Zach.

"You destructive moron!" Mr. P yelled as Mill chased after him. Their neighbor got within ten feet of Zach before Mill grabbed him and yanked him back. "You need to be locked up for life. You destroyed a one-of-a-kind gazing ball! *One. Of. A. Kind!*"

Mr. P seemed to lose his momentum at that point, his shoulders slumping as he allowed Mill to usher him back to his porch.

"I feel kind of bad for him," Cara muttered quietly. "We were responsible for Zach being on his porch after all."

"Sure, but remember when he called the cops on us because he measured a piece of our grass with a ruler and it was an eighth of an inch longer than allowed by city ordinance?" Molly asked, still peering at the scene outside through an opening between the window frame and the edge of the blinds. "Or when we were kids and spent weeks building that little tree house in the cottonwood that's right next to his yard, and he destroyed it when we were at school? I mean, it was pathetic and probably would've led to us falling to our deaths, but there was still no excuse for him smashing it to bits with a sledgehammer. Oh! And when we saved our money to get rainbow Christmas lights, and he cut the plug off every single strand during the night because he didn't want decorations that 'promoted homosexuality' in the neighborhood?"

"Fine! Fine," Cara put her hands on her head as if protecting herself from an onslaught. "I was wrong. He doesn't deserve my pity. My pity for Mr. P has officially dried up."

Norah smiled a little at the memories Molly had brought up. "I loved those Christmas lights. They were so *bright.*"

"Yeah." Judging by Molly's sigh, she was feeling nostalgic too. "I wish he'd gotten electrocuted when he took his garden shears to them."

"Molly!" Cara sounded both legitimately shocked but also like she was trying not to laugh, which took some of the impact away from her scolding.

"Fine," Molly grumped. "I wish he'd gotten a solid, painful— but not deadly—shock. Is that better?"

"We should decorate the house for Christmas again this year," Norah suggested absently as she watched Mr. Petra wave his arms as he talked to Mill.

"Oh, let's." Molly sounded so gleeful Norah was surprised she wasn't rubbing her hands together like a cartoon villain. "That'll be brilliant."

"Especially if we leave them up until July." Cara looked serious, but the corner of her mouth twitched, making Molly lose it completely.

When she finally regained control of herself, Molly wiped her eyes and returned to her surveillance spot at the side of the window. "And you thought I was wicked for wishing he'd been electrocuted. You want to *torture* him for months instead."

Cara just offered a tiny yet smug smile. "A quick death is too good for him. I loved that tree house."

More amused than she should probably be at a discussion about torturing their neighbor, Norah peeked through the blinds. She was careful not to get too close so she didn't bump them. Neither cop was looking their way, but she didn't want to be obvious about it and draw their attention.

The uniformed officer had returned Zach to the safety of the back seat and was speaking with Mr. P and Detective Mill. Without being able to hear what they were saying, Norah's mind drifted. She wondered where Dash ended up holing up for the afternoon. This probably wasn't the way he'd wanted to spend his day off.

The cop turned away from his huddle with Mill and Mr. Petra, striding over to the driver's side door of his squad car. After a few more minutes of what looked like Mr. P lecturing Mill, judging by the amount of times the smaller man's finger poked the detective in the chest, their neighbor gave Mill a final stab and walked into his house.

Norah and her sisters grew quiet and still as they watched the last remaining man standing on Mr. P's front walk.

"Just get in your car," Molly mumbled, making Norah bite back a chuckle. It almost sounded as if Molly was trying to hypnotize the detective from a distance. "Get in your car, and follow the nice, competent cop back to the station."

Molly's hypnosis skills obviously needed work, because Mill's gaze locked on Norah and her sisters' house. Glancing down the road as if making sure the other cop was out of sight, he strode toward their front door. Norah's stomach clenched.

"C'mon." Molly was at the top of the stairs before Norah had even processed the fact that Mill was coming to their house.

She hurried to follow her sisters down the stairs but froze when she reached the bottom. What did the detective want? Why was he trekking over to their place? She swallowed hard. Did he know something? Was there a hole he noticed in Dash's improvised story?

Molly moved to the security controls and deactivated the alarm. The familiar screech of the screen door opening made Norah's stomach twist into an even tighter knot, but Molly's expression was calm as she walked to the door.

As she yanked it open, Detective Mill was revealed. His fist was raised as if he'd been just about to pound on it. Wanting to back up her sister, Norah moved closer, noticing that Cara did the same. Even though Mill hadn't been arrested like his partner, no one in their family trusted him one bit—especially since he seemed bound and determined to catch them doing something illegal.

"Detective Mill." Molly bared her teeth in what couldn't quite be considered a smile. "How...*lovely* to see you."

Even as her stomach tightened, Norah had to hold back a snort. The word "lovely" had positively dripped with malice.

"I have some questions for you about an incident at your neighbor's house." Mill didn't even bother with the niceties as he pushed open the screen door wider, moving as if to step inside.

Molly didn't move, continuing to block the doorway. Norah moved closer, adding to the barrier.

"Why don't you want me inside?" Mill asked with an unpleasant, sneering smile. "What are you girls hiding?"

"First of all..." It was Molly's turn to step forward, and Mill automatically took a step back, yielding the space to her. From his immediate frown, he wasn't happy about it. "We are not *girls*. Second, there's no reason for you to come inside to talk about something that happened at the *neighbor's*. We can talk out here."

Although Mill scowled, he backed up another step so that Molly, closely followed by Norah and Cara, could step out onto the porch. Norah pulled the solid door closed behind them, not allowing Mill even a peek into their home. Warrant, who'd wandered up behind them to greet the visitor, gave her a hurt look when she closed the door in his face, and she mentally promised the dog an apology treat once Mill was gone before focusing on the detective again.

"What can we help you with *this* time, Detective?" Molly asked in a long-suffering tone.

Norah hid her chuckle in a covered cough. The way she'd phrased it made it sound as if the police were constantly asking for their assistance with open cases. From the darkening patches of red creeping up Mill's neck from his shirt collar, he didn't find that as funny as Norah had.

"Does the name Zach Fridley ring any bells?"

Norah felt the churning in her stomach start up again. After the day—weeks—she'd had, she wasn't going to have any stomach lining left after the acid chewed it all away.

"He's a local criminal," Molly answered.

At first, Norah was a little surprised her sister admitted to knowing him, but then she realized Zach's name would be in their car-theft report as the main suspect.

"He burglarized our place a few weeks ago," Molly continued.

"Why is he out already then? Is he one of your bail jumpers?" The way Mill phrased the question made it seem like the Pax sisters collected skips, like adopted cats, rather than returning them to jail.

"Insufficient evidence," Molly said. It sounded like she was clenching her teeth around the words. "The investigators seemed to be more interested in our mom's crime than in the one committed against us."

"What does he want at your neighbor's place?" Mill asked, sounding less aggravated and more thoughtful.

Molly shrugged, and Norah was impressed by how well her sister pulled off casually clueless. "How should I know? As you could probably tell, we're not on warm and fuzzy terms with Mr. P."

"Did you see what happened?"

"Not until we heard the siren, then we saw you and the other cop arrive." The corner of Molly's mouth tucked in, and Norah recognized that tell. Her sister was trying to hold back a smile. "We looked out the window in time to see the wrestling match."

Mill's molars clamped together with an audible *clack*. He waved toward Dash's SUV sitting at the curb, the tenseness of the gesture revealing his irritation. "Whose vehicle is that?"

Crossing her arms across her chest in a Charlie-like move, Molly demanded, "What business of that is yours?"

Rather than look offended, Mill got that focused gleam in his eye as if he thought he'd cornered them. "I'm investigating a crime. It's parked on my crime scene."

"It belongs to my boyfriend," Norah blurted out, worried that stonewalling Mill would just make him more likely to run the plates. If he saw Dash's name on the registration, then their whole story would collapse.

Mill's eyebrows leapt to his forehead. "*You* have a boyfriend? Since when?"

"Her private life doesn't have anything to do with your crime scene," Molly said, her voice as cold as frost.

"Where is he?" Mill didn't seem put off by Molly's ice-cold warning tone. "Maybe he saw something next door."

"He's not here." Norah's brain spun as she tried to keep her expression relaxed. This was why she didn't usually do fieldwork. She was so bad at improv. "I had some errands to do, so he's letting me use his SUV while he's at work."

"What's his name?"

"That's none—" Molly started, but Norah cut her off.

"Davies." The name of Dash's employee burst out of her. He was the first guy she could think of who wasn't a felon or a skip. At least she didn't *think* he was a skip.

"That his last name?" At her uncertain nod, he asked, "What's his first name?"

"He goes by…" She only paused for a microsecond, but it felt like a yawning pit of silence to her. "Bruiser." The name came out in a rush of relief, quickly followed by the realization that no one named Bruiser Davies existed. "That's his nickname."

"Bruiser?" Mill repeated the name like it tasted bad.

"Yes." Norah set her jaw, even as she ignored her sisters' eyes. Knowing them, they were fighting laughter. She held Mill's skeptical gaze instead. "He's an MMA fighter. So he…you know, *bruises* people. Just in fights though," she hurried to add. "None of it is illegal bruising. It's all…um…consensual." She fought the surge of heat that wanted to surge up her neck into her cheeks.

"MMA fighter, huh?" From Mill's tone, he didn't believe a word of it. "Where's he working?"

"Porter Sports." There was no way she could think of a different gym name on the spot. Thinking up "Bruiser" while Mill glared at her had already melted her brain.

Immediately, his brows bunched together. "Porter Sports? As in Dashiell Porter?"

"Yes, that's Bruiser's boss?" Her voice rose, turning her statement into a question, but she couldn't help it. It was a wonder she was still able to make words at this point.

"Isn't that a coincidence," Mill muttered, scratching his cheek as he continued to study her.

She tried her best to look innocent and not like she'd just beaten up a guy who'd jumped out of a closet at her.

"You're a member there?"

"Yes." She waited a beat, but the detective seemed to expect something more. "That's how I met Bruiser." Saying his name was getting more comfortable, as if she was settling into her imaginary relationship with Bruiser Davies.

"How well do you know Porter?"

Her heartbeat sped up again. "Uh…not well?" She knew that didn't sound convincing at all, so she tried again. "He's very…gruff. And intimidating." It wasn't exactly a lie. He was indeed gruff, and although she didn't find him intimidating, she knew others did—including Mill, if the way he tightened his lips as he gave the faintest of nods was any indication.

"You expect me to believe that it's just a coincidence that Porter—who you're already acquainted with—was in *your* neighborhood at exactly the right time to stop a burglary?"

Molly cleared her throat, and Norah could tell her sister was swallowing the last bits of laughter at the whole "Bruiser" thing. When she spoke, her voice was impressively grave. "This is Langston, Detective, not Denver. Everyone pretty much knows everyone here."

"Unless…" Cara didn't do as good of a job as Molly in hiding her amusement. "Maybe Dashiell Porter has a thing for you, Norah. Could he be running by our house, hoping to catch a glimpse?"

"Oh no." Norah shot a glare at her smirking sister. "We barely know each other. Besides, I'm dating *Bruiser*."

"Still, he sees you at the gym. Maybe he has a crush." Cara was barely holding back her laughter, and even Molly was obviously trying not to grin. "And the fact that you're dating his employee… Well, some guys want what they can't have."

"I'm sure Mr. Porter wouldn't do that to Bruiser."

"Let's stay on track here," Mills interjected before Cara could poke at Norah any more.

"Of course, Detective." Molly smiled in a way that clearly said she was out of patience. "Do you have any other *relevant* questions for us? As much as I'd enjoy sharing conspiracy theories with you all afternoon, we have work to do."

Mill glared at them each in turn but eventually shook his head. "Not right now, but I'm sure I'll be back here again soon. You *girls* just can't seem to stay out of trouble." Before any of them could respond, he turned and stalked toward his car.

It was probably good he left, Norah figured, before Molly could punch him in the face. She had a wicked right hook, and their family didn't need Molly in jail for assaulting an officer on top of everything else.

They waited on the porch as the detective did a three-point turn and then drove away, none of them moving until he turned left at the first cross street and his car disappeared. Norah glanced at Mr. Petra's house, but it looked like he'd gone inside.

"Call your boy," Molly ordered in a quiet voice, opening their front door. Norah was already pulling out her cell phone.

"Let him know the cover story, and ask him where he is. We'll pick up his keys and take his SUV to him."

They moved inside, Warrant greeting them as if they'd been gone for days. Norah held her phone to her ear, her stomach dropping when she heard Dash's gruff greeting. She knew she had to tell him about her new fake boyfriend, but it was going to be excruciatingly embarrassing.

Bracing herself, she forced words out of her mouth. "If Mill asks, I'm dating your employee, Bruiser Davies."

To his credit, there was barely a pause before he responded. "Davies's name isn't Bruiser. It's Leon."

"Well, I didn't know that." Realizing that she was getting snappy with the wrong person, she closed her eyes and took a calming breath. It didn't do much to help her nerves. "Besides, Bruiser is his nickname."

"Bruiser is not his nickname."

"It is if Mill asks."

This time, the pause was a hair longer. "Fine. Why are you dating Davies?" His voice had a bit of a growl to it that made Norah shiver, but not in a scared way.

"I'm not. I just had to explain why Bruiser's vehicle was parked outside our house."

His grunt didn't sound happy. "So Davies gets you *and* my car?"

"Well, it can't be *your* car, since that would've blown your story."

"True."

His admission sounded resigned although still a bit grumpy,

so she continued her explanation as Molly waved her into the kitchen and then nudged her through the door into the garage. "I figured since Davies is your employee, that would explain why the SUV is registered to you if Mill runs the plates."

"So Davies gets you and the car, but I have to *pay* for it?" There was a hint of humor in his voice now, although his words were still grumbly.

"It's kind of a stretch," Molly joined in the conversation even though she could only hear Norah's half. "Mill was already suspicious, and he hadn't even run the plates yet."

"Hopefully he stormed off before he could get the plate number." Even as she said it, Norah knew it wasn't very likely.

"Doubt it," Molly and Dash chorused.

Despite everything horrible that was happening, Norah had to smile at how Dash seemed to be fitting seamlessly into her family.

"Where are we going?" Molly asked as she backed out of the driveway.

"Sorry," Norah said with a grimace. "I haven't asked yet. We were still talking about me dating Bruiser."

"Stop saying that." Dash had passed grumpy and was now sounding positively surly.

Norah wanted to explain that the more they discussed it, the more natural Dash's answers to the detective's questions would be, but their car was now idling in the middle of the street as Molly stared at her expectantly. Besides, she was pretty sure Dash understood the importance of supporting her cover story. He just didn't care for her fake dating Bruiser for some reason. "Where are you?"

"Bubbles Diner on Rock Street."

At the name of the restaurant, Norah's stomach reminded her that she hadn't eaten since her quick breakfast. "Bubbles," she told Molly.

"Yum. I love their burgers." Apparently, her sister was hungry too. "Let's eat there after we get Dash's car."

"Bruiser's car," Norah corrected, drawing a laugh from Molly and a growl from Dash. "Did you eat already?"

"Twice, but I'll stay while you eat."

His words made her stomach warm. "Okay. We're going to get your SUV first so Mr. P doesn't see you driving off in it." She was tempted to mention Bruiser again but decided she'd teased him enough. It was just funny how unexpectedly annoyed he was by her imaginary dating situation.

He just grunted, but it sounded more like agreement this time and less like his grumpy inner badger was speaking for him.

"We're turning onto Rock Street now. See you in a minute." At his sound of acknowledgment, she moved to end the call but then hesitated. "Dash?"

"Yeah?" He must've heard something in her tentative tone, because he responded with an actual word.

"Thank you for everything."

"You're welcome."

Two words! Ending the call, she rested the hand holding her phone against her thigh, looking out the side window so Molly couldn't see her smiling.

"You're so gone on this guy." Molly practically sang the words, and Norah had to laugh. Of course her sister already knew.

TEN

CARA DECIDED SHE NEEDED SOME fries too, so she rode along in Molly's car while Norah drove Dash's SUV to Bubbles. She didn't want to mess up his settings for such a short trip, so she perched on the edge of the driver's seat, stretching her leg to reach the pedals. It reminded her just how *big* Dash was, and she found herself flushing for absolutely no sensible reason for the entire drive.

As she parked in the diner's small lot, she blew out a relieved breath and turned off the engine. She'd worried that something would happen while she was responsible for the vehicle, but she'd managed to get it here without adding any dents or scratches.

As she climbed out of the driver's seat, she looked around, trying to be subtle about it but probably failing. Not only was she extra paranoid lately thanks to Leifsen, but now she had to worry about whether Detective Mill was lying in wait somewhere, ready to leap out when he saw her and Dash together.

The only other people in the lot were an older couple slowly making their way to their car. Norah gave them her usual awkward stranger-greeting smile before hurrying toward the entrance. She knew she wouldn't relax until she was inside, away from all sorts of spying eyes—whether real or imaginary.

The bell on the door jangled as she pushed inside, relieved to see that the small restaurant was mostly empty. It was a strange time—midafternoon—to be having a meal, and she figured it was late enough for most of the lunch crowd to have finished and left. She spotted Dash and her sisters at a table in the corner, and she smiled reflexively at the sight of him.

Dash watched her approach. His scowl and intense stare would've frightened off just about anyone else, but she found it oddly comforting. That was just how Dash looked. He had resting grump face.

He stood as she arrived at the table and pulled out the chair next to him for her. She eyed him sideways as she sat. "Is this like a not-swearing or car-door-opening thing?"

"Manners, you mean?" The corner of his mouth twitched up as he took his seat. "Yeah, my gran's ghost would smack me on the back of the head if I wasn't polite."

Fighting an answering smile, she glanced across the table at her sisters, who were watching, fascinated. "What?" she asked self-consciously.

Molly and Cara exchanged a look before chorusing, "Nothing."

Wanting the attention off her, Norah grabbed the small menu from the holder in the center of the table.

"Don't you have that memorized?" Molly asked good-naturedly, turning her chair a little so she had a better view of the room. "We come here enough that I bet I could recite it word for word." Pseudo casually, she glanced around, taking in the room. Molly hated having her back to strangers.

For a moment, Norah was surprised that Molly hadn't taken her seat, but then she realized that her sisters had left it open for her because it was next to Dash. Flushing at the thought that this was sort of like a date—a well-chaperoned one—she studied the very familiar menu even more thoroughly. "They might have added something new," she answered as her face heated even more. She knew without looking up that her sisters were smirking at her down-bent head.

"Mm-hmm," was all Molly said, but Norah could feel her amusement from across the table.

"Oh, here." Remembering she still had Dash's keys, she pulled them from her pocket and handed them to him. Feeling the devil on her shoulder give her a bit of a poke with his pitchfork, she added, "Tell Bruiser thanks for lending it to me."

With a look that just about set her hair on fire, Dash wrapped his fingers over not only the keys but her entire hand. "I'll do that."

The threatened retribution in the growled words made her want to squirm, but she forced herself to hold still. The feel of his hand enveloping hers sent a buzzing prickle along the length of her spine, and her heart beat quickly in her chest. It was a scary feeling but safe at the same time, like watching a horror movie or riding a roller coaster. She knew in her gut that Dashiell Porter would never hurt her.

Molly's voice reminded her that they weren't alone. "Since I don't have popcorn, I'm going to need some fries."

Norah tried to pull free of Dash's grip, but he had her hand fully and utterly caught. Very slowly, he released her and snagged his keys from her now-exposed palm. It took her a few seconds before she dropped her hand.

Her sisters were both grinning at her. Cara opened her mouth to say something, and Norah braced herself for the teasing comment that was coming. Cara had been channeling her twin's sense of humor lately. Luckily, their server, Taren, arrived at their table just in time.

"The usual?" she asked, taking them in. The three of them nodded as Taren scribbled on her order pad, her bejeweled nails catching the late afternoon sunlight. Looking at Dash, she sighed. "You want *more*?"

The last word had a disbelieving edge, making Norah glance at him with a raised brow. How much had he already eaten to faze the typically unflappable Taren?

Dash gave a short shake of his head. "Coffee. Thanks."

With a nod, Taren hurried off, and Norah tried to put her menu back in the most inconspicuous way possible. When her sisters started laughing, she sighed. She should've known they would notice. Wanting the attention off her, she turned to Dash. "So how much have you eaten?"

"A couple burgers."

That didn't seem like much. He was a huge guy who worked out all the time.

"Fries."

Still, that wasn't an unreasonable amount of food.

"A few milkshakes."

Okay, the milkshakes were enormous. How had he managed to finish *a few*?

"Onion rings."

Norah just blinked at him.

"A salad."

She didn't even know they offered salad, and she'd just been burning holes in the menu with her eyeballs.

"Flatbread pizza."

He had to be messing with her. She studied his deadpan expression, wishing she knew his tell for when he was joking. The problem was he'd have to joke for her to notice it, and that was very, very rare so far.

"Pie."

Now things were getting ridiculous. "A whole pie?"

"No, a slice."

That was at least a little more reasonable.

"A few slices."

From the snorts and chortles coming from across the table, Molly and Cara thought this was hilarious, but Norah couldn't stop staring at Dash.

"And a cupcake. Forgot about that. It was small." He reached up and rubbed his cheek. The movement was seemingly casual, but Norah saw the slightest crinkle at the corners of his eyes and knew he was hiding a smile behind his hand.

"You're just messing with me." She was almost disappointed. Consuming that amount of food would've been an impressive feat.

"No, I ate all that." Dropping his hand, he let her see his smile. "The look on your face is entertaining."

She was back to staring at him with a sort of disgusted awe. "How are you still alive? Shouldn't you be having a heart attack right now?"

Lifting his shoulder in a shrug, he said, "I'll burn it all off tomorrow."

"That's true." The thought of him working out at the gym made her gaze drift to his bowling-ball-size biceps, but she caught herself mid-gawk and abruptly turned to face her sisters. They were both grinning knowingly at her. Although she felt her cheeks grow warm for what felt like the thousandth time just that day, Norah managed to not drop her gaze. "Should we...um...discuss..." She trailed off as everything—Leifsen, Chloe, Zach Fridley, Mr. P, Detective Mill—churned around in her thoughts. With all that was happening, she didn't know where to start. Finally, she just spread her hands and went with "Everything?"

"First off, let's go over what happened with Detective Mill."

When Molly spoke, Norah let out a relieved huff of air. This was why Molly was in charge of the business and Norah was happy to just be a research monkey in the background.

After a glance around the diner to make sure there weren't any nearby eavesdroppers, Molly fixed Dash with her bossy big-sister look and asked, "Are you clear on the story in case he contacts you?"

Although he tipped his chin in a nod, Dash looked annoyed. Norah figured it was because he was being ordered around until he spoke. "Norah's dating Davies." His expression grew even more thunderous. "*Bruiser* Davies. My employee. Who drives around in *my* car. That I'm paying for. I barely know Norah, and only as a member of my gym. That it?" It seemed it wasn't Molly's questioning that had rankled but that Dash was still irrationally hostile about her imaginary boyfriend.

"Pretty much, yeah." Giving him an approving look, Molly asked, "Did you let Davies know? Is he willing to play along?"

Still looking immensely grumpy, Dash grunted an affirmative. "If Mills contacts him, Davies'll confirm our story."

"Perfect." Appearing satisfied, Molly continued, "Cara and I also might have implied that you're stalking Norah because you want to steal her away from Bruiser, but you can save that card in case the whole coincidental just-happened-to-be-running-by thing falls through."

Except for crossing his arms over his chest, Dash didn't outwardly react to that nugget of information.

"Okay!" Molly slapped the table lightly. "One thing down. Let's talk about that slimy weasel Zach Fridley next."

"He's been arrested, but he'll likely make bail tomorrow," Cara said before waving a subtle hand toward the approaching server. They waited until Taren had unloaded their drinks from her tray and had walked out of earshot before picking up the subject again.

"Can you keep tabs on that situation?" Molly asked Cara, who nodded as she took a drink of her water. "Let us know when he's out. I have a feeling he's going to be annoyed with us." Turning to Dash, Molly added, "Especially you. Be prepared for retaliation, possibly from two idiots named Dane Sanders and Eddie Cord. He likes to send his minions to do his dirty work."

Dash just gave Molly a slight nod, looking less bothered by the fact that there could soon be any number of people out to get revenge on him than he was by Norah fake dating Davies.

Molly's mention of Zach's dislike of getting his hands dirty made Norah frown in thought. "Why do you think he broke in?" she asked, immediately gaining everyone's attention, which made her try to inhale and talk at the same time. The sound that came out was almost a quack, and she quickly cleared her throat as she felt heat creeping up her neck. "Rather than sending someone else I mean? And why did he come alone? He was with Mom up until just a few days ago. Think they started fighting again?"

Both her sisters appeared thoughtful as they considered that. Dash seemed...more intense than usual? Maybe? Although she was getting better at reading his expressions and body language, she still felt like she couldn't tell what he was thinking most of the time. Glancing back at her sisters, Norah saw someone entering the diner. Her eyes widened as she recognized the woman, and she bit back a panicked squeak that wanted to escape.

"Could he ha—" Cara, who was oblivious to the horror that had just arrived, started to say, but Norah interrupted.

"Cara," she hissed under her breath, drawing her sister's startled gaze. "Switch places with me! Hurry!"

To her credit, Cara didn't hesitate, quickly sliding out of her seat. Before the swap could take place though, Laken Albee spotted them. With an enthusiastic wave and huge smile, she made a beeline toward their table.

"Too late," Norah sighed, settling back into her chair next to Dash. "Thanks though."

Cara took her seat again, twisting around to see what had caused Norah's panic. "Ugh."

"What is… Oh." Molly had turned to look as well. "That woman again? What's her deal? Is she stalking you too?"

"Stalking Norah does seem to be the rage recently," Cara said quietly so that a quickly approaching Laken didn't overhear.

Norah just sighed.

"Who's that?" Dash asked, his scowl firmly back in place.

"Someone who used to bully Norah back in high school." Molly positively growled the words.

"Junior high," Norah corrected weakly, knowing there was going to be a horribly uncomfortable confrontation in just a few seconds. "She outgrew it by high school. I'm giving her a chance to show that she's changed."

Despite her denial, Dash looked at Laken with an ice-cold gaze. Norah thought it was interesting how his indifference appeared even more intimidating than his usual scowl.

"Norah!" Laken cooed. She came right up to the table, either braver than Norah had thought or oblivious to the three people who wanted to rip every strand of hair out of her head. "I'm so glad I ran into you! I wanted to get together again, but I forgot to get your cell number." She finally glanced around the table, but her smile didn't waver. "Sorry if I'm interrupting. How about I join you?"

She turned as if searching for a chair to pull over, and Norah held back a groan. If she didn't do something, Laken was going to be murdered.

"Sorry, but this is a business meeting," Norah rushed out.

"Aren't these your sisters?" Laken gave a trill of laughter that made Norah wince. "You still live with them, don't you? Doesn't that make *every* meal a business meeting? You need some relaxation time. Remember, all work and no play makes Norah a dull girl."

Molly opened her mouth to say something, and Norah hurried to give her leg a warning kick. It wasn't a hard bump, but Molly still appeared shocked enough by the uncharacteristically aggressive move from Norah that she didn't say a word.

Laken paused, her gaze scanning over Dash, lingering on his broad chest. "Mm-hmm. I wish I had this kind of *business*." Reaching across the table, she offered her hand to Dash, her voice dropping to a low, husky tone. "Laken Albee. And you are?"

Norah stared at Laken's outstretched arm, trying her hardest to remember that she was giving the woman the benefit of the doubt.

Glancing at Laken's hand with utter indifference, Dash didn't make any move to shake it as he met her eyes. "I'm in a meeting."

"Oh!" As little as Norah's attempt at a brush-off affected Laken, it seemed to make a much bigger impact when Dash delivered the snub. Laken pulled back her hand, her fake smile faltering for the first time since she'd bustled over. "Well, I'll just grab Norah's number and get out of your hair then."

"Or you can just f—" Molly broke off as Norah kicked her again. She was going to have to use the kicking technique more often to silence her sisters. It seemed to be surprisingly effective.

Norah held her hand out for Laken's phone and quickly entered her number. As she went to hand it back, she saw that the woman's flirtatious gaze had settled on Dash again, despite the fact that he looked completely disinterested.

"Here," Norah said a little too loudly, making Laken's attention snap back to her.

"Perfect." Laken tapped at her phone, and a buzz came from Norah's pocket. With a satisfied nod, Laken tucked the phone back into her purse. "Now you have my number. Feel free to share it with any *business associates*." She winked at Dash—actually *winked*—as if she were starring in a rom-com.

A tiny part of Norah actually admired her utter confidence, although the rest of her was simmering with steadily growing annoyance. A possessiveness she didn't even know existed inside her ballooned to enormous proportions, and she resisted the urge to grunt *mine* like a jealous cavewoman.

"Why? I can't imagine any reason we'd need to contact you," Cara said, her words chilly.

"Sure, *she* can talk without getting kicked," Molly muttered.

"Bye, Laken," Norah said, her teeth showing in what she hoped passed as a smile.

"See you soon, Norah," Laken said with a tiny wave before her voice dropped to that husky tone she reserved for Dash. "Goodbye, Mr. Mysterious." She walked toward the door much more slowly than she'd approached their table, and she added a sway to her round hips.

Their table stayed silent until the door swung closed behind Laken.

"She didn't eat," Molly said, scowling. "Why was she even here?"

"That is odd." Cara cocked her head. "How could she know we'd be here? Maybe she secretly chipped Norah?"

The idea, ridiculous as it was, made her stiffen. "Why would you even say that? Do you never want me to sleep again?" she asked Cara, who gave a rough laugh.

"Sorry." Twisting around in her seat, Cara glanced at the diner door again as if she was expecting Laken to come flying back in, guns blazing. "I just can't figure out what she wants."

"What everyone wants," Norah said with a small shrug. The small hope that Laken actually wanted to be friends had pretty much been snuffed out. "The necklace."

Dash was still scowling heavily even though Laken was gone. "Why'd you give her your number?"

"Seemed like the fastest way to get rid of her." Norah didn't care what happened to Laken, but she didn't want to cap off this endless day by bailing her sisters out of jail. "Besides, this way, I can dodge her calls."

"That's true," Molly said, and then her face lit up as Taren carried a loaded tray toward their table. "Food. Finally."

They were all quiet for a bit while they dug in. Glancing at Dash, who just had his coffee mug, Norah nudged her plate toward him. Even though he'd just eaten three-quarters of the diner's menu, she still felt bad eating in front of him when he didn't have any food...especially since he'd been stuck there for hours in order to help her and her sisters out. Giving her a crooked smile, he grabbed one of her fries.

"So…" Cara wiped greasy fingers on her napkin and then took a drink. "What were we talking about before Miss Mean Girl interrupted? Leifsen?"

"I'd like to talk about Norah kicking me under the table to shut me up," Molly said through a mouthful of burger.

Norah put on her most innocent expression. "I have no idea what you're talking about."

"Norah kicked you?" Cara looked doubtful. "Are you sure it wasn't…" Taking in Dash's raised eyebrow, she stuttered to a halt. "Uh…*Norah*! How could you?"

Norah gave a small shrug. "If I'd known how well it worked, I would've done it before."

Molly tried to pretend as if she were offended but then gave the game away by laughing. "Why do you think the rest of us do it all the time?"

"Back to Leifsen," Cara reminded them.

"Dash wants me to make friends with Chloe," Norah blurted. In all the excitement following their abbreviated stake-out that morning, she'd temporarily forgotten about that plan. Now, the mention of Leifsen brought it all back, and anxiety rose in her again.

"Wait…what?" Molly asked.

She and Cara stared at Norah as Dash gave an amused grunt and took another one of her fries. Glancing down, she saw that he'd eaten all but four of them while she'd focused on the conversation with her sisters. She looked pointedly at her plate and then him, and he stopped with the purloined fry halfway to his mouth.

"I'll get you some more," he said, sliding out of his chair, presumably so he could track down Taren and replace her missing fries.

When Norah looked away from his retreating back, returning her attention to her sisters, she found they were both watching her with matching gleeful expressions.

"Let's put the Chloe explanation aside for a moment," Molly said, leaning forward. "I want to hear about that." She gestured between Norah and where Dash had just been.

"What about it?" Norah asked warily, wishing for Dash to make a speedy return. Suddenly, a refill on fries didn't seem as critical as ending this conversation.

"Everything!" Cara tossed her hands up as if encompassing the whole universe, and Norah swallowed hard as her mind blanked. "This came out of the blue, so while you two are busy exchanging secret smiles and private jokes, we're flummoxed on this side of the table."

"*Flummoxed,*" Molly repeated with a nod.

Norah struggled to find words to explain when she herself didn't really know what was happening between her and Dash. All she managed were a few squeaks and various vaguely monkey-like noises. Finally, she just settled on, "I don't know?"

That didn't seem to satisfy her sisters. "How'd it start?" Molly pushed. "Did he make the first move? Did you? This is blowing our minds here, Norah. You need to throw us a bone."

"Make a move?" The thought of instigating something with Dash made her entire body cold with panic. "Noooooo, there was no move made. There haven't been any moves."

"No moves?" Cara sounded rather disappointed by that. "But there's something happening between you two. It's obvious."

"So obvious," Molly chimed in.

Norah eyed her sisters. "Why are you doing the twin thing when you're not twins?"

With a shrug, Cara said, "Charlie's been gone a lot lately. I needed a fill-in twin."

"No changing the subject." Molly rerouted the conversation back to its original, unpleasant path. "Do you and Dash… Ah, here you are, Dash! I was just wondering if you'd found…um…fries."

Dash had reappeared next to their table like the supersize ninja that he was. Tilting his head slightly, he eyed Molly, and Norah felt her face heat up as she wondered how much of their mortifying conversation he'd overheard. Without commenting on Molly's clunky attempt to cover up the fact that they'd been talking about him, Dash took his seat and slid a basket of fresh fries in front of Norah.

"Thanks," she said, still feeling incredibly awkward, and then jammed a couple fries in her mouth so she wouldn't have to say anything else. They were hot enough to make her eyes water, but she just chewed determinedly. The slight pain was better than explaining what they'd been talking about.

"So…Chloe Ballister," Cara said, and Norah could've kissed her for tossing out a safe topic. "What'd you find out?"

———

By the time Norah had almost finished her second order of fries, with Dash only stealing about a third this time, everyone was caught up on their surveillance and the burglary in progress they'd interrupted. Dash had paid the entire bill over their objections, simply handing his card to Taren before they had time to pull out their money.

"I think it's a good idea to make friends with Chloe," Molly said, turning her empty water glass in circles. Her gaze was focused on what her hands were doing, but it was obvious her thoughts were elsewhere, working out the next steps in their plan to bring in Leifsen. "Even though it's doubtful she has anything to do with Leifsen anymore, she's really our only lead right now. Do you know what her day job is or if she has one?"

"Not yet." Norah hadn't investigated Chloe much beyond her connection with Leifsen, just basic details like her home address and her band's venues.

"See if you can find out more about her schedule so you can arrange another *accidental* meeting."

Cara chuckled. "Your turn to be a stalker, Norah."

With a grimace, Norah dropped the last fry back on her plate. With the renewed churning happening in her stomach, she didn't want to eat any more. Dash snatched it up almost before it hit the plate.

"Norah?" Molly prodded.

Although she heaved a deep sigh, Norah nodded, resigned to the plan. A part of her had hoped she could have Chloe as a true friend, but it was critical to bring in Devon Leifsen before he hurt anyone else. Molly and Cara had packed schedules, and it seemed like her sisters were fine with Norah doing fieldwork now that she had her own beefy bodyguard.

As if she'd read Norah's mind, Molly gave her a stern look. "Research only unless one of us—or Dash—is with you."

"Yes, Mom." At Molly's pained expression, Norah hurried to clarify. "I didn't mean Jane but an actual mom-type mom. A *good* mom." She didn't think she'd actually made sense, but Molly was grinning at her, so at least she wasn't offended.

"Okay!" Molly stood up. "Good meeting, team. Dash, thanks again for everything today and especially for watching out for Norah. If you hurt her in the slightest, we'll kill you slowly and painfully." She delivered that last bit in the same cheery tone as the first, and Dash acknowledged the threat with a relaxed nod. "We'll leave first and check the area, just in case Detective Mill doesn't have anything better to do with his Sunday than follow us around. We wouldn't want him to see you driving off in Bruiser's SUV."

Dash hadn't blinked an eye at the idea of her sisters torturing him to death, but the mention of Bruiser had his lips tightening into a straight line. Molly and Cara headed toward the door, but Norah felt like she should say something. Dash, being Dash, didn't help smooth over the awkward moment but just watched her with those intense eyes.

"So...um...see you Tuesday?" She realized she was playing with her medical alert bracelet and dropped her arms to her sides. At his affirmative grunt, she gave a stiff wave and then hurried after her sisters. Knowing he was watching her leave made it impossible to walk normally. Was she swaying her hips too much...or not enough? She was so focused on not looking ridiculous that she barely managed to avoid running into the corner of a table. Refusing to look behind her to see if Dash had seen that graceless maneuver, she scuttled for the door instead.

As she stepped out of the diner, she rolled her eyes at how silly she was acting. She'd always considered herself a logical, reasonable person, but Dash flustered her. She knew she could never again make fun of the way Molly, Cara, and Felicity mooned over their guys.

Their guys? Her brain stuttered over the phrase. *Does that mean I consider Dash* my *guy?* She stopped walking, the idea taking her breath away. The *beep* of Molly's car horn reminded her of where she was and got her moving again, but her thoughts continued to churn. It wasn't a bad thought, keeping Dash as her very own. In fact, it made warmth spread from her middle all through her body.

Mine. With a smile she quickly erased before her sisters could see and question her about the cause, she hurried to climb into the back of Molly's car.

The drive home was fairly quiet. Instead of trying to wheedle more Dash details out of Norah, Molly and Cara were focused on making sure no detectives—or stalkers—were staking out the diner or following them home.

Once they arrived at the house, Norah hurried inside. After greeting Warrant, she jogged up the stairs, wanting to get started on her Chloe research. As soon as she stepped into her bedroom, she froze, knowing something wasn't right. Standing stiffly, her heart racing, she scanned the room. Even though there was nowhere to hide in the tiny space and she knew that plastic storage bins filled the space under her twin bed, not leaving enough room for a squirrel, much less a fully grown human, she still couldn't slow her breathing. All her instincts were screaming that someone had invaded her space.

When she spotted what didn't belong, it should've been innocuous. A single pen sat in the center of her neatly made bed. Even without seeing the writing utensil up close, she knew it wasn't her pen. The unfamiliarity made it terrifying.

Forcing herself to take a step closer to the bed, she glanced down at her feet. An illogical part of her brain, one that had been molded by childhood nightmares and horror movies, was determined that a hand was going to reach out from under the bed and latch on to her ankle if she dared look away.

"Don't be ridiculous," she told herself, forcing her gaze back to the pen. "No one is in here but me."

But someone else *had* been there earlier.

Had it been Zach, or did he have an accomplice after all?

With fingers that wouldn't stop shaking no matter how many times she told herself she was being silly, Norah picked up the pen. She realized she was holding her breath and let it out in an audible puff. That unreasonable part of her refused to believe that it was just a pen and not a trigger for explosives or a miniature gun.

As she moved it closer to her face, she realized it was a promotional item with the name of a business printed on it. Spinning it around so she could make out the words, her breath caught in her chest again.

"Porter Sports," she whispered. *Dash's gym.*

ELEVEN

"You're not taking this seriously enough," Norah said, bracing her hands on her thighs as she tried to catch her breath. The training session had been brutal. Every one of her sweat glands was working overtime, even the ones between her fingers and toes. One saving grace was that Dash had cleared the gym for her, so he was the only one to see her punch and kick and throw elbows until her muscles were floppy noodles.

"Yes, I am." His fierce inner badger was evident in his narrowed, furious eyes, but he was angry for the wrong reason. "He was in your *bedroom*."

"That's not the important point." Sure, it was extremely creepy that someone—Zach or another of his criminal buddies—had been poking around in her room, but she wasn't the target of the implied threat. "You need to be careful. They're going to try to go after you to get to me...*us*." She stumbled over the last bit, knowing it revealed just how devastated she'd be if something happened to Dash. He'd done nothing but help her, and in return, she'd dragged him into a dangerous situation.

"Let them." His casual half shrug made her absolutely wild. He needed to be cautious, not literally shrugging off any threat toward him. "I'll squash them and then dump them on your porch."

"Of course, that would be the ideal resolution," she said, straightening as her breathing slowed to normal—or at least closer to normal than the fish-out-of-water gasping she'd been doing. "But Zach is my mom's friend, so I know how he operates. He's sneaky. He doesn't care about fairness or morals or anything except for money and staying out of prison. He'll play dirty."

That annoying shrug reappeared, joined by a small smirk that made her want to stomp her foot in frustration, which was something she'd never done in her entire life. "So can I."

"At least keep some backup around. Bruiser, maybe?"

His eyebrows drew together into a grumpy frown. "I don't need *Davies* to help keep you safe."

She stared at him, trying to come up with a logical argument that might get through to him, unlike all the *other* logical arguments she'd tried that hadn't penetrated his stubborn skull. "I don't want you to be hurt."

"I can't promise that I won't be." His expression softened as he reached out to catch her sweaty hand. "But I *can* promise to hurt Fridley—and whoever he sends after us—more."

As sentimental promises went, it was unorthodox, but for some reason, it caused a whole herd of butterflies to take flight in her belly. Her feelings must've been evident, because he took a step closer, his eyes darkening in a different way than his earlier anger at Zach. His free hand cupped her jaw, his fingers as gentle as if he was cradling something precious. Her breath caught as sensations overwhelmed her—the burning heat of his hands, the flare of desire in his eyes, the way her own body seemed to ignite as if his fire had engulfed her.

She couldn't look away as he leaned closer. Usually in unfamiliar situations, her thoughts would race around chaotically like go-carts on a track, but now her mind was oddly clear. She was focused on one thing, and that was Dash.

He hadn't even touched her except for her hand and face, but she was already addicted to the experience. Not only was her body fizzing with energy and anticipation, but her brain was giving her a rare break from the constant mental monologue of self-doubt and anxiety. She'd thought she'd be nervous and stressed in this moment, but everything in her was calm and certain. All she wanted was the man in front of her.

He was so close that she could see every detail of his fascinating face, but then he hesitated, staring at her as if trying to read her thoughts. Rather than say anything and possibly break the spell of settled certainty that had fallen over her, she gripped a handful of his T-shirt and yanked. For the split second before that final gap between them closed, she saw his lips quirk up in that tiny smile that was so *Dash*, and the glow in her chest warmed even more.

Then they were kissing, and that was all she could feel.

As their lips explored each other, she wondered how she'd

ever lived without this connection. For her, touch had always been something she avoided. It had made her feel trapped and awkward when she'd been enveloped in an unwanted hug, her skin prickling unpleasantly until she shied away. When she'd occasionally wondered how it would feel to be kissed like this, she'd figured her thoughts would be occupied the entire time with how uncomfortable and unsanitary and just plain weird the whole process was.

That wasn't how it was at all though.

She couldn't imagine anything more natural or wonderful or weirdly *comfortable* than kissing Dash. From the way he groaned deep in his throat as he pressed closer, he couldn't imagine anything better than kissing her. His hands moved to her waist and then skimmed down over her hips to her thighs. He hoisted her up, lifting her until their faces were level. The movement startled Norah, and she broke the kiss for a moment. He held her easily though, as if she weighed nothing, and she quickly adjusted to her new height. Wrapping her legs around his waist and her arms around his neck, she marveled over her newfound confidence as she leaned in to resume kissing him.

The new position was even better, she quickly discovered, making it so he didn't have to lean over and she didn't have to crane her neck back. When he turned and walked a few steps, she barely noticed, even when he pressed her back against the wall. Tightening her legs around him, she slipped a hand up the back of his neck and over his closely shorn hair. Dash seemed to like this, judging by his rumbling groan and tightening fingers.

He deepened the kiss, pressing her back harder against the

wall as he reached for her ponytail, wrapping it around his hand. He tugged gently, and she tipped her head back, allowing him to run his lips down her neck, leaving a line of tingling, oversensitive skin in his wake.

"Whoa!"

A male voice that wasn't Dash's brought her back to earth with a thump. Peering over his shoulder, she saw Davies whirl around so his back was to them.

"Sorry, man. Just let myself in since it's after eleven, and the guys are getting restless out there."

Dash closed his eyes, looking pained and extremely irritated at the interruption. "Tell them—"

"Nothing! You don't have to tell them anything. We're done," Norah hurried to interrupt. Releasing her legs from their hold around his waist, she tried to slide down, but he still held her pinned. When she gave him an entreating look, he huffed out a frustrated sound but slowly lowered her to her feet.

He turned to face Davies. "Might as well let them in," he grumped.

When Norah tried to wiggle around him to get her bag, he hauled her back to his side. The feeling of someone's arm over her shoulders usually made her count the seconds until she could skitter away, but it was different with Dash. His enveloping arm made her feel cocooned in warmth and safety, and if she hadn't been feeling mortified by Davies walking in on them, she would've been all too happy to stay tucked against him.

As Davies headed to unlock the door, she wiggled away.

Dash frowned at her. "Are you embarrassed to be seen with me?"

"No." The sheer absurdity of anyone being embarrassed to be seen with the ever-so-impressive Dashiell Porter almost made her laugh. "I'm just weirded out that Davies saw us kissing and…" She wasn't sure how to describe the most incredible event of her life so far, so she just sketched a hand in the air. "And everything."

His lips quirked up at the corners, hinting at a smile. "I'm glad he saw."

"You are?" She looked at him out of the corner of her eye. "That's kind of pervy."

An actual crack of laughter escaped him. "It's not pervy. This way, he knows he'll never be more than the *fake* boyfriend."

"Hey!" It was the guy who'd tried to chat her up after her last training session and had been shut down by Dash. He bounced toward them, beaming, looking so much like an enthusiastic golden retriever that Norah couldn't help but smile back. "Hot girl's back!"

"No," Dash said with such a stern expression that happy golden-retriever man did an abrupt ninety-degree turn.

"I'll just go work on my side kicks." He scurried away like a scolded puppy.

Although Norah wanted to laugh at how Dash sent the man on such an abrupt detour with a single word and a glare, she also felt a little bad for the golden-retriever man.

"No," Dash said again, but he was looking at her this time.

Confused, she blinked at him. "What?"

"Quit smiling at him. You can't have Tucker as a second fake boyfriend."

This time, she laughed out loud. "I don't want a second fake boyfriend. I didn't even want a *first* fake boyfriend. What would I do with two?"

His grunt didn't sound convinced.

"I was smiling because he's just so bouncy and happy. Can you even imagine going through life so…exposed like that?" Feeling brave, she patted Dash's arm.

He immediately grabbed her hand and tucked it into the crook of his elbow. "No. I can't."

As he started toward the cubby where she'd stashed her bag, she gave him a sideways glance. The way she held his arm was more suited to a formal occasion than a stroll across a gym filled with sweaty, grunting men. If Dash was about to sweep her into a waltz, she should be in a long, flowing dress rather than her shorts and wilted tank top.

"Again with the manners?" she asked dryly, hiding how much she liked their running jokes. Usually, people didn't understand her humor, or she didn't get what others thought was hilarious. With Dash, she got to be in on the joke with him. It was a novel and frankly addictive place to be.

He just slanted her a look that pretended to be dark but actually sparked with amusement.

Smiling, she released his arm to grab her bag. Moving to the door, she gave him a stiff wave. As comfortable as she was starting to feel with Dash, there were still awkward moments when she wasn't sure how to act…like right now. After their make-out session, how was she supposed to say goodbye? Had the kissing door been left open so every encounter between them would begin and end with a peck? On the cheek or mouth? She wasn't about to initiate it, and he wasn't leaning in, so she figured her odd little wave had sufficed. Just to make sure, she added, "See you later."

"You have a ride home?" He was scowling as he pushed the door open, scanning the empty alley as his frown deepened.

"I'm meeting Cara at that Thai restaurant we went to." He still looked unhappy, and she wasn't sure why, so she asked. "Why are you extra grumpy?"

"Extra grumpy?" His expression lightened a bit before his eyebrows crashed together again. "I don't like the idea of you walking alone, but I can't be away from the gym since Davies has to leave early today."

"I'll be fine." Even though they were in an alley, it was a wide, clean one in a good part of town. Besides, the warm fall sun was almost too bright, banishing any sinister shadows or possible hiding places in which a stalker could lurk. "It's broad daylight, and lots of people will be out. Leifsen is a chicken. He's not going to bother me unless I'm alone, and even then, he hides behind his electronics."

Dash rubbed his cheek, not seeming convinced. The quiet rasp of his palm against his jaw made her shiver, reminding her of how that same stubble felt against her skin. He dropped his hand and grumbled, "Text if you need me."

"I will." Still she hesitated, not wanting to leave yet. "You too."

That brought out his crooked grin. "I will."

"Okay. Bye." The awkward wave reappeared, making her wince as she turned to go.

"What are you doing tonight?" he asked before she'd taken three steps.

"Tonight?" she repeated, turning so she could see him again. "Eating dinner, researching, and then sleeping. Unless something surprising happens. Why?"

"The gym closes at ten. Meet me after." Although he said it like an order, there was a question in his eyes. That rare tentativeness gave her a warm feeling in her chest.

"Meet you here?"

"Yeah." He pointed at one of the second-story windows. "I live upstairs."

"You live above the gym." Even as she said it, she could see how it would make sense. The gym seemed as much a part of Dash as his grunts and the scars that marked the left side of his neck and jaw. "Okay."

"Good." A real smile curled his mouth, making him look younger and sweeter than she ever imagined he could. "Will you need a ride?"

"No. I'll meet you here."

He dipped his chin in acknowledgment as she started down the alley again. It seemed a bit cold for her to just walk away, so she waved over her shoulder. Yet again, it was so awkward. It felt just like it had at Bubbles, with Dash getting the rear view of her as she struggled not to walk in a weird way or sneak a peek to see if he was still watching. When she finally reached the street and turned out of his view, she let out a breath that was partly relief but mostly disappointment.

"You're so contrary," Norah muttered under her breath, drawing a glance from the older man walking past. Clamping her lips shut, she quickly walked toward the restaurant where she was supposed to meet Cara. A glance at her phone showed that she was running late, which she absolutely hated. Still, a part of her whispered that spending extra time with Dash had been worth it. Shaking off a smile that she knew even without seeing was much too mushy, Norah sent a quick text to Cara to let her sister know she was on her way.

Slipping her phone back into her bag, she wove between pedestrians who were moving slowly as they basked in the warm fall sun. Just as she'd told Dash, the beautiful weather had brought out the hordes, and no one would be able to harass her without it being witnessed by dozens of people. Even so, a tiny chill made the fine hairs on her arms stand up. She rubbed at the goose bumps, glancing around in a way she hoped came off more casual than paranoid to anyone watching.

Anyone watching... The thought bounced around in her head. Maybe Leifsen wouldn't approach her, but that didn't mean he wasn't following her. As expected, Zach was out on bail, so it wasn't just one guy she had to worry about. Norah was suddenly glad that the gym had solar shades on all the windows so no one could see inside. She moved a little faster, wanting to get off the street. Everyone she saw seemed suspicious now. They could easily be one of Zach's cohorts or another fortune hunter wanting a chance at finding the necklace.

She blew out a relieved breath when she reached the Thai restaurant and hurried to open the door. Cara waved from the same booth Norah had sat in with Dash, and that little thing made her smile. Her knees were still a little wobbly as she wove through the tables, but she blamed her intense workout rather than her panicked thoughts on the walk from the gym.

"Hey," Cara greeted as Norah took the seat across from her. "You're a mess. What happened?"

A cursory glance at her rumpled and sweaty gym clothes showed that the stressful speed walk over hadn't improved matters any. Her face was probably red from exertion, and her hair almost certainly looked like she'd survived a tornado. With a shrug, she said, "Intense workout." It had been intense, especially the kissing that had immediately followed the working-out part. She pulled a hoodie from her bag and put it on as the hostess dropped off menus and waters. Norah gratefully drank half the glass in one go.

"Uh-huh." Cara rested her chin on her hand, her eyes dancing with laughter. "Tell me about this *intense workout* you just had with your lovely trainer, Dash. The one that made you so *thirsty*."

It was like her sister could read her mind. Norah was glad that she was already beet red from exercise so her embarrassment was hidden for once. "I warmed up by running a mile on the treadmill and then jumped rope—"

A wave from Cara cut off her step-by-step recitation. "Never mind. If you're not going to tell me the fun stuff, I don't want to hear about the boring stuff. Felicity makes me live through enough of that torture."

Norah hid her triumphant smile behind her menu.

"Don't think I don't know what you just did."

Obviously, she hadn't hidden it well enough. "What's the plan with Chloe?" she asked, more than ready to change the subject. "Stakeout at her work?"

"Nope." It was Cara's turn to smile wickedly, and Norah's heart sank. "I have a much better idea."

———

Norah hesitated outside the music store, feeling the same sense of overwhelming dread that she'd had the first time she'd gone to Dash's gym. *That ended up turning out well*, her mental cheerleader reminded her, but it didn't matter. Her fingers were still clammy with sweat, and this time, she didn't have exercise to blame.

The door swung open, and Norah hurried to step out of the way as a younger guy in a beanie left the store. Spotting her standing there, he held the door for her. She hesitated long enough for the moment to grow awkward.

"Are you going in?" he asked, and she made an affirmative noise in her throat before diving into the store just to get away from the now-uncomfortable interaction. Once inside, she came to an abrupt halt as she looked around, getting her bearings.

"Can I help you?"

At the familiar throaty voice, Norah turned slowly, using the time to try to wrestle her ping-ponging thoughts into a coherent sentence. "Ah…" was all she managed to get out before Chloe's eyes widened along with her smile.

"Norah! Why haven't you texted me?"

"Um, because I haven't needed beat-down backup?" she answered tentatively, her own smile starting. Despite her true reason for being here, something about Chloe made her feel more at ease. "I saw you at Dutch's."

Of all the things she could've said, that was one of the weirder and more random choices. Norah wanted to squeeze her eyes closed and pretend she was no longer there—or at least no longer visible. By sheer force of will, she managed to keep from cringing.

"Yeah? What'd you think?"

"It was… You were amazing." *Great.* Now she was gushing. "Since you were playing at Dutch's, I thought it would be more…death-metal-y? But your songs were easy to dance to." Worried that she'd sounded shallow, she added, "And your voice is stunning."

To Norah's shock, that babbling mess of words made Chloe's smile widen until she was beaming. "Thank you. People— especially musicians—tend to take themselves too seriously. I like to add a pop-y edge. It's hard to be pretentious when you're jumping up and down. Helps keep me grounded."

That made quite a bit of sense. Even after their encounter at Chico's, Norah hadn't expected her to be so easy to talk to. "Do you write your own songs?"

"Sure do." Chloe boosted herself up to sit on the counter, and Norah marveled again at the woman's apparently shatterproof confidence. This was the type of person she would've expected Dash to date.

At the thought, a rush of possessiveness roared through her that shocked her with its ferocity. She had to calm her inner beast by reminding herself that she'd just invented the competition in her mind. Chloe didn't even know Dash, much less want him. She forced herself to get out of her head and tune back in to what Chloe was saying.

"Donner—he's the drummer—has a carnival brain, so he's great to collaborate with. He knocks me off my comfortable musical path and into the deep, dark woods."

Norah cocked her head. Something about Chloe eased her anxiety, so she was comfortable enough to ask, "What does that mean?"

With a laugh, Chloe shoved her hair over her shoulder. It was loose today except for two thin braids encircling her head like a crown. It was very Renaissance-looking, which made an even more interesting contrast to the tattoos exposed by her strappy sundress than her usual milkmaid braids. "It means he comes up with ideas I would never think of, even in my wildest imaginings. He doesn't just make me think outside the box, he drags me out and then drop-kicks me into Fun House Land."

Although she still wasn't completely clear as to what Chloe was talking about, Norah just nodded.

"But you didn't come in here to listen to me talk about Donner. Can I help you find something?"

"Uhh…" All band names and every song she'd ever heard completely abandoned her, leaving her brain empty. She glanced around the store, but her thoughts were too chaotic for anything to register. Desperate, she settled on a version of the truth. "No,

I actually just came in here to ask…if your band will be playing somewhere this weekend?"

"Yeah, an outdoor show in Saturn Canyon on Saturday night." Norah must've looked blank at the name, because Chloe chuckled as she continued. "It's a pretty small event in the mountains west of Denver. Closest town is McCann, which I know you've never heard of, because almost no one has—well except for the forty-two and a half people who live in McCann."

"Forty-two and a half?" Norah echoed, making Chloe laugh again.

"Don't ask. Not a huge crowd and doesn't pay much, but the people are friendly, and the staff's amazing. Performing outdoors is a nice change too—smells so much better than Dutch's."

"Saturn Canyon by McCann." Norah mentally filed away the name and location. That could be another opportunity to possibly catch up to Leifsen. Even though it looked less and less likely that Chloe willingly spent any time with him, he did turn up at her last gig. There was a good chance he'd come to this one too. "I'll see if I can make it. Sorry if coming in here just to talk to you was too stalkery of me."

Chloe laughed so hard she almost fell off the counter. When she'd recovered enough to speak, she reached over and gave Norah a slap on her upper arm. "Don't worry about it, but you could've just texted me."

Norah tried very hard not to grimace at the huge hole in her excuse. She *could've* just texted, but this way, she could possibly spot Leifsen if he was lurking around Chloe again.

"Don't worry about it. It's good to see your face. If I was

going to be stalked by anyone, I'd definitely choose you." Leaning back on her hands, Chloe looked so open and carefree and comfortable in her skin that Norah felt a pang of envy. She knew people weren't always as confident as they projected on the surface, but Chloe seemed authentically solid.

Norah was trying to figure out how to respond to that, but another woman approached the register. Hopping off the counter, Chloe gave a small wave.

"Work calls, but it was great to talk to you, Norah." She headed for the register, calling over her shoulder, "See you Saturday!"

Norah returned the wave, although she was pretty sure hers looked stiff and strange compared to Chloe's. She squashed that little tendril of envy again. "Bye. Thanks. Okay, bye."

Chloe laughed in response, but it wasn't mocking like Laken's. It was warm and appreciative, as if Norah's babbling was meant to be a joke just between the two of them.

As Norah walked outside on autopilot, she headed toward where Cara waited in the car a half block away, startled to realize she was now in on not only one but *two* inside jokes. The most incredible part was that she hadn't had to magically become a different person to accomplish that. As a kid and then a teenager, she'd imagined she'd have to go through a rom-com makeover montage, but for her personality rather than her appearance, in order to have any kind of social life. Now though, she was still the same severely introverted, extraordinarily awkward, seriously weird Norah Pax—only now she was the Norah Pax with two very interesting potential friends.

TWELVE

FOR THE SECOND TIME THAT day, Norah was eyeing a door as if it were about to fall over and smoosh her. It was four minutes after ten, and the alley had developed the eerie shadows and pockets of stalker-hiding darkness that it'd lacked during daylight. Still, her anxiety took precedence over her worry about her personal safety at the moment. Normally, she just walked in, but that was when the gym was officially open. She wasn't sure whether she should knock, since this was Dash's home, and she wouldn't just walk into someone's house without knocking.

And for the second time that day, the decision was taken away from her when the door jerked open. Dash started to charge through but stopped abruptly before running her over.

"Norah."

What was the response to that? She went with, "Yes."

"You're here."

"Yes."

"You look nice." His voice sounded gruffer than usual, and she glanced down at herself. She'd showered away the sweaty day and agonized over what to wear until she'd finally asked Molly to pick out something for her, swearing she'd wear whatever her sister chose. Molly had raided Felicity's closet, deciding on a pretty blue dress and flats. Although it felt strange to wear a dress since her usual uniform was jeans and hoodies, the cut wasn't revealing enough to make Norah uncomfortable, and she liked how the skirt felt when it flared and swung as she moved.

A little belatedly, she said, "Thank you."

"Why didn't you come in?" Stepping back, he waved her inside.

"I was about to knock."

"Knock?" He gave her a sidelong look. "You don't need to knock. Just come in next time."

"But this is your home—upstairs at least. It seemed rude." She glanced around as he locked the door behind them. The gym looked dim and shadowy with the lights turned off, but it smelled the same as it always did—like sweat and vinyl. There must be something wrong with her, since she was starting to kind of like the stink. It reminded her of her sessions with Dash. "Did you need something outside?"

"What?"

"You were going outside just now, but I blocked your way."

His usual half shrug looked the tiniest bit sheepish. It always struck her how incongruous any type of hesitation or insecurity looked on him when he was so large and confident. "Just going to check if you were there."

"It's only four minutes after ten." *Probably five now,* her mind corrected, but she ignored that pedantic voice.

"I know." He scowled harder, but she was pretty sure it was just to cover that tiny fissure of insecurity in his hard outer crust. "Come upstairs."

She almost smiled. It was good to know she wasn't the only one who changed the subject when answers got uncomfortable. Curious to see his home, she followed him through a door and up some stairs. He held open another door at the top, filling the space in the doorway with his large frame so she had to brush against him as she slipped by. Her skin buzzed from the contact, and she mentally shook her head at her reaction. She was so giddy around him. It was ridiculous, really.

She stepped into his living room and immediately approved. The space was lofted but still felt cozy somehow. For some reason, she'd thought it would just be a continuation of the gym, with weight machines and mats as the only furniture, but now she realized how silly that mental picture was. His floors were a pale wood, mostly covered by an area rug. Tall windows with white sills were covered by closed blinds, but she imagined how the place looked during the day when it was filled with sunlight. The overstuffed couch and chairs were a soft-looking dark brown fabric that could only be described as plush. The flat-screen TV mounted on the wall was a completely reasonable size and framed by two packed bookshelves that reached the ceiling.

The kitchen, set on the other side of the open space, was also surprising. The white cabinets reminded her of something she would see in a farmhouse, although the granite island and countertops fit her idea of what a loft would have.

Dash cleared his throat, and she realized she'd been standing there, silently staring at his home for who knew how long. "I like it," she said.

His grunt sounded satisfied as he put a hand on her lower back as if to usher her farther in. She resisted his light touch long enough to take off her shoes and then let him nudge her to the couch.

"It's surprising but also not." She wasn't sure if that made sense but continued anyway as she sank into the cushy depths of the sofa. "It reminds me of you."

"Surprising but not?"

"Yes." She watched as he settled next to her, far enough away that they weren't touching but close enough that it wouldn't be hard to make contact if they made the slightest effort. "You're made up of bits and pieces that shouldn't fit together, but it all somehow works."

His brows drew together as he made a thoughtful sound in his throat. "Not sure if that's a compliment."

"It is," she assured him, meaning every word. "I like both you and your home."

His eyes narrowed and darkened in a fascinating way, so fascinating that she couldn't look away as he leaned closer. Her heartbeat picked up speed as she tipped toward him. She hadn't thought they'd get to the making-out part of the evening so quickly, but she didn't really have any dating experience to pull from, so maybe they were following the usual schedule.

Before their lips could meet, he pulled away, making her frown. Even though she hadn't expected the kissing part to come so quickly, she definitely wasn't *opposed* to it.

He grimaced slightly as he stood. "Forgot to ask. Want a drink? Hungry?"

For a moment, she blinked at him, more taken off guard by the reason he'd moved away from her than his verbal shorthand. She wasn't thinking about food or drink at the moment. Would it be rude to just ask for more kissing instead? She figured it probably was, or at least it would be awkward. "Um…water?"

With a clipped nod, he moved to the kitchen area. Pulling her feet up and crossing her legs, she turned sideways so she could watch him over the back of the couch. She loved how he moved, so smooth and ninja-like. It was another one of those shouldn't-fit-but-it-works-for-Dash things, since she'd assumed such a big, muscle-bound guy would make some noise when he walked.

"How'd your thing with Cara go?" he asked, pulling out a water pitcher from the fridge.

"Really well, actually." She beamed as she thought of how unexpectedly *nice* Chloe had been and how easy—well, once she got past the awkward part—it'd been to chat with her. "I talked to Chloe. I like her."

Pausing with two glasses in his hands, he looked over his shoulder as if checking to see if she meant what she said. After a moment, he set the glasses on the counter. "Good. Think she's wrapped up in Leifsen's…nonsense?"

As usual, his effort at not swearing was endearing, a part

of what made up Dash. His question quickly erased her smile though. "I don't know." Drawing up a knee, she rested her chin on it. "I hope not. She's so much better than him."

His grunt sounded like agreement as he poured the water and returned the pitcher to the fridge.

"We should probably go see her band play on Saturday just in case he shows up." Jitters made her nerves feel electrified when she realized she was in the process of asking Dash out on a date. It might have a work element to it, but if being with Dash at Dutch's could feel like a date, then going to an intimate concert under the stars would certainly qualify.

"Where?" Walking back over, he handed one of the glasses to her before retaking his seat on the couch. It might have been her imagination, but she was fairly sure—at least sixty-five percent sure—that he'd placed himself slightly closer to her. If she moved her left knee even a half inch, they'd be touching. Knowing that made it impossible to move a muscle, but at the same time, she felt like she'd burst out of her skin if she *didn't* move.

"Um…" It took some effort to recall the question. "It's an outdoor show at Saturn Canyon, close to McCann, which is a tiny town with an illogical number of residents." When Dash looked at her blankly, she hurried to add, "In the mountains west of Denver."

During the following pause, Norah thought that her heart would stop. If he rejected her, she didn't think she'd ever be able to get up the nerve to ask anyone out ever again.

"I'll drive us."

Just like that, her heart started beating again. Their date was planned. Maybe their fourth? She mentally ran over their lunch and then Dutch's and tonight—but should she count their last training session? There had been kissing after all—

A *crash* of glass cut her thoughts off abruptly. The heavy blinds covering the left-side window billowed toward them, and something heavy thudded onto the floor right below the sill. Norah stared at the dark shape, her mind trying to process what was happening, but Dash was already up off the couch. He moved so he was standing in front of her, blocking her view of the object and that entire wall of the apartment. The silence after seemed extra loud until Norah couldn't take not knowing what was happening anymore.

"What is it?" she whispered, wincing at how loud her voice sounded in the echoing quiet.

"Looks like a rock. Stay there."

A rock? She immediately wanted to ask more questions, but she managed to keep her mouth closed and her seat on the couch as he moved even more soundlessly than usual to the entrance. The room went dark, and Norah's heart pounded for a few beats of panic before she realized that he'd intentionally shut off the lights. Her brain seemed to be functioning a step behind how it usually worked, and she took a few breaths, frustrated by her inability to figure out what was happening.

Her eyes gradually adjusted to the dim ambient light coming through the small kitchen window—the only one without blinds covering it. She saw Dash's dark form slip over to the window next to the broken one and shift the blinds slightly so he could peer out onto the alley below.

Another slightly more muffled crash came from behind the door next to one of the bookshelves, and Norah jumped in place. She needed to do something rather than just sit there as all of Dash's windows were broken—probably by one of her stalkers. Why had she come to Dash's home when she suspected Leifsen or Fridley were following her? She clenched her fists until her short nails dug into her palms. It was her fault Dash had been dragged into all this.

She needed to do something. "Should I call the police?"

Even though she'd barely whispered the words, Dash must've managed to hear her. "Go ahead."

Fumbling to pull her phone out of her dress pocket, she winced at the brightness of the screen as it lit up. Her fingers felt huge and extraordinarily clumsy, but she managed to tap the three numbers and then *call*.

"Nine-one-one. What's your emergency?" The male dispatcher's voice sounded too loud, and Norah had to resist the urge to hush him.

"I'm at..." When she realized that she didn't know the street address, she mentally switched gears. "We're in the apartment above Porter Sports—the entrance is in the alley behind the building—and someone's throwing rocks through the windows."

"Okay, ma'am." As the dispatcher spoke, she could hear the tapping of keyboard keys in the background. "Someone is throwing rocks at your windows?"

"No, *through* the windows," she corrected. "The rocks are breaking the glass and—"

A *smash* behind her cut her off. Ducking, she turned halfway around to see that the kitchen window was broken.

"Ma'am?" The dispatcher sounded more alert now, making her wonder if he'd heard the crashing noise. "Is anyone injured?"

"No."

Dash flew to the door, yanking it open, and she mentally qualified her answer. *Not yet at least.* Once Dash got ahold of Leifsen or whoever was throwing the rocks, someone was about to get pounded.

"Lock this behind me," he ordered, halfway out the door. "And stay away from the windows. Got it?"

She nodded but realized it might be too dark for him to see, so she said out loud, "Got it."

The dispatcher was asking her questions, and she tried to focus on answering him as she hurried to lock the door. Just as she'd flipped the dead bolt, a *thunk* came from the kitchen. Turning, she saw a flicker of light and instinctively turned her back, hunching as something exploded behind her.

She froze in place for several moments after her ears stopped ringing. As she came back to what was happening, she did a quick mental check of all her parts, making sure she was still intact before straightening. A faint voice echoed from somewhere a few feet away, and she realized she'd dropped her phone. The apartment was much brighter than it had been just seconds ago, and she was confused until she turned to see that patches of fire were scattered around the kitchen.

Fire! the panicky portion of her brain screamed even as she moved to grab the fire extinguisher hanging on the wall. Before she could pull the pin, a *thunk* from the other side of the room made her turn her head. A clear glass liquor bottle rolled toward one of the overstuffed chairs, and the research part of her brain identified it immediately.

Molotov cocktail. Otherwise known as a gasoline bomb or a poor-man's grenade.

Time slowed down to a crawl. She wondered why she was so calm, but nothing about this situation seemed real. Here she stood in the kitchen of the man she'd just asked on a fourth date, holding a fire extinguisher while one or more of her stalkers hurled bottle bombs through the windows.

Get down, dummy! a voice in her brain shrieked, the panicky voice that usually wasn't much good for anything. Right now though, it made sense. She ducked behind the counter, crouching in as small a ball as she could manage, just as the bottle exploded with a *crash*.

This time, she kept her head and stood as soon as the sound had dulled to a quiet roar. Straightening, she swallowed, her dry throat hurting as it convulsed.

Fire was everywhere.

She took an uncertain step toward the living area just as another explosion from the other room made her jump and almost drop the extinguisher. There were too many patches of fire, and it was spreading fast. She watched in horror as it raced across the rug and spread over the couch, whatever accelerant that had been in the bottle egging it on.

That is not how I expected to burn up the couch tonight.

The irreverent thought made her choke on a hysterical laugh, but she fought it back.

Just pick a spot and start extinguishing! Her panicky voice was offering some solid advice tonight. Pulling the pin, she ran over to the couch and sprayed foam over the flame. The chair was next, and then she covered just a quarter of the rug before the extinguisher was empty, spitting air and useless flecks of foam.

The remaining flames were growing faster than ever, licking their way across the floor and up the bookshelves, eating the books that she hadn't even had a chance to do more than glance at. A pang hit her at the sight of Dash's cozy apartment being ruined, but smoke crawling into her lungs and making her cough brought her back to her main priority—she needed to leave.

Dropping the empty fire extinguisher, she turned to the door. The apartment was hazy with smoke, making her eyes sting and water and her lungs itch. She tried to hold back her cough, knowing she'd just suck in more smoke on the inhale. Old elementary school lessons about what to do in a fire resurfaced, and she dropped to her hands and knees.

The air did seem easier to breathe down lower, so she stayed on all fours as she crawled toward the door. Despite the light from the flames, the haze and her watering eyes made it hard to see, forcing her to feel her way. Her progress felt infinitely slow. Even though she knew the door wasn't very far away, it felt like she'd been crawling for blocks before she finally bumped into a vertical surface.

Sliding her hand over the wall, she felt her fingers collide with the molding around the door. She stood, groping the door until her fingers fumbled over the dead bolt. Norah hesitated before flipping the latch, Dash's command to keep the door locked echoing in her head, until she realized that was stupid.

Unlocking the bolt, she twisted the knob and yanked open the door. Clean, fresh air brushed against her face, and she sucked in a desperate breath. That same influx of air made the fire roar behind her, reminding her that she wasn't out yet. His apartment might be the only thing on fire at the moment, but that could quickly change. She needed to get out of the building altogether.

Closing the door behind her in the hopes that would slow the spread even a little, she blinked her blurry eyes even as heaving coughs made them water again. The stairway was dark, so she shuffled her feet, taking tiny steps to feel for the drop-off that would indicate the first step. Her hands waved in front of her, groping for the wall or—better yet—the railing.

A hand grasped her wrist, tugging her forward.

"Dash?" she croaked, relief flooding her. He'd come to save her. Of course he had. After all, leaving her in his apartment to die of smoke asphyxiation would be the height of bad manners. Her semihysterical burst of laughter at her mental joke came out in a cough. She blinked rapidly, trying to make out his features, but the dark shape in front of her was…wrong.

This isn't Dash.

Setting her feet, she pulled back against the hold on her arm, her stomach twisting as she realized the person in front of her, the one who had her in their grip, was much too small and slight to be Dash. The hand tightened, fingers digging into her, painfully grinding the bones of her wrist. Her instinct was to keep pulling back, to try to yank away so she could run…but there was nowhere to go that wasn't on fire.

The training session with Dash replayed in her brain, and she forced herself to lurch forward, toward the person who held her so cruelly. The darkness made it hard to judge the distance, so her shoulder plowed into them. Norah heard a muffled grunt as their bodies collided, and the pressure on her wrist immediately lightened. Not allowing herself to resume the pulling contest, she immediately sent a palm-heel strike toward their nose—or where she thought their nose might be.

By the hard bone she hit as well as the clack of teeth hitting together, Norah was pretty sure she'd hit a chin rather than a nose, but she still plowed through the motions she'd practiced over and over with Dash. Her stomp landed, but it didn't seem to cause any damage, and she wished she were wearing boots rather than being uselessly barefoot. Without wasting any more time, she swung her free arm, sending the elbow toward the person's midsection.

It actually worked. The grip fell from her wrist as not-Dash grunted. From the sound, she'd hit them hard enough to make them instinctively bend at the waist. Reaching out, she grasped the back of the person's head with both hands, yanking down as she drove her knee up toward their face. This had been her favorite part of this exercise when she'd practiced with Dash, and she realized she was actually smiling fiercely as she felt her kneecap connect with something both hard and squishy and a little bit wet.

The sensation was unexpected and off-putting, and she released her grip as she jumped away. From the groan she heard, her hit had hurt, and Norah was a little shocked at how glad she was about that.

Now run. It was Dash's rumbly voice in her head, telling her over and over that the whole point was to get away. She'd unconsciously retreated until the heat of the closed door radiated against her back, and she knew she needed to get past the person and down the stairs while they were still incapacitated. If they caught her again, it would be harder to escape, because she'd have lost the element of surprise. Now they'd be expecting her to fight back.

Go. Just go. Taking a deep breath that was tinged with smoke, she forced her feet forward in a rush, staying to the right of the still-groaning form. One heel hit the edge of a step before sliding painfully to the next. The thump as she hit vibrated through her body, but she ignored it as she scrambled down the rest of the stairs.

Her first step on the landing was heavy and hard, since she'd expected more steps, but she recovered quickly, hunting for the next set of stairs with her toes. She located them just as a roar of anger echoed from her attacker, and clattering boot soles thundered down the steps toward her. Not allowing herself to look behind her—since all she would see would be darkness—Norah flew down the rest of the stairs and hit the release bar on the door with both hands.

The door swung open, revealing the gym. Even though just the emergency lights were on, it was much brighter than the smoky apartment or the inky black stairwell. Norah dodged through the equipment, the familiarity of the space weirdly reassuring, allowing her to race confidently toward the door.

Just before she reached it, it swung open, and Norah tried to skid to a halt. She'd been traveling too fast and wasn't able to stop in time. She crashed full force into the huge shape filling the doorway. Panic snapped through her as strong arms latched around her, holding her tightly. In an instant, however, she recognized Dash, and her terror leaked out of her in a rush, leaving her limp against him.

"Are you hurt?" His hands roamed over her urgently as if checking for injuries.

"I'm okay." She was pretty sure she was at least, although she imagined that adrenaline plus the reassurance of being held safely in Dash's arms could mask a whole lot of pain. "There's someone chasing me though, so we might want to move." With Dash there, whoever had grabbed her at the top of the stairs didn't seem like such a threat anymore.

His whole body stiffened as he growled out one word. "Who?"

"Not sure." She tried to shrug, but he was holding her too tightly against his chest. "It was dark. He was right behind me though." Despite the strong urge to bury her head in the sand—or Dash's well-developed pectoral muscles—and pretend no one else existed, she turned as well as she could in his grip and looked behind her.

The gym was empty...or at least it appeared that way.

"Maybe they're still on the stairs?" she suggested, peering

into the shadowy corners. "Or they went into one of the dressing rooms."

"Or out the stair exit." Reluctantly releasing her, he moved between her and the rest of the gym. "Come on."

He gave one last glare around the gym before ushering her outside. The fire above them lit up the building, flickering red, yellow, and orange in a display that was both too bright yet caused deeply dark shadows in the alley around them. She shivered as she glanced around, wondering if someone was lying in wait for them. As much as she believed in Dash's strength and fighting skill, there were ways he could lose—too many opponents, an ambush, or a gun would bring him down like Goliath.

Headlights lit up the space around them as a squad car turned into the alley, followed closely by several fire trucks. Dash guided her to the far side of the alley across from the neighboring building so they weren't directly next to the gym.

"How'd they know there was fire involved?" she asked, her voice shaking a little as she spoke loud enough to be heard over the sirens. The last few words echoed in the sudden quiet as the vehicles cut their sirens.

"Someone probably saw the flames and called it in," Dash said.

"Oh. I did too, but I only got to the broken window part before I dropped my phone. Although the dispatcher might've figured it out before my phone burned up." Norah's gaze went back to the flickering flames in the broken windows of his apartment, the fire glowing brightly even in the red and white flashes from the emergency vehicles' overhead lights. "I'm sorry about your home. I tried to put it out, but the fire extinguisher didn't hold as much foam as I needed."

His grunt was displeased. "You shouldn't have even tried. You should've left at the first sign of fire." Before she could respond to that, he continued. "I should've brought you with me when I left. I just thought you'd be safer up there." He looked at the smashed-out windows as his hand ran up and down her arm. He hadn't stopped touching her since he'd caught her running out the door. Norah didn't mind. It was reassuring, reminding her that he was right there.

"Did you catch anyone?" she asked, watching as the emergency vehicles parked, the police car pulling closer to where they were standing while the fire trucks stopped on the other side of the building, keeping the space right in front of the gym clear.

"No." He didn't sound happy about that. "As soon as I stepped outside, someone clocked me in the back of the head."

A worried sound escaping her, Norah turned away from the flames to look up at Dash. "You're hurt? Do you have a concussion?" She reached up toward the back of his head before hesitating. If it still hurt, he wouldn't want her prodding at it, and if it were bleeding, she would just add her germs to the mix, which wouldn't be helpful. Lowering her hand back down, she frowned, hating this feeling of helplessness when Dash was hurt.

"It's fine." He patted her as if she were the one who needed comfort. "Just dazed me for a minute. Long enough for them to set everything on fire though."

A random thought occurred to her. "You never mentioned how gross it feels to knee someone in the face."

He stared at her before grinning. It didn't last long, but she held on to the memory of that broad smile. "Pants help."

"Okay. Next time, I'll wear pants."

Two uniformed officers approached them, neither looking familiar to her, and Norah held back a groan as she realized something. Being at Dash's apartment was going to severely mess with their Zach Fridley story.

One crisis at a time, she reminded herself as Dash wrapped his arm around her. She leaned into him, feeling as if she was a hundred times stronger with him at her back. Together, they'd get through this police interview and every other crisis after that.

THIRTEEN

SUNLIGHT BEAT DOWN ON NORAH's eyelids, making it impossible to fall back asleep. Prying open her eyes, she blinked at her wall clock until it came into focus. It was two in the afternoon, but her stiff and sore body didn't think she should move. Thirst and a demanding bladder forced her out of bed though, and she knew her sisters were going wild waiting for an explanation.

When she'd dragged herself into her house in the wee hours that morning, bruised and jacked up on adrenaline and smelling like smoke, her sisters had demanded she tell them the whole story. She'd managed to get them to wait until she'd had a shower and a few hours of sleep, but midafternoon the next day was probably pushing it. Norah figured they'd be barging into her room at any moment to hammer her with questions.

To her surprise, they waited until she stumbled into the kitchen. Cara even handed her a mug of hot coffee. Norah's thank-you came out as more of a grateful groan.

"Are you okay?" Molly asked, always the mother hen.

Norah did a mental self-check. Now that the adrenaline rush had worn off, every muscle in her body ached, but nothing felt broken or in danger of falling off. She'd discovered a few tiny cuts on the backs of her arms and calves—from flying glass, she assumed—when she'd checked herself over in the bathroom after her shower. They'd stung when the hot water had hit them, but they'd stopped bleeding by the time she'd discovered them. Her throat still felt raw from the smoke, and her knee was sore from hitting someone's face, but overall, she was surprisingly fine. "Yes," she answered truthfully.

"What *happened* last night?" Cara leaned forward in her chair.

Molly was standing propped against the counter, but Norah had a feeling her sister would be stress pacing before she got too far into the story. She figured it'd be easiest to just rip off the bandage and get the worst part out first.

"Someone broke Dash's apartment windows with rocks and then threw in gasoline bombs, setting his place on fire."

As her sisters goggled at her wordlessly, she remembered there'd been several other pretty bad parts that night.

"Then someone tried to grab me on the stairs, but I kneed them in the face." She was inordinately proud of that. "It felt hard yet weirdly wet and squishy, but Dash told me just to wear pants next time." That reminded her of something else that had gone wrong. "I'm going to have to tell Felicity I ruined her dress. It smells of smoke and probably has someone's spit on it."

"You…what…gasoline bombs?" Although she still wasn't very coherent, at least Molly was managing to get words out now.

"Yes." Blocking out the memory of exploding glass bottles and fire licking across Dash's floor and over his bookshelves, Norah kept her mind firmly on the technical term. "Also known as Molotov cocktails or bottle bombs. Petrol bombs too, but I think that's more a European term."

With each synonym, Molly's eyes grew wider and wilder.

"Uh…you might want to quit listing off bombs," Cara suggested with an uneasy eye on Molly's face.

Rather than explain she was talking about different names for the same type of incendiary device, Norah just gave a nod and continued, wanting to get all the bad parts out at once. "Also, if Detective Mills reads the police report, we might've blown the whole fake-boyfriend story, since I was at Dash's place."

"Eh…" Looking moderately calmer, Molly waved a hand, dismissing the last concern. "That's minor. Let's discuss the rest of it. Like the *bombs* and the *fire* and the part about *you being attacked!*"

Norah realized she'd been a bit premature thinking Molly had calmed down. "Um…okay." She figured she'd hit the important points, so she hesitated before asking, "What else did you want to know?"

"Ev-er-y-thing," Cara said, drawing out the word into four definite syllables. "From start to finish. Who did this? Were they caught? Arrested? Is Dash okay? What happened *exactly*?"

Norah tried her best to fill in the details. "We were talking on Dash's couch…" She paused for a split second, expecting one of her sisters to make a suggestive comment, but they were both silent, listening intently with serious expressions. That really brought home how upset they were about the whole thing. "Someone threw a rock through the living room window. Dash turned off the lights and looked outside but couldn't see anything, since they'd apparently broken out all the lights in the alley. Then another rock came through the kitchen window, so Dash ran out to try to catch them. When he got outside, someone bashed him in the back of the head."

Both of her sisters winced. "Is he okay?" Cara asked.

"Yes. The paramedics took a look." Norah's stomach twisted with remembered worry. Dash was so stoic she could see him saying he was fine, even if he had to carry his decapitated head around under his arm. "He didn't lose consciousness, just was dazed and distracted for a few minutes."

"Long enough for whoever it was to start throwing bottle bombs through those broken windows?" Molly asked grimly, and Norah nodded, glad she didn't have to cover that horribly scary part in detail.

"So I tried to put out the fires, but the extinguisher was too small to do much good." She very firmly kept her mind focused on the unemotional facts of the story rather than allow herself to relive every terrifying moment. She was rather proud that her matter-of-fact tone didn't waver. "I left the apartment, closing the door behind me to keep the fire from spreading into the stairwell too quickly. At the top of the stairs, someone grabbed my wrist. I thought it was Dash at first, but then my eyes started to adjust to the darkness, and I saw they were too short and not…"

"He-Man shaped?" Cara offered, making Norah huff a surprised laugh.

"Pretty much." The moment of levity, even as short as it was, relaxed her enough to continue. "I remembered Dash showing me how to move in closer if someone grabs me rather than pulling back—"

A pained sound from Molly interrupted her retelling.

Norah eyed her sister uncertainly. "Should I go on or…"

"Just let me finish mentally dismembering someone," Molly muttered.

Norah met Cara's raised-eyebrow look with one of her own.

After a final deep, audible breath, Molly dropped her hands and stood straight, shaking her hair back over her shoulders. "Okay, I'm good now. Please continue."

"Uh…okay." Despite her sister's reassurance, Norah gave Molly a careful look before picking up her story where she'd left off. "So I elbowed the guy and then stomped his foot, which didn't do much since I was barefoot and he wasn't—"

This time, Cara was the one who interrupted. "I thought we agreed after I was kidnapped in my socks that we'd wear shoes all the time except in bed?"

"I didn't want to wear shoes in Dash's apartment. It was really clean, and that would've been rude." It *had* been clean. Norah didn't want to think about the state of it now.

"Why didn't you put them on when you left?" Cara asked.

She seemed a bit stuck on the shoe thing, but Norah understood. If she'd been forced to run sock-footed from her kidnappers in a semiarid high-plains landscape with rocks and cacti and other sharp things, Norah would probably have a shoe-wearing obsession too.

"It was dark." She didn't want to go into any more detail about the heavy smoke that stung her eyes and made seeing even the doorway impossible, much less her flats. "I didn't want to stay in a burning apartment hunting for them."

"Good point," Molly said, seeming to be fully recovered from her earlier mental murder spree. "I think escaping the burning building had priority in this situation."

"Fine." Cara gave a grudging nod. "But next time, just wipe your feet really well before you go into someone's house rather than taking off your shoes."

Norah hesitated, not sure she could make that promise, and Molly waved her arms in an exaggerated *move on* motion.

"Okay, so I pulled the person's head down and kneed them in the face." Viscerally remembering how that had felt, Norah gave a little shudder. "They let go, so I ran down to the gym and met Dash at the outside door." She didn't want to say anything about how he'd held her or how she'd felt safer than she'd ever experienced before, so she quickly skipped ahead. "We went outside, and the police and fire department arrived soon after. I didn't recognize the cops, but they seemed halfway decent. Better than Detective Mill at least. I think they would've arrested whoever it was if they'd caught them throwing bottle bombs."

"How low our law-enforcement standards have fallen," Molly said mournfully before refocusing on the events Norah had just laid out. "So you didn't get a glimpse of who was responsible?"

"No." Norah felt a pang of guilt for that. "Not even the stairway person. It was so dark that I was barely able to tell the police an approximate height and build—oh, and the texture and length of his hair when I grabbed it."

"Plus he'll have a broken nose or fat lip," Molly added, and Norah felt that same spurt of pride for successfully taking on an opponent. "Or a black eye, depending on where your knee landed."

"It has to have been Zach and his buddies, right?" Cara asked. She'd pulled her laptop toward her and was frantically typing what Norah assumed were notes. "He's got to be holding a pretty big grudge after being knocked out, dragged over to Mr. P's house, and arrested."

"That would explain why Dash was targeted." Moving so she could see the screen over Cara's shoulder, Molly tugged her bottom lip as she read what Cara was typing.

"The person on the stairs was too small to have been Zach." Norah paused, hesitating to say anything, since it seemed a little egotistical to think that everything was targeted at her, but she knew there was a chance it hadn't been Zach after all. "What about Leifsen? He left that note in my pocket when he saw me and Dash together at Dutch's." She left out the dancing part of that story, since Molly and Cara appeared to have recovered enough from their worry to resume their usual teasing. "And we still don't know who left that pen from Dash's gym on my bed."

"Hmm…" Molly moved her gaze from the computer screen to Norah's face. "Good point. Do you think they're working together?"

"Um…" Although she hated the pressure of putting forth theories that might be entirely and ridiculously wrong, she preened a little at being asked her opinion. She'd always been part of the business, but that part had—until very recently—been in the background. That had been where she'd wanted to be, so she didn't have any resentment toward her sisters about that, but now it seemed like a whole new path was opening up to her. "Maybe? I can search for any connections."

"Leifsen was arrested for deactivating security systems for a burglary ring," Cara said, her voice sounding distracted as she spoke and typed at the same time. "That might be a good place to start searching for a link between those two."

"Good idea." Molly gave a nod. "Let's come up with a list of Zach's usual accomplices and try to get a glimpse of each of them before the bruises fade. We need to see whose face is messed up."

Norah felt another little pleased glow, this time because she might've left evidence behind, a trail they could follow.

"Did you feel anything break?" Molly asked. "Nose? Maybe knock some teeth loose or out?"

"Maybe?" Norah ran the knee strike through her mind again, ignoring the squelch of distaste at the memory. "I think I hit their nose, not their mouth, and I thought I heard a crack."

"Doctors then." Cara's typing turned to tapping on the touch pad. "ENTs or plastic surgeons, do you think? Maybe ERs?"

Molly's reply was interrupted by a heavy pounding on the door. "Cop knock," she said, her eyes narrowing. "Unless it's John, but he's not supposed to be back until tonight."

"He has a cop knock?" Cara asked, her voice hushed as she stared in the direction of the front door.

"Yeah." Molly moved toward the kitchen doorway, and Norah got up to follow. "He has a really nasty cop knock. I keep telling him he needs to work on that, but he doesn't believe he has one."

Cara closed her laptop and rose, staying close behind Norah. "The worst offenders can never hear their own cop knock."

"Isn't that the truth." Molly peered through the peephole just as another round of thunderous knocking made the door shake. "Uggghhhh."

"Who is it?" Norah was pretty sure her sister wouldn't make that noise upon spotting her own boyfriend at the door.

"Our good friend Detective Mill." Moving to the alarm display, Molly disarmed it.

Cara looked at the door in distaste. "Can't we just hide and pretend we're not home?"

"I can hear you girls in there!" Mill's shout through the door answered Cara's question. "Open up, or I'll get another warrant."

"I'm almost tempted to let him, but then we'd have to actually allow him in," Molly muttered before jerking open the door just wide enough to block his view into the house. "Why, Detective Mill, what a pleasure! What brings you here to see us *girls*?"

Even though he probably couldn't see her where she was standing, Norah bit the inside of her lip to hold back her smile at Molly's heavy sarcasm.

"I need to talk to Norah Pax," he said, and she lost any urge to smile.

"Why?" Molly demanded, but Norah knew why. They *all* knew why after the conversation they'd just had.

"You're not Norah, so that's none of your business."

"It's okay, Molly." Norah had known since the previous night that she'd be answering Mill's questions. She figured she might as well get it over with so Mill didn't get a warrant or pick her up the next time she left the house and bring her to the station as a "person of interest." At least at their house, she was somewhat in control of the situation, and she had her sisters there with her for support. Slipping past Molly, she ignored her sister's sound of protest and stepped onto the porch.

The move brought her face-to-face with Mill, and she was instantly uncomfortable. Resisting the urge to shrink back or drop her eyes, she took a couple of steps sideways toward the porch swing.

"You're Norah Pax?" he asked, following her, which opened up enough space for Molly and Cara to step outside as well. They shut the door behind them, and Norah swallowed a sour taste at how accustomed they were to getting questioned by the police and one grudge-holding detective in particular.

"Yes," she said, his flat stare making her realize she hadn't answered him.

"You called that fire in last night." Although he said it as a statement, not a question, she still shook her head. "You didn't call it in?"

"Not the fire." Even though she knew she was being pedantic, she couldn't let something not quite true slide. "I told the dispatcher about people throwing rocks through the windows, but I dropped my phone before the fire started. Someone else must've seen the flames and called in the fire. Or Dash thought the dispatcher might've heard the explosions before my phone was burned up."

Molly muttered something inaudible, and Norah gave her arm an awkward pat of reassurance. From listening to her sisters' harrowing stories, she knew how hard it was to hear about them being in danger. It had to be even worse for Molly, since she'd always been the one to take care of the rest of them.

Mill blew out a breath as if he was already frustrated with the interview. Norah just blinked at him innocently. If he didn't want the truth, he shouldn't ask her questions. "Dash as in Dashiell Porter, the guy who supposedly stopped a burglary at your neighbor's last Sunday?"

"Yes." It was easier to hold his gaze when they were talking about Dash. It felt as if she was defending him rather than herself, which brought out her bravery for some reason. She even gave a small, proud smile at how he'd covered for them. "That's the same Dash."

"I thought you two didn't know each other."

Ignoring the skepticism heavy in his words, she put on her best confused face. "Of course we do. I belong to his gym."

"Uh-huh. What happened to your story that you were dating his employee?" He glanced down briefly at his small notepad as if checking his notes. "*Bruiser* Davies."

This was the question she'd been dreading, but it was surprisingly easy to answer now that all her hackles were up in defense of Dash. "Watching Dash handle that burglar on Sunday made me…want to get to know him better." She heard Cara's soft exhale. It was only because she knew her sister so well that Norah could tell she was attempting to stifle a laugh. Norah tried not to blush as she replayed her last sentence in her head. From how her face warmed, she didn't think she succeeded very well.

"What about Davies?" It was hard to tell if the detective believed her. Mill had a decent poker face. "How does he feel about you just dumping him for his boss?"

"We weren't serious," Norah said, being careful to stay truthful while implying something else. She knew she was a terrible liar, and the detective would call her out immediately if she tried. "Bruiser's fine with it."

"Pretty big coincidence, don't you think?" He folded his arms across his chest.

A few weeks earlier, Norah might've been intimidated by the man's authority and size, but steady exposure to the much bigger and gruffer Dash had inured her to large, scary men—even ones who could potentially arrest her.

"What is?" She cocked her head while holding his gaze. "That Bruiser isn't mad about me spending time with Dash?"

"That the same guy who allegedly interrupts a burglary in progress at your neighbor's house is the one you're boning less than a week later when his apartment is torched."

"We're not boning," Norah rushed to say. Not that she would mind if they were, but it felt a bit like stolen valor. They'd only kissed so far—as intense and amazing as those kisses had been—but she didn't want to take undeserved credit for luring Dash into bed when it hadn't happened...*yet*. Just the idea of it made her skin feel hot again. "We were just sitting on his couch and talking. There was no boning."

Detective Mill broke his stone-faced expression to roll his eyes. "Fine. The guy you were *talking to* while the two of you were alone in his apartment. Still a pretty huge coincidence, don't you think?"

"Not really?" Norah responded, but it came out sounding tentative.

"I think you're forgetting again how small Langston is," Molly chimed in, and Norah was grateful for the assist. "You're used to Denver. Around here, we're tripping over the same people all the time, especially in our line of work."

"And it's not like I hadn't noticed Dash before I saw him at the neighbor's," Norah burst out, not sure if what she was saying was helpful or not, but her nerves didn't let her hold it in. "I mean, have you seen his hands? They're very…sinewy."

Cara's stifled laugh sounded more like a choke this time as Molly turned her head away to stare at the porch floor. Norah had a suspicion that if the detective wasn't there glaring at them, they'd be rolling on the ground, laughing their heads off.

Still, she couldn't stop talking. "The whole thing at Mr. P's house gave us a topic of conversation. Things…escalated from there." She forced her lips to clamp shut before the truth untwisted into something that didn't fit the story they were spinning for Mill's benefit.

Despite the embarrassment it caused her, Norah's babbling seemed to have worked to convince Mill—or at least to make the detective uncomfortable enough with the topic to change his line of questioning.

"Who was behind the alleged attack last night?" he asked.

All her earlier flustered feelings evaporated at that word. "It wasn't an *alleged* attack," she said fiercely. The heat warming her chest wasn't an embarrassed flush anymore. It was sheer rage. "Dash has a huge bump on the back of his head and a torched apartment to prove it. He had to stay at Bruiser's house last night since his place is all sooty and smoky…and a crime scene." She'd offered him a bed at her house, but the cops had kept him on the scene for questioning much longer than they had her, so he'd declined and sent her home after a final hard squeeze and kiss pressed to her temple.

"Fine." He raised a hand as if warding off more verbal attacks. "Who was behind the…attack last night?"

With some effort, she ignored that taunting pause before *attack*. "I don't know."

"You must have some suspicions."

"Of course." She raised her shoulders in a shrug, suddenly feeling exhausted by everything that had happened, and the craziness showed no signs of slowing down anytime soon. "Zach Fridley, the guy he stopped in the middle of a burglary, is out on bail."

"Anyone else?" Mill actually sounded genuinely interested in her answer rather than just hoping he'd trip her up and trick her into telling him the truth.

"Devon Leifsen." This wasn't anything she hadn't told the officers who'd questioned her the night before. "He's one of the skips we're after. He likes to hack into my computer and send me creepy messages with lots of menacing smiley faces."

Detective Mill raised an eyebrow.

She shrugged a little at his unspoken comment. "Yeah, he doesn't seem like the type to throw rocks and bottle bombs into someone's apartment, but he made it clear he doesn't like seeing me with other guys." She decided to leave out the note he'd slid into her pocket at Dutch's, since she had been supposedly still seeing Bruiser at that time. "Stalkers can be unpredictable."

As if on cue, a white Lexus rolled up to the curb in front of their house. Norah had been so distracted by Mill's questions she hadn't even seen the car approaching. When Laken Albee popped out of the driver's seat, Norah didn't know if she should groan in dismay or cheer the interruption. It was almost impossible to choose whether she'd rather talk to the detective or her junior high bully. *Neither*, she decided firmly. She really was too tired and sore to deal with either.

"Norah! There you are!" Laken waved enthusiastically over the top of her car as if seeing Norah on the porch of the house where she lived was a wonderful surprise.

"Who's that?" Mill asked as both Molly and Cara gave low groans.

"Just an old acquaintance," Norah said, not really wanting to get into her school-aged traumas with the suspicious detective. "I can get rid of her if you have more questions for me?" It was a close call, but talking to Mill was *slightly* less heinous than having to deal with Laken's transparently fake affection.

Mill studied her for a long moment before tucking his small notebook in his shirt pocket. "If I do, I'll stop back again." It was as if he knew she was dying to find a reason to dismiss Laken and refused to do her any kind of solid. "You're not far from the station. As you said"—he gave Molly a mocking nod—"Langston is a small town." Turning, he walked down the porch steps.

"You okay dealing with her?" Molly muttered quietly as her eyes shot lasers at the pair passing on the walkway. "I want to call John and fill him in on all this."

"Same," Cara said, glaring just as hard as the detective reached his car and Laken approached the porch steps. "Only Henry, not John."

"Glad you're not trying to steal my man."

Cara snorted at Molly's joking comment. "As if he'd ever look away from you long enough to even see another woman. Even if he did, Henry's plenty for me. I'm not greedy."

Norah laughed, grateful to her sisters for reducing the tension. She relaxed a little, less worried about the upcoming conversation but still dreading it. "Go ahead. I'll be fine."

Her sisters slipped back into the house, closing the door behind them. Although she'd just told them to leave, Norah envied them. If she'd had a chance to escape the oncoming nightmare, she would've grabbed it with both hands too.

"Norah! Why aren't you answering my texts?" Laken slapped her on the shoulder. Although it was done teasingly, Norah's sore muscles still protested the hit.

She hid her wince behind a forced smile. "I couldn't. My phone burned up."

"Burned up?" Laken's expression blanked with honest shock.

Norah registered the reaction with interest. It wasn't as if she'd honestly suspected Laken was the one throwing rocks and bottle bombs, but there had to be a motive behind the woman's interest. No one tried this hard to catch up with someone from high school—especially when they hadn't even been friends.

"Yes." Ignoring the hint to give more details, Norah got straight to the point. "What were your texts about?"

"You still owe me a night out at Dutch's!" Laken's broad smile of exaggerated friendliness fell back into place.

There was something about showing that many teeth that made her seem threatening instead of disarming. Norah had to make an effort not to take a step back. This wasn't the time to show weakness to a predator.

"How about tomorrow? It's Ladies' Night—not that we ever have to pay for a drink." Laken winked, and Norah thought how strange it was that Chloe could make the same expression look fun and cute but it just seemed contrived when Laken did it. Also, she wasn't sure why Laken didn't think Norah paid for her drinks. It was just a weird thing to say.

She realized she'd hesitated too long when Laken's eyes lit up with anticipation. Then again, maybe this outing was needed to expose what her junior high nemesis was really after. Norah could shoot down her hopes at finding the necklace, and then she'd hopefully be free of any future unwanted social obligations—at least those involving Laken. Going to Dutch's without backup wasn't an option though. The thought of seeing Dash again made a fireworks show launch in her belly, but she quashed the excitement, telling herself to save it for later, when she was alone.

"Fine," she said, knowing she'd regret it later. It had to be done though, like a dentist appointment. "I'm bringing a date."

A strange expression flashed over Laken's face before she reverted to her usual game-show host smile. "That delicious, muscle-bound man from the diner?"

Norah gave a short nod, not liking to hear someone else describe *her* Dash in that way.

"Ooooh, can't wait." As if wanting to leave before Norah could change her mind, Laken clattered down the porch steps impressively fast for someone in heels. "See you tomorrow! Let's say nine!" she called over her shoulder, not waiting for confirmation on the time before hurrying around to the driver's side of her car.

Norah watched her drive off. If she'd known that agreeing to go to Dutch's would mean such a quick departure, she might've said yes sooner…although this also meant she had to spend an evening at Dutch's with Laken.

Groaning, Norah reflexively reached for her cell phone, making a face when it wasn't in her pocket as usual. No, it was likely a blackened lump on what was left of Dash's apartment floor. Even if it hadn't been burned, the firefighters had surely doused it with a hefty amount of water. Heaving a mournful sigh, she headed inside. This meant a trip to the phone store in Denver, and she hated the phone store with a passion.

She dragged herself into the kitchen. Cara wasn't anywhere in sight—probably upstairs—but Molly was digging through the fridge as she talked on her phone to John. No matter what they were discussing—even if they were arguing—Molly always had that underlying lovey-dovey edge to her voice whenever she was talking to her boyfriend. Norah settled at the table and took a sip of the coffee she'd started before the detective had interrupted them. Wincing, she swallowed the lukewarm brew. She wasn't sure why she'd expected it to still be hot after Mill's interrogation and Laken's visit.

By the time she'd dumped the remainder in the sink and rinsed her cup, Molly wasn't showing any signs of wrapping up her conversation with John. Too antsy to wait any longer, Norah grabbed one of the disposable phones they kept on hand for informants. She scribbled the number down along with "going to Denver to get a new phone" and stuck it on the fridge. Molly walked over to read the note and interrupted what she'd been saying to John.

"Take Dash with you."

Norah felt her stomach squeeze with both excitement and nerves. "He's working."

"Then wait until he can go, or I'll go with you tomorrow." Molly listened to whatever John was saying. "Norah needs to get a new phone. Hers burned up." There was another pause before she spoke again. "Get in line. I get first crack at whoever did this." Yet another pause. "That's not fair. She's my sister. I should get dibs on torturing—"

Knowing from experience that the argument would take a while, Norah just scribbled out the first sentence she'd written and changed it to "going to talk to Dash." This new plan got an approving nod from Molly, who tossed her the keys to the weed-mobile. Norah fumbled the catch, as always, but managed to grab them before they hit the floor. With a wave of thanks, she headed out before Molly could reconsider letting her little sister leave her sight.

The drive to the gym felt too short as Norah tried to plan out what she'd say to Dash once she saw him. When they were together, it wasn't usually stilted or awkward, but that didn't stop her from fretting about what she should say to him after their harrowing experience the night before.

Parking on the street, she was halfway down the alley before she saw the police tape blocking the gym door.

"Of course it's closed," she muttered, stopping and turning back in the direction she'd come from. "The building was on fire, dummy."

As she hurried back to the car, her stomach churned. She hadn't thought about Dash losing his home and—at least temporarily—his livelihood at the same time. Since it was likely Norah had dragged him into the situation that led to the previous night's events, it was her fault he had nowhere to live and his business was shut down.

Sitting in the driver's seat, she locked the doors but didn't turn on the car. Digging out her burner phone, she stared blankly at it as she thought. The unfamiliar ring made her jump and fumble the phone, dropping it into her lap.

Once she'd recovered it, she recognized Molly's number on the display. Relieved and feeling a bit silly for being startled by her own phone, she answered. "Hello?"

"Hey, Norah. Dash called."

"He has your number? Why?"

"For situations like this?" Molly said. "Or in case you forget to turn your phone on or something."

The second one made more sense. Even Norah, who worked

for a group of bounty hunters, couldn't have predicted the previous night's mess. "What did he say?"

"The gym's closed. He's on his way to meet you there."

"Yeah, I should've figured out that it wouldn't be open." She was a little abashed by her lapse in logic, but she'd just wanted to see Dash, so she hadn't thought further than that.

"Good news is he's not working, so he can go with you to get a new phone."

Norah thought that was an optimistic way of looking at it.

"You should leave my car parked by the gym and take Dash's." Molly's voice had an undercurrent of laughter, as it always did when she was being an instigator.

"Okay," Norah said slowly. "Why?"

"My car's so recognizable that you know our detective buddy is going to notice it. It'll drive him up a wall when he can't figure out where we went."

Norah snorted at her sister's machinations but just said, "Fine. As long as Dash is okay with it."

"Stay safe. You have your pepper spray and your Taser on you?"

"Of course." As she spoke, she heard a voice in the background on Molly's end.

"Cara's reminding you not to take your shoes off for any reason."

"Why would I take my shoes off at the phone store?"

"Just promise her," Molly urged. "It's easier."

"I promise." Glancing in her rearview mirror, Norah saw Dash's SUV pull up behind her. "Dash is here. See you later."

"Bye. Be careful!"

"I will." She started to lower the phone from her ear as if that would encourage Molly to end the conversation.

"Tell Dash if you get hurt in any way, we're holding him responsible."

"Yeah, I'm not telling him that." Just the thought of it had her face warming with imagined embarrassment.

"It's okay. I already did when he called earlier."

Norah tipped her head forward to rest on the top of the steering wheel. *Of course Molly did.* "Okay. Bye. I have to talk to Dash and also die of humiliation." She ended the call before her sister could say anything that would make her blush even more.

A tap on the window made her lift her head to see Dash, his scowl heavier than usual. She moved to lower the window but then realized the car wasn't on, so she reached for the door handle instead. As soon as the lock disengaged, Dash pulled it open the rest of the way.

"You okay?" he asked immediately. When she looked at him in confusion, he offered her a hand. "Your head was down."

"I'm fine. Molly was embarrassing me." She accepted his hand even though she didn't really need help getting out of the car. Then her stiff muscles screamed at her, and she reconsidered, gripping him a little harder as she straightened to standing.

His gaze flicked over her as he frowned even more severely, and she knew she hadn't managed to hide her grimace. "What hurts?"

Everything. She knew that wouldn't do anything except

make Dash even more worried, so she shrugged and said, "Just a little sore. Nothing serious. How's your head?"

He waved a hand, effectively dismissing the fact that he'd been bashed over the head hard enough to daze him less than twenty-four hours earlier. "I'm fine. You need a phone."

"Yes." Apparently, asking Dash how he was feeling got him to quit fussing over her. "Do you mind driving? I'll pay for gas. Molly wants Detective Mill to see her weed car here and spend the day futilely searching the area for one of us."

That made his mouth crook up in a smile. "I can drive, and you're not paying."

FOURTEEN

It ended up that when Dash had told Norah she wasn't paying, he meant for *anything*. She almost started throwing elbows in the phone store when he used his height advantage shamelessly to block her from the counter until he'd handed the clerk his credit card.

"Your phone was destroyed in my apartment," he said as they left the phone store. The late afternoon sun glared right into their eyes. "It's covered by my insurance."

"But it was most likely one of my stalkers who caused the fire," she argued. "If it weren't for me, your apartment wouldn't have burned in the first place. You'd be at your open gym right now, having a normal day of Norah-free bliss."

He snorted, turning her toward another store in the strip mall with a light hand on her elbow. "There's no such thing as Norah-free bliss."

This flustered her enough to silence her until they reached a restaurant. She blinked in surprise, not having expected they'd go out to eat after phone shopping. Her stomach gave a grumble, reminding her she hadn't eaten all day.

"Fish tacos okay?" he asked, holding open the door for her.

"Sure." She walked inside. The place was only a third full. Even though they were in Denver and the chances of her seeing someone she knew were low, she still scanned the other patrons. As they approached the counter, she said firmly, "I'm paying."

He grunted, otherwise not even bothering to respond. Knowing he would use that same size advantage on her again, she sent him a sideways glare. When she saw he was smiling, she was distracted from her annoyance.

"What's funny?"

He just lifted a shoulder in one of his shrugs. "Nothing. Just happy to be with you."

Feeling a little like she'd been punched in the stomach—but not necessarily in a bad way—Norah came to an abrupt halt.

Dash stopped too, raising his eyebrows. "What?"

"Nothing." It wasn't *nothing* though. It was far from nothing. It was the first time someone had said that her presence made them happy. She was pretty sure her sisters enjoyed her company most of the time, but none of them had ever come right out and said it before.

The employee at the counter cleared her throat, pulling Norah out of her tumultuous thoughts. She started walking again but then paused. She didn't want Dash to think she'd just blown off what he'd said like it hadn't meant anything. It'd meant so much that she couldn't even start processing it while deciding what kind of fish tacos she wanted. Before she could think of the potential for rejection and humiliation, she reached toward Dash and took his hand. After a moment of stillness during which she almost died several times, his fingers wrapped around hers in a firm grip.

With her face warm and dragon-size butterflies dive-bombing her stomach, she turned to order. It wasn't until the clerk smiled back at her that Norah realized she had a huge smile on her face.

Yeah, being with Dash makes me happy too.

They held hands while ordering, while Dash handed over his card, and even while she gave him a glare for not letting her pay in order to ease some of the guilt she felt for dragging him into her enormous mess of a life. They continued to hold hands while he easily ignored that glare. It was only when she needed both of her hands to get her fountain drink that they let go of each other.

Norah was beginning to understand why Molly, Cara, and Felicity got so sappy with their respective guys. Kissing and hand-holding and even just staring at him for inordinate amounts of time were surprisingly enjoyable. It often felt like she and Dash were in their own bubble, separate from anyone else. She made a mental promise not to make so much fun of her sisters when they got mushy.

Once they had their drinks, they made their way toward a table in the back by unspoken agreement. Between her stalker and a general distrust of…well, most people, she felt more comfortable being able to see the restaurant. Dash obviously felt the same, since they sat on the same side of the table with their backs to the wall. When the side of his thigh pressed against hers, she appreciated another aspect of sharing a side rather than sitting across from each other.

As she looked around the restaurant, everyone looked very normal and not at all suspicious, but a part of her still had to wonder if she was being watched. Maybe the two college-age guys blowing straw wrappers at each other had been hired by Zach to follow her. Or maybe the woman sitting by the window wasn't really texting but was actually taking pictures of Norah and Dash. A little of her earlier elation seeped away.

"What's wrong?" Dash seemed to pick up on her mood change immediately.

"Just being paranoid." She took a drink, trying not to assign anyone else in the restaurant imaginary ulterior motives.

"The number of enemies you have, it's probably smart to be paranoid."

Wanting a distraction from that all-too-painful truth, she asked, "What about you? Is there anyone who has a grudge against you—besides Zach Fridley I mean?" She realized she didn't know much about Dash's history. The cops had separated them before questioning, so she hadn't heard him list off possible suspects. Maybe there was a chance she *wasn't* the reason his place had been firebombed the night before.

"Not that I can think of." He killed her tentative hope with a partial shrug. "I'm not especially likeable, but no one that I know of hates me enough to risk prison time."

"I think you're very likeable," she blurted out, making him

smile. Her face warmed as she tried to refocus on the point of their conversation. "I kind of wish you had past Mafia ties or something."

"What?" He barked out a laugh.

"I feel so *guilty*," she admitted. "Your nice apartment burned, having to close your gym... If you'd never met me, then Zach Fridley wouldn't know who you are."

He waved a hand, dismissing the attempt on his life with the casualness someone would give to shooing a fly. "But then I wouldn't have met you."

Their food arrived, giving her a chance to recover from that bit of incredible sweetness. By the time she'd eaten three tortilla chips loaded with pico de gallo, she'd regained enough of her composure to speak again.

"Have you always lived in Langston?" It seemed impossible she could've stayed unaware of his presence if they'd grown up within miles of each other.

"No. Phoenix."

"When did you move here?" She'd researched him and his gym when she was looking for a trainer, but she hadn't looked into him personally. Now she regretted it, feeling weirdly like she wanted to know absolutely everything about him immediately. All she knew was that he'd bought the gym four years ago when the previous owner retired and that he had a stellar reputation as a trainer. When she'd started, that had been sufficient information. Now that seemed not nearly enough to satisfy her curiosity about him.

"College."

She gave him a look. He wasn't making this easy for her. Not that she'd expect Dash to be one of those people who spilled his entire history ten minutes after meeting someone, but it'd be nice to have answers longer than one word. "How old are you?"

"Thirty-one." There was a pause before he asked, "You?"

"Twenty-three." She was tempted to say that she was almost twenty-four, but that attempt to bump up her age seemed too juvenile.

"Hmm."

She took a bite, waiting for him to elaborate on that thoughtful sound he'd made, but he stayed quiet, sending her curiosity off the charts. "Is that older or younger than you thought?"

"You look your age, but your brain seems older."

"Oh." She took another bite so she'd have time to process that, unsure whether that was a compliment. Did having the brain of a forty-year-old make her less appealing or more? From his enthusiasm when he'd kissed her, she didn't think it was less. She finally decided to ask. "Is that good?"

"Yeah." There was no hesitation before he answered. "The way your brain works is really interesting."

She smiled, thinking back to her first impressions of Dash. "I think your face is really interesting."

He paused, staring at her.

She watched him back, not sure what he was waiting for, so she just remained quiet.

"Is that good?" he finally asked.

"Oh yes." Her face heated. She couldn't help it. "I like... interesting."

One side of his mouth slowly curled up into a smile. "Me too."

———

It wasn't until they pulled up behind Molly's weed-mobile that Norah remembered she hadn't mentioned the following night. "Um...remember Laken Albee?"

"No."

"She came into the diner while we were eating last Sunday?"

"Right. Her." His lip curled slightly, and Norah had to bite back a smile. She'd never seen a straight male have that particular reaction to Laken before, and it was kind of a treat coming from Dash.

"She really wants me to go to Dutch's with her tomorrow night."

"I don't trust her." Dash's growl was back.

"Me neither." She reached over to pat him reassuringly lost her nerve halfway, so she ended up patting the air betw them. "I know she has an ulterior motive in trying to 're nect' with me. I just want to know what it is."

"I could get her to tell me," he offered, making her on a laugh.

"No torture." She felt like she was talking to on sisters.

"Then you wouldn't have to go out with her."

"Are you sure you don't have Mafia roots?"

"Pretty sure." He shrugged. "I could ask my great-aunt though."

She laughed, tickled by the thought of this surly beast of a man having a sweet little auntie who'd been involved in organized crime.

His answering smile came and went quickly. "I'm going with you tomorrow."

She blinked. That had been easier than expected. "I was hoping you would."

"What time?"

"Nine."

"I'll pick you up at seven. We'll get food first."

"Um…okay?" Somehow, an unpleasant few hours trying to figure out why an old acquaintance was being so persistently friendly had turned into an official date…not that she minded at all.

He leaned over the center console and kissed her firmly before getting out of the SUV. The kiss was so unexpected and intense and fast, it took a few seconds for her to come down off her Dash-inspired cloud. By that time, he'd rounded the hood and was opening her door for her.

Even without seeing it, she knew her scowl was unconvincing. "One of these days," she told him as she took his proffered hand and stepped out of the SUV, "I'm not going to fall for that trick."

He gave her his full-fledged smile, and it dazed her just as much as his kiss had. Keeping hold of her hand, he led her to the driver's side of Molly's car. When Dash didn't immediately move to open her door, she glanced at him, surprised by the un-Dash-like hesitation. He was glaring across the road at a nondescript sedan. When Norah followed his gaze, she saw Detective Mill was in the driver's seat, watching them.

"Wonder if he's been here all afternoon," she said under her breath as she reached for the door handle. The detective's stare made the little hairs on the back of her neck stand up, and she wanted to be out of his view. Before her fingers touched the handle, Dash's big hand made it there first. Without looking away from Mill, he opened the door and ushered Norah into the car.

"What's his deal with you?" he muttered, glancing at her as if to make sure she was in before closing the door with a solid thump. His scowl had returned, and his muscles vibrated with an annoyed energy that Norah didn't think she should find as attractive as she did. She started the car and rolled down the window so she could answer.

"His partner was dirty, and we were part of the reason he was arrested." Norah condensed the long, scary event into one sentence. If she mentioned that his arrest had been preceded by her wearing a belt full of explosives and Molly and John being shot at as they dodged booby traps, she had a feeling Dash would never let her out of his sight again. That wouldn't be *bad*, but she was sure he had insurance claims to file and all sorts of other things to do that didn't involve babysitting her.

"There's more to that story." It was like he could read her mind.

"Yes," she admitted. "You're not the only one who can answer truthfully while leaving a lot of important things out."

She smiled at him to show she wasn't really annoyed. In fact, she was looking forward to doing some research on him. There was nothing she liked better than solving an interesting mystery.

He smirked at her before leaning in for a final kiss. "Stay safe. Text me if you need me."

The different definitions of *needing him* bounced through her mind, and she knew she was blushing yet again. All she could manage was a flustered nod and one of her trademark awkward waves before rolling up the window. As soon as he stepped away from the car, she pulled forward, wanting to get away from Detective Mill's watchful gaze almost as much as she didn't want to leave Dash.

Tomorrow night, she reminded herself, unable to hold back a smile. Who would have thought she'd be smiling about spending time with Laken Albee, but the woman didn't seem to matter much anymore—not when Dash would be with Norah.

An unfamiliar beep made her jump. As soon as she was out of sight of Detective Mill, she pulled over and checked her new phone. It was just a spam text, and she deleted it. She started to put her phone down but then hesitated.

"Just do it, you chicken," she scolded herself before pulling up Chloe's contact info.

Hi. This is Norah. She was tempted to add a smiley face, but Devon Leifsen had ruined them for her. Before she could reconsider, she quickly sent the text, her heart thumping as if she'd done something terrifying. Putting her phone in the cupholder, she moved to put Molly's car back in drive when she heard the beep of an incoming text.

Her stomach was jittery but settled instantly as she read it and laughed. Norah!!! Finally!!!

Norah barely had three letters entered before a second text from Chloe showed up.

Can you sing?
Um...not like you can, but I'm okay. Why?
You and me. Chico's. Tomorrow. Open mic night!!!

Her stomach instantly clamped down again before she remembered her plans at Dutch's. Can't. Have a date.

Poo. Next week?
I'd rather stab myself in the face repeatedly than sing in front of strangers.

Chloe sent a line of laughing emojis before giving in. Fine. We'll be spectators then.

Next week. No singing.
Promise.

Norah doubted that, since Chloe followed it up with a devil emoji. Norah tried to frown but didn't quite manage it. She'd somehow found herself a boyfriend and a friend and a burgeoning social life. Her smile broke free as she headed toward home.

FIFTEEN

WHEN SHE ENTERED THE KITCHEN early the next morning, only Molly and Cara were there—well, and Warrant, who was stretched out in his favorite place under the table. Norah's eyes darted to the empty chairs. "Charlie, Fifi, and Bennett aren't back yet?"

"No." Molly scowled, worry evident in the deep line between her brows.

She looked intensely tired, making Norah wonder if her sister had even gone to bed the night before. Feeling almost guilty that she'd slept like a baby after a blessedly Leifsen-free evening of researching Dash, she topped off her sisters' mugs before getting her own coffee.

"Where are they now?" She hoped the information she'd pulled from the security video hadn't sent them on a wild goose chase across the country. The house felt too quiet without them.

Molly made a face that was interrupted by a yawn. "Charlie

gave the latest update last night, so all we know is that they're safe somewhere in one of the Dakotas."

"Well, they're safe at least," Cara said with forced optimism, sounding as if she was trying to convince herself. "You look like you're dressed for a workout. Training with Dash?"

"The gym is still closed—" Norah started, but Molly interrupted before she could continue.

"Is it still a crime scene? What's taking them so long?"

With a negative shake of her head, Norah said, "The police released the scene. Dash doesn't think there's any damage to the gym, but he can't reopen until the insurance company checks it out."

Cara leaned over as if trying to see through the kitchen doorway. "How do you know all this? Do you have Dash stashed away in your bedroom?"

With a snort, Molly attempted—poorly—to hide her smile behind her coffee mug. "Have you seen Dash? There's no way he'd fit in Norah's bedroom."

"True."

There was a lilting note to Cara's voice that told Norah more teasing was coming, and she tried to control the blood rushing to her cheeks. Quickly, she shook her head. "He texted me this morning."

Anything more Cara was going to say about the whole Dash topic was cut off by a glance at her phone. "Eep! Gotta go, or I'll be late for class." Shoving her laptop into her backpack, she flew toward the door to the garage.

"Be safe! Got your weapons?" Molly called after her.

"Yes!" Cara answered before the door closed behind her.

"Bye," Norah said, but she doubted her sister heard her, since she'd already disappeared.

"No training session today then?" Molly picked up the conversational thread they'd dropped to tease her.

"No…I mean, kind of." Norah's dreaded blush was back. Talking about anything to do with Dash seemed to bring it on. "Not a regular session. We're going to go for a trail run."

Molly perked up, some of her tiredness seeming to fade. "That actually sounds good. With Fifi gone, I've been slacking, and I'm feeling like a blob. Mind if I come along?"

"Sure." With all the time she'd been spending with Dash, Norah hadn't seen her sister as much as she usually did, and she missed Molly. "He's coming here, and then we're going to run the main south trail loop."

Molly stood just as her phone beeped with a text. Glancing down at her phone, she gave Norah a sheepish look. "John's on his way over. Mind if he tags along?"

With both Molly and John there, that meant they would be divided into couples, which meant the run would feel a lot like a double date. Actually, Norah's brain corrected her, Molly and John were family, so it would be more like a family get-together kind of run. Although Molly had met Dash before, John had not, and he could be a bit of a wild card. Norah liked Molly's boyfriend, but the man had no brain-to-mouth filter and loved to tease. Who knew what he'd say to Dash. Norah's stomach butterflies began swooping around again as sweat prickled along her hairline.

Molly must've misread her hesitation, since she started to tap on her phone. "It's okay. I'll tell him we'll meet up later."

"No, it's fine." When Molly paused, fingers poised over her phone screen, to look at her, Norah gave a firm nod, not letting any of her hesitation show. "It'll be nice to spend some time with you and John."

She was rewarded by a broad smile. "I'll go get ready."

Taking a last sip of coffee before switching to water, Norah tried not to fret about how their family run was going to go. It'd be fine. John wouldn't act like an overprotective father figure, and Molly wouldn't give Dash the third degree as Norah went all flustered and tongue-tied and red-faced—*oh no.*

Her head hit the table with a soft *thunk.* That was exactly how it was going to go.

Feeling penned in and claustrophobic in the kitchen as she came up with one disastrous scenario after another, Norah went out to the porch swing to wait. Warrant followed her, settling with a canine grunt in his dog bed next to the swing until John arrived. Popping up, Warrant ran down the steps to greet him and was rewarded with a thorough belly rub.

"Norah! My favorite sister!" He only called her that when none of her other non-Molly sisters were around, but it still made her smile. With Warrant following, he climbed the steps wearing his usual exuberant grin.

"Hey, John." She gave him a little wave.

He leaned against one of the support posts holding up the porch roof. "So I hear you've found yourself a man."

Her face flamed hot. She tried to respond, but nothing came out. *So it begins...*

"Don't worry." His voice softened a little, like he could see her mortification. "I'll be gentle with him. Molly told me he knocked out a guy for you and then took the heat for it. I'm inclined to like him for that, but if he steps out of line, you need to tell me so I can hurt him."

He delivered the last line with such a bouncy, happy cadence that it took a few moments to register.

"Um…Molly already called dibs on murdering him." She worried that the way she'd phrased that made it sound like Dash had already done something wrong, so she hurried to clarify. "If he…only if he does something wrong, I mean."

"He's behaving himself then?" His tone was light, but she could tell he was watching her face carefully.

The question actually made her smile despite all her building anxiety. "Yes. He's *really* into manners."

That made him cock a quizzical brow. "A guy who can take a burglar down with a single punch and also knows what fork to use? Sounds like a winner."

Although she was pretty sure the humor in his voice was just because he was John and thought life was consistently entertaining rather than because he was making fun of Dash, she hurried to correct him. "More like he opens car doors for me." She almost added that he didn't swear, but that was *their* inside joke. Other people might not understand why she found that quirk so endearing. Unfortunately, she couldn't think of any other examples with her thoughts churning like they were, so she ended with, "And other polite things. Not that he has bad table manners. He doesn't. He's just not hung up on proper fork usage or anything."

"Good to know." There was definitely a laugh trying to escape John now. "Not sure I have much fork-related conversation in me. There might've been an awkward lull."

Norah was pretty sure there had *never* been an uncomfortable silence within ten feet of John. He was the very definition of an extrovert. "You could always talk about punching people. You're both very good at that."

He let out a big belly laugh as Dash's SUV pulled up behind John's car. Norah's stomach butterflies, which had been smothered in a blanket of general anxiety up until this point, took flight, and she found herself smiling as he headed toward them.

Dash's scowl was firmly in place, his gaze focused steadily on John.

"Hmm…" John murmured, still not losing his grin, although he'd straightened from his casual lean to a more ready position. "Not exactly what I expected. You're a deep little pond, aren't you, sis?"

Norah wasn't sure what he meant by that or how to even begin to respond, so she stayed quiet. Watching the two of them as Dash approached, Norah was reminded of a wildlife documentary, two dominant males meeting for the first time. Warrant didn't seem to share any of the men's wariness, happily trundling over to greet the newcomer. Dash rubbed Warrant's ears without dropping John's gaze.

As Dash climbed the steps, John said, "You must be Dash." He held out his hand.

After a microsecond of hesitation, Dash accepted it. From the way the men's tendons stood out on their forearms, the shake was more of a strength contest than anything. She half expected to hear a clash of antlers.

"I'm John Carmondy, Molly's boyfriend."

Dash gave a tip of his chin as he released John's hand.

"Hi," Norah said, standing up from the swing and bringing Dash's attention to her. His scowl immediately lightened, and his soft expression made the butterflies in her belly go wild. "Ready to go?"

"Sure."

"Molly and John are coming along," she said, wishing she'd texted him about their expanded group. Maybe if he'd been forewarned, the moment between him and John wouldn't have been so charged. She immediately dismissed the idea though. Two bossy, protective guys were going to feel each other out. There wasn't any way to avoid an initially tense meeting.

Dash looked at John again, assessing him for a long moment before finally saying, "That's fine."

"Sorry to hear about what happened to your place," John said. Some of the tension eased from his posture, making Norah think Dash had passed the initial meeting.

"Thanks." Dash shifted toward Norah, so close their bare arms brushed. "Just glad no one got seriously hurt."

She frowned up at him, reminded that he'd nearly had his head bashed in. "*You* were hurt pretty seriously. Are you feeling up to running?"

"I'm fine." The corner of his mouth lifted in a half smile. "No headache even. How about you? Still sore?"

"Sore from what?" John asked quickly before she could answer. "I thought you weren't injured."

"I wasn't hurt. I mean, I'm fine." She wasn't sure which question to answer first, so she kind of muddled them together. "Just some strained muscles yesterday."

Neither man looked satisfied, so Norah was relieved when Molly bounced out the door, distracting them from questioning her further.

"Hey, sweetness." Molly stood on her toes to kiss John. After an intense moment that was even more charged by the fact that Norah's arm was touching Dash's, Molly turned toward them. "Hey, Dash. Good to see you. Thanks for letting us join your run. Whenever Fifi's not here to boss us, I tend to only run when I'm chasing a skip."

He just gave her a chin lift, but it was somehow friendlier than the prickly one he'd offered John earlier. "Ready?"

"Just one sec." Catching Warrant by the collar, Molly steered the reluctant dog back into the house and set the alarm. As she pulled the door shut and locked the dead bolt, John gave an exaggerated frown.

"Warrant can't come?" he asked.

Dash tipped his head down to murmur, "Your dog's name is Warrant?"

The feel of his breath on her ear made it hard to focus on his question. Dash had her so flustered and distracted she wasn't sure *what* her dog's name was. Clearing her throat, she made a desperate grab for some rationality. "Yes."

He smiled, and that hard-won logic was gone, replaced only

by the thought of how beautiful the man next to her was when he smiled.

"Of course not," Molly answered John, pulling Norah's attention away from Dash. "You want to actually *run*, right? Not slowly amble a few feet with frequent stops for sniffing?"

John looked like the second option didn't sound so bad. Norah had to agree. She'd take a meandering dog walk over a run any day, but with all the enemies she and her family had acquired recently, running was an essential skill.

They made their way down the steps and across the yard, falling into pairs with Dash and Norah in front of the other two. As they moved toward the trailhead at a slow warm-up pace, Norah glanced at Mr. P's house and noticed the blinds on one of his windows pushed aside slightly, just enough for her to see his accusing eyes glaring at them. Glancing at the side of Dash's face, she realized why Mr. P's stare was more venomous than usual and grimaced.

"What's wrong?" Dash asked, apparently noticing her reaction even though his gaze had been focused forward.

"Mr. P's watching." She resisted the urge to look back at her neighbor's window.

"Ugh," Molly groaned. "You know he's probably on the phone to the cops right now, letting them know he saw Dash with us. He probably has a whole conspiracy theory cooked up already."

"A conspiracy theory?" John repeated thoughtfully. "Like one where his bounty hunter neighbors dragged an unconscious man to his porch and picked his lock in order to prevent the cops from searching their house again?"

"No," Molly said. "He'll think of a far more nefarious reason. He believes we're the spawn of the devil."

"Well," Norah said. "That *is* a reasonable assumption for someone who knows Mom."

Dash gave her a slightly startled look, but Molly started laughing. "Very true."

They reached the start of the wide trail and increased their pace slightly before John asked, "How's the search for Norah's stalker going?"

She sensed Dash's tension at the question, almost as if his muscles had swollen an extra two sizes instantly. "Which one?" she asked, which didn't seem to settle the man on her right.

"How many do you have?" Although John sounded like he was amused, she heard the steel thread of anger in his words.

"Just two?"

"Three," Dash corrected, his voice growlier than usual.

"Leifsen and Fridley...who's the third?"

"Albee. The woman we're going to meet tonight."

That didn't seem quite accurate. She frowned. "Can we really consider Laken a stalker?"

"Yes," all three of the others chorused.

Norah supposed that following her around and popping up wherever she happened to be *was* rather stalker-like behavior. "Fridley isn't strictly mine though. He's more of a shared stalker."

"Still counts," Molly piped up as if she were the ultimate referee of stalker determination. "You have three stalkers, minimum."

Dash rolled his head, and his neck popped audibly. "Three too many."

The discussion seemed to be stressing him out, so Norah refocused on John's original question. "We're dealing with Laken tonight, and then we'll look for Leifsen Saturday night."

"What's Saturday?" John asked.

"Chloe's band is playing an outdoor show in the mountains west of Denver." She got a happy jolt saying the words so casually, as if they were already friends. Even though she knew she might be setting herself up for disappointment if Chloe ended up being involved with Leifsen, she couldn't help hoping Chloe was just as amazing as she seemed to be.

"Who's Chloe?" John gave a frustrated-sounding grunt. "I leave town for one night and end up out of the loop."

"Chloe's a possible link to Leifsen." Norah's stomach twanged as she heard her own words out loud. It felt wrong to define Chloe so dismissively. "An old acquaintance. She seems really nice and not creepy or felonious at all. He showed up to her last gig, but that might've been because he followed me there."

Dash grumbled under his breath.

"So we're all going to see Chloe's band on Saturday?" John asked, making Norah's heart sink a little. That was supposed to be her and Dash's fourth—fifth?—date. It was hard to keep track when each one kept going off the rails. If someone tried to kill them in the middle of it, did it still count as a date? Norah thought it did. After all, the intention to spend time together was still there, even if it ended up being interrupted by bottle-bomb-wielding sociopaths. In any case, having John and Molly along on a run in public was fine, but having her sister and pseudo brother along on an actual date would definitely put a damper on the kissing and…other activities.

"We can't," Molly said, and Norah tried not to look relieved. Dash sent her a funny sideways glance that made her think he was just as glad as she was that it hadn't evolved into a family affair. "I'm helping you pick up that guy in Pueblo on Saturday. Even if everything goes according to plan—which it never does with you—there's no way we'll be back in time."

"What are you saying?" John's offended tone was spoiled by the laughter in his voice. "I follow plans beautifully."

Molly snorted. "*Sure* you do. Like when you tackled that guy on the boat and both of you ended up in the reservoir?"

"That was called *improvising*." John drew out the last word. "Sometimes, you have to make a new plan in the middle of an old plan—"

"How is that following the plan?"

"I'm following the *new* plan! You just don't know it yet, because I just came up with it."

Dash gave a huff of quiet laughter. "They always like this?" he muttered.

"Always," Norah said before adding for the sake of honesty, "Unless they're making out." Although her cheeks warmed a little, she was glad she'd said it when another soft chuckle escaped him.

While they'd been talking, they'd arrived at the fork in the trail that started the south loop. The popular trail was surprisingly quiet, with just a few other early morning runners sharing the path. Although Norah had worried when Dash had first suggested a run that she would struggle to keep up with him, they stayed shoulder to shoulder as they fell into an easy pace. She knew he had to be holding back for her sake, but it was surprisingly pleasant to run next to him like this, even with the affectionate bickering happening behind them. The sunshine filtered through the trees, dappling the trail in front of them, and leaves scattered over the rocky trail crunched satisfyingly underfoot. It smelled amazing, like pine and fall and Dash.

Another runner approached, and Norah shifted over automatically. As the man got closer and his features were easier to make out, she recognized him.

"Bruiser!" she said, the name just popping out of her mouth before she could stop it. "Uh...I mean... Hey, it's Davies." Her weak attempt to save herself embarrassment made Molly and John laugh so hard they stopped running. Norah glanced sideways at Dash, but she couldn't read his expression. If she had to guess, she would've said he was torn between annoyance and reluctant amusement, but he went stone-faced before she had a chance to really examine him.

"Davies," he greeted as the man slowed to a stop in front of them.

"Porter." There was a suspicious redness darkening Davies's cheekbones, and he seemed to be avoiding looking at Norah.

She immediately felt bad she'd embarrassed him. Of all people, she knew what that was like. "Sorry. For calling you Bruiser I mean. I just think of you as Bruiser now." Dash grumbled something low in his chest, and Norah could feel the creeping heat of a flush warm her face. *Great. Now Bruiser and*

I match. "Not that I think of you very often? I mean, just when I'm talking to Detective Mill, and he's asking about us dating—*pretend* dating—not that Mill knows it was pretend. So…yeah."

With a strangled-sounding cough, Davies gave a small upward jerk of his chin. Norah wasn't sure if that was an acknowledgment of her apology or just a hello nod. He was definitely blushing though.

"Thank you for going along with that." For some reason, words kept flowing out of her to this stranger who she'd pretended wasn't a stranger. Normally, she couldn't manage to say anything when she was in an awkward situation, and this was nothing if not awkward, but now she couldn't manage to shut herself up. "It must've been a shock to learn we were dating when you didn't even know who I was."

"I knew," he said gruffly, but even that interjection wasn't enough to stop Norah's once-in-a-lifetime unstoppable avalanche of words. She could feel the heat of Dash's gaze, but she didn't look at him, focusing instead on poor, uncomfortable Davies.

"Oh well, it was still probably an odd thing to suddenly learn you were fake dating me, so thank you anyway." What was *wrong* with her? "Plus you had a brand-new nickname that made you sound like a cartoon character from the fifties. That can't have been fun."

"It's…fine." Davies was looking embarrassed *and* a little panicked at this point.

"It's over now though," she hurried to say, wanting to reassure him. "The detective knows we're no longer together. We've fake broken up so I can fake date Dash now."

"*Real* date," Dash corrected in a grumbly tone, making her gaze fly to meet his.

His interruption startled her enough to make her stop talking, and she was grateful to him and also a bit thrilled he'd announced their relationship in front of Molly, John, and even her fake ex.

"Right. Real date." She couldn't hold back a smile.

"Okay." Davies, who looked like he wanted to be anywhere but there, started backing away from their small group. "Uh… later." With a final flustered lift of his chin, he skirted around them and took off down the trail at a rapid pace just short of a sprint.

"Oh, Norah…" Molly's voice was still shaky with laughter. "I think you broke that poor man."

Biting her lower lip, Norah watched the rapidly retreating figure. "I know. I feel bad. I just…couldn't stop making it worse."

"I was impressed." John had stopped laughing, but he still wore an enormous grin. "I didn't think there were that many words inside you, little sis."

Norah could only manage a small groan in response.

A snort came from Dash that sounded like a muffled laugh. When she looked at him though, he'd regained his usual poker face. "C'mon," he said, catching her hand in his in order to tug her forward. "Let's go."

Norah gave the distant Davies a final, regretful glance before picking up the pace next to Dash. He held her hand for several strides, giving her fingers a gentle squeeze before he released her. That small sign of affection settled her nerves, although she knew she'd replay every excruciating moment of the encounter as soon as she was alone.

A renewed chuckle came from Molly. "I'm so glad we got to meet your fake ex."

This set John off again, although this time he managed to run and laugh at the same time. "Thanks for inviting us along on your run, Norah. I would've hated to have missed Bruiser."

Norah shot them a look over her shoulder, making them burst into fresh laughter. Giving up on subduing their mirth, she peeked at Dash out of the corner of her eye. "Tell him I'm sorry next time you see him." She was suddenly glad the gym was closed so her mortification had time to fade a little before she had to see Davies again.

"For what?" he asked, looking honestly puzzled.

"For...*that.*" She didn't even know what to call it, so she just waved a hand behind her in the general direction Davies had run. "I didn't mean to embarrass him."

His chuckle wasn't muffled this time. "Not your fault." Before she could argue that it was very much her fault, he kept talking. "Davies gets flustered whenever he gets within six feet of a woman."

"So it wasn't just the Bruiser thing or the fake dating thing or my talking about both of those things way too much?" His words soothed the burn of her embarrassment, but she still had her doubts.

"Maybe a little, but mostly it's just because you're hot and you were talking to him."

Norah studied the left side of his face—her preferred side, since it was less perfect than the other—looking for any sign he was hedging the truth in order to make her feel better. Then she realized this was *Dash*. He never skirted the truth just to spare her feelings. That was why she'd liked him immediately when she'd met him and a big part of why she liked him even more now.

"Okay," she finally said, her anxiety calming as she settled into a steady pace.

Molly and John were chatting behind her about the skip they were planning to pick up in Pueblo, and their voices merged into a steady background noise as Norah got lost in the regular beat of her feet hitting the ground and the warmth of the dappled sun on her skin. Running had never been her strong suit, but the man next to her somehow made it enjoyable. He made her feel comfortable yet amped at the same time, and she shifted slightly closer to him.

He gave her one of his crooked, one-sided smiles that she returned with a beam. It didn't matter if one or more of her multiple stalkers were watching her, plotting something dastardly. For now, she was happy to just be alive with Dash at her side.

SIXTEEN

DASH MUST'VE FELT SOMETHING SIMILAR, since he didn't seem to want their time together to end. Groans from Molly and John when the run extended too long eventually turned to serious whining. After a shared glance, Dash and Norah turned toward home.

"Next time, we should run the north trail. It has those neat little hills that feel like a baby roller coaster," Molly said as they all stretched in their backyard, hiding from Mr. P's view.

John grunted from where he was flopped out on the grass, not stretching anything from what Norah could see. "I thought we agreed we're never running with these two again."

"I don't know." Molly switched legs to work on her other quad. "It's not so bad now that we've stopped."

"That's the problem," he grumbled, eyes closed. "They never stop. They just keep running and running and running—"

"C'mon," Molly interrupted, rolling her eyes. "Let's go to your place to shower. Our water heater will beg for mercy if we try to take four showers here." She offered John a hand up, and Norah immediately saw the flaw in that plan. Sure enough, John accepted her hand with an innocent look before immediately pulling Molly down on top of him.

"Stop!" Molly was laughing as she tried to avoid being pinned. "No sparring! No fair! You know I'm not at my best on the ground!"

Watching the two with a small smile, Dash moved closer to Norah. "You weren't kidding about them always being like this."

"Not at all." Norah shrugged and headed for the house. "They're either fighting or...uh...making up." For the millionth time, she cursed her fair skin that showed every hint of a blush.

Dash chuckled, and the rare sound made her embarrassment worth it. "Thanks for letting me clean up here. Davies's shower is tiny."

"Least we can do when I was probably the reason your place is currently uninhabitable."

His frown returned. "No, the only ones to blame are the... ones who did it. You're an innocent victim."

He left her side to jog to his car, and she felt his words poke at a mental bruise she didn't even know was there. As he popped his trunk and grabbed a gym bag, her thoughts firmed into a resolution. She didn't want to be the innocent victim—or even an innocent bystander—anymore. These past few weeks with Dash had shown her that as terrifying as being in the middle of the action could be, it was also exhilarating. She didn't want to go back to her quiet, peaceful, boring, Dash-less existence. She wanted…more.

He jogged back over to her, slowing as he took in her expression. "You okay?"

"Yes. Better than okay. I'm *wonderful.*" Driven by her new resolve, she grabbed his hand and towed him toward the house. He followed for about two steps before moving next to her, but he didn't let go of her until they reached the front door.

When he held out his hand, she unzipped her shorts pocket and pulled out the house key. Not quite sure why he wanted to be the one to unlock the door, she mentally shrugged and went along with it. It was likely one of Dash's weird rules of etiquette. Once they were inside, she relocked the door and silenced the warning beep of the alarm, resetting it to *occupied.* Turning from the control panel, she saw Dash was prowling toward the kitchen as Warrant wandered out to greet him. Giving the dog an absent pat, Dash glanced at her and gestured silently for her to stay where she was. At least she was pretty sure that was what his hand motion meant.

Leaning against the wall, she waited as Dash checked the kitchen and even the garage before soundlessly climbing the stairs. It wasn't really a chore, since she could watch him move in that jungle-cat way for hours. Warrant meandered over to sit next to her, and she scratched behind his ears without taking her eyes off Dash. Once he disappeared upstairs, she got a little jittery, imagining him being ambushed by fortune-hunting burglars hiding in her sisters' closets. Tense, she stared at the ceiling, straining to hear any creak or hint of sound to indicate where he was and if he was in trouble.

"It's clear." As welcome as they were, his words made her jump.

Relieved, she grabbed the bag he'd dropped by the door and crossed the living room to meet him on the stairs. She expected Warrant to follow, but he headed for his doggie door instead. Handing over Dash's things, she gestured toward the second floor. "Bathroom's up there."

"I saw." There was a teasing glint in his eye as he moved over to let her pass and go in front of him. "You can shower first."

"Um…" Resolutions were all fine and good when she was making them in her head, but their execution was a lot more terrifying. Still, she was determined. "You can too."

He shook his head, and the thought of him turning down her offer made her chest feel like it was caving in. "It's your house, your shower. You go first."

Her first thought was that he would've insisted she go first even if they were at his house, but then overwhelming relief swamped her as she realized he wasn't rejecting her offer. He'd just misunderstood. Despite knowing that, asking the second time wasn't any easier than the first, especially since she wanted to be very clear about what she was offering.

"Do you want to shower with me?" The words came out in a rush before hanging in the air, so brash and revealing she couldn't just leave them there alone. "Together. Shower together. If you want. Or we don't have to. If you don't want. Up to you. Because I want. But not if you don't want."

His eyes widened in surprise, and she was just about to rescind the whole offer—forget those resolutions to be brave and seize the day and all that—when he gave her the hottest, most searing look she'd ever seen. His voice wasn't much more than a growl as he answered, "Yes."

"Yes?" Her head was spinning a little, everything moving faster than she'd expected, just like during their first training sessions when she was practicing blocking. For some reason, that memory jarred her out of her shock. Even back then, when she barely knew him, she trusted him enough to not even move when his fist was flying toward her face. Every single time, he stopped it millimeters away, just as she knew he would. It was the same feeling now, that he would never hurt her, would always protect her, and that she could end everything she'd just started with a single word. Somehow, knowing that made her even more eager *not* to stop. This was what she wanted, and this time, her answer came out sure. "*Yes.*"

As soon as the word left her lips, the world swooped around her as he picked her up, lifting her right off her feet with an arm around her hips. She gave an embarrassingly high-pitched squeak of surprise. Still holding her with that one impossibly strong arm, he rushed up the stairs and down the hall.

His eagerness loosened some of the tightly wound strands of anxiety inside her, and she started to laugh. He was normally so stoic that seeing him hustle into the bathroom like he couldn't wait for their shower made her feel wanted and sexy and like she was the coolheaded one for once…not that her head was especially cool. It was the first time he'd let down his guard enough with her to act this eager, and she really, really liked it.

He set her down in the bathroom, and her worries about

awkwardness returned for just a fraction of a second before Dash grabbed the back of his T-shirt and yanked it over his head. Once that happened, her brain turned off all thoughts except the ones admiring his defined chest and abs and arms and… She could go on for hours, since everything about him was absolutely perfect.

Although he stood still, letting her look her fill, there was the slightest insecurity in his expression that she noticed, mainly because it was so unusual for the ever-confident Dash.

"You okay?" she asked.

"Yeah." His hand rubbed over his collarbone and up his neck to his jaw, all the places where shiny pink patches of scar tissue interrupted the smooth tan stretch of skin. "Sorry. I know it's ugly."

"What's ugly?" She almost laughed at the idea that anything on Dash could be described as ugly. "The scars? I like them."

"You…like them." Although he looked a little bemused, he dropped his hand to his side.

"I've always liked them. They're part of you, and I like looking at you. You're very interesting. I've told you that before." When he just continued to stare at her, she wondered if she'd sounded a bit sociopathic, so she tried to clarify what she meant. "I don't like that you were hurt when you got them, but now that they're a part of you… I just really like all this." She waved her hands, indicating his entire muscled, scarred, gorgeous, protective, manners-obsessed form.

A hint of a smile touched his mouth, and she really liked that too.

"How'd you get them?"

"Pulled my buddy out of a burning car."

"Did he live?"

His smile grew, softening his expression. "Yeah."

"Well, now your scars are even more interesting." She sucked in a breath and, before she could lose her nerve, pulled her shirt over her head, leaving her upper half in just a sports bra. Even though he already knew what her body was like from training together, this was different, more intimate. She felt exposed and vulnerable, but she also felt safe, cocooned in this small, familiar room with Dash.

The way he was staring at her made her catch her breath. "You're beautiful," he said, his voice a low growl in his throat.

Although they weren't touching, she could almost feel the vibrations of that sound, and the sensation made her shiver. His eyes dropped to her goose-bumped arms, and he moved to turn on the shower.

She wondered if he thought she was cold. The idea almost made her laugh. She was the very opposite of chilled, with heat running through her like her blood was on fire. Taking the opportunity to undress while his back was turned, she stripped off the rest of her clothes. From the way his eyes flared when he turned back around, he hadn't expected her to be naked. Her arms twitched, wanting to cross over her chest, but the stark need and appreciation in his eyes kept her from covering herself. The way he looked at her was clear proof that his earlier words hadn't been an empty compliment. He truly believed she was beautiful.

The knowledge gave her the confidence to brush by him and climb into the shower. The hot water felt amazing on her overheated skin, and she closed her eyes as she tipped her head back to rinse the sweat from her hair. She could hear the slight rustle of fabric, and she felt her belly warm at the thought of Dash undressing completely.

The curtain rings clattered lightly against the rod as he pulled it closed, making her open her eyes again. She drank all of him in, the entirety of his beautiful, huge, fully bare form. When her gaze returned to his face, she saw he was smirking.

"Well?" he asked as if she were examining a painting and he expected her to give him a full critique.

"You're even more interesting naked." She smiled at him, a little surprised that any flush to her cheeks now was due to arousal and hot water. She must've borrowed some of his infinite confidence.

"I'm happy to please." He stepped closer so their fronts were almost touching, close enough she could definitely feel that growl in his voice.

She lifted her hand and let it hover over his chest. When he went still, she glanced up to see his eyes were hot, his face a mask of need, but he didn't move, allowing her to make the decision of where and when to touch. Without looking away, she brushed her fingers over his pec, feeling a strange sort of power rush through her at his responding groan. She'd done that. *She'd* caused that reaction with just the smallest touch.

Wanting to explore more of him, she grabbed the bottle of body wash and squeezed some onto her palm. Rubbing her hands together, she started to spread the sweet-smelling foam across his skin.

"Sorry." Was that her voice, so throaty and breathless? "You're going to smell like a sugar cookie after this."

"I like sugar cookies. After this, I'll *really* like sugar cookies."

She felt his words under her fingers and smiled. Even though he was as still as a statue except for the quickening rise and fall of his chest with each breath, she could feel the static tension just under his skin. He felt so *alive*. It was a strange thing to be surprised about, she knew, but quick hugs and arm pats and even his arm over her shoulders hadn't prepared her for the way his muscles tensed and released as she swept suds over them.

She washed him almost everywhere, losing her nerve and letting her hands skip away when she drew close to his groin. The difference in texture between his scars and the surrounding unharmed skin fascinated her, but she glanced at his face, her fingers hesitating as she asked, "Do they hurt?"

He gave a short shake of his head along with a strained quirk of his lips that looked more like a grimace than a smile. "That's not what's hurting right now."

It took her a second, but she finally got his meaning and ducked her head—not to hide a blush but to conceal her pleased smile. She, Norah Pax, had aroused him to the point of pain. Standing on her tiptoes, she slid her hands up the back of his neck to urge him to bend down. When he obliged, she kissed him.

It was like she'd shot a starter pistol. Dash went from immobility to motion in a flash, lifting her off her feet and pressing her against the shower wall. She barely noticed the chill of the tiles against her back, too focused on returning his kisses, their mouths meshing almost frantically, clutching at each other as if they were trying to climb inside the other's body.

Norah moaned, both from the intense sensations and from the feeling that she couldn't get close enough to him. She'd never really wanted to be physically close to anyone, but now the thought of losing the press of Dash's skin against hers was unbearable. Running her hands across his shoulders, she gripped him tightly, digging her fingers into the muscles working under her palms, and she knew she'd never grow tired of the way he felt—or the way he made her feel.

When he pulled back and set her on her feet, she gasped, his absence shocking her like she'd been dropped into icy water. She reached for him to pull him close again, but he held her off, smiling wickedly. "My turn."

He picked up the body wash as she watched, curious now that the initial wrench of him pulling away had faded a little. Starting on her arms, he soaped her body thoroughly, his hands careful and curious as they ran over every inch of her skin. The way he looked at her, the way he touched her, made her feel like she was the most beautiful and precious thing in the world to him.

Her skin grew hot under his touch as he discovered sensitive spots she'd never known about. She leaned into the contact as he washed her and learned her body at the same time. Her skin was almost humming, so alive under his touch, and by the time he slipped his soapy hand between her thighs, she was so ready it only took the slightest brush to her clit before she was coming. The orgasm was quick but strong enough to soften her knees, the shock of pleasure startling a cry from her. He caught her against him, supporting her as she recovered.

Once she was able to hold herself up again, he reluctantly finished washing her skin and started shampooing her hair. As his fingertips massaged her scalp, her eyes drifted closed, and she marveled at the way her feelings for him could flip back and forth between wild need and comfort. Both were alluring in their own way, the almost platonic head massage just as addicting as his frantic kisses and the surprise orgasm…well, maybe not quite as addicting as *that*.

"What caused this smile?" he asked huskily, kissing her gently as if he couldn't resist.

As cheesy as she knew it'd sound, she had to tell him the truth. "You did."

From the way he kissed her again, deeply and thoroughly, he didn't think it was cheesy at all.

By the time the last of the conditioner was rinsed from her hair, the water was lukewarm. Norah knew from painful experience the final drop to frigid would happen very soon. She shut off the water, squeezing excess water from her hair as Dash watched with hooded eyes. With the shower off, some of the hazy, dream-world feeling faded, and she felt a little shy under his frank and openly appreciative appraisal.

Dropping her gaze, she gave a small shrug. "Our water heater's ancient. We have a new one on our wish list, but it still kind of functions, so it's not a priority."

"How does that work with five women living here?" he asked, pulling the curtain aside and snagging a towel. She expected him to start drying himself off, but instead he handed the towel to her.

As she rubbed it over her skin, she was struck by what a commonplace action it was, something she'd done almost every day her entire life, but now it was full of lovely tension and undercurrents since Dash was here, watching her as he grabbed his own towel. It took her a few moments to recall his question, and she had to clear her throat before she could answer. "Five women and one man now—Bennett's staying with Fifi in what used to be Mom's room. We have a strict shower schedule when everyone's here. Fifi's really good at organizing that sort of thing. It's much easier now that Mom's gone too." As she said the words, she was struck by how true they were. It wasn't just sharing the bathroom either. Everything was easier...except for the mess Jane had left behind.

Pushing away thoughts of bail bonds and treasure-hunting burglars, she pressed the worst of the moisture out of her hair before wrapping her towel around her. Dash wore his low around his hips, and the sight was almost more alluring than when he was completely nude...*almost.*

She caught sight of her damp mess of a mane in the mirror and reached for a comb. When Dash took it out of her hand, she stared at him, confused, even when he started combing out her tangled hair. He started from the bottom, holding the handful so the motion didn't pull on her scalp.

"Why are you so good at this?" she asked, allowing herself

to relax into the very different sensations of his fingers and the teeth of the comb. Opening one eye, she peered at his closely clipped head. "Did you used to have long hair?"

"No." He started on detangling another section, intently focusing as if combing her hair was the most important task in the world. "I have a little sister."

"Yeah?" Although he'd tipped her head forward so he could work on the strands covering her nape, she peeked up at him, charmed by the thought of him caring for a small girl who looked like him. "What's her name?"

"Daphne."

"Is she still in Arizona?"

"Minnesota. She's a doctor at Mayo."

He finished working through the tangles and ran the comb from the crown of her head to the ends of her hair. It felt so incredible that Norah couldn't hold in a groan. The comb froze, and she felt Dash go still behind her, his body radiating that same feeling of immobile vibrating tension he'd had when she'd first touched him in the shower.

She glanced up at him and then couldn't look away, caught by the ferocious need in his eyes. "Do you...want to see my bedroom?" she asked, her words sounding to her own ears like a corny cliché.

When Dash answered with a growled "Yes," it felt like it'd been the exact right thing to say.

She led the way down the hall, Dash so close she felt like she was being hunted. Instead of making her nervous, having that solid wall of muscle stalking behind her sent her stomach butterflies into a good sort of wild frenzy, her heart jumping from the thrilling, seductive danger of it all.

It wasn't until he stepped into her bedroom that she remembered how very small it was, her hobbit-size closet with its *extremely* tiny bed. She looked back and forth between the bed and Dash, completely unsure as to how things were going to work, logistically speaking, until Dash's full-throated laughter drew her attention.

Entranced, she stared at him, fascinated by the way his smile transformed his face. Even though she really liked him while he was wearing his usual scowl, there was something about him looking so *happy* that awakened an answering joy inside her.

"Don't worry," he positively growled, although there was still an amused current to his words. He pulled the door closed behind him, making the bedroom seem even more minuscule, which Norah hadn't thought possible. "We'll make this work. I want you so bad, I'd make *anything* work."

Her mouth dropped open a little at his raw admission, and then he was on her, kissing her fiercely. Her head spun with the intensity of it, and she took a half step back to catch her balance. That was all it took for her calves to meet the edge of her bed, and then she was falling backward.

Dash somehow turned her before she smacked into the wall, instead landing with her head on the pillow. He came down on top of her, taking his weight on his hands, his arms caging her in a way that felt both thrilling and weirdly safe.

"Good thing Warrant didn't follow us up here," she said breathlessly, not sure why she was talking about her dog when there was a gorgeous hunk of man currently hovering over her, his eyes positively *smoldering*. "With him on the bed, you definitely wouldn't fit."

Another laugh burst out of him, and before Norah could decide whether seductive Dash or happy Dash was more attractive, he lowered his head and kissed her. Instantly, she was caught up in a whirlwind of want, everything in her focused on Dash and how his lips felt against hers. Since the first time they'd kissed, she'd wondered a few times during moments alone whether she'd exaggerated the intensity of how she'd felt when they'd been together like this, if her mind was putting a romantic sheen on something that had, in reality, been rather ordinary. Now, in the moment, she could definitely say that kissing Dash was even better than she'd remembered.

He lowered his body until his chest pressed against hers, just a single layer of terry cloth separating their skin. Even that one towel felt like too much, and she pulled at it where it was tucked into her side. Although he was just resting a portion of his weight on her, it was enough to trap the towel. She wanted him to stay where he was, but she also wanted to feel his skin against hers.

As if he'd read her mind yet again, Dash pushed off her so she could pull the towel loose. It dropped to either side, leaving her bare. She tugged on his biceps, wanting him to kiss her again, to feel his skin against hers, but he resisted, staring down at her with hungry eyes. His intensity reminded her that she was completely naked, all her flaws exposed to the one person whose opinion in this matter she actually cared about. She gave a shy wiggle, dropping her gaze to the side.

"Hey." His voice was a low rumble, bringing her eyes back to his. "You're so beautiful. I didn't expect… I mean, I thought about it a lot, but actually seeing you…"

His inability to finish a sentence made her smile. She'd managed to fluster the great Dashiell Porter. That was impressive.

He smiled right back at her, not at all embarrassed by his uncharacteristic verbal stumbling. "You're more stunning than I could've ever imagined."

Even though she could feel her face heat, she didn't look away. Her heart felt full to the point of being stretched, as if it would burst with one more sincere word from him. Not wanting to risk it, she looped her hands behind his neck and tugged him down. This time, he allowed her to pull him into another kiss.

This one felt different. It was as hot as fire, as usual, but there was a sweetness to it as well. Leaving her mouth, he kissed along her jaw and down her throat, interspersing nips with gentle touches of his lips and tongue. She never knew which would come next, wicked or soft, so by the time he reached her collarbone, she was quivering with anticipation and raw need.

He wasn't stopping though. He scored the tips of her breasts with his teeth before soothing them with his tongue. Shifting lower, he laid a path of kisses across her belly and then nipped at her hip bone. Norah realized she was making small, needy sounds, and a part of her was surprised. Her default was silence, but apparently not while Dash was exploring her body with his mouth.

Even when he shouldered his way between her thighs, his

wide bulk pushing her legs so far apart her muscles ached pleasantly with the stretch, her earlier shyness didn't return. Despite the newness of the experience, the awkwardness she'd expected just…wasn't there. All she felt was fiery need and eagerness for the next touch, the next kiss, the next teasing nip as those dark, dark eyes caught hers. She liked this, liked everything they'd done so far, and she hadn't expected to. It shouldn't have surprised her so much, she thought. After all, she'd liked pretty much everything she'd done with Dash. He seemed to be the key to her comfort and pleasure.

"You okay?" he asked, his breath hot against her center.

She was pretty sure she couldn't be any more okay. "Yes."

His mouth tipped up, his usual crooked smile holding more than a hint of wickedness. "Good." Lowering his head, he gave her an open-mouthed kiss, showing her how very wrong she'd been. She could be much, much more okay.

Her orgasm wasn't quick this time. Instead, it lasted for what seemed like forever, a suck or nip or lick from Dash sending her pleasure to crest again just as she thought it was receding. Norah was pretty sure she screamed as she came, but she wasn't at all abashed by it. Even if the sound made Mr. P call the cops and tell them someone was being murdered at Norah's house and an entire SWAT team came crashing through her bedroom door, she didn't think she would care. She felt too good to be bothered by anything.

Dash crawled up her body, and she gave him what was certainly a dopey grin. He looked positively smug as he kissed her quickly and then got off the bed.

"Wait…" Her brain struggled to function in its floaty post-orgasmic state. "Where are you going?"

Leaning over, he kissed her again, a little longer this time. The flame in her belly reignited, jumping back to instant life like a smoldering campfire. "I'll be right back."

Grabbing his towel, he wrapped it around his hips and then slipped out the door, moving in his usual ninja-like way. Still feeling like her muscles were all overstretched and floppy rubber bands, she managed to push up onto her elbows, still confused as to why Dash had left. Before she could cover herself with the towel still wedged underneath her or even come up with a few worst-case scenarios to explain his disappearance, he was back, carrying his bag.

Closing the door behind him with his elbow, he dug something out and held it up.

"Ohhh," Norah said as she recognized the small packet. "Good planning." She couldn't believe she'd completely forgotten about condoms. She scolded her practical side for missing that. Although in her defense, she hadn't expected a group run would turn into a shower together and then sex in her tiny bedroom.

Tossing his bag into the corner, he gave her another one of his crooked smiles—which seemed to be coming a lot more frequently lately—and yanked his towel free. When he basically *leapt* on her, she made a sound that was shockingly close to a giggle. Then he was kissing her again, their hands roaming freely, and she forgot everything else.

Since he had the condom, she expected him to get right to business, but he didn't seem to be in any hurry. Instead, he touched and kissed what felt like every inch of her body. Then he flipped them so she was on top and offered himself up for exploration.

Explore she did. She marveled at the differences between his body, so solid and hairy and rough, and hers. At the same time, there were surprising similarities, like the silky softness of the skin of his belly and the way kissing him right behind his ear made him shiver, just like it made her. His obvious desire for her fueled hers, and by the time he rolled on the condom under her fascinated stare, she was more than ready.

Holding her hips, he helped her ease down over him. The feel of him inside her was like nothing she'd ever experienced before—the stretch, the dull ache, the *fullness*—and she stilled, processing it.

"Okay?"

The word was just a breathless grunt, and she focused on his face. He looked…almost desperate, which strangely made her smile. Experimentally, she moved, lifting her hips a little and then lowering back down again, and he groaned, his fingers working on her hips as his eyes rolled back in his head.

Every nerve inside her was awake. It wasn't just the physical sensations though, as incredible as they were. It was the sense of power, euphoric and addictive, that she was able to make him feel such intense pleasure. Not only that, but her focus was pinpointed on this, how each drag and bump of their bodies against each other felt. All the anxious thoughts that seemed to spin continuously in her brain were just…gone. Everything was so simple, just her and Dash, joined together.

She began to move more quickly, goaded by his grip on her hips, harder and deeper until she was coming yet again. Her body clenched around him, the feel of him inside her driving her higher. It must've triggered something in Dash too, since he made a growly sound, and then she was spinning as he flipped them over.

She'd thought her climax was easing, but this new angle shot her right back to the top of the roller coaster. She wrapped her arms and legs around him, holding on for dear life as he drove into her and yet another wave of pleasure crashed over her. His muscles tensed under her gripping limbs, and he let out a long groan. Even in the throes of sensation, she still smiled at the sound. *She'd* done that. She'd made him feel so good, made his muscles turn to Jell-O just like hers had.

His weight sank her into the mattress, heavier and heavier until she changed from feeling warm and secure to just a bit squished. Her arms were still wrapped around him, and she couldn't imagine letting go anytime soon, so she patted him lightly on the back, tapping out like they were sparring.

He immediately raised his head, his eyes heavy-lidded but alert enough to figure out what she was silently telling him. "Sorry," he said, lifting off her.

She immediately felt cold and exposed, and she worried he was going to leave, but he didn't go far, just settling on his side next to her. The small bed forced them to stay close, and Dash angled his body, gathering her against him so he partially covered her without squashing her into the mattress.

They were both quiet then, but the silence held none of the

awkwardness Norah dreaded. She floated in a comfortable daze, drifting but not asleep as one of his hands played idly with her hair. It was just…nice.

Of course it ended too soon. In the quiet, the squeal of the screen door was obvious. Dash stiffened, his muscles taking on that vibrating readiness as he moved off the bed and quickly dropped the tied-off condom into her tiny trash can. Grabbing a pair of sweats out of his bag, he yanked them on.

"Molly?" Cara's voice carried up the stairs and through the closed bedroom door. "Norah? I know someone's home, since the alarm's set for occupied."

Not wanting her sister to barge into her bedroom, Norah gave a silent sigh and rolled to her feet. Maneuvering past Dash, who seemed to have grown like the Hulk while in protective mode, she cracked the door. "Hey, Cara. I'm upstairs. I'll be down in a minute." Closing the door again, she turned to see Dash's raised eyebrows. Guessing at what his expression was about, she gave a small shrug. "I didn't want to have a yelling conversation about you. She'll see you soon enough and figure it out."

"Want me to go out the window?"

Glancing at the tiny pane of glass that even *she* wouldn't fit through, she laughed. From his rather proud half smile, that had been his intention. Forcing her face back into a serious expression, she said, "Would you? That'd be great."

His eyes widened for just a moment before he gave a teasing growl and grabbed for her. Giggling, she tried to dodge, but the bed tripped her up. He followed her down and immediately started tickling her.

"Sorry! Sorry! I give up!" She'd never been able to win a tickle war. "Mercy! Uncle!"

He stopped but stayed hovering over her, his eyes starting to heat again.

She was tempted, but the thought of Cara one story below them made her give his chest a little push. "Not with Cara here." Not when she'd just discovered how vocal she was during sex.

Dash actually pouted—a look she found strangely adorable on him—but stood and helped her up. His tug on her hand was strong enough to pull her right into his arms, and she went with it, all too happy to be pressed against his bare chest again.

He kissed her, quick but intense. "I *like* you, Norah Pax."

"I *like* you too, Dashiell Porter." She didn't hesitate saying the words. "I also like having sex with you."

His laugh was a bit rough as he tightened his arms around her. Leaning into his hug, she let herself enjoy the moment. She could deal with nosy sisters and stalkers and skips later. Right now, there was just Dash.

SEVENTEEN

"I've forgotten why I thought this was a good idea," Norah said as they approached the front entrance of Dutch's. The lot was full, forcing them to park on the street a block away, and there was a short line of people waiting for the bouncer to check their IDs at the door.

"I never thought this was a good idea," Dash grumbled, his gaze moving around them, scanning the shadows as well as the people scattered around.

Norah ignored his mutterings, too occupied with trying to see who the bouncer was. "Think we'll not get in?"

"Don't think we'll be that lucky."

His persistent grumpiness was almost funny. "Well, we did almost get kicked out last time. And the bouncer gave me the *I'm watching you* fingers."

Dash's attention shifted back to her as his brows rose.

"You know." She demonstrated.

His huff of laughter quickly disintegrated into another

growly mutter as they joined the end of the line at the door. "No one gets banned from Dutch's. One of these days, I'm taking you on a date to a *nice* place."

"We've been to nice places." Standing on her toes, she could see the bouncer's shaved head, but that didn't necessarily mean it was the same guy. Although her experience with bouncers was limited, she was fairly certain having a shaved head was part of the traditional uniform. "I liked our run."

The look he gave her was hot enough to light her hair on fire. "I liked how our run ended."

"Me too." She knew she had to change the subject before she jumped him in Dutch's parking lot. "I love that Thai restaurant we went to. And your apartment is nice...*was* nice." She corrected herself with a pang.

"It doesn't count as a date if the cops or fire department has to be called."

Giving up on trying to get a glimpse of the bouncer, she turned to him, honestly interested. "Do you think so? I was wondering about that same thing, but I figured what constitutes a date has more to do with the intentions of the parties involved rather than if there's a violent interruption or not."

His expression had lightened a little. "You deserve every date to be nice and nonviolent." His frown returned as he scanned the lot. "With no stalkers."

She smiled, imagining it. "That'd be nice."

With the sun long gone for the night, the temperature had dropped. Although Norah had dressed in pants—just in case she needed to knee someone in the face again—and a jacket over her blouse, she still shivered a little from cold and anticipation. Without dropping his gaze from the people around them, Dash wrapped his arm around her and tucked her against his side.

She stiffened, not expecting to be touching him so suddenly. It was different in public than it had been in the privacy of her bedroom. After a few moments, she began to relax. He was extremely warm and, despite his rocklike conformation, surprisingly comfortable to lean against. As they slowly advanced toward the front of the line, Dash kept her close. Norah would never have guessed that in-line cuddling would be a perk of dating that she enjoyed, but she didn't want to pull away from him, even when they reached the bouncer.

It was the same one, and Norah immediately looked at her feet as she held out her driver's license for him to see. She was sure the bouncer was about to pick her up by the scruff of her neck and physically toss her out of line, likely combined with shouted warnings to never return, and then Dash would have to kill him for touching her, but all the bouncer did was grunt in a displeased way.

Handing back her ID, he warned, "No trouble." But that was it. No tossing or shouting at all. It was almost anticlimactic.

When Dash was allowed through with the same treatment, Norah had to admit that he'd been right—apparently, no one got banned from Dutch's. That was both a relief—since she hadn't looked forward to being tossed across the parking lot—and a little intimidating. Who knew what kind of troublemakers frequented a place where literally *anyone* was allowed to go?

Dash tugged her behind him, pulling her out of her musings, and she latched on to the back of his belt. Even when she had a firm hold of him, he didn't move his hand, keeping it resting on her hip as if to reassure himself that she was still with him.

Dutch's was packed, busier than she'd ever seen it before... although this was only the third time she'd been at the bar. She looked around, searching for a glimpse of Laken, but she was too short to see much of anything. Dash must've spotted someone though, since he made a sharp left and worked his way through the crowd, plowing a path for her like one of those ice-crushing boats in the arctic.

He stopped by a table, and she moved to his side.

"Norah! You came!"

Dash had indeed led her right to Laken. Part of her—a very large part of her—wished that Dash was just barging his way to the dance floor or something. Forcing a smile, she gave Laken a little wave in response to her enthusiastic greeting.

"You remember Kenslee, Carson, and Pike, of course!" Laken made a sweeping gesture toward the three sitting with her at a high-top table close to the bar.

Losing even her weak attempt at a smile, Norah just nodded stiffly at her three former classmates. They didn't look much different from when she'd last seen them five years ago, except Carson was currently trying out a very strange facial hair arrangement. The two guys offered her chin lifts while Kenslee gave her a wave and her trademark pageant smile.

This was a bad idea. Norah couldn't argue with the voice

in her brain, but she was determined to get this over with. She needed to find out exactly what Laken wanted—although she had a pretty good idea it had something to do with the necklace her mom had stolen—and somehow convince the woman there was no way Norah could help her.

"Who's this?" Kenslee asked, giving Dash a slow once-over that made Norah want to smack her.

It was such a strong urge that she grabbed her right hand with her left to keep her body from overruling her common sense. *This is a nonviolent date*, she told herself, repeating it like a mantra. *This is a nice, nonviolent date.*

When Dash just gave Kenslee one of his typical scowls, Norah figured it was up to her to introduce him. "Dash," she said, but it was lost in a surge of crowd chatter. Raising her voice, she tried again. "This is Dash." When Kenslee gave him another heavy-lidded look, she added, "My boyfriend."

That earned her a sideways half smile from said boyfriend. She could feel her cheeks warm slightly, but she straightened her shoulders. Even though they hadn't specifically defined their relationship, he felt extremely boyfriend-like to her. Also, he was the one who said they weren't fake dating.

"Here!" Laken shoved a drink toward her. "It's on me! You have some catching up to do."

Occupied by claiming Dash as her own, Norah hadn't even noticed Laken leaving the table, but she'd obviously made another trip to the bar. A little of the bright pink liquid sloshed over the rim of the glass, and Norah shifted back against Dash, both so she didn't get splashed and also because she really didn't want to take the drink. She wasn't a big drinker in the first place, and she didn't trust Laken enough to accept anything from her.

"No, thank you." She held up a hand as if to physically block the drink from entering her body. "You enjoy it. I'm just going to have water."

Although she pouted, Laken stopped shoving the drink at her and put it down on the table in front of her own seat. "I'll get you a water then."

"No, I—" It was too late to protest, since Laken had already darted toward the bar again.

Reluctantly, Norah turned back to the others. Even though Laken was annoying, she was chatty and could've served as a bit of a buffer between Norah and the remaining three. She sent a quick glance at Dash, but he was keeping an eye on the crowd around them. It looked like there was an argument building between two guys three tables away, and she could tell most of Dash's focus was on them.

Except for Laken's, all the available seats were taken, so Norah just stood awkwardly next to the table. Dash took up the space behind her, close enough that she could feel his body heat but not touching. None of the others said anything, so Norah searched her brain for something to talk about. It was interesting how awkwardly quiet things could seem even in a noisy crowd. She finally settled on an innocuous question she was fairly sure wouldn't be considered strange. "Um…how long are you going to be in Langston?"

"Just tonight," Kenslee answered, although her gaze kept

flicking to Dash as she stirred the remains of her cocktail. "I live in Colorado Springs now."

"Oh." *What is there to say about the Springs?* Scrambling for a response, Norah just said, "That's…nice."

"What've you been up to?" Pike asked. "Heard you're a bounty hunter now. You must have some interesting stories."

There was an odd note to his voice, but Norah wasn't sure if it was amusement or derision or possibly horniness, so she ignored it and just nodded. At least some of Dash's attention must've been on their conversation, since he stiffened. When Norah glanced up at him, she saw he was glowering at Pike. Either the man didn't notice or he ignored it, because Pike's gaze stayed fixed on her. The other two at the table were watching her closely as well. It was more than a bit unnerving, and she found herself leaning back against Dash, finding courage in the press of her back against his front. He ran his hand over her upper arm, and that was very nice too.

Despite the comfort of Dash's touch, Pike's question rankled. *Not this again.* Laken had been all about the "interesting stories" too, making Norah think that it was code for "tell us the one about your mom stealing a very expensive necklace, and make sure to include the part about where she hid it."

"Not really." Norah gave her standard answer, knowing that she was a beat or two too late. "I'm just a researcher. No field-work for me."

Pike and Carson exchanged a look while Kenslee studied Norah like she was a particularly interesting bug she was about to squash with her very expensive heel.

"I heard about your mom," Carson said. When his lips moved, so did the weirdly caterpillar-like hair above and below his mouth. It was both disconcerting and distracting, making it hard to concentrate on what he was saying. "The whole stealing that necklace and taking off thing. That must suck."

Kenslee slapped his arm. "Rude! I'm sure she doesn't want to talk about her loser mom."

Blinking, Norah wasn't sure whether she should thank Kenslee for that save, since it was also kind of a kick in the face.

"It's not good to hold things in though," Pike offered, taking a drink without looking away from her. "Maybe she wants to vent."

She felt Dash's chest move with either a chuckle or a grunt. Knowing him, it was almost certainly a grunt of derision directed at the three in front of her. She glanced up at him, but she couldn't get any idea of his thoughts from his expression. The arguing pair at the other table was getting loud again, and he was staring in their direction, his usual scowl in place.

"The line at the bar took *forever*." Laken slid back into her seat. Twisting off the cap of a water, she held out the bottle. "Here."

Norah accepted it, although she gave the cap in Laken's hand a confused look, unsure why the woman had opened it for her.

Following Norah's gaze, Laken gave a little laugh and held out the cap. "Sorry. Mom habit. I have a three-year-old, so I'm always opening drinks for her—although that usually involves poking a straw into a juice box."

Hearing that Laken had a daughter made her seem a bit more human. "What's her name?" Norah asked, taking a sip of water. It was cold and made her realize how dry her mouth was, and she gave Laken an honestly grateful smile before taking another long drink.

"Isla." Digging in her bag, she pulled out her phone and held it out so Norah could see the picture on the screen.

"Cute." It was true. The little girl looked like a miniature, sweeter version of Laken. Norah looked at the other three, Laken having unknowingly gifted her with a conversation topic. "Do any of you have kids?"

"No," Kenslee said quickly, looking so horrified by the idea that Norah almost laughed.

"Two." Pike was the next to answer, although he didn't elaborate. Seeing the grim set of his mouth, Norah decided not to ask.

Carson shook his head. "None that I know of at least." He laughed as he said it, making Norah stare at him, trying to tell if he was truly joking or if there really was a chance he'd left fatherless mini Carsons all over Colorado.

"Enough about us though," Laken said before Norah could ask Carson to clarify. "We want to catch up with what's going on with *you*."

"Not much." Norah's brain instantly froze, deleting any ideas for innocuous replies to Laken's question. The only thing she could think of was Dash, and she had a sudden flash of terror that she'd blurt out *we had sex* or *Dash washed my hair and then we had sex* or *Dash washed my hair and then we had sex and I really liked it.* Her fear was so strong she clenched her jaw so none of those words could escape.

"Come on." It sounded as though Laken was clenching her teeth as well. "You have the most interesting job of all of us... and the most interesting family. You've got to have some stories to tell."

"No." Relieved she hadn't allowed anything embarrassing to slip out, Norah was emboldened to continue. "Dash is the one with the interesting job. He owns an MMA gym."

"Yeah?" Carson sounded intrigued, and Norah gave a sigh of relief as his attention focused on Dash. "You fight?"

Dash gave her a teasing gentle pinch on her hip, most likely for throwing him under the conversational bus. "Used to. Now I just train."

Norah was surprised he'd answered in actual words, since she expected a glare from him at the most. She realized he'd spoken to take some of the pressure off her, and she melted at the sweetness of that gesture. She gave the hand on her hip a squeeze of thanks.

Carson started talking about his gym, and Pike and Kenslee joined in. Only Laken didn't contribute to the conversation, instead listening with no sign of irritation. As the minutes ticked by, however, Laken began tapping her perfect nails against her glass. She wasn't drinking, and Norah wondered if she was the designated driver for the other three, who were tossing their alcohol back freely.

"We still haven't heard about *you*, Norah." Laken interrupted Carson's literal blow-by-blow story of a boxing match he'd won. "How's your mom holding up? Is she still living with you?"

Norah was suddenly tired of all the fake smiles and stilted

conversation. Her stomach was beginning to feel queasy, and she was pretty sure it was from all the anxiety this forced socializing had caused. All she wanted was to go home and sleep, preferably with the big guy she was currently leaning against. She took a drink of water, sad to see the bottle was almost empty. There was no chance she was going to endure the crush at the bar to get another, and she doubted Laken would get it for her after what she was about to say.

"I don't have the necklace," she stated bluntly. "I don't know where it is. It's probably with my mom, but I don't know where she is either. I can't help you find it."

All four froze in place, and despite Norah's discomfort at being so confrontational, she was fascinated by a glimpse of honest emotion from Laken. Anger, frustration, and—oddly— fear flashed across her face for just a split second before she recovered and plastered on a look of offended innocence.

Dash gripped Norah's upper arms, giving her a squeeze of support. When she glanced up, she saw his crooked smile, telling her as clearly as words that he was proud of her. It bolstered her, giving her the strength to deal with the instant chorus of denials from the other four. In fact, she ignored them altogether as he leaned down, close enough for his breath to brush her ear.

"Ready to go?"

"Very ready." A flush of nausea engulfed her, and she felt a bit dizzy. It passed after a few seconds, but it left her exhausted. The thought of bed was even more tempting now.

"You okay?" he asked, his fingers tightening as if he was preparing to hold her up if needed.

"I'm fine." She would be as soon as she left her current company and the hot, crowded bar. Finishing off her water, she said, "Just let me run to the bathroom, and then we can go."

"Want me to come with you?" he asked.

She laughed at the thought. "Thanks, but you'd probably get beaten and then kicked out."

Although he didn't look happy about letting her go off on her own, he stepped back enough to let her skirt around the table.

"Bathroom?" Laken asked, hopping off her stool, as chipper as if she hadn't just been acting horribly hurt that Norah would ever question her motives.

"Oh, me too." Kenslee joined them.

Norah gave a resigned sigh. It looked like she'd have to put up with a group bathroom visit before she could escape. She was tempted to skip it altogether and wait until she got home, but she didn't want them to think she was running away, not after her show of bravery. Besides, she was thirsty and planned to refill her bottle with tap water. Turning, she headed toward the bathroom.

Just as she reached the hallway where the restrooms were located, she heard a shout that escalated to a roar. From the sound of it, there was definitely a fight happening. Looking behind her, she couldn't see Dash, and she hoped he wasn't in the thick of it. Even though she knew he could take care of himself, there was always the danger he could get hurt in the melee.

"Every time," Kenslee said, rolling her eyes as she took the lead, pushing open the door to the ladies' room. "I don't think we've ever come here when there *hasn't* been a fight."

Laken gave a little shrug, entering behind Kenslee and holding the door for Norah. "It's Dutch's," she said as if that explained everything.

Norah muttered her thanks before heading for a stall. The bathroom was busy, but thankfully there wasn't a line. As she peed, she felt sweat beading along her hairline, and nausea rose in her again. She swallowed, really not wanting to get sick here. Laken and Kenslee would fake fuss over her, and it would be awful.

As she straightened, pulling up her pants, her head swam, and she flattened her hand against the side of the stall to catch her balance.

"You okay in there, Norah?" Laken asked, sickly sweet.

Norah had to swallow again before she could speak. "Fine."

Her head cleared enough for her to let go of the wall. She took a few deep breaths, and by the time she left the stall, she felt mostly fine, although a little lightheaded. Mentally, she ran over what she'd had to eat that day, wondering if her blood sugar was low. She really hoped she wasn't coming down with something, not when she'd just discovered the joys of trading germs with Dash.

Laken and Kenslee were touching up their makeup in the mirror, talking together in low tones that Norah couldn't hear over the chattering of the other women. Norah made her way to a sink and washed her hands before clasping her wet hands to her cheeks. The cold water felt good against her flushed skin, but she noticed the two women looking at her strangely, so she reached for a paper towel.

Another dizzy spell hit her hard, making her stagger. The room spun around her, voices rising and falling but not making any sense.

"Are you okay?" The question made it through her confusion, and she tried to focus on the person who asked. Norah tried to shake her head, to ask for someone to go get Dash, but it was hard to tell if she was just thinking things or actually doing them.

"...Daaash," she heard herself slur, and the helpful stranger just looked confused.

"Oh, Norah." That voice she knew. Laken laughed that awful, beautiful peal of sound as she gripped Norah's arm. "I told you not to do that last tequila shot."

Kenslee appeared on her other side. "Don't worry, sweetie. We've got you."

The stranger's face immediately smoothed, the worried lines disappearing. Norah tried to say they weren't her friends, and she wasn't drunk. This was something so much worse. Her thoughts spun, and words wouldn't come together coherently. All she could manage to say was Dash's name, and that didn't help.

With Laken and Kenslee each holding an arm, they led her out of the bathroom. *Good,* her bleary mind thought with relief. *Dash is out there. They'll bring me to Dash.* Instead of turning left toward the bar and Dash though, they turned right.

"Nooo." Norah tried to turn, but her muscles seemed to

have lost all coordination and strength. Just staying upright was an effort, and she couldn't manage to pull away from the two women guiding her the wrong way down the hall. "Dash…that way."

The words didn't sound right out loud, but her sense of hearing was distorted, so Norah hoped she'd managed to speak clearly enough to be understood. Either she'd failed, or the two escorting her were ignoring her, because they continued hauling her toward the emergency exit.

"What you need is some fresh air," Laken said.

Norah tried to struggle, but nothing was working right with her body. Her distorted gaze fixed on the "alarm will sound" warning plastered across the door. *Alarm*, she thought. *Alarm is good. Dash will hear, come running.*

Her hopes were quashed as Laken shoved the release bar down, and the door opened with barely a sound. Time started skipping, slowing and then speeding up again. Suddenly, she was in the darkness of the alley behind Dutch's, her back pressed against the wall. Laken and Kenslee were right in her face, their happy pageant masks gone. They glared at her, spitting questions she couldn't make sense of. They were just scattered words, skipping through her brain without letting her catch them.

"…tell us…necklace…know…" Kenslee bared her teeth in what looked like frustration when Norah just stared, having a hard time focusing on the other woman's face.

Laken started talking again, and Norah turned her head. The entire alley spun around them, and she forced her gaze to lock on Laken's before the whole universe spun away. "Try…

remember…" Her voice was a little gentler, but her eyes hardened when Norah just looked at her. "Where…necklace?"

Norah choked out a laugh even as everything did a pause and restart that made her feel like she was under a strobe light. "Told youuu."

"What?" Laken asked urgently, Kenslee leaning even closer as if not to miss Norah's answer.

"Told you…you were after…the neck-a-lesssss." She spread the word over three syllables, playing with it with her tongue. It was a funny word, *necklace*. Her mouth wasn't working right, so it felt even stranger on her lips. Everything suddenly slowed down. Rather than losing bits of time, now it dragged, each second stretching like taffy, the other women's voices disturbingly distorted, although at least now she had time to hear every word.

Kenslee gave a muffled shriek. "This is *useless*! You gave her too much."

"How did I know she'd drink it all?" Laken retorted. "I thought she'd just have a few sips."

"Well, obviously not." Kenslee threw a hand toward Norah as if indicating exhibit A. Norah snickered at that, which seemed to make Kenslee even more livid. "See! She's not even capable of telling us her name, much less where the necklace is."

Laken's chin jutted as she faced down Kenslee. "We'll just wait a few minutes until she comes down a little. We need that information. Do you have any idea how much my divorce lawyer costs? There is no way I'm losing custody of Isla."

At least her motive isn't terrible, Norah thought. *She just wants to keep her daughter.* Her calm thoughts bothered her. Norah knew her reactions weren't normal, that she should be freaking out and fighting to get free, but she just couldn't work up the urgency. Besides, now that they were arguing with each other, it was almost comical.

"Quiet," a new voice—a male voice—commanded. "I could hear you two halfway down the alley."

Norah forced her head to turn to see the newcomer, and the anxiety she couldn't feel a moment ago bubbled up inside her at the sight of his too-familiar face…a face marred by a swollen nose and two black eyes. Time snapped back into place, fear giving her a clarity she didn't really want.

"Leifsen," she said, still slurring but feeling suddenly much more awake.

"*Norah.*" There was a false intimacy to the way he crooned her name that made her stomach lurch. "You can call me Devon."

"Laken gave her too much," Kenslee hissed. "She can't even talk right now. We need more time to get information out of her."

"This isn't the place," he snapped. His gaze was fixed on Norah's, making her feel like a mesmerized mouse, unable to move away from a snake. "I'll work on her."

"You need to tell us what you find out," Laken insisted. "That was the agreement. We get the necklace's location, and you get her."

"I'll tell you. I don't want that necklace." Moving to Norah's side, he slid an arm around her.

She tried to scream, but all that came out was a pathetic

squeak. A mouse noise. Crouching a little, he swung her up into his arms. *Bridal style.* The term for the hold ran through her head unbidden, and she fought to shake the thought loose, since it only increased her horror at the situation. There was nothing romantic or caring about this.

"I just want Norah," he said softly, almost fondly.

Panic roared through her, cutting through the muffling layers that'd been protecting her from what was really happening. She tried to kick and squirm, but he subdued her weighted limbs with embarrassing ease. He even chuckled as he held her close in a parody of a caring partner.

"Dash!" Again, her attempt at a yell barely made it to her ears, but the name did make Leifsen frown. He gave her a shake, making her head loll over his arm as the world spun around her. She felt her gorge rise, and she didn't attempt to swallow it back, hoping that would get him to let her go. If vomit was her only weapon right now, she would use it.

Nothing would come up though. Even that bodily function failed her. Frustration made a tear slip over her temple, tickling as it ran into her hair. She tried to master her wobbling limbs, wishing for just one solid elbow or heel strike or kick, but her muscles wouldn't cooperate, and their surroundings wouldn't settle long enough for her to get her bearings.

His footsteps got quicker, and she focused on turning her head. A car was parked twenty feet away, and he seemed to be heading for it. Even though it was shadowed and blurry, she knew it was a 1999 green Toyota Corolla. She'd done her research on him after all.

The sight of the car made her renew her struggles. She did not want him to put her in that car. If he did, she knew her chances of making it back to her sisters, back to Dash, back to their beloved house at the edge of the forest, would drop dramatically. Forcing her weighted arm to swing at his face, she managed to shove his chin, knocking his head to the side.

"Stop it." He gave her another shake before hefting her higher. His breathing was heavy, and her hazy mind took a little satisfaction in the fact that either carrying her or her struggles were causing him to have to exert himself.

"Dash..." She tried to organize the words in her mind. Drugged as she was, it was a hundred times worse trying to sort through her spinning thoughts than normal.

"Stop saying his name." The falsely tender note was gone from his voice, she noticed with another zing of fierce pleasure.

"Dash...wouldn't be..." The right words came close but then darted away like shy fish when she grabbed at them. Finally though, she managed to cobble together a sentence. "Dash doesn't...suck air like you...when he carries me." The words were rough and slurred, but she knew he understood them when his arms tightened painfully around her. She didn't mind the hard press of his hands. It helped keep her from drifting off. "Dash's...sssstrong."

"Don't say his name!" His words were raised, not quite a shout but loud enough that she gave an inner cheer.

"Yurrr jealous." Her tangled brain struggled to come up with a plan, any plan, but she could barely think in a straight line, much less strategize. "That...why you...burned down his...his gym?" Even though her mind wasn't producing a workable plan, it did make the connection between the damage to Leifsen's nose and the memory of her knee hitting a wannabe abductor in the face.

"I'm not jealous of that meathead." Leifsen gave an offended huff that made Norah want to laugh for some drug-induced reason. "And I wasn't responsible for the damage to his place. That was all Fridley."

Her scoff sounded off, but she didn't know if that was because her mouth or her ears were malfunctioning. "So there'ssss…" She stalled out on the *s* sound and had to refocus to get the rest of her thought out. "Some other…some other stalker with a noken brose?" A snort of laughter escaped her, that false happy, floaty feeling threatening to overtake her again. She forced herself to focus on getting the words out correctly. "I mean…broken nose."

"I was there watching you when Fridley started playing with fire," he said, sounding smug again. "Couldn't let such a great opportunity pass by, now could I? It didn't quite work out, but that's okay. I'm a try, try again type of guy, and look at this." He jostled her in his hold. "Success! Now there'll be nothing stopping us from getting to know each other…really well."

Her stomach lurched, and she rolled her head to the side in case she was finally able to vomit. Her heart immediately plummeted when she saw they were just steps away from Leifsen's car. "Daaaash!" This time, she almost managed to yell. "I need a rescuuuue."

She decided she wasn't even going to try to pretend she

wasn't a damsel in distress. No, she was fully tied to the railroad tracks as Leifsen curled his nonexistent mustache. After all, what good was a very strong boyfriend who knew how to fight if he couldn't rescue her once in a while? Even as the thoughts played out in her head, a heavy ball of dread collected in her belly. A rescue would be wonderful, but it was looking less and less likely the closer they got to Mr. and Mrs. Leifsen's 1999 green Toyota Corolla.

Her teeth started chattering as he stopped next to the car and shifted her weight. Maybe if he put her down to open the door, she could belly crawl away or even underneath the car. Anything to delay her kidnapping long enough for the drug to wear off a little more.

Instead of setting her on her feet though, he managed to open the driver's door without relinquishing his hold. Crouching, he fiddled with something on the floorboard. She heard a heavy click before he straightened, and her skin went clammy.

She knew what that sound was. He'd opened the trunk.

Twisting and flailing as wildly as her uncoordinated body could manage, she put up a desperate final attempt to save herself. "Not the trunk! Not the trunk!" The plea echoed loudly in her head, but she didn't know if she'd managed to say the words out loud. Despite everything she was doing, his slow, methodical steps continued to move to the rear of the car and its gaping black trunk.

"Norah!"

The roar echoed through her head and the air around her. Leifsen stiffened, letting her know it wasn't just a figment of her drugged imagination. Then she was falling for what felt like forever before she hit the pavement with a thump. She lay still for a long moment, feeling the impact of the hard surface vibrate through her, not even hurting so much as stunning her into stillness.

The sound of a scuffle—grunts and smacks of knuckles on flesh and shouts and growls that made her smile because they sounded just like Dash—seemed close but still remote. A pebble dislodged by someone's skidding boot flew in the air before it stung her cheek. The tiny pain was sharp enough to remind her that she needed to move. She couldn't just lie there until Leifsen picked her up and stuffed her in his truck.

Moving was incredibly hard though. It felt like she had to force each muscle to work with the others to drag her inch by inch across the pavement. Her fingertips bumped something—a tire. That was good. She needed to get under the car, and that meant she was close. Pushing herself forward with her knees and elbows, she managed to get her head and shoulders under the Toyota before hands caught her waist.

She kicked out, more from muscle memory and reflex than from actually directing it. Her foot connected with something, and she heard a grunt. The sound made her go still. She knew that grunt.

"Dash?" Her voice shook as she told herself not to hope, not to be an idiot. She needed to get under the car, not have audio hallucinations. She couldn't make herself move a muscle though. Not until she knew if Dash was there.

The hands around her waist tightened, lifting her slightly

before pulling her clear of the car. Part of her wanted to wail that all her slow, hard, painful work was for nothing, but another, larger part recognized those huge hands and that effortless strength.

Once she was out from under the car, he rolled her over. She stared at the man towering over her, backlit by a streetlight that made his silhouette look even larger.

"Dash…" She could still hardly let herself believe he was there. "You look like Thor."

That choked bark of a laugh though…that was all Dash. It wasn't until he lifted her up and cradled her against his chest and she smelled his slightly sweaty but so wonderfully familiar scent that she knew for sure. Her arms clumsily tangled around his neck.

"Thanks for coming to find me." Her voice was still slurred, but her thoughts were slightly clearer. "I owe you a rescue."

Wrapping those thick arms around her, he pressed his face into the spot where her shoulder and neck met. Squeezing her tightly but ever so gently, like he was holding a precious egg, he said right against her skin, "Let's never do this again."

"Deal." Even in her semi-lucid state, that seemed like a no-brainer. She could've stayed locked against him forever, but then she remembered they weren't alone in the alley. Pulling back a little so she could peer over his shoulder, she asked, "Did you kill him?"

"No." He sounded a bit put out by this. "I wanted to, but I didn't know if you'd get the bounty if he was dead."

As fuzzy and tangled as her thoughts were, she honestly

didn't know the answer to that at the moment, but she made a vague mental note to check later. It seemed like something she should know—and probably Dash should too if he was going to continue to be her boyfriend and regular rescuer.

With a heavy sigh that blew hot breath across her neck, Dash released her, although he kept his hands on her arms as he looked into her eyes. "Can you stand here for a second?"

She honestly wasn't sure, but she didn't want to cause any more problems for Dash that night, so she said, "Sure."

As if he doubted her answer, he slowly released her but kept his hands close as if to grab her if she started to drop. Norah concentrated on standing upright without swaying, and she managed to do an adequate enough job that Dash took a step back, although he was frowning heavily.

While she watched, he grabbed the limp shape she recognized as Leifsen's unconscious form, and she took a brief but fierce pleasure in how helpless he looked. Dragging Leifsen across the pavement to the car, Dash crouched and got a good grip on the other man. With a grunt, he lifted Leifsen and dumped him into the still-open trunk. He slammed the trunk with more force than really necessary, but Norah didn't begrudge him the satisfaction he obviously got from locking her would-be kidnapper in his own trunk.

Dash returned to her and wrapped an arm around her, pulling her into his side. It was a relief to lean into him and not have to concentrate on balancing on her own feet anymore. He pulled out his phone with his free hand, tapping at the screen with his thumb.

"Who're you calling?" The slur was back, worse than ever, and Norah wondered if that was because she was safe, so panic wasn't fighting the effects of the drug anymore.

"Dispatch. We need a deputy."

"Why not the coppers?" She giggled at the term, feeling like a mobster from the thirties. "The po-po?"

"I'll ask for them too." His voice sounded amused, and she liked that she made him happy. "The deputy'll pick up your skip."

"Ohhh." As he talked to the dispatcher, she remembered she had a call to make too. Digging out her phone was complicated, but she finally succeeded, only to have it plucked from her fingers. "Hey!"

Dash must've finished his conversation with dispatch, since his phone was nowhere in sight, and he held hers out of reach above her head. "I'll call your sisters for you. Right now, you'll just freak them out."

She pouted for a second and then shrugged. Even with her brain not functioning on all cylinders, she knew he was right. She held up her thumb, and he touched the phone to it. Once it was unlocked, he made the call.

"No, it's Dash." There was a pause before he added, "She's fine now. Just not fully coherent yet. No. Drugged."

Norah was glad she had gotten out of making the call, as Molly's voice on the other end got louder and higher pitched the more Dash told her. "Thought the plan was *not* to freak her out," she muttered, making him give her a sideways look.

"Laken, working with Leifsen."

Molly's voice said something Norah couldn't make out, but she could tell that her sister had switched from frantic mode to straight-up rage.

"He tried to take her. I stopped him."

Molly asked a question.

"Not dead. Unconscious. Stuffed in his trunk."

Norah was starting to feel impossibly exhausted, so she leaned heavily against Dash. He took her weight, pulling her closer without missing a beat of his phone conversation.

"Alley behind Dutch's."

She tipped her head up and saw his eyebrows quirk.

"No explosions. Why?"

"She's always getting almost blown up," Norah tried to explain, but that didn't calm down Dash's eyebrows.

"Yeah. Okay. We're closer to Petunia Street."

Something about Dash saying "Petunia" struck her as funny, and she started to giggle. He looked at her with an odd look on his face as he ended the call.

"Thanks for doing that," she said, trying to stop laughing but only succeeding in giving herself the hiccups. "If I'd called—*hic*—it would've been a disas-*hic*-ter."

"Yeah, pretty much." He was half smiling as he said it, and she stared up at his interesting, fantastic face, her feelings striking her hard.

"I love you—*hic*—so much."

His half smile turned into a whole one. "Love you too."

Completely contented, she burrowed closer into his side. "Now that that's sett-*hic*-led, is it okay if I pass—*hic*—out?"

Without waiting for permission, she let her eyes close and darkness drop over her, knowing that Dash was there to keep her safe.

EIGHTEEN

I'D BEEN *DAYS* SINCE SHE'D passed out in his arms, and Norah had long since recovered, but it was becoming more and more obvious that Dash hadn't yet.

"You're *sure* you're up for this?" Dash stared at her from the driver's seat as if he was trying see right under her skin to check for hidden injuries.

She held his gaze so he could see she meant what she was saying. "Yes. If I had to stay home any longer with all four of my sisters, one brother-in-law, and two boyfriends-in-law checking on me every two minutes, I would've done some sort of damage. I'm fine."

"You passed out."

"I was tired." She waved a hand, dismissing that. "I woke up as soon as you started poking at me."

"You were *hospitalized*." He said the word like it hurt him.

"I know." Reaching across the center console, she patted his clenched fist. "But that was just to check me out and see what

I'd been drugged with. They sent me home soon after." *Home to be watched over by four overprotective sisters and one* extremely *overprotective Dash.*

He blew out a rough breath, and she patted him again. If their roles had been reversed and he'd been the one drugged, almost kidnapped, and then hospitalized—even briefly—she would've wanted to keep him wrapped in very soft blankets in a secure location too, so she could empathize with how he felt. Still, she didn't want to be trapped at home forever, so she brought out the big guns.

"Didn't you want to take me on a nice, nonviolent date?"

"Yes." The answer was grudging, almost sullen, and she weirdly found that—and him—adorable. She was so gone on him, it was ridiculous.

"Well, here's our chance." She gestured toward the busy, well-lit path leading away from the Saturn Canyon parking area. *Well, nonviolent anyway.* She was reserving judgment on the *nice* part, since she wasn't exactly a nature person, and the rocky cliffs loomed ominously above them, matte black against a star-studded sky. Plus, outside the venue lighting, bunches of evergreens created shadowy potential hiding places for stalkers, and she was still wary after the whole thing with Leifsen watching her.

The police had found feeds on his laptop from three high-resolution cameras Leifsen had planted the first of several times he'd broken into her house—in the kitchen, living room, and her bedroom. She was relieved he hadn't put one in the bathroom; knowing he'd watched her in her bedroom was traumatic enough. Every time she'd changed her passwords and upped her security, he'd been watching. It was no wonder he'd been able to hack into their laptops. It'd been extraordinarily satisfying to find, remove, and reprogram the cameras for her sisters to use in the field. Charlie had suggested smashing them with a hammer, which would've also been pleasant, but she couldn't waste such expensive tech. Plus, there was something especially gratifying about Leifsen funding equipment to help them bring in other skips.

Dash's skeptical grunt drew Norah's attention away from their ominous surroundings. "Please? I really want to hear Chloe's band...and dance with you again." She channeled Warrant and offered Dash her very best pleading puppy eyes.

His only response after a long pause was another grunt, but she knew a *yes* when she heard it. With an excited *meep!*, she reached for her door handle, only to pause at his "Wait."

She rolled her eyes the entire time it took for him to get out and round the front of his SUV, but she did what he asked. When he opened her door for her, she tried to hold an exasperated expression, but she was too excited. The whole way along the trail, she clung to Dash's hand and barely kept herself from bouncing.

Dash kept glancing at her, seeming reluctantly amused by her excitement, although she could tell the majority of his attention was on their surroundings. Except for a possible stray mountain lion or bear, she was pretty sure they weren't in any danger, but she knew he wouldn't let his guard down where her safety was concerned for a long time...probably not ever.

The entrance was a natural gap between two boulders. The bouncer checked their IDs and accepted the cover charge perfunctorily, which was a nice change from the one at Dutch's. Her gaze drifted to his shaved head, and she had to cough to hide a laugh.

Once they were out of the man's earshot, Dash leaned close to ask, "What's funny?"

"Guess it *is* part of the bouncer uniform." When he gave her a strange look, she ran a hand over her head, and his mouth crooked up as if he understood.

"No hair to grab in a fight."

"Very logical." She looked around, taking in the space. The canyon was a natural small amphitheater, the rocky ground sloping slightly upward away from the stage. Even the long bar to the side of the stage fit the setting, looking as if it'd been carved out of the rock surrounding it. Although the canyon was well-lit, the stars were still bright and clear, seemingly closer than in Langston. The place was crowded, and Norah was still uneasy in the midst of all the people, but having Dash there made it bearable. In fact, when he squeezed her hand and gave her that smoldering look he seemed to reserve just for her, everyone around them faded away.

Dash worked his way through the people, and Norah latched on to the back of his belt more from habit and for comfort than because she was actually concerned with being separated from him. There were a couple of stools at the bar open, and Norah climbed onto one and took a better look around as Dash ordered drinks for them.

The other end of the bar butted up to the side of the elevated stage where the band was setting up. She spotted long blond milkmaid braids and raised her hand to wave, only to pause in the middle of the motion, worried that Chloe would just look at her blankly, not recognizing her.

"Chloe!" Dash's voice was gruff but still carried across the space.

Chloe turned, scanning for who'd called out for her. When her gaze snagged on Norah and Dash, she grinned and waved her arms over her head. "Norah, my favorite! You came!"

Flushed but pleased, Norah offered a return wave as Dash gave her hip an encouraging squeeze.

"Come find me after!" Chloe called, giving her one last smile before returning to setting up.

Turning on her stool until she faced Dash, Norah realized she was grinning.

He raised a teasing eyebrow. "Should I be jealous?"

She shrugged, too happy and too comfortable with him to be embarrassed by her girl crush. "Probably. If she invites me to run away with her in her van, I'd give it serious consideration."

Dash just smiled at her as he slid a drink in front of her. She looked at it, a little wary since her last drink at a bar had been doctored. "It's just Coke. Figured you'd rather have this than water."

"I would, thanks." She took a sip as her nerves settled. Dash had gotten the drinks, and there was no way he'd let anything happen to her again. He'd apologized at least a hundred times for focusing on the arguers rather than their table when Laken had given her that water with the cap removed. She knew he felt horribly guilty about not protecting her, but she also knew she should've been less trusting, especially with Laken of all people.

She and Kenslee were both out on bail after being arrested for their part in Leifsen's plan, but Norah didn't think they'd bother her. Her sisters had been loud about hoping the two women would skip out on their bonds so the Paxes would have an opportunity to tackle them and drag them back to jail. Norah couldn't blame her sisters. She would've felt the same if Laken and Kenslee had targeted any of them.

Pike and Carson had been released after extensive questioning by police, since they'd sworn up and down they'd thought the plan was to try to charm the location of the necklace out of Norah. They had no idea who Leifsen was, and the two men had no part in planning her drugging, interrogation, or attempted kidnapping.

By the time her glass was empty, the band had started playing, the natural acoustics of the canyon filling the night air with music, and Norah was bouncing along to the beat.

Dash slid off his stool and offered his hand as he leaned in, his mouth against her ear. "Dance?"

She didn't think that would ever *not* give her good shivers, even if they were together for decades. She smiled at the thought.

He took that as the agreement it was and towed her into the crowd in front of the stage. They danced to the rest of the fast-paced song before the next one slowed dramatically. Glancing up at Chloe, Norah saw the singer give her a wink before starting to croon the lyrics of a ballad. Leaning against Dash's chest as they swayed to the beat, Norah clung to him, enjoying the moment of happiness and contentment. After all, she knew the craziness that was her life recently would start up again as soon as this night was over.

Pushing away thoughts of her mom and skips and stolen necklaces and burned apartments, she decided to live in the moment, just for one evening with Dash. Tipping her head back, she looked up to see him smiling down at her—his real smile, the one it seemed like he reserved for her.

Too soon, the song ended, and the band crashed into another one with a rollicking beat. Reluctantly shifting away from Dash, she started bouncing along, laughing when he did as well, his liquid jungle-cat moves even more mesmerizing when he was dancing than when he was stalking someone.

Song after song, they danced, never looking away from each other for long. Norah felt euphoric and giggly, even though she'd only had a Coke to drink, just from having Dash's entire focus.

"I'm so happy we decided to come here!" she told him loudly.

Leaning close—which she was starting to think he did just to have the excuse to touch his lips to her ear—he said just loud enough to hear, "I'm happy too."

When she looked at him, she saw that was true. He looked really, truly happy, his scowl erased for the moment. She'd caused that. Her. Introverted, anxious, quiet Norah Pax. It was an incredible feeling to know she wasn't the only one feeling love fizzing in her blood.

Clasping either side of his face, she pulled him down for

a short, intense kiss. As the song ended, so did their kiss. He stared at her, his mouth slowly curling into a wicked grin.

"Now I'm even happier."

Tipping her head back, she gave a laugh of true joy.

"Norah!" It took her a moment to realize Chloe was saying her name into the mic. "Miss Norah, get your cute little butt up here. If you're not going to sing with me at open mic night, you're going to sing with me right now."

Instant anxiety crammed all her words into her throat, so she could only make a choked *ack* sound.

With an amused snort, Dash took her hand. "C'mon. Let's get you onstage with your girlfriend." He sounded resigned.

Any other time, she would've been entertained by his teasing, but now her entire brain was frozen by the thought that she was going to be *onstage* with *Chloe Ballister* to *sing* in front of *all these people.*

She automatically followed him, the crowd parting for them good-naturedly, until they reached the stage. Dash turned toward her just as she mouthed "But…"

He leaned in, and she took reassurance from the familiar warmth of his breath on her ear. "You know you'll kick yourself later if you don't take this opportunity."

At the moment, she really doubted the veracity of that stateme—

"*Ack!*" She made the same strangled sound again as Dash grabbed her around the waist and lifted her effortlessly to sit her on the edge of the stage.

Then Chloe was there, smiling devilishly, and there was no

way Norah couldn't smile back at the woman who looked like a tatted-up milkmaid. She let Chloe help her to her feet, and then she was standing on the stage as the band kicked off the next song, a well-known cover Norah knew every single word to, and then she was leaning toward the mic and...*singing*? With Chloe? And maybe smiling? And...actually having fun?

It was impossible not to have a good time with that bouncy beat and Chloe's grin surrounding her like a warm, friendly hug. When Norah started thinking about the crowd watching, she just focused on Dash. He didn't take his gaze off her the entire time, and his steady, affectionate regard made her relax enough to let go and enjoy this amazing, unthinkable thing she was doing.

Feeling brave, she let her gaze sweep over the crowd. They weren't even focused on her. They were dancing and singing along and having just as much fun, except... Her smile faded a little as she watched a guy at the bar, hunched on the stool closest to the stage. His face was tucked down, so she couldn't get a good look at him, but there was something familiar about him that made the back of her neck prickle in warning.

Then Chloe was pulling her into a hug, and Norah realized the song was over. Pushing away the weird feeling seeing that guy had given her, she squeezed Chloe back. Normally, she avoided hugs like the plague, but this felt right.

"Thank you for that," Norah said sincerely. She would've never thought she'd enjoy it, but Dash had been right to encourage her.

"I'm just glad that man of yours dragged you up here."

Chloe winked at her, and Norah gave a sheepish smile. "You're not allowed to leave. We're having a drink together when I'm done." Chloe narrowed her eyes in a mock glare that somehow managed to look impossibly happy.

"Okay." Giving a little wave, Norah moved toward the edge of the stage where Dash waited. She couldn't stop grinning. It had been the best night.

"We're taking a five-minute break," Chloe told the crowd.

"Did you have fun?" Dash asked, looking up at her, his tiny smirk saying an obvious *I told you so*, but she was too elated to even care.

"Yup." She grinned down at him. People had drifted away, heading toward the bar or clustering in groups, leaving the space right in front of the stage empty except for Dash. A little shriek made her glance toward the bar where a woman was fishing ice out of her cleavage. With a sympathetic wince for how cold that spill must've been, Norah started to turn back to Dash when a movement from the hunched guy at the end of the bar caught her attention.

His hand slipped under his jacket, and he turned his head toward the stage, but the brim of his baseball hat shadowed his face. There was a tenseness to him, a readiness that didn't fit in with the relaxed, semi-drunken vibe of the crowd, and her body stiffened. Part of her wondered if she was imagining things, but her instincts were all blaring alarms. Somehow, she just *knew* that this man was a danger.

Right as she was about to point him out to Dash, the guy's chin tipped up, revealing his face.

Zach Fridley!

Before she had time to do anything except suck in a shocked breath, he pulled his hand out from under his jacket. The lights of the bar made it hard to see what was in his grip, but her stomach seemed to know even before her brain did.

"*Gun!*" This time, the word made it out of her mouth as Zach's arm extended, pointing the pistol at the man right in front of her. Dash seemed so vulnerable, set apart from the crowd, with nothing between him and the weapon in Zach's grip, nothing but useless air to slow down an oncoming bullet.

Before she could even think of what to do, her body burst into motion. She sprinted toward the side of the stage, her mind blank except for an all-encompassing need to keep Dash alive. She'd just found him. There was no way she was letting him die, not if she could stop it.

Time seemed to slow as she ran, as if her legs were caught in quicksand. She saw every detail, Zach's squint and twitch as he extended the gun in front of him, his head slightly cocked as he sighted down the barrel, a small, ever-so-evil smile touching his face. Someone's scream set off another, but it sounded muted to Norah, all her narrow focus pinpointed on Zach and the gun pointing at Dash.

Reaching the end of the stage, Norah didn't plan, didn't hesitate, but just flung herself off, diving straight toward the man about to shoot Dash. Her arms, outstretched in front of her, hit Zach in the chest first. He grunted at the impact as they both tumbled to the ground, the world spinning and jolting around her as something exploded with a *bang* right next to her ear.

There was no time to think. Her body went on autopilot, muscle memory kicking in from all those sessions with Dash. When she finally went still and took what felt like her first breath since she'd spotted the gun in Zach's hand, she realized she had him pinned on his back.

For a moment, she just stared into his angry eyes, shocked that she'd actually managed to subdue him, but then Dash was there.

"Good job." Although his voice was calm, there was an extra gravelly growl underpinning it that told her how much he wanted to rip Zach's head off. "Mind if I borrow him for a sec?"

She didn't look at him, not wanting to be distracted from the guy on the ground. "You can't kill him, Dash."

"I don't see why not."

"I don't want you dead *or* in prison."

A couple of bouncers bent over them. "We've got him."

Norah let Dash help her to her feet as the two security guys grabbed Zach none too gently. Before she could even steady her knees enough to support her, they weren't needed any longer. Dash pulled her against his chest, his arms wrapped tightly around her. At first, Norah thought she was the one shaking, but then she realized he was too.

"Are you okay?" She couldn't get the image of the gun pointed at Dash out of her head. She ran her hands over whatever parts of him she could reach, checking for bullet wounds.

"Am *I* okay?" He barked out a rough laugh before clutching her closer. "You're the one who dove off the stage and tackled someone holding a *gun*—" His voice broke on the last word, and then his hands were on her shoulders, setting her back just enough so that he could see her. "Are you hurt? The gun went off. Did you get hit?"

She took the opportunity to look him over as well, her body sagging with relief when he appeared to be wholly unharmed. He gave her shoulders a small shake, and she looked back up at his face. "Oh, sorry. I'm fine…I think. Zach broke my fall, and he's pretty doughy." Glancing down at herself, she saw the skin of her upper arm through a hole in her sleeve. "Oh, my shirt's ripped."

Dash's hand smoothed over the tear as if soothing an actual hurt. His fingers were trembling. "I thought we agreed this would be a *nonviolent* date."

"Well, I couldn't just let him *shoot* you." Giddiness bubbled up in her now that she was starting to realize she'd done it. Dash hadn't been shot, and she'd escaped without any obvious injury. She hugged him convulsively, trying to reassure herself that he wasn't hurt. "Besides, I owed you a save. It was your turn to be tied to the railroad tracks."

His laugh was more of a growl as he hugged her back. "No more. This is the last time. Can we agree on that?"

Leaning back, she frowned. "I don't know if I can promise that. If you keep hanging out with me and my family, things tend to get a little…chaotic."

"Well, I plan to keep hanging out with you," he said. "Just try to keep the near-death scares to a minimum."

"I will if you will." Despite everything, she couldn't hold back a smile. "So does that mean you want to try again to see if we can have a nice, nonviolent date?"

"Well, yes." He sounded as if any other answer would be ridiculous. "I love you. Of course we're going on more nice, nonviolent dates."

"You do?" Her smile grew to a beam, even as he, Dash Porter, Mr. Stoic, actually *rolled* his *eyes*.

"I already told you this."

"When?"

"In the alley behind Dutch's," he said. "Do you not remember? You *were* pretty out of it."

"Oh, I remember." She remembered the many embarrassing things she'd said while under the influence of whatever Laken had dosed her with. "I just thought you were humoring the drugged girl."

"Didn't *you* mean it?"

"Of course." When he just raised his eyebrows expectantly, she huffed a laugh and repeated it. "I love you." It was shockingly easy to say, even without the roofie.

He hugged her yet again, and she leaned against him happily until a yell made her pull away enough to turn.

"Norah!" It was Chloe of course, using her projection powers for good. "You badass! That stage dive was awesome!"

"Thanks." Even after everything that had happened, Norah felt a little bashful. "I didn't really think about it. I just saw the gun and reacted."

"C'mon." Chloe grabbed her hand and hauled her toward the two boulders marking the start of the trail to the parking area.

Norah realized that while she'd been caught up in Dash, the

canyon had mostly emptied, and the few patrons who hadn't immediately run for the exit were being herded in that direction.

"Once they let us back in," Chloe said, "I'll buy you a congratulatory shot."

Norah glanced behind her, and of course Dash was right there. "Don't think we're getting back in here tonight," he said with a shrug. "We'll have to wait for the local cops."

"Next week then. I'll get one for you too, big guy," Chloe said as they followed the stragglers out of the canyon.

The chatter around them turned from shocked and dazed to excited as people recounted what had happened. Once they reached the parking area, Norah leaned back against Dash, who stood as close behind her as he could get, and soaked up his warmth in the chilly night. "Want to hear something weird?" she asked.

His grunt sounded like a yes.

"Despite everything, this has still been our best date so far."

His laugh was warm against her ear. "Yeah." He kissed her temple, holding his lips there for an extra moment. "It has. But I promise you even better ones. Thousands of them."

EPILOGUE

EVEN THOUGH CHARLIE WAS FINALLY lying in her own bed after spending the majority of the last five weeks fruitlessly chasing after their mom, she couldn't sleep. She frowned at the glow-in-the-dark stars on the ceiling Molly had given her and Cara on their tenth birthday. On her twin's side of the room, the stars were placed neatly, spaced so evenly it was obvious Cara had used a ruler. On her side, Charlie had stuck them on haphazardly, so there were bunches separated by long stretches of plain ceiling.

"It's more astronomically accurate," Charlie muttered out loud. "Nature loves chaos." There was no chance of her words waking Cara, since her sister was spending the night at Henry's. Charlie was happy for her, and she already adored her sister's boyfriend, but after a lifetime of sharing a room with one sister and a house with four, it was just…different.

And the difference made it hard to sleep.

With a huff, Charlie gave up on getting any rest. Flinging

her covers to the side, she slid out of bed. Once in the hallway, she stopped abruptly, realizing she didn't know where she was headed. She wasn't hungry or thirsty, so the kitchen was out. She didn't want to sit in the dark, silent living room either, alone with her thoughts. She was bored.

She eyed the closed door to what had been her mom's room. Now, Felicity and her new husband, Bennett, were using it. A few weeks earlier, their mom had broken in, and Felicity had caught her searching for something in her closet. Norah and Cara had turned the closet inside out after their mom had run again, but they hadn't found anything. Even though she trusted her sisters and knew they were more methodical than she was, Charlie was still tempted to try her luck.

The only problem was that the bedroom was occupied.

Charlie paused, debating whether she should risk going in or if she should play it safe and go back to bed to stare at the ceiling, bored out of her mind.

The answer was easy. Charlie had never played it safe in her life.

Pressing her ear to the door, she heard her sister's deep breathing that meant she was sleeping. Bennett wasn't making a peep, so he was either snoozing uncharacteristically quietly or was awake. Satisfied they weren't in the middle of sexy times— Charlie had interrupted those when the three of them had been on the road, and even one time was too many—she eased the door open and peeked inside.

Bennett was indeed awake, watching her with a cocked eyebrow as he held her sleeping sister tenderly against him.

Although Charlie couldn't read his expressions as well as Felicity could, she did know that look—wary curiosity with a touch of humor.

Charlie pointed to the closet—as if that explained her presence—and crept through the shadowed room to the goal. Without moving anything except his eyes, Bennett kept his gaze on her. Easing the door open, she slipped into the closet and closed the door behind her. Once she was shut into the tiny space, she turned on the light.

She knew Norah and Cara had gone over all the walls, ceiling, and floor with a fine-tooth comb, searching for secret cubbies or hidden hiding spaces. Still, she did all of it again, tapping ever so lightly to check for hollow-sounding spots as she ran her fingers over the smooth, painted drywall. As expected, she didn't find anything. The closet, as boring as it was, was strictly what it was built to be—a small space to hold clothes.

Frowning, Charlie checked everything again. She even unscrewed the light fixture and examined the inside of the wooden door but still found nothing. Her sisters had cleared out all their mom's clothes and shoes, so there wasn't anything else to search.

Hands on her hips, she glared at the white space. The only reason their mom would've taken the risk of breaking in would be if there was something she needed desperately. There was a slim—very slim—chance that Jane had managed to grab whatever it was between Zach Fridley knocking Felicity unconscious—Charlie silently snarled in fury at that memory— and the rest of the family returning to the house. But it was unlikely. There just wouldn't have been time for Jane to get whatever she needed and also make it over to Mr. Villaneau's *and* convince him to smuggle her out in that minute or two window of opportunity. Charlie was certain whatever it was her mom was after was still there.

Think, think, think. She checked for vents and outlets, but there weren't any. Just blank walls, ceiling, floor, door, rod to hang clothes on... Her gaze snagged on the thick wooden dowel that stretched the length of the closet, and a smile touched her lips. Examining the spot where the rod met the wall, her grin grew. The screws at the top of the mounting were tarnished and old, matching the age of the house...or were they? Charlie knew all Jane's tricks, including how to make something new look like it'd always been there. She ran the edge of her nail over one of the screw heads. Sure enough, a flake of dull paint peeled off, revealing the shiny silver of a brand-new screw.

She reached for her pocket, but her fingers slid over silky, pocket-less material.

Right, she remembered. *Pajamas.*

Turning off the closet light, she waited a few seconds for her vision to adjust and then stuck her head out the door. Bennett's eyes were still open, so she whispered, "Flathead screwdriver?"

Carefully moving his arm off Felicity, he reached for the bedside table and pulled a multi-tool from the top drawer. In the same motion, he tossed it to Charlie and then immediately resumed cuddling his wife.

She grinned as she caught it. After spending time with Bennett chasing Jane, Charlie knew he was never far from his multi-tool—or an impressively wide array of weapons. Not only did he worship her sister, but he was also a very handy guy to chase skips with. "Thank you," she mouthed before retreating back into the closet.

After turning the light back on, she made quick work of unscrewing the brackets holding the clothes rod in place. It fell toward the floor, but Charlie caught it before it could land with a Felicity-waking clatter. Her heart thumping with excitement, she checked one end—solid—before flipping it around to look at the other side. At first, it looked just like the first end, and her breath left in a huff of disappointment. Upon closer inspection, however, the wood grain didn't quite line up about an inch from the end.

Her triumphant grin returned as she pulled off the cap over the end, revealing a hole drilled into the rod. The opening was a good inch and a half in diameter and two inches deep, the hiding spot just deep enough for the key placed inside.

Feeling like the winner of a treasure hunt, Charlie fished out the key and held it up. It didn't have any identifying marks on it, meaning it could fit in any lock in any building in any town in the country, but she was still optimistic. Their mom had risked coming back to the house, even though she knew her daughters were searching for her. That meant this key was important.

"I'm sick of chasing you, Mom," Charlie whispered, closing her fingers over the very ordinary yet extremely precious key. "Your turn to come to us."

Anticipation bubbled inside her, and she knew she couldn't keep it to herself. Holding back an excited giggle, she slipped out of the closet. Bennett's eyes narrowed immediately, and he gave her a warning glare promising death if she woke up Felicity.

Giving him her most innocent look, she moved toward the door, reversing at the last second and sprinting toward the bed.

"Charlotte Calamity Pax!" he whisper-yelled, but she just grinned as she pounced, landing on the bed next to her sister.

"Wha?" Felicity's eyes flew open, and she tried to sit up, but Bennett's hold kept her in place long enough for her to realize Charlie had woken her. Relaxing back against him, Felicity gave her sister a glare that matched the one Bennett was giving her. "Charlie, what are you doing? It's the middle of the night! This better be good, or you're going to be doing twice as many burpees as everyone else."

"It's good," Charlie promised, holding up the key.

Felicity tried sitting up again. This time, she managed as Bennett reluctantly released her. "A key? What's it for?"

"That what you were looking for in the closet?" Bennett rumbled, still looking peeved at Charlie for waking his wife.

"I wasn't sure *what* I was looking for, but this was hidden in the clothes rod, so I'm thinking it was what *Mom* was searching for." She dropped the key into Felicity's outstretched hand. "Think she wants it bad enough to come get it?"

Felicity looked up from the key and met Charlie's gaze. "Bait the trap?" she asked, starting to smile.

"Yep." Charlie grinned back at her, feeling a bone-deep satisfaction at the idea of finally, *finally* bringing in their mom. "Let's catch our skip."

ABOUT THE AUTHOR

A fan of anything that makes her feel like a badass, Katie Ruggle has trained in Krav Maga, boxing, and gymnastics, has lived in an off-grid, solar-and-wind-powered house in the Rocky Mountains; rides horses; trains her three dogs; and travels to warm places to scuba dive. She has received multiple Amazon Best Books of the Month and an Amazon Best Book of the Year. After spending over a decade in Colorado, Katie now lives in Minnesota with her family.

Website: katieruggle.com
Instagram: @katieruggle
Threads: @katieruggle
TikTok: @katieruggle

THE SCENIC ROUTE

Why date a mountain man? Because climbing
him will leave you breathless.

Felicity Pax loves her job. She craves excitement, and being a bounty hunter gives her that in spades. So when her estranged mother disappears with a small fortune in tow, Felicity chases her like she would any other skip. Too bad she didn't barter on having increasingly infuriating (and infuriatingly hot) PI Bennett Green on her tail.

Bennett's got a job to do, and if that means shadowing Felicity...well...he's had worse assignments. Even if he's 99% sure the increasingly intriguing bounty hunter is leading him on a wild goose chase through the Rockies.

If she has to drag her PI tail through endless quirky mountain towns in order to shake him, that's what she's determined to do...but it isn't long before Felicity's intended distraction turns up a mystery worth solving—and Bennett becomes the unexpected partner she never realized she needed. As things heat up, Felicity will have to decide what's most important to her: staying one step ahead of the "enemy" or giving herself freedom to experience the adventure of a lifetime.

"Ruggle kicks off her latest series, Beneath the Wild Sky, with a novel offering a delicious romance, laugh-out-loud banter, and edge-of-your-seat suspense that will keep the pages turning."

—*Library Journal*

For more info about Sourcebooks's books and authors, visit:

sourcebooks.com

FISH OUT OF WATER

Why date a mountain man?
Because he knows how to pitch a tent.

When Dahlia Weathersby's sister disappears on what should have been a simple day hike, Dahlia immediately heads deep into the Colorado Rockies to find her. Knowing she'll never survive the mountains alone, she convinces the local hermit—adorably grouchy survival expert Winston Dane—to be her guide. All it takes is a good helping of Dahlia's charm…and just the teeniest bit of blackmail… before she's got all six-foot-something of him wrapped around her finger. But even with her very own mountain man in tow, things aren't going to be easy. There are:

Long hikes through gorgeous wilderness? **Check.**
Bears? **Check.**
A single shared sleeping bag? **Check.**
Enough sparks to set the Rockies ablaze? **Check, check, check.**

With everything the wilderness has to throw at them, it'll take more than charm and some city girl ingenuity to make this trek anything but a disaster waiting to happen…and an adventure she'll never forget.

"Romance lovers will have no trouble rooting for this raunchy heroine and her strong, protective hero."

—*Publishers Weekly*

For more info about Sourcebooks's books and authors, visit:
sourcebooks.com

ROCKY MOUNTAIN BOUNTY HUNTERS

Four bounty-hunter sisters in the Rocky Mountains track down bad guys and solve the mystery of their family's downfall—finding their own happily ever after along the way.

In Her Sights

Tough-as-nails eldest sister Molly Pax falls for fellow bounty hunter and #1 competition John Carmondy. But does he really want her, or is he just using her to track down her criminal mother?

Risk It All

Just as Cara Pax is ready to move on from the family business, she's tasked with tracking down Henry Kavenski, a man who's got innocence to prove. When bounty hunter falls for bounty, what happens when it's love at first catch?

"An unpredictable, high-octane action adventure tale...This fast-paced romance is laced with humor and a bit of heat. Fans of Janet Evanovitch's "Stephanie Plum" series will enjoy."

—*Library Journal*

For more info about Sourcebooks's books and authors, visit:

sourcebooks.com

ROCKY MOUNTAIN
K9 UNIT

These K9 officers and their trusty dogs
will do anything to protect
the people they love.

Run to Ground

K9 officer Theo Bosco lost his mentor, his K9 partner, and almost lost his will
to live. But when a ruthless killer targets a woman on the run, Theo and his new
K9 companion will do whatever it takes to save the new family neither can live
without.

On the Chase

Injured in the line of duty, K9 officer Hugh Murdoch's orders are simple: *stay
alive*. But when a frightened woman bursts into his life, Hugh and his K9 companion have no choice but to risk everything to keep her safe.

Survive the Night

K9 officer Otto Gunnersen has always been a haven: for the lost, the sick, the
injured. But when a hunted woman takes shelter in his arms, this gentle giant
swears he'll do more than heal her battered spirit—he'll defend her with his life.

Through the Fire

When a killer strikes, new K9 officer Kit Jernigan knows she can't catch the
culprit on her own. She needs a partner: local fire spotter Wesley March. But
the more time they spend together, the hotter the fire smolders...and the more
danger they're in.

"Gripping suspense, unique heroines, sexy heroes."

—Christine Feehan,
New York Times bestselling author

For more info about Sourcebooks's books and authors, visit:
sourcebooks.com

SEARCH AND RESCUE

In the Rockies, lives depend on the Search & Rescue brotherhood. But this far off the map, secrets can be murder.

Hold Your Breath

Louise "Lou" Sparks is a hurricane. A walking disaster. And with her, ice diving captain Callum Cook has never felt more alive...even if keeping her safe may just kill him.

Fan the Flames

Firefighter and Motorcycle Club member Ian Walsh rides the line between good and bad. But if a killer has his way, Ian will take the fall for a murder he didn't commit...and lose the woman he's always loved.

Gone Too Deep

Survival guide George Halloway is a mystery. Tall. Dark. Intense. And city girl Ellie Price will need him by her side if she wants to find her father...and live to tell the tale.

In Safe Hands

Sheriff Deputy Chris Jennings was a hero to agoraphobe Daisy Little, but one wrong move ended their future before it could begin. Now he'll do whatever it takes to keep her safe—even if that means turning against one of his own.

On His Watch

Ice rescue diver Derek Warner never meant to be a hero. But when two little girls go missing, he's the first in line to bring them home—even if that means scouring the wilderness with the woman he once loved and lost, Artemis Rey.

After the End

Now that the murderer has been caught and the arsonist is behind bars, the town of Simpson, Colorado has returned to its sleepy, picturesque former glory. Yet for the heroes of Search & Rescue, work is never done...especially not if the extraordinary women if their lives have anything to say about it.

"Vivid and charming."

—Charlaine Harris, #1 *New York Times* bestselling author of the Sookie Stackhouse series

For more info about Sourcebooks's books and authors, visit:

sourcebooks.com